WITHIN
THE
WAKE

S.A. Cummins

RSC Publishing

WITHIN THE WAKE
Copyright © 2023 by S.A. Cummins.

ISBN 979-8-9888919-0-1 (softcover)
ISBN 979-8-9888919-1-8 (hardcover)

Copyediting by Kristen Stein and Jennifer D. Munro
Cover illustration by James Cummins
Cover layout and design consultation by Carmen Andonian
Interior design by Tod McCoy

Published by:

RSC Publishing

https://withinthewake.com/about-the-author

In death, spirits lost in longing
Relinquish joy in search of home.
No use of time, horizon bound
To the light they are drawn.
All with hope of substance
To fill the space between.

—*The Changing Veil*

2004

Chapter 1
The Emerald City

The gray, damp fog of the morning was a disguise for spring in the Northwest. James hated the vengeful clouds of pollen carried on the breeze, intent on finding their way into the house his great-grandfather had built. Raw at the edges, the headache anchored in his skull, with ringing in his ears as shards of glass framed his vision, making it difficult for him to move.

The world revolved around him in a haze, and he winced and reached blindly, fumbling with the everyday objects on his nightstand that now seemed foreign. In his quest, he came upon a pair of reading glasses and his old Timex watch, its second hand ticking happily away, before finding the two aspirins his wife had left for him. It warmed him that after all their years together she still had an uncanny way of knowing what he needed when Mother Nature in all her blooming glory crept in.

The sounds of the morning, familiar and comforting, announced another day in a city that valued the young and considered over forty out of touch and old. At forty-eight, he was educated and fit for the most part, with only a few extra pounds and a full head of hair women still swooned over. James Allen Jr., no matter his attributes, was labeled a dinosaur. The label was also a proverbial nail in the coffin of anyone whose career had not advanced past middle management.

Nonetheless, James was happy with his life: the safety and security of an advanced education, work, charts, lists, plans, and all the seeds planted for a cultivated future in a place where he had set down roots in a measured, careful way.

Whether or not others considered him dinosaur, he was an established, successful, mid-level engineer with a solid fourteen years at the same national firm specializing in home security. Still, he believed he could do more, that he could achieve something bigger in his career and create a better future for his family. In his spare time, he loved researching the latest cutting-edge technology, simultaneously working new ideas that floated in his head as he experimented with various ongoing projects. Occasional programming fails were sprinkled in with an electrical short circuit here and there as he spent hours in his sixteen- by twenty-four-foot garage, built in the backyard.

He affectionately called his garage the Geek Shed—geek was worn as a badge of honor in a world where referring to "graphical user interface" and "doing multiple overlays from the sensor" was common-speak. In this sacred workspace, software, circuit boards, gadgets, wires, nuts and bolts, discarded display screens, and monitors, all dusted with time, were waiting to come to life and be put to use once again.

The detached garage had two small casement windows and an open-joist ceiling, giving some freedom from the confined rectangle designed for just one car. To keep the floor less cluttered, bare oak beams were draped with extra electric cords. Two eight- by four-foot plywood sheets were placed over the rafters to provide support for various old boxes, which included Christmas decorations and two mysterious steel film canisters no one knew anything about or where they came from. As a child, James had imagined they were secret military films or videos of the lunar moon landing, hidden away for safekeeping. The garage door was manual and dated back to the early 1970s, when it replaced the original carriage-style doors that had deteriorated.

The space was much more suited for tinkering than parking, and it had taken some time to talk his father into removing the 1964 wood-paneled Chevy station wagon, nicknamed The Glorious Rust Bucket, so James could use the space for projects.

The day floated up to meet him as he rose from bed, a lofty task at James's height of six feet, four inches. Leaving his bedroom, he descended the stairs slowly, hoping that each stair would give the aspirin more time to work so he could pull off the expected Morning Dad routine. Morning Dad was happy, fun, and ready to take on the day no matter how gray the mood or weather.

The kitchen was large, bright, and cheery, with the original cornflower-blue and white-tile floor. It had been built to be the gathering place and the heart of the house and was rich in memories. It was the center of the family's special moving universe. An earthy and robust aroma of coffee, cocoa, cereal, peanut butter, and fresh strawberry jam added delicious redolence to the room. The whirling buzz of family amplified the bump, squeak, and laughter of cartoons coming from the old Sears portable television on the counter by the kitchen window. Sprawled on one end of the large, old, plank table were two school backpacks, their contents spilling out, fighting for space with the dishes and silverware. The table had been built for the room and was flanked with mismatched and well-loved, handcrafted, farmhouse-style oak chairs.

Jessica was already in the kitchen, humming to herself as she prepared for the day. He'd fallen in love with her when she had walked into Mr. Peterson's biology class his senior year of high school. To this day, he still saw her as that perky freshman girl with the freckles he loved to count. Petite, with gold chestnut curls and eyes the color of glossy, dark green grass in the spring, she was the yin to his yang, and he was the sugar in her coffee. Jessica, known as Jess to her family, had dreamed of having four or five children. However, due to a late start, difficulties conceiving, numerous visits to fertility experts, and various tests, that dream vanished after an emergency hysterectomy with the birth of their second child, Alena. But dreams move and expand like water finding its level; her love of children was channeled into a teaching certificate, and she turned her passion for molding little lives into a career as a sixth-grade teacher. Their two children, Jack and Alena, both smaller versions of their parents, completed the family.

Ten-year-old Jack's gravity-defying, disheveled curls lent an additional inch or two to his height. He had a broad smile, a spray of freckles capping the bridge of his nose, and warm hazel eyes that were always expressive, whether happy or sad, as they crinkled at the edges. As with most children his age, he stood on the crest of a world that might eventually crush his dreams, but for now he still believed in Santa and that superheroes really had the ability to save the world.

Alena, age six and wise beyond her years, was small, precocious, and filled every room with her thunderous giggles. With unbridled hair, the apples of her cheeks rosy and full, an upturned nose, and wide green eyes, she had the mischievous look of a garden pixie intent on causing chaos. Imaginative by nature, she was a self-anointed ruler of what she called the creatures of her grand kingdom—also known as the backyard. One special inhabitant of the yard was a squirrel who had lost part of its tail, most likely during a fateful dash across the road. A neighboring cat by the name of Ms. Matilda Cunningham found the extra treats shoved deep in Alena's pockets an enticing reason to be part of the visiting nobility. Hummingbirds, warblers, wrens, and an occasional, red-breasted nuthatch made up the royal feathered air battalion, keeping Jessica in constant motion filling the feeders with seeds, nectar, and suet, no matter the weather or season.

Their Queen Anne Hill neighborhood loomed above a city rich in culture and history, with destination-worthy sweeping views of Puget Sound, Lake Union, and the famous Space Needle. The top of the hill was still a snapshot of nineteenth-century Seattle—grandeur and elegance apparent in homes built to capture the wealth and dreams of their owners in a newly expanding city, a city that shone like the rich green jewel for which it was nicknamed. The homes on the block were grand, but not as large as the nearby mansions that faced the iconic misty views.

Built at the turn of the twentieth century for a growing family, the Allen house was considered an American Foursquare Craftsman. Originally painted white, the current color was a frosty gray, reminiscent of a Northwest winter sky. With three stories, it stood taller than the homes on either side. The front-entry porch was wide enough for a porch swing, yet his great-grandfather never got around to hanging one. Deep, wide-tread stairs were flanked by aged boxwoods, groomed in perfect three-foot rectangles, which added graceful elegance. From a distance, it was obvious that balance and symmetry had been painstakingly planned. The substantial front door included two nineteen-inch, leaded, beveled-glass panels, casting fluctuating prisms of light into the entry hall when touched by the rays of the sun. Two large, multipaned bay windows filled much of the first floor, giving an ample view of the world outside from the kitchen and living room. A row of smaller windows on the second floor, topped with two double-hung dormer windows on the third floor, gave the home the appearance of a lit wedding cake at night. James felt a swell of family pride in ownership every time he put his key in the lock. He was, however, keenly aware of the value of the gift of generations. In an area where even a small home was worth over a million dollars, he reminded himself daily just how lucky he was.

Seattle's growing corporate metropolis of Microsoft, Amazon, Starbucks, Expedia, Boeing, and a myriad of others known for changing the world and the way people live, also affected his neighborhood simply by existing just down the street. When he was young, families consisted of one stay-at-home parent and one who was a schoolteacher, mailman, or worked at the local hardware store. Now, two-income corporate presidents, executives, and movers and shakers occupied the homes surrounding the Allen family. Gone were most of the friends and families he had grown up with, dwindling one by one as they sold their homes for huge profits, paving the way to an early retirement. The familiar faces moved away as fast as the new families descended, bringing with them their bulging bank accounts and fancy cars, looking for their little piece of heaven on the hill.

Chapter 2
Goals

"Good morning, Jimmy." Jessica met him sleepily at the kitchen doorway, lifting her face, lids half closed and a smile in her voice, a greeting that made him feel as warm as the breakfast smells that circled the room. "Coffee has been on for a bit, but I'm sure you can't cut through it quite yet. How about some breakfast? Come on, come on, sit down. The eggs are fresh."

Jessica had a way of making the simplest meal a feast, using details like a garnish or an extra sprinkle of cheese to make each plate special and delicious. With purpose in her voice, she nuzzled him gently before lightly kissing him. She pulled back, giving him a direct look and brushing his hair back from his eyes.

"How's your head this morning?" Her hands remained on his cheeks so she could assess his honesty when he answered.

"I'm fine, Jess." He rolled his eyes. James had been down this road for almost twenty years of marriage and knew a wink and a nod would avoid the interrogation and the suggestion to go back to the doctor for more allergy testing. "I'm right as the rain that I'm sure is around the corner." He gave her a cheesy grin that made her giggle.

"OK, but I'm calling Dr. Cooper if you have the same problems as last year," she said, with a sigh, her concern fading.

"Good morning. How's my favorite family on this fine, and lovely day!" James smiled from ear to ear as he settled in, grabbing *The Seattle Times*. Morning Dad had flipped the switch and was now on. Jack and Alena sat were sitting in their normal spots at the kitchen table. Jack, in his own world, sat mindlessly eating cereal, his nose in a book. Alena hummed a made-up tune as she pushed a rogue oat circle that had escaped her bowl toward the intended goal of the floor.

"Dad, look!" Jack chirped with a mouth full of crispy oat cereal. "Dad, I figured it out!"

In one hand he held the book of the week high in the air in triumph, and in the other hand he waved his cereal spoon, milk running down his wrist and splattering the table. "I guessed the end of the story!" he blurted with an excited shout. It was a treasured game that father and son had played since Jack was old enough to read.

"I told you I knew the ending! So what do I get this time?" Jack squirmed in his chair as he waited for his dad to announce his prize.

James had a difficult time coming up with new rewards for Jack, who continuously and magically figured out the endings of most of the books he read. While James and Jessica knew their son was bound to the agreement of "no peeking," there was obviously no guarantee. At the end of the day, he was, after all, only ten. What was important to his parents was his growing love of literature.

"How about dinner at Spikes tonight?" James answered, knowing his son's love of pizza.

"Spikes!" Jack exclaimed with a flourish, up close and in his sister's face, his spoon making circles the size of a medium pizza around her head. He knew what Alena thought of Spikes, and this was another way to push her buttons and get a reaction from her.

"Dad, I hate Spikes! I'm tired of pizza." Alena fidgeted and whined, kicking her legs in protest of the inevitable cheese with extra pepperoni, Jack's favorite and his predictable choice. Alena hadn't figured out her own game yet, or at least one she wanted to play every week. She preferred the world of make-believe, with no end or rules. Jack led in the weekly prize category and, as Alena grew older, she was very aware of the discrepancy.

"Alena, we'll make sure you have your own plain cheese, so no worries." Jessica glanced over her shoulder, the butter knife in her hand poised for another swipe of peanut butter to finish the PB&J sandwiches for school lunches.

In response, Alena glared at her brother, who continued to gloat. Neither Jack nor Alena ever seemed enthusiastic as they faced the school day. Alena, agitated by her lack of a way to win prizes, sulked, while Jack mulled over various escape routes for afternoon recess, with the hope of avoiding the always-dreaded encounter with the school bully.

"Ugh, look at the time. Come on, kids, grab your lunches and backpacks, and giddy up," Jessica barked as she lifted her messenger bag strap over her head, a piece of overcooked toast still in hand. She was often the last to eat and did so most mornings on the run.

With Jessica and the kids off to school, James looked out on the Seattle morning, another of those cold-around-the-edges days that defined Seattle in the early spring: warm in the middle, with frost still clinging to winter, unwilling to relent to the heat until the late afternoon.

James often worked from home, a perk that most in the tech industry embraced. He enjoyed the solitude, uninterrupted focus, and the ability to wear flannel pajamas into the afternoon.

James's home office was small, but he didn't care. The little room might have seemed lonely to some—located in the back of the house, with no closet and no room for more than a few people—but that was the main reason James made it his office. It was an island of beige walls that were his choice, bare of clutter and simply furnished, with nothing to distract him except for a small window looking out to the backyard. The only furniture was a desk left to him by his grandfather, an old oak chair, and a green glass banker's lamp. The desk was large and had been in the room for as long as he could remember; no one had wanted to try to move it. James couldn't explain the love he had for the desk, worn at the edges; the patina of time called to him, holding years of family and the wisdom of decisions that changed the course of all who lived there. It served as the ship that kept him focused and afloat as he navigated each day.

The morning aspirin hadn't done the trick to eliminate his headache. James considered another cup of coffee to take the sharpness of the pain away and help him stay focused. A shuffle and stroll to the kitchen, cup in hand, might give him the time he desperately needed to get back on track. To the right of the front staircase was a hallway that ran the length of the home to the kitchen, then extending to the back of the house. Framed family photos told a story from one end to the other and gave a sense of time travel. Each picture was hung with care, including all the celebrations, milestones, and firsts—first birthday, first haircut, first day of school—most often with all of the family included. They would need to extend or reconfigure the hallway if they were to include the upcoming years.

James was proud of his family and paused to revisit his favorite memories as he moved along the hall. He entered the kitchen, now still and abandoned. It was as if the air had gained in density with his family gone. They had a magical ability to lift the energy with their laughter, and now the quiet seemed overwhelming.

The coffee was still warm and had turned the dark color of molasses. A quick thirty seconds in the microwave would get it hot, and all would be right with the world—at least he hoped. Leaving the kitchen, time travel complete, James sat at his desk, head in hand, for what seemed like hours. All of these allergy-infused mornings were not proving to be productive. Working on a software update was tedious work when there was a ring of itchy fog that blurred everything.

The newest security system James was working on provided an IR motion-tracking system with facial recognition and body scanning capability—something not currently on the market. Issues with CCT, known for distorted grainy images, was creating new opportunities for innovation and the right vision. In a world coming to life, thanks to new scientific and technological advancements that controlled everything and anything, knowing who was in your home at any given moment was a bonus to the navigation of busy lives.

With any expanding technology, working out the bugs was part of the process. The latest glitch that James was solving involved four-legged pets being mistakenly recognized by the software as two humans, albeit small humans. Once he got the system to recognize one set of four legs as Fido or Garfield rather than two kids, an entire group of animal lovers would flock to purchase a security system that ensured their beloved pet had made it through the pet door safely. James was counting on inventive engineering and a new marketing campaign that would give him and his career the boost he needed to put the younger developers on alert: this dinosaur wasn't prehistoric residue, and he could still leave a lasting positive imprint on the company.

Possibilities flitted through his mind. The goal would be a program that would not only greet everyone who entered, but have interactive capabilities, as well as various reminder notifications of things to be done. He heard it clearly in his head: JACK, WELCOME HOME. REMEMBER TO DO YOUR MATH HOMEWORK; YOU HAVE A TEST TOMORROW. And WELCOME HOME, JESSICA, CALL ME IF YOU NEED ME TO PICK UP DINNER. Simple programming options that allowed preprogramming or remote changes with a phone call. Monitoring and stored playback would also be available without the intrusion of a video feed. Gone would be the need for notes and notepads— not to mention nagging parents, who could now take a step back from being the source of daily canned messages that kids heard when they stepped through the front door after school. James knew that if he could make it all work smoothly, he could advance his company and his career.

But first, platform adjustments and program additions needed tending. Hours disappeared, and, with most of the code revisions complete and his headache gone, there was time for a late afternoon jog and then Spikes for pizza.

Chapter 3
Vermin Patrol

S pring flew by, and weeks gave way to warmer days. The familiar rhythm was always a constant blueprint of stability, giving James a sense of comfort. Adding to this, the crest of summer worked its magic as the late nights of work became longer. With his allergies getting worse, expanding past spring, James decided this was the year to make the Geek Shed more comfortable. A HEPA filtration system for dust and airborne debris would make working easier during the warmer months when he spent more time there.

"Jess, I have a project." With his most dashing and pleading smile, James crawled into the bed and leaned into Jessica, his head resting on her shoulder as he waited for her to pause in her reading and acknowledge him.

"Huh, Jimmy, you always have a project." Jessica rolled her eyes, then bent the corner page of her book before setting it down on the bedside table. She shrugged, giving him a narrow look as she tried to dislodge him, then arranged the pillows behind her head and sighed.

He continued to stare at her.

"OK, what?" She turned to him, so they were nose to nose.

He kissed her cheek. "The Geek Shed needs better ventilation for it to be in decent condition. Well, really, so I can breathe easier. You know how I like to breathe, right? Want to help me clean out those dusty, molding boxes and decide what we should keep?" He waggled his eyebrows, his cheesy grin even more exaggerated.

"Those boxes have been there for decades. Do you think there's anything left to keep?" She shuddered, pulling up the covers as if protecting herself from dust, mold, and the possibility of something worse. "There could be rats or mice living in those boxes, and you know I'm deathly afraid of things with beady eyes and long tails. I hate them." Jessica shook like a dog fresh from a dip in the lake.

With a smile of victory, he nuzzled closer and whispered, "I'll be your champion and defend you against the beady-eyed little monsters. You have always been able to count on me for vermin patrol." He puffed out his chest.

"I know, you are my King of the Vermin and always have been. When do you have this project on the calendar? You always have the date and details figured out before *yes* escapes my lips." She chuckled as she snuggled in for sleep.

"Soon. I was thinking this weekend, maybe Sunday. Does that work for you and the kids? Jessica?"

His wife's eyes were closed, a deep breath escaped her, and she was still.

Moving to his side of the bed, he pulled the covers up to his chest, turned off the bedside lamp, and whispered, "We'll talk about it this weekend." He reached out, searching for her hand. Upon finding it, he let his settle over hers and gave it a light squeeze.

"Love you honey," he said, his words intertwined with a sigh as he joined her in the magical Land of Nod.

Chapter 4
The Geek Shed

The Geek Shed looked much more magical at night. Filled with the yellow glow of an old overhead fluorescent tube light and the luminescent buzz of multiple computer screens, the electrical radiance floated out to the corners of the shed like ripples on a pond where a pebble is tossed, giving a fluid atmosphere when entering. But during the day, the dust and grime showed in the weak light from the two small windows and lent to the gloomy grayness of the garage.

James, Jessica, and the kids stood looking at the small garage. Stepping forward with a groan of effort, James lifted the manual door into place overhead. The interior looked older once exposed to the light of day, and the aged and forgotten castoff treasures of almost eighty years no longer hid within the shadows. The movement of air and dust created a cascade of sneezing that took minutes to get under control.

"Are you OK, Jimmy? Want me to get your inhaler?" Jessica asked.

"No, I'm good. Let's let the dust settle for a minute," James said with a sniffle, followed by a loud blow into his grandfather's handkerchief. James had carried that handkerchief with him since he was a boy, and it was one of his treasured possessions. Before placing it back in his pocket, he gently touched the frayed edge and blue embroidered letters as a sentimental reminder of a man who was kind to a fault and whose meticulous care and landscaping was seen everywhere in and around their home. "I'll pull out the large garbage can and shift some of the summer stuff off to the side so it's easier to move in there."

"How on earth you stay in there for hours is beyond me." Jessica waved her hand in front of her face in a desperate attempt to keep the dust and airborne debris from settling on her.

"Dirt, dirt, dirt, Dad," said a small voice from behind a large black garbage can. Alena's face appeared with a disgusted expression, as if she were sucking on a sour pickle. "Yuck, I'm not going in there, Momma." Her eyes narrowed and her upper lip almost touched the tip of her nose.

"No, baby, you don't have to go in there," Jessica said with a sideways wink to James. "We'll find the treasure all on our own."

"Treasure! I want to find treasure, too." Alena's protest became louder, her feet pounding in place, hands gripping the garbage can, moving it slightly back and forth as if getting ready to roll it at an invisible enemy if she didn't get her way. Her brother decided he would be first to explore, pushing her out of the way and knocking over the can while she decided whether the danger of possible monsters lurking in the corners of the garage was worth the adventure.

"Hey, Momma, Jack pushed me!" Alena's yell escalated to level seven on a scale of ten.

"All right, everyone," James said. "It's a family treasure hunt. Just give me an hour to get the treasure down from the rafters, OK?" He had a way of making mundane and tedious chores fun for the kids, but his exasperation was beginning to show. He didn't doubt there would be something of interest to them. Some of the boxes were from the 1950s, the contents mostly forgotten.

Jack and Alena sat side by side with their legs crossed, faces resting in their hands like two mirrored book ends, both staring into the gloom with anticipation. Jessica did most of the work once the boxes and film canisters were inspected by James and on the ground. She said she wanted to make sure there were no rats or mice in any of the boxes, and then they could help. The first three boxes were falling apart on one side. It was apparent there had been a water leak at one point, and James thought it might have been from a storm that had blown off some of the roof shingles in the late 1980s. The tape still held the top of the boxes in place, so Jessica used a pair of old pruning shears to cut the tape and pull the tops off, but only after feeling certain no critters were living within.

The first box was filled with items wrapped in old newspaper, edges brown with age, the faces from old advertising ads crumbling at the edges, looking out as they protected their contents from time. On the back side of the box, James made out three initials, the first faded due to the water damage, but the last two were clearly *J. A.* For the most part, the box contained loved objects stored with care, nothing thrown or hastily tossed in, including an old pair of boy's roller skates with one wheel missing, a green baseball jacket with a tiger on the back, a chess set, two worn baseballs with a slight mildew stain on one of them, a few old slot cars, a box with an old segmented toy track, and a separate box with the words *power supply* scrawled in black ink. James thought those tracks could carry cars in circles to any child's delight, and maybe some items could be sold for a few bucks, maybe more, depending on how rare. Jack wasn't having any of that, and he grabbed at an old cast-metal car, the green paint chipped, and the number *8* stenciled in white paint on each door.

"Ah, Racer 8," James said as he watched his son. "Racer 8 was the name my uncle gave to his favorite special car. Well, that's what my dad would say." Picking up an old newspaper, James walked to the garbage can, looking around for any other bits and pieces as he cleared the walkway that separated the Geek Shed from the backyard.

"Who do you think this belonged to?" Jessica gently touched the box with the two initials.

"I'm pretty sure it belonged to my Uncle Harold," James said as he also touched the box slowly, letting his eyes settle on each item as if taking in every detail. "Harold James Allen Jr. The H is gone."

"Harold? Oh, yeah, your dad's older brother," she said softly. "I think I've only seen a few photos of him, but I'm not sure. Your family is big." She knew there was something she didn't get, something her husband wasn't telling her.

"We can talk about it later," James said, looking over his shoulder.

Jack was playing with the toy car with enthusiasm in front of Alena while singing a made-up tune.

"The treasure is boys' stuff, it's boy stuff, not girl stuff," he sang, knowing she would pout and maybe cry if he kept it up long enough.

"Alena, we still have six boxes left, so there is much more treasure, baby," Jessica assured the now emotional and upset little girl.

The next box contained a baby book, with all the specifics, including hospital name, baby footprint in ink, identification wristband, and a card announcing *It's a Boy*, showing a stork flying with a baby dangling in a diaper. A haircut clipping, lovingly tied with a ribbon, yellowed at one end and faded to a brilliant sky blue on the other, was kept in an envelope marked as *Harold's First Haircut*. Also in the box were a white and yellow bib with a sad clown, a red pompom for his nose; a metal rattle that was almost completely rusted, which had been originally painted like a circus tent, a dash of green and red paint still clinging to the bottom; and a pair of bronzed baby booties fixed to a small whiteboard, with a label showing the time, date, and weight of a baby boy:

Harold James Allen Jr.
June 22, 1944, 6 lb. 4 oz.

Reading the name out loud, Jessica took a deep breath before glancing around to find her husband. She saw the sadness like a shadow that even his million-dollar smile couldn't break through.

"His things bring him close and make him more real somehow," she said as she touched the lock of hair peeking out of the envelope.

"My grandfather wouldn't talk about him much," James said in a hushed voice. "The story is tragic. Let's talk about it later." He gave her a glance as he jerked his chin in the direction of Jack, who was now poking around in the first box.

Alena, seeing the colorful bib and rattle, lit up, asking if she could use them while playing with her dolls. Jessica looked to James for approval, lifting her shoulders questioningly. He forced a thin smile, knowing the emotional value of his Uncle Harold's baby things. However, the bib being played with to feed one of Alena's many magical doll subjects wouldn't do any harm. It would give her a sense of inclusion in the treasure hunt.

"Sure," he said, turning to watch Jack play with his uncle's things.

The third and fourth boxes held a myriad of school papers: PTA announcements; a painting of a three-legged cat (or at least what looked like a cat and a tree); and a papier-mâché Santa Claus boot filled with old macaroni that must have been a necklace at one time, but the string had disintegrated, leaving only small segments rattling freely at the bottom. James, remembering the macaroni necklace Alena had proudly brought home just last year, laughed at the cohesive and familiar school projects that were obviously timeless. There were books that seemed to span a young life, including an 1885 copy of *Adventures of Huckleberry Finn*. James thought this might be worth something other than sentimental value, especially if it were a first edition.

The remaining boxes were filled with Christmas decorations, various tablecloths that seemed to span every holiday on the calendar, and old vinyl records, most of which were warped due to time and heat. It was obvious someone had loved Bing Crosby and Perry Como, as well as other smooth crooners of the time.

The last box was still in remarkably good shape. Most of the other stored items suffered water damage, but this one seemed to have escaped it. This box contained nothing but photos, some so old they were on tin and had most of the subjects wide-eyed and looking scared, likely due to the length of time it took to create the exposure. By the time they got to this box, both Jessica and James had lost the energy to look at the vast number of nameless faces, whose identification would take time and might be difficult, if not impossible.

It can wait, James thought, closing the box. "Let's look with new eyes, maybe tomorrow. Somewhere in this box may be an addition to the hallway wall," he said out loud, mostly to himself.

"Maybe we can travel further back than we first thought," Jessica said as she looked over his shoulder while moving some of the boxes to the corner and out of the way. "We can move the timeline up the stairs, before you get to the hall?" She gave an inquisitive smirk.

"Maybe, just maybe," James responded with a kiss on her nose before hoisting the box containing the photos onto his shoulder. "Let's close and lock up for tonight. This treasure hunting took longer than I thought it would. We can finish the cleanup tomorrow. I'll need to do something with these." He nudged the edge of one canister with his boot, then bent over, examining the faded and illegible label. "They're probably old home movies. Not sure if the film survived or not."

Jack, eager to play, asked to go to his room. There, he wasted no time building a ramp made of books and salvaged album covers for his newly acquired Racer 8 car. Alena cared little for toy cars, yet she followed her brother. She was smiling her elfin smile and humming, her few small treasures of the day tucked under one arm, accompanied by her beloved Mrs. Kelly, a stuffed squirrel named after her favorite teacher, who happened to love squirrels as much as Alena did.

His head congested, James headed to the shower to wash the dust off. When he returned, he found Jessica at the stove making spaghetti sauce. The cutting board held cloves of garlic, ready for cutting and crushing into the simmering minced tomatoes.

"Do you want to tell me about your Uncle Harold?" Jessica asked softly as she stirred the sauce, giving James space to decide on whether it was a good time to fill her in.

"Pfft." The escape of air was more than a sigh; it was a release. James sat down slowly at the table and rubbed his forehead, as if to clear away a veil that clouded his vision. "Well, I don't have a bunch of information, other than he died back in the late '50s," James said, staring at the saltshaker in the shape of the Space Needle. It provided a good focal point as he walked the halls of his memories, able only to recall bits and pieces from one relative or another.

"Uncle Harold, or Little Harold as the family called him, was around twelve at the time, I think, maybe eleven." He looked up at the ceiling as if he would find the answer there. "I'm sure we'll find his death announcement somewhere in the second box. I remember my father talking about it. It had something to do with a pick-up baseball game and the neighbor boy. There was an argument and a fight, I'm not sure over what exactly; some say the next-door neighbor was a bully, and the other boys didn't like him. They were arguing one minute in front of the house and in the street the next. The car didn't even have a chance to stop."

"Anyway, Dad was always, I don't know, secretive," he continued, his eyebrows pulled down in remembering. "He kept a picture of Little Harold on the table upstairs. One night he got upset when he thought someone moved it. Dad never let us go up to the attic, for some reason. He said to never go in, never move Little Harold's things." He shrugged, looking down at his hands.

Jessica set down the serrated knife she was using to cut onions, her heart wrapped in the pain she heard in her husband's voice, and she moved to be close, sitting next to him. She leaned in and touched his hand with a pat of reassurance, then stood, pushing her chair away from the table. Returning a moment later, she placed a cold beer in a pint glass in front of him, then moved back to the stove, crushing garlic, and chopping basil.

"Thanks." A smile tugged at the corners of his mouth, and he wrapped both hands around the glass as if drawing strength from the chill.

"Years ago, when Dad died, my mom cleaned up the attic and moved a bunch of Little Harold's things to the garage, I guess to make room in the attic for our stuff. You know, new stuff. God, there's a spot in the attic just for the dozens of board games alone. I was told my grandparents treated anything belonging to my uncle with reverence." He gave a nod, agreeing with his own last statement. His voice lowered with heaviness. "I can understand that. Dad basically lived in the shadow of his older brother and was never allowed to go near the street, so he stayed mostly upstairs in his room or the backyard." Arching his back to stretch his muscles, he took a deep breath, then sat back in his chair, finishing the last of his beer. He tilted his head, examining the foam that clung to the sides of the glass before setting it down.

The bubbling *plop, plop, plop* of the spaghetti sauce simmering calmed Jessica, giving her something to focus on as she looked down at her reflection in the pot of water she had placed on the stove to boil.

"Is it cold in here?" she asked, shivering. Jessica was sensitive to any tragedy, especially one that involved a child and her husband's family. Wrapping her arms around her shoulders for warmth, she turned to James. "I'm so, so sorry. I know it was a long time ago, but, still, it's so tragic. I find it strange about the room and his things. Don't you? I mean…" She sighed, searching for words. "I mean, why haven't you told me about any of it?" She gestured at the ceiling in the direction of the attic.

"It was a long, long time ago." James lowered his eyes, setting his jaw and dismissing with a wave of his hand the sadness that now permeated the air. He stood, reaching for her and sliding his hand down her arm, intertwining his fingers with hers. "I'm starving. It smells delicious. How much longer?"

Letting go of her hand, he bent over the spaghetti sauce and inhaled deeply, then turned back to her. Jessica closed her eyes, one tear catching in her lower lashes. He reached out to touch her cheek with his thumb, silent understanding moving between them as they tucked the subject of his uncle away for the night.

Chapter 5
Big Dreams

James was habitually a do-it-yourself kind of guy when it came to home repair, and shoring up the Geek Shed was easier and more satisfying than expected. The reflective fiberglass insulation went up easily and kept the dust to a minimum, which helped his head greatly. A HEPA filter was added, and now all he needed was to install his security system.

He intended to use his home to demonstrate that his innovative new technology worked. If there were no hitches, it would be his launchpad to reach upper management and the recognition he needed. As one of the main designers of his company's latest motion SGC-series facial recognition software, his focus was creating a system able to recognize not only facial characteristics with a higher level of accuracy, but also to recognize each person in their entirety, with an artificial intelligence component for interaction. Every person stepping through the door would be recognized: visitor, family, or intruder.

At times, Jessica would visit the Geek Shed, bringing late-night snacks with the occasional piece of pie. She never stayed for long, as it was all so foreign. The details of his work flew over her head, as she usually had more on her mind involving her own students. James made strides over the summer. The longer days gave him more time for work at night, once the kids were asleep. By the end of August, James had finished the code and improvements, which meant he was almost ready to give the system a try.

Jessica and James enjoyed the slow-motion quality that was the calm before September. Taking full advantage of the kids' summer activities, they spent extra time lingering over coffee and the morning paper while discussing small home projects on the honey-do list, which was in a perpetual rotation. Lightbulbs needed replacing, the lilac and forsythia cried out for pruning, and the box hedges needed constant care to retain their shape. Each time they went over the list, old things were crossed off and new items added.

"Hey, Jess," James called out after looking around the kitchen and, hoping she was within earshot. "Now that the equipment is finally installed, I'd like to connect the new virtual occupant recognition program today, boot up the system, and give it a test run. Any chance of taking the kids to the lake for a few hours so they won't be in the way?"

James tilted his head back, glancing at the newly installed IR motion tracking camera and speaker, then listened for his wife's distinctive footsteps and general location as she finished a few of the morning chores. The main hall above the kitchen always gave away the location of who was there. The creaks and movement of the cedar floorboards were as familiar to James as if the house were a part of him.

"Is today the day?" Jessica asked as she descended the stairs with the plastic laundry basket under her arm, joining him in the kitchen. "How exciting. You've been working on it for a long while now. Thank God you finished the installation. I thought I would be looking at wires dangling from the ceiling forever." She waved her free hand above her head, then pointed vaguely toward the front of the house. James cocked an eyebrow and glanced at the IR camera in the corner above her head.

"C'mon, Jess, don't you have faith in me?" He wrapped his arms around her waist, pulling her close. "I'm the geek man, king of the Geek Shed, remember?" He kissed her lightly before any protest left her lips.

"Mmm, I do believe that you, sir, are the king of the Geek Shed. So, yes, I have complete and utter faith in you," Jessica said, pulling back. "If I'm to wrangle the kids and get out of here, I'll need to finish what I'm doing, big boy." She winked, then leaned around him, looking in the direction of the kids, who could be heard shouting in the back yard.

"OK, OK," he said, letting her slip from his hands and turning her in the direction of the mudroom, which was home to the plastic laundry basket.

His security system was a labor of love. The challenge was with the full-spectrum IR projection and motion-tracking system. One or two IR motion-tracking cameras would be needed, depending on the size and shape of each room, including hallways. The attic space was primarily for storage and dust bunnies. So, along with the closets, James didn't think they needed to be monitored. The three bathrooms were considered private, personal space, and, therefore, would also be left out. The Geek Shed was off the list as well, as it was separate, and additional electrical upgrades would be needed to include it. To enhance the system, he had added a graphene lattice matrix to the filter pack, which had conductive use as well as optical properties. He needed to boost the optic sensor in the camera to enhance low light, IR, and a spectrum of light response for motion tracking. This would give a head-to-toe image and work with the facial recognition and 3D body-scan software.

The data would be stored on a separate server with a backup link to a password-protected work system. This would protect the integrity of the program if any malfunctions were to take place, or if there was a loss of power. When Jessica and the kids returned, he would call a family meeting to explain the system in the easiest and simplest way possible, and then he would take facial scans, assigning identity markers for each.

The installation of some software had taken more time than expected. Hallway corners and small spaces were challenging and left areas off the map. The Craftsman was bigger than the average home, and, while built-in nooks and spaces lent charm, they were a logistical nightmare for James. However, he knew that with time the bugs would all be smoothed out.

Later that evening, with his family back home, James gathered everyone into his small office and began the process of bringing his creation to life.

"What if I change my hair? Or gain weight?" Jessica questioned, looking at the keyboard as he uploaded the information into the program. "Can't it be, well, fooled?" She knitted her brows together as she moved her focus to the monitor.

"The system has a biometric readout that is ninety-eight percent accurate. Even though some things may change, your nose, eyes, and facial dimensions stay basically the same," James answered, not looking away from the screen. "The 3D body-scan technology I added has been under development for a while with my company, but the powers that be feel it's far enough along that they're allowing me to include it as a feature. It'll provide additional means of recognition, which other companies in the security market don't have. As far as I'm concerned, nobody will be able to touch my system for accuracy. You'll be able to see everyone in the house from an overhead, three-dimensional view. You'll not only know who is in the house, but you'll know what room they're in. This, combined with the perimeter security sensors, lets us know the home is secure. It will absolutely revolutionize home safety." He straightened in his chair and pointed to the left-hand side of the screen, which showed a basic outline of the house that could be moved or adjusted using the IR motion tracking cameras installed at various locations throughout the house, depending on the view he sought.

"So, for instance," James said, swiveling in his chair and looking at Jessica with the grin of a child who had just won first place at the science fair, "if Jack is to clean his room after school, you can look to see if he's where he's supposed to be."

"You mean, we can spy on the kids with more accuracy?" Jessica asked skeptically, then glanced at Jack and Alena, a look of puzzlement on their faces as they stared at the computer screen.

"Well, yes," James answered with a wink. "Bond is my middle name." He laughed as a smile tugged at the corner of his mouth.

Not wanting to dampen his triumphant mood, Jessica kissed his cheek, glancing at the control panel and then the monitor. "We'll see how things go," she said quietly.

***

The few remaining adjustments only took a few minutes. With the system upload complete, a test run was in order. Jessica had champagne on ice and had gone to get more sparkling apple cider for the kids. Jack and Alena were already mesmerized as their father tried to explain what they could expect now that the basic system was operational.

"Will you always see us?" Jack asked, looking at the monitor, which rumbled with a low vibrational hum as the power pulsed through it.

"We'll always be able to watch over you, yes," James said, patting Jack on the head.

Alena, curious now but oblivious as to why the fuss, chimed in, "Can you see Mrs. Kelly in my room?" Her nose was an inch from the screen.

"No, sweetheart, this only watches over the family," James said softly.

"But she is family, Daddy," Alena said, poking out her lower lip in a defiant pout.

"Well, maybe one day I can figure out how to add Mrs. Kelly." He rubbed her back as he adjusted the monitor.

Jessica entered, carrying the last two glasses of the kids' cider. Though the days were still long, evening seemed to come a bit earlier in the back of the house.

"So, are we all here?" James asked, looking around the room.

Jessica picked up her own glass, then checked to make sure everyone had a glass in hand. "Yep, all accounted for. Let's do this," she said with childlike glee. All were facing the monitor as James, with eyeglasses propped on the end of his nose, reviewed his checklist.

With his quick keystrokes, the monitor screen bloomed with color. The perimeter of the house and the interior walls were a bright green; the interior was a dark gray showing the room and hall space. Each floor was represented side by side, and the images could be configured based on the system owner's preference. Once uploaded, the virtual-occupant data of each home was represented by a stick figure of the approximate size comparable to the others in the household.

In the small room titled OFFICE, four bright blue figures appeared on the monitor. JESSICA, JAMES, JACK, and ALENA showed at the edge of the screen and, when clicked, their identity was highlighted.

"There we are!" James said with a large toothy grin. "Now, Jack, why don't you go to your room, stay there for a few minutes, and then come back." James patted his son on the shoulder as he gently turned him in the direction of the hall.

Once Jack exited the office, the remaining family focused on the small, moving figure identified as JACK on the monitor, as Jack himself began the journey from the back of the house, down the hallway, and then up the stairs. The stick figure on the monitor was now showing in JACK'S BEDROOM.

James felt a surge of excitement. He tipped his head back and yelled, "Jack, can you wave for me?"

The glowing, animated figure on the screen waved a slow and steady arc above its head. James adjusted the view, which gave two different angles. With a squeal of delight, Jessica lifted her arms in the air as if to signal a touchdown.

"It works! It works!" James was out of his chair, and he grabbed Alena, lifting her off the ground in one gliding swoop, her feet kicking with excitement. Jack, hearing his father's elation, flew downstairs and worked his way under his dad's arm to be part of the celebration. Jessica was her own private whirling vortex as she spun and danced, holding the glass of champagne high overhead.

"It works," they chanted in unison, "it works, it works!"

***

James spent his evenings over the following weeks working on integrating and entering data into the virtual response system. Each day, tasks and responses were cataloged and uploaded for each virtual occupant, also known as Identified Virtual Occupant (or IVO). Completion of each task schedule allowed the uploaded occupants to receive a list of instructions upon entering the home. The programming parameters would be adjusted and reviewed during the testing phase, based on feedback from the time-lapse interaction data and response from the IVO.

The task schedule was designed to be clear and direct. When Jack and Alena entered the house, the IVO response software would engage, and then the preprogrammed instruction software would respond via three key points set in the house. These points were chosen for their location and proximity to each level of the home. The first was located off the main hallway between the living room and the kitchen. Speakers were installed in all rooms, radiating out from each location and motion-tracking camera. Once the IVO was engaged, the listed tasks would be distributed via the speakers. The programmed tasks could only be silenced by entering an assigned coded response into a system keypad. Depending on the size of the location, additional keypads could be added for convenience. This took some getting used to, and Jack and Alena did not like being continuously reminded of homework or chores.

Like most kids their age, running off to their room was a way of ducking out of the dreaded chore list. But the new system always knew where they were, and their acknowledgment of the task message was currently the only way to stop it, if the system was set to REPEAT. The REPEAT feature allowed messages that were programmed to repeat every thirty minutes to an hour and could be adjusted based on the needs of the security system owner. Some IVO messages, however, could be programmed to announce only once. Often these messages were simple: REMEMBER TO CLOSE THE DOOR BEHIND YOU. Or REMEMBER TO TAKE OFF YOUR SHOES.

Chapter 6
Scotch Broth

Summer marched into fall, marked by the chill of cooler evenings. Days became shorter and leaves transitioned, hanging onto life with brilliant shades of gold and red, which gave the illusion of warmth against the evergreens. Knowing time waited for no man, James focused on his security system revisions, wanting to tweak and adjust the prototype so it would be running smoothly by the first of the year. This would allow him to generate several months of operational data to determine how well the system was working.

Remnants of warmer days still littered the yard: the small, now-deflated pool and a portable badminton set, short a racket and with only one remaining shuttlecock, had a sad misfit look as they lay in the yard. Their discarded state irritated James. He believed that everything had a place and should be cared for. He was a creature of habit when it came to organizing the family games, bicycles, helmets, sporting equipment, and camping gear. It was a ritual to oversee and rotate the family's treasured possessions. It gave him a sense of fatherly duty as he moved and replaced items throughout the changing seasons.

James maneuvered the green and blue collapsed lump of plastic under one arm, with the racket, shuttlecock, and portable net under the other, into the Geek Shed. He hung them on preassigned hooks, behind three discarded computer monitors, on the left wall under the window. Against the opposite wall sat the large box of family photos, flanked by the two mysterious film canisters, which leaned in the corner. There was considerably more room since throwing out old, damaged, and broken items. At Jack's urging, Little Harold's remaining things were neatly repacked, marked as pirate booty, and transferred to his room for safekeeping until he determined what treasures he would keep.

With the summer fun tucked away, James thought it might be a good time for a family project, yet another reason to continue cleaning out the Geek Shed. He hoisted the box of photos to one shoulder. "Guess who's in the photo?" he said out loud to himself, as if testing the suggestion before heading into the house for dinner.

He dropped the box of photos on the kitchen counter. It landed with a thud, narrowly missing a large container of Parmesan cheese and a tray of cooling sourdough biscuits.

"Let's have fun after dinner!" he said, grabbing a beer from the refrigerator and taking his seat at the kitchen table with Jack and Alena. Jessica gave her husband a razor-sharp look as she grabbed two potholders from a drawer next to the stove. She glanced at the large cardboard box, shaking her head, then opened the oven door, a warm rush of hot air hitting her face as she removed the casserole dish containing her special vegetarian lasagna. Using the heel of her shoe, she kicked the oven door closed, then set the piping hot dish to a waiting brass trivet in the middle of the table. The smell of garlic, basil, and tomato sauce wafted up, eliciting a "yum" response as hungry stomachs rumbled.

"Really?' Jessica sat down next to James, her eyes shifting from her husband to the box, which now had the kids' full attention.

"Couldn't you have waited until after dinner to bring that dirty thing into my clean kitchen? Good God, I can smell the dust and mold from here."

"Ick, Daddy, it's dirty." Alena held her nose, screwing up her face as if she was in physical pain from the presence of the box.

"Do you think it has treasure like the other boxes?" Jack asked.

"Not sure," James answered, "but I think there might be something of value somewhere in there. There could be a photo of someone famous, you never know, so let's hurry up and eat. Then we can dig in!"

After dinner, Jessica took the initiative, wanting to help the evening along. She moved the surprisingly heavy box of photos to the table. With one fluid motion, she lifted the lid and turned the box on its side, dumping the contents out but making sure to avoid any remaining dishes. "Let's see what we have now, shall we?" She continued to clear the table. "Hey, what about those film canisters? Should we see if we can have them transferred to, I don't know, something we can watch?" She set the empty casserole dish in the sink, filled it with water, then returned to the table, where the kids sat motionless, looking to their parents for direction.

James knew the chance of finding anything of value in the box was slim to none, but he wanted to keep the kids entertained. He shrugged. "I think the film might be disintegrating at this point, but I'll ask around at work and see if I can find someone to take a look."

He began separating the large mound of photos into piles as he gave instructions. "OK, Allen family, grab your stack, and any photos that have a name or date on them, please place them here." James pointed to the end of the table, moving plates out of the way. "Color photos with no name or date, place here." He gestured to an empty area at the other end, then added, "If we can sort everything in less than an hour, I'll take us out for ice cream, and, yes, Mrs. Kelly is invited."

"No cool stuff." Jack said, exhaling with disappointment. "Not like the other box with the jacket and Racer 8."

The sorting game lasted approximately forty-five minutes. Before the photos could be organized and cleared, an argument had begun over what was the best ice cream flavor.

"All right now, stop arguing, or no ice cream," James said with a direct look that meant business. Jessica, who loved to organize, let her eyes move over the table, then slipped away, leaving her husband to handle the chocolate-versus-vanilla debate at the Baskin-Robbins at the bottom of the hill. She returned to the table with labels and three smaller plastic bins, which she organized into categories. She labeled the bins with name, date, newer or older photos, and color or black-and-white. She placed a few newspaper clippings into a large manila envelope and taped it to the lid of the box containing color photographs.

It's the best I can do, she thought as she placed the lids on each box. *One mystery at a time.* Her hand slowly touched each box as she stacked them. Using a small hand truck, she moved the boxes to James's office and set them in the corner next to the desk. The mudroom door creaked and closed, startling her, the voices of her family returning. The animated giggles of Jack and Alena moved above her head in time with their light footsteps. She refocused on the task at hand and glanced through their contents one last time before leaving, turning out the light.

"Hello, husband. I take it the kids are happy and full of ice cream. Oh, and the photos are tucked away for the night," Jessica said in a quiet, weary voice as she entered the kitchen to find James reading *The Seattle Times*, a freshly chilled bottle of beer in front of him. "The kids brushing their teeth?" She picked up the remaining dishes before noticing the sink half full of warm, sudsy water and the open dishwasher neatly loaded.

"I wasn't sure if you were finished. There's one piece of pie left with your name on it." James smiled and winked, looking over the edge of the paper.

"I'm good, thanks," she said, dunking a dish once, twice, then turning on the faucet to rinse away the clinging suds. Drying her hands, she glanced at him. "Thanks for cleaning up. I didn't realize I took so long. There's something intriguing about those photos, and I found myself looking again, especially at the older ones with no names. Who do you think they are?"

He lifted his head, eyes narrowed in thought, letting the newspaper fall forward. His attention was somewhere off in the distance, remembering. "Well, let's see, there's my Grandma Lillian and Grandpa Harold. Oh, and Great-Aunt Jenny, that's Grandpa Harold's sister who passed away of pneumonia in 1978. There's also lots of photos of Dad as a small child. They called him Baby Jimmy for the longest time, I was told, which gave Dad a complex." He snorted. "Then you have the fringe relatives no one remembers. So many lives, and these are their memories. I feel we need to honor them in some way. I'm just not sure how." He folded the newspaper and sighed.

"I don't think we have enough wall space for all that time travel," Jessica said as, from behind him, she wrapped her arms around his neck, her cheek to his. "There were so many of your Uncle Harold, but then so few of your dad and your great-aunt Jenny. Did you notice? I thought it was sad, as if your dad and his sister didn't matter as much." Jessica took a seat next to James.

James sat very still for several minutes, thinking about the story the photos told. The sadness was evident in his eyes. "Yes, I think, as it would with any parent, the loss of Harold did irreparable damage. Some things can't be fixed. I think the pieces never line up in a heart with a hole in it." He took both her hands in his. "How would we ever heal from something like that happening to our two?"

Pulling her hands to his lips, James kissed the back of each before letting go. "I don't think we would fare well, either," he continued. "I know they did the best they could under the circumstances. Dad said they had a good life, but the loss left an indelible mark."

***

News of a proposed visit by Jessica's younger sister came in an email. Only a few years apart, Jessica was close to Tracy when they were young, and they leaned on each other through boy crushes, track meets, and homework. Yet the difference in life choices had become more obvious through the years: Jessica lived in Seattle, while Tracy lived in New York City. Jessica chose a family life, while Tracy was a single free spirit wearing the Crazy Aunt badge with honor. Never empty-handed, she always arrived bearing gifts. She was so loved that nobody in the family spoke of her quirky eccentricities. Jessica at times envied Tracy's nomadic life: Tracy traveled the United States with various art exhibitions, staying months at a time in one city or another. Even with a full life, however, she always made time for her beloved side gig of tarot card readings, paranormal investigating, and an occasional Ouija board session.

Jessica embraced her sister's differences, no matter how different Tracy's insight into otherworldly realms was from Jessica's grounded, logic-based earthiness. The paranormal was exciting compared to grading papers, tooth fairy assignments, and listening to the soccer moms lining the streets of her neighborhood.

"I smell your famous Scotch broth. What's the occasion?" James asked as he stepped in the door after a day of meetings with his implementation team at the office.

"Now why would you think that?" Jessica placed a freshly constructed apple pie in the oven.

"Well, you hate to cut up so many vegetables, and your pie crust takes elbow grease. Add that on top of a long week of school tests and all the grading you have to do…" He grabbed her around the waist as she slammed the oven door, turning her to face him. "Well?" James raised one eyebrow in suspicion as a smile tugged at the corner of his mouth.

"OK, OK," Jessica sighed. She avoided his inquisitive look before letting the words spill out in one breath. "Tracy is coming for a visit in about a month." She placed both hands on his chest, twisting the fabric of his shirt between her fingers, not yet looking up at him. Playing coy was a game she excelled at when she wanted her way with little pushback. "OK, my love?" She tilted her head up now, looking into his eyes in a hushed and pleading voice, fluttering her eyelashes dramatically.

"Is that it?" James loved the attention and would milk the game-like flirtation, which they both admitted took them back to their high school days.

"She's going to have an exhibit at the Seattle Art Museum, and I thought, well, it would be fun for her to stay with us," she said, now playing with his shirt buttons. "Besides, you know the kids love their Auntie." A coquettish smile crinkled her eyes. She locked her fingers around his neck and kissed him lightly, hesitating, breathing him in, tasting a hint of his last cup of coffee lingering on his lips.

"How long, exactly?" Wanting to keep her close, he feigned concern, pulling her tight, loving the feel of her as he looked into her eyes. *God, she is still as beautiful as the first day I noticed her,* he thought.

Managing to slip his grip, she moved to check on various pots that occupied the stove, some on the verge of bubbling over. A popping, sizzling clatter filled the air.

"She says no more than a few months." Her eyebrows furrowed as she stirred the simmering, golden stew, then lifted the spoon to her mouth for a taste. She closed her eyes and licked her bottom lip. "It depends on the success of the exhibit." She gave him a sideways glance and shrugged.

"I mean, it will be great. She can help around the house and with the kids," she continued, lifting another spoonful toward James, her free hand hovering under the spoon so not to drip on the floor.

"After all, she's flexible when it comes to her work schedule So, what do you think?" She passed the spoon just below his nose, a dimple pulling up her mouth in a smirk. "The way to a man's heart, you know."

He opened his mouth, and the rich aroma bloomed as the warm spices filled his mouth. It was delicious. "OK, Jess, but remember she was with us for almost six months during her last Modern Masters art exhibit." He knew in the end he had little choice, and he still loved the dance after so many years.

Chapter 7
Racer 8

The fog and rain kept the light at a minimum, which delayed the need to move from the warmth and coziness of their bed. With a second jolt of her alarm clock, Jessica reluctantly sat up, moving slowly, finding her slippers with her eyes still closed. Breathing deeply, she grabbed her robe and turned to find James with one eye opened as he followed her progress.

"You make the coffee, and I'll wake the kids," he said, flinging the covers aside.

"Deal!" She shuffled to the door, the belt of her robe dragging behind her.

James headed down the hallway just as Alena peeked her head out of her door. Her curls stuck out in every direction, with one flat spot on the right side giving away her favorite sleeping position.

"Good morning, sunshine," James said. "Time for breakfast. Why don't you head downstairs and I'll wake up your brother?"

Without a word, she headed down the hall; Mrs. Kelly, held by the tail, swung back and forth. Always a morning soul, she was the first in front of the television to watch *SpongeBob* while waiting for breakfast.

In the kitchen, Jessica pulled Alena to her, one arm around her tiny shoulder, squeezing her gently. "Morning, sweetie. Where's Daddy?"

"He's waking up Jack," Alena answered in a small, crackly morning voice, switching on the television.

James entered the kitchen, directing his sleepy son with one hand on his back. Jack was the opposite of his sister. It often took time and a bit of breakfast before he would utter a single word. Jack walked mindlessly toward the counter, where Jessica had lined up the family's easy breakfast choices. Grabbing his favorite, Toasti O's, he nudged his sister on his way to his chair.

"You took it. I know it," he said in a higher-than-usual whine.

His sister, engaged in her favorite undersea world of pineapple condos and burger-flipping crustaceans, ignored him.

"Mom, she took Racer 8, the car that I found in the Geek Shed." This time, on the verge of a meltdown, Jack hammered his fist on the table. His tone climbed an octave.

The underwater bubble Alena had immersed herself in was now broken. Turning, she glared. "I didn't touch your stupid car," she said calmly. Alena's response and range of whining was always more advanced in parental manipulation.

As if on cue, Jack reached across the table and grabbed Mrs. Kelly by the tail. Before Alena could hit a glass-shattering scream, her stuffed companion was airborne, landing with a splash in the sink's dirty dishwater.

"Stop it now!" James, at the counter pouring a cup of coffee, narrowly escaped a direct hit from the flying squirrel. His better-stop-or-else dad look froze Jack's spoonful of Toasti O's that was ready to launch at his sister.

"Don't even think about it, mister." Jessica grabbed the spoon from his hand, placing it back in his bowl. "It's probably under your bed. I saw it next to your pillow last night. You know your sister doesn't play with cars."

"Fine," Jack said, glaring up from the table. "She keeps moving my things, and nobody listens." Pushing back from the table with no further protest, he edged around his mom and disappeared.

"What's with him?" James shot Jessica a look of concern before turning to the sink to recover the soaked Mrs. Kelly. He squished her between his hands, ringing her out gently, then placed her on a kitchen towel to dry. "There, she'll be dry in an hour or two, baby girl, so no worries."

With the heroic rescue complete, he peeked into the various bowls and pans scattered throughout the kitchen, wondering what there was to eat. Knowing before he asked that the answer would be cereal, he grabbed a bowl and the box of Toasti O's and returned to the table. Alena had already forgotten the morning donnybrook and was again engrossed in her underwater world as the pink starfish made his morning entrance.

***

Jack's room was small. His twin bed positioned in the corner left only two sides open to the room. This gave him a sense of security, but he didn't know why. The walls were not overly cluttered. Two shelves took up most of the wall opposite the closet. Several Little League trophies gleamed on one end, and a mechanical T-Rex, missing a right arm, sat in suspended animation, looking the worse for wear. Books were piled with no sense of order, some open. His prized possession, a signed football from Seattle Seahawks linebacker Chad Brown, was front and center on the bottom shelf, so it could be easily shown off. A small desk stood to the right of the closet. Above it hung a small corkboard, empty aside from a picture of Spiderman, his favorite action hero, who appeared to be jumping from the page in perpetual motion, staring back into the room.

He sighed and flung his pillows from the bed with one hand

and pulled back his red rocket bedspread with the other. He looked under the bed, finding a bunch of dust, one sock, a baseball cap with a cartoon goat holding a slice of pizza, and a few tiny plastic buildings that were remnants from a sleepover game of Monopoly. Opening the closet, he shoved aside the box that had been found in the Geek Shed's rafters. He tossed his sneakers, one pair of dress shoes, and a set of shin guards from Little League to one corner.

Defeated, Jack returned to his bed, head in hands. As he stared at the floor, he noticed the green jacket, previously packed away with the rest of the treasures, now hung on the back of his desk chair. Smelling the mustiness of the coat, he tilted and turned his head to get a better look, trying to make out the writing on the back, which was cursive and faded. He shrugged, thinking it weird, but it wasn't his focus. He wanted to find his new favorite treasure. He wanted to find Racer 8.

Standing in the doorway, Alena held a damp but relatively un-harmed Mrs. Kelly. "I didn't take it," she said again.

"Yeah, right," he answered, looking up through his eyelashes and rolling his eyes mockingly.

"Maybe your friend took the car with the eight upstairs?" Edging into the room, Alena took a step aside and leaned against the wall, ready for a quick exit.

Jack was puzzled and frustrated, the tips of his ears turning pink. "I haven't had anybody over since JJ's birthday." He screwed up his face, looking at the ceiling as he tried to remember.

A distinct look of annoyance brewed in her eyes. "I saw him go up the stairs to the playroom."

"No way! Why would anyone wanna go up to that dirty, stupid room?" He dismissed her as he returned his gaze to the floor. "It's all your play clothes, and dolls, and...well, icky stuff."

"It's your icky stuff, too." She kicked the wall mindlessly with her heel, eyebrows furrowed, then moved to the doorway.

"Yeah? What stuff do I have up there?" He let his hand drop

from his chin as he looked up in the direction of the attic.

"You know, the racetrack. The one that was in pieces." With a finger, she drew a figure eight in the air and made a rumbling *vroom* noise.

Jumping up from the bed, Jack shoved past his sister.

The playroom was a small, twelve-by fifteen-foot space on the right side of the attic, with one brick wall containing the chimney. On the left, the larger attic room was open, included the staircase landing, and held unused furniture as well as most of the family's mementos and holiday decorations. Two small dormer windows, one in each room, offered inadequate light, creating a need for several floor lamps. Inside the playroom was an old, blue, leather-belted, duck-cloth steamer trunk, which held long-loved—but discarded—toys, along with clothing often used for dress-up. A frayed wool carpet, relocated from storage to protect young knees and elbows, covered much of the unfinished pine floor.

Now the room held an additional item. In the middle, just as Alena had described, was a racetrack. The Scalextric track was set up in an under/over in a figure-eight shape, like one of thousands sold in the mid-to-late fifties. The room was in shadow, but, on the farthest end of the track, a green race car—with the number eight clearly visible—was illuminated by light from the window.

Chapter 8
Testing 1 2 3

In his office, James was eager to overload the new system in order to find and reveal any hiccups or flaws that needed revision prior to rollout. False alarms and disappearing objects had more to do with the house's many nooks and crannies than the software itself. However, the system needed to be flawless, regardless of how large, unique, or old the home happened to be. The company wanted the usage and testing monitored for at least a year while they worked on a marketing plan and assessed the feasibility of upgrading their current subscribers.

To check the system, James ran test commands. One day, he had six scheduled interactions for Jack alone. It started with JACK, TAKE OFF YOUR SHOES WHEN YOU ENTER and moved throughout the house, scanning Jack's movement. When leaving the hallway to enter the bathroom, Jack was given instructions to make sure to PUT THE SEAT DOWN. James loved that one and chuckled while he created it. When he entered his room, Jack was told to START YOUR HOMEWORK, followed by the standard TAKE OUT THE GARBAGE when he entered the kitchen.

James believed that the system would include all of these messages. The user would check those and assign them to the appropriate avatar.

James was proud of the system's abilities and thought some preprogrammed interactions would make the system easier for the user. Jessica, on the other hand, found it to be a bit intrusive and didn't think the general public would approve. James was especially excited about the voice modulation simulator that would mimic the programmer's inflection, cadence, and tone. There could be up to four voices loaded at any one time and included language options. Each day, the voice modulator could be set when assigning programmed interactions.

Most subscribers would want to include every important room in their house, so dealing with a smooth transition to and from NO PROFILE areas was imperative. These areas on the location map would be dark when presented for the viewer. In addition to closets, many would opt out of having bedrooms included, uncomfortable with the monitoring and backup of their actions on a company hard drive. When a virtual occupant entered a NO PROFILE area, their avatar would appear to step off into space.

Like most security systems, several monitoring options could be set. The AT HOME setting could include a perimeter activation, while turning off the voice interaction monitor. However, James liked using it while they were home in order to witness timing firsthand and work out any glitches. The AWAY mode would send any motion-sensor activation to the owner's computer as well as to the monitoring company.

James wanted the new system to give an AI experience, but without the sci-fi creepiness of a maniacal supercomputer looking to keep its humans under its control. He imagined the voice processor would help eliminate that fear by being familiar.

Weeks went by, and James made adjustments here and there. Some errors were coding issues and easily fixed, while other strange and reoccurring events stumped him.

One such event occurred at night in the front entry hall. A PNI, or person not identified, caught on a stored video feed, appeared and then disappeared in several other areas of the house. Being aware of such glitches was imperative during the various developmental stages of the system, and many had gone unnoticed within the overall activities of his busy household. James checked all perimeter and interior systems, yet found no real issues. The monitor displayed full movement. These events were unnerving to Jessica.

Most times the glitches happened when the family was together in the kitchen, but an occasional disembodied voice would sometimes float up from the entry hall while they were sleeping. The only comforting fact was that the intruder alarm was never activated, nor was there any evidence of a sensor breach.

One night, they had just settled into bed, with the security system set on AT HOME mode, when they heard a chime followed by: PERSON NOT IDENTIFIED, PLEASE REMOVE YOUR SHOES.

"Again?" Jessica groaned, getting angry. "And what is that vibration? Shit, James, you really need to figure out that glitch. It feels like a giant car is idling in our crawl space." She turned to the clock on the nightstand and glared back at her husband before pulling the blanket high on her chest, as if chilled. "Good God, it's after midnight. I'm really getting sick of this." She pulled her pillow out from under her head and covered her face dramatically while elbowing her husband.

"Ouch, Jess! Maybe it's a small earthquake," he mumbled, rolling onto his back, closing his eyes, and listening to the house. "We *are* due for a big one, you know."

"Fix it, would you?" She hit him with the pillow as she pulled the blanket up farther under her chin and curled into herself.

Exhausted from a long day, he struggled to figure out this pesky continuous error. His canned response of *I'll figure it out, dear* wasn't cutting it anymore. James gave her a pat on the hip as he sat up, throwing back his covers. "I'll turn off the voice announcements. OK, babe? I know it freaks you out."

As he reached the bedroom door, another monitored system response rang out downstairs: PERSON NOT IDENTIFIED, PLEASE REMOVE YOUR SHOES. Grumbling under his breath, he slipped through the door and down the hall to the second-floor landing. At the top of the stairs, he bent to get a good view of the entry hall. Below, the night-light cast shadows that seemed to expand and waver like waves on a desert highway in hundred-degree heat. The strange thrumming tingled in the soles of his feet. Out of the corner of his eye, he saw a movement for a fleeting second. He stopped midstep. His chest expanded with an intake of air, and the hairs on his arms stood up. Realizing he was holding his breath, he exhaled. Did he hear someone calling him? He saw the green light on the front door security pad. *No tripped alarm, no breach in the system,* he thought, calculating the chance of an intruder.

"C'mon Jimmy," he said quietly, nervously shaking his head. He hugged the wall as he descended the stairs. There was a strangeness in the air, as if a physical void held the space in front of him. Narrowing his eyes, he leaned forward, scanning the floor below, but saw and heard nothing. Reaching the bottom of the stairs, he opened the front hall closet and grabbed the old Louisville Slugger he kept for protection. He stood listening to the house he knew well. The golden glow from the range hood above the kitchen stove spilled into the hall before him. The light was steady. *A good sign,* he thought. Anyone in the kitchen would need to pass in front of it if their goal was to escape.

"Get it together, Allen," he said as he moved with greater urgency, flipping switches and turning on every light he came to, hoping to dispel the darkness and reveal any possible hiding place.

His office was its usual sea of green light as he checked the system for malfunctions and sensor hiccups. The soft illumination of the monitor added to the eeriness of the room. James looked at the screen, his name pulsing slowly. "Well, there I am."

He pulled up the event history and hit Replay. There, in the hallway, was the PNI and, at the top of the stairs, he saw the figure marked JAMES approach as the PNI disappeared.

"What the hell?" He leaned close to the screen as he hit Replay again. "What type of glitch has arms, legs, and looks around?"

Turning off the voice announcement system, James sat in his office contemplating what to do. *I'll need to figure out the problem soon,* he thought, scratching his head, then rubbing his brow. He felt one of his stress headaches creeping in. Jessica was beginning to push him for answers, as this sort of thing was unnerving her. For the first time, it was beginning to unnerve him as well. This would also be irritating to the corporate talking heads, who were eager for progress. He pinched the space between his eyebrows and stood up, hitting his knee on the desk. "Shit." He glanced one more time at the system monitor and headed back to bed.

Chapter 9
The Arrival

Tracy loved to fly early in the morning when traveling to the West. It allowed her to spend more time getting settled when she landed—she called it her best form of time travel. "Home, home, home," she'd whisper before exiting the plane. The Emerald City was, and would always be, home.

As the taxi turned the corner near her sister's house, the canopy of oaks was full, the leaves bright orange, gold, and red as they transitioned into fall. *Damn, this city is still so beautiful,* she thought.

"Can you go around to the back?" she instructed the driver.

To own a house like this would be a dream come true, she thought, wishing her parents would have held onto her childhood home. This would have given her an additional anchor and reason to stay. But, like it had for many, the housing boom presented early retirement options and warm horizons in the Arizona sun for her parents.

Armed with the security code from her sister in case no one was home to greet her, she entered the house. "Hello?" The echo seemed large, almost mocking, as if the void would draw her in and tap into her life force.

After entering the mudroom off the kitchen, she heard the soft beeping and saw the alarm panel to the left of the door. She entered the code, and a bell-like chime rang out. She thought it sounded like a harpsichord being tuned. The tone was soft, then, from above, a female voice announced: PERSON NOT IDENTIFIED, PLEASE REMOVE YOUR SHOES.

"What the hell?" she hissed through pursed lips. "Hello? Jess? Is that you?" Dropping her bags, she stood waiting. The silence that answered her was heavy, the weight of it frightening.

"Ha!" Laughing, she picked up her bags, made a 360-degree turn, and surveyed the area near the kitchen.

"OK, this is funny. Sis, what are you up to?" Tracy called out, hoping to elicit a response from the disembodied presence that sounded like her sister in tone.

Not flustered easily and rarely scared, she was nonetheless unnerved. A cold sweat ran down the center of her back, and her breath came faster as the air moved around her. The house didn't feel empty, and she was aware that something was different. Something was wrong.

Quirky, she owned her sensitivity in all things of the ghostly realm. Her abilities were respected by those who knew her, those who knew exactly what she was capable of. She had a way of finding any type of missing thing. On more than one occasion, she had found a lost pet, predicted political race results, helped locate a lost piece of jewelry; the list went on. In addition, Tracy also had the gift of precognition, a heavy burden even for the strongest of mediums. In college, she was not the most popular girl when it came to dating, as many a young man feared she'd expose their secrets.

"Well, you have a bunch to explain, sissy." With a sigh, she resumed her journey from the back of the house to the second-floor guest room. Reaching the top of the stairs, she noticed the round black lens of what she assumed was a camera of some kind just under the crown molding at the end of the hallway. A red light to the right blinked on the outer edge of the lens casing. The apparatus was no bigger than the standard makeup compact.

"Can you see me?" she wondered aloud as she entered her room.

She tossed her travel clothes in the corner hamper, quickly exchanging her moto boots and jeans for a well-used pair of WSU sweatpants and T-shirt she had purchased as a freshman in college. She called it her comfort uniform and wore it for cleaning, lounging, and sleeping.

With her suitcase unpacked and toiletries tucked away, Tracy figured a quick nap would relieve the jet lag, which was sure to dampen the excitement of the much-anticipated family reunion scheduled to take place within a few hours.

Jessica and the kids arrived home, Jack pushing his sister to the side as they made a beeline upstairs to surprise their aunt, the chime greeting each by name.

"Hey, hey. Slow down and knock before you run over your aunt," Jessica yelled as they disappeared up the staircase. "OK, here we go." She knew chaos was on the menu, along with eggplant Parmesan.

James was through the door minutes later, a bundle of kindling and wood balancing precariously in his arms; it was his job to build a fire when the chill crept in with the sunset. "Everyone upstairs?" he called as he moved the fireplace screen slightly to stack the kindling behind it.

"Yep." Jessica entered the room and patted his shoulder, bending to kiss his cheek. "I like it when you smell like a tree." She chuckled, dusting off a few pine needles clinging to his shirt and redirecting her attention to the commotion coming from above.

"I'm starting dinner," Jessica yelled, chin up, hoping to be heard above the kids' manic chatter. "Sis, get your butt down here and help!"

Tracy joined her sister in the kitchen. The kids held fast and close, not wanting to miss a moment. The smell of garlic, basil, and Parmesan permeated the room as Jessica set the table.

"Here, let me help." Tracy grabbed napkins and plates.

"Mmm, I'm thinking a nice Chianti?" James chimed in as he entered the room, dusting away small pieces of wood splinters that clung to the front of his pants.

"Yes, I love a good Chianti," Tracy answered, looking at Jessica, who responded with a raised and a grin.

Hours disappeared. Everyone talked eagerly over each other as if they would burst into flames if they didn't urgently share their stories. Jack shared his latest book review, knowing his aunt loved the classics as much as he. Alena was much more content with just being part of the girls' club, all while James traveled between his office and the Geek Shed to review the data errors within the new security system. He occasionally stopped by the kitchen table to listen in on the latest adventure of his much-loved sister-in-law. Both Jessica and Tracy fell into their usual companionable rhythm, picking up where they had left months earlier.

* * *

"Hey, you." Tracy looked up at James, who was standing next to the table. She readjusted on her chair while she sipped her tea, pulling one knee to her chest. "Sit and visit, dear brother. Everyone else has called it a night." She motioned to the chair across from where she sat. Just then, giggles echoed from above as Alena settled into bed. Both James and Tracy looked up, listening.

"Past her bedtime." James said. "She's excited to have her favorite auntie here."

"So, tell me about this new system you designed?" Tracy asked. "It's a little creepy when you have no fair warning, don't you think?" She sipped her tea and warmed both hands on her cup.

"C'mon, I'll show you." He stood still for a minute, as if the room was about to tilt and catch him off guard. "I know it's been a long day, but it's important to share some of the basic features so we can avoid the creep factor." He patted her on top of her head.

Tracy gave him an upward glance and an eye roll but followed him down the hall to his office.

Simplifying engineer geek-speak to the average human was something at which he excelled. Not everyone within his company understood the code and engineering infrastructure of their systems, and they would become stupefied at meetings that included too much technology and not enough highlights simplifying functionality. As he and Tracy entered the room, the small, antique, green desk lamp that had been his grandfather's enveloped the room in a rich glow, making him feel as if he were underwater. The lights of the security system beeped, displaying SYSTEM NOT ENGAGED in the center of the monitor.

"First, let's take some pictures, then give you a scan and get you in the system." James picked up a handheld device, much like a camera, that he used to map each home occupant. He instructed Tracy to stand against the wall with her arms out at a forty-five-degree angle, and an image appeared on the monitor. James proceeded to take headshots, front facing and in profile. He assigned the name TRACY and included her information in the data file.

"There, we're done!" James said with what enthusiasm he had left as he looked at his watch. "Now, just know everyone living here is identified upon stepping through the door. There will be two modes, like with most systems, AWAY and AT HOME. I'm setting the system to the latter now that we're all present and accounted for." He peered over the top of his eyeglasses, trying to gauge if she were following along before continuing. "When there's a break or trip in the perimeter sensors by someone with no alarm code, then the system will sound a very loud alarm. As for testing the system, simple commands are included in the beginning, because I want to observe how they work and if there are any issues with multiple entries or movement. It can be simplified and customized by the user."

Tracy pointed to the monitor as James typed away, adding her digital outline to the list of family members. She touched the screen, where her name glowed and exhaled slowly. The rudimentary stick figure had no discernable features other than her name.

"So, I'm now a part of this virtual home forever?" she asked, moving her gaze to the home footprint and inner walls identified in a multilevel diagram. "How exactly does the system know we are there, or is it here?" She pointed to the floor in front of her, then back at the screen.

"Yes!" James exhaled, scratching his head with a pause, looking to where her hand now rested on the screen. "Well, in a nutshell, the IR motion-tracking cameras and speakers are mounted at key points throughout the house and are the eyes of the house, so to speak. The way it works is each level of the house—be it a hallway or a room—is basked in a million pinpoints of light. Those pinpoints of light are then used to measure distance."

He pointed to the screen where the three levels indicated where the cameras were positioned and continued. "What the cameras are seeking is a head, shoulders, knees, and toes: whether human or beast. It's looking for a three-dimensional figure as the light moves across the space and, when those million points of light are interrupted, if that pattern measures a human shape, it communicates the information—along with the facial recognition software—and the data is relayed back to the system that there is, in fact, a figure standing there."

One corner of his mouth pulled up in a wry grin. "It's not what you would consider artificial intelligence, or AI; it is more like a digital interactive system that connects and supports function and safety." He sounded like a commercial advertisement. "I promise that nothing is creepy, and I can turn off the interaction with any uploaded inhabitants, so it doesn't get annoying. We'll work out all the bugs and keep the interactive responses to a minimum. The only message I'll leave on all the time is for a newbie who enters to remove their shoes; the family knows better. Well, I'm off to Bedfordshire. I'm exhausted." With a wink, he was gone out the door, his footsteps fading as he disappeared down the hall.

"If you say so, Jimmy." She sat in his office chair and whirled around, head lolling against the backrest. Lifting her head, she stopped mid-revolution, noticing the film canisters and boxes in the corner of the room. Curious, she got up and lifted the lid of the first box with the manila envelope taped to the top.

The smell of time, mold, and degrading paper leapt from the container of family photos. With care, she placed the first box on the desk and opened an envelope that contained various newspaper clippings and announcements. The first article featured a photo of two young boys, standing side by side, under the headline: *Tragic Accident Takes the Life of Two Seattle Boys.*

The first boy had a pleasant face and a flat-top haircut popular in the 1950s, but his eyes had a sad, faraway look. The other boy smiled pleasantly, his mop of curls cropped short above the ears.

"Too young and so sad," she said under her breath. Her eyes stopped at the name of the second boy—Harold Allen Jr. With a sharp inhale, she placed her hand over her mouth as if she'd revealed a secret by reading his name.

"Harold," she whispered, transfixed, not able to look away. One curl seemed to stand alone, as if to escape the top of his head; she thought of how his mother must have worked hard to keep his curls under control. Using one finger, she traced the line of his cheek and then continued to read:

The Seattle Times, June 26, 1956

Tragedy at play today when two boys, Jeffrey Simmons, 11, and Harold Allen Jr., 12, both of Seattle, were struck and killed by motorist Ezra Johnson of Shoreline. Seattle Police

Chief Fredrick Calputto stated that a full investigation will be completed and released shortly. Allen died at the scene; Simmons died several hours later at Harborview Medical Center. Several witnesses have given statements noting that the driver may not have had time to stop and most likely will not be held at fault.

"I'm sorry, Harold," she said as she set the various clippings aside. A chime rang out, followed by something that sounded like escaping air and a flash of light: PERSON NOT IDENTIFIED, PLEASE REMOVE YOUR SHOES.

Jumping, she spun around to see a figure appear on the monitor. PNI was blinking red as if in warning. The figure was small, standing in the front entry of the house.

"What the hell?" she muttered, moving closer to the monitor, as if it would clarify what she was seeing. "Where did you come from?" On the monitor, the alarm was set to HOME, the entire perimeter secured.

"Who are you?" she said under her breath as she slowly stood, keeping her eyes on the monitor. The PNI moved, turning first left and then right before stopping. Then, with a forward motion, the figure disappeared.

Adrenaline took over, prompting her to move. She was at the hallway door, then running to the front of the house, stopping abruptly when she reached the middle of the entry hall. Her heart fluttered, thumping loudly in her chest, making it difficult to listen for movement. She stood in the soft golden glow of the night-light placed along the baseboard near the staircase. The smell of ozone lingered in the air, giving it weight as it filled the space around her like smoke rising above a bonfire. Planting her feet, she struggled for balance, swaying as if the home was adrift on a stormy sea.

"Shit, fuck." She uttered the words with a breath of realization: She had experienced this feeling before. Someone or something was moving between dimensions. She was being pulled in. "I'm in a motherfucking wake!"

Her heart fluttered, then slowed, as did the sound of blood rushing in her ears, allowing her head to clear. No sounds or movement from above. She was stupefied. It had felt like the sudden impact of a lightning strike. How on earth did they not hear it? Looking up at the hallway that led to the bedrooms, she stood for a few minutes, her hand on her heart as if to monitor its erratic behavior.

Strange things happened to her even as a small child. She would try to share these events with her parents, but they dismissed her with a pat on the head and a comment on her colorful imagination.

Her energy drained as she stood trying to get her bearings. Her legs felt as if warm lead encased them. Her body still thrummed as she reached the staircase, pausing once more to listen to the house. She heard the faint ticking of the kitchen clock as she grabbed the banister. Pausing, she shook to shed any spectral remains, like a dog shaking water from its fur.

Chapter 10
The System

The morning light crept in, with thin pale slivers framing the curtains. Shafts of light lifted the darkness of the room. Tracy had been laying there for hours, waiting for sleep to take her away, but the sandman and his magic dust failed miserably. *What time is it?* Tracy thought. She knew Jessica would be up soon and felt it was best to avoid the family and the sister who could read her with a glance.

"One early morning meeting coming up," she said as she dug through her suitcase for a quick change. She needed an exit in order to process the ghostly unveiling from last night that clung to her like a spiderweb.

She dressed in classic New York chic—hair in a top bun, minimal makeup, leggings, and an oversized sweater with a pair of white sneakers that seemed out of place in the rainy fall weather. Grabbing her gray peacoat and neoprene tote, she crept down the stairs as quietly as she could. Upon reaching the entry hall, she stopped and surveyed the silence. As she turned toward the door, a voice came softly from behind her.

"Want a cup of coffee before you run away?" Jessica stood in the early morning light of the hallway wearing light-blue flannel pajamas. Her hair was disheveled from sleep, and she was grasping a cup of coffee with both hands. Raising one brow, Jessica gave Tracy an inquisitive what-are-you-up-to? look.

"Good morning, sis. No, I'm good. I'll grab a coffee downtown. God knows there's a coffee shop on every corner in this city." Tracy laughed nervously, not wanting to make eye contact with her sister. "I have an early meeting at the museum and need to get a jump on things. Since when do you get up when the frogs fall silent? Sheesh." Fumbling for her cell, she concentrated on calling a cab, with hopes of appearing distracted rather than obviously avoiding her sister. Looking up at the speaker in the upper corner near the front door, she waited, expecting the creepy chime.

"What…what are you listening for?" Jessica asked, head cocked as if she could read her sister's mind.

"I was waiting for your system to tell me to have a good day, or don't forget your umbrella, since it might rain." Tracy rolled her eyes and shrugged.

"Oh. I turned off the system when I started the coffee," Jessica said, still half-asleep as she stepped closer. "So, will you be home for dinner?"

"Let me see what I need to get done today," Tracy answered, brows pulled down in concentration as she focused on her phone.

"Yellow Cab." The voice on the other end seemed miles away, as if coming from under the city somewhere.

She lifted the phone to her ear, at the same time addressing her sister, who stood looking quizzically at her. "I'll try to be home by seven, but don't wait for me. I love leftovers, anyway." She held up a finger as she gave their address to the dispatcher.

"The kids will be disappointed, but I'll let them know you'll be home as soon as you can." Jessica moved in, hand outstretched, grabbing the sleeve of Tracy's coat and pulling her in for a sleepy, half-hearted, one-armed hug, careful not to spill the coffee sloshing in her cup.

"Love you, Trace," she whispered before disappearing down the hall.

"Love you, too," Tracy said in a lost, disconnected voice as she gazed at the space where last night's visitor had stood. She turned and walked out the door, melting into the damp Seattle morning, not knowing how to deal with the knowledge she held and the dangers she felt were lurking within the house.

Returning later that evening, she climbed the front porch, hesitating as she placed her hand on the doorknob. Placing the key in the lock, the door opened with a low rumbling creek. She saw the light from the kitchen, a brilliant glow that bloomed from the heart of the house, down the hall, and to the front door. One tote strap was over her shoulder, the other hanging freely, and it caught the doorknob as she entered, spilling the contents of her bag everywhere.

"Shit, shit, shit," she grumbled sharply as she bent to pick up the mess and put her bag back on her shoulder.

A melodic chime, followed by HELLO, TRACY, came from above. She muttered, cursing under her breath, and yelled, "James? Must you use Beethoven's harpsichord as a lead-in for your disembodied message?" She lifted her head and looked up as if questioning God himself. She hung her coat on one of the hooks that lined the right side of the hall, kitty-corner to the foot of the stairs.

A shadow filled the hall as James shuffled out of the kitchen, a large glass of red wine in hand. "Good evening to you, and I like Beethoven, by the way." He glanced at the small speaker mounted in the corner of the ceiling while handing her the wine.

Tracy took it, accepting his peace offering.

His eyes settled on her. "If you hate it, I can deactivate you, but I really would like to see how the system works out." James glanced up at the small red light on the IR motion tracking camera in the corner next to the front door.

Tracy smiled, taking a long sip and closing her eyes as she inhaled deeply. "God, I needed this. What a long, long day. It's OK, though, your system can stalk me as long as it doesn't take my soul." She rolled her eyes.

"Auntie Tracy!" An explosion of energy came as Alena squealed, running at her with a piece of yellow construction paper gripped tightly in one hand. "I made this for you." She wrapped her arms around Tracy's waist and dropped her creation to the floor. "Look, it's our family."

Picking up the picture, Tracy found a typical stick figure collage painted in watercolor that included a house, a family, and what looked like a squirrel. "Thanks, baby. Is that Mrs. Kelly?" She squinted one eye, picture in one hand and wine in the other. "I love it!"

The strain and sleep deprivation were apparent in every line of Tracy's face. *How do I ignore what happened last night?* she wondered as she walked to the kitchen, followed by James and Alena. Something still felt off. The Craftsman she'd come to know as a second home felt strange, and she couldn't shake it. *Has it always been this active?* She stood in the hallway, looking into the kitchen, her trancelike focus on the gleam of the blue tiles that ran the length of the counter.

"Tracy? Hello. Tracy?" The questioning voice of her sister came from the kitchen table. Jessica sat with Jack, working on his math assignment. "Come sit down. Have you eaten? There's cherry pie, and it's still warm."

Shoulders slumped, her energy drained, Tracy crossed the kitchen and took a seat at the table. "Sorry, I am tired this evening. Hey, mmm, this looks delicious, is it all for me?"

Picking up a fork, Tracy pulled the pie tin close in a protective gesture, raising the fork as if she were about to plunge in and eat what remained. This, of course, was a direct effort to delay any real conversation.

"No," Jessica said as she flicked Tracy's hand. "There's an entire half of pie left, and one piece is for Jimmy's lunch, so grab a plate and I'll cut you a slice." Jessica cut several pieces.

A chime sounded softly. DON'T FORGET TO BRUSH YOUR TEETH, JACK. Followed by another DON'T FORGET TO BRUSH YOUR TEETH, ALENA.

"Damn Beethoven," Tracy grumbled, looking up as if the voice hovered in mid-air above her. "What's that? The kids aren't getting ready for bed just yet, are they?" she asked her brother-in-law, who was entering the kitchen.

"Hey, some parents will find great value in the new system," James said, pulling up a chair. "I was just running some tests. I think reminding kids to brush their teeth is a good thing. Just ask the Tooth Fairy." He chuckled, glancing at Jack, who was busy working on his homework and didn't look up.

Tracy gave him a direct look. "Yeah, I guess, but I'm glad I don't have to worry about it. I mean, think about all the things kids have to be reminded to do on a daily basis. Some households will have messages going all day and night!" She snorted as she licked cherry pie off her fork.

"I think it'll be a big hit, or at least I'm counting on it." James glanced at Jessica, who was smiling proudly at him. Reaching out, she touched his hand and gave it a tender squeeze.

"I want a new bike," Jack chimed in with a smile and leaned over the table, placing himself at the center of attention. "Dad said if the new system is a hit, then I can get a new bike."

"I get a new Easy-Bake Oven." Alena leaned in and whispered in her aunt's ear, wanting to emphasize her wish but not looking to compete with her brother for attention.

"Wow, those seem like amazing things. I hope you both get them," she said conspiratorially, poking them as they giggled.

"Hey, what's this?" Tracy noticed a faded green coat hanging on the back of Jack's chair. Picking it up, she examined it, turning it one way, then the other. Upon closer inspection, she noticed moth holes in a few places but, overall, the wool was in decent shape. The back of the coat had a yellow circle with a matted, cartoon, brown and white tiger in the center. Below the tiger was *Seattle Crest Tigers* in faded red lettering.

"Who are the Tigers? Are you playing baseball?" She smiled, noting the prickly energy crawling up her spine.

"Nah, I found it in a box in the Geek Shed. It's old and stuff, but I like it." Jack shrugged "It smells funny and has the name Harold written on the inside." He grabbed the edge of the jacket still in Tracy's hand. "See, right here." Jack pointed to the faded writing just above the inner pocket. "He's my great-great-uncle or something like that. Dad said he wouldn't mind if I wore it."

A sound much like air escaping a long-sealed jar echoed throughout the kitchen. The sisters locked eyes. Then, a sudden feeling of decompression, followed by a thrumming vibration, filled the room. The lights flickered, and the space they occupied brightened for a brief second.

With urgency, Tracy whipped around, looking for the source of the strange event. "Jess, we need to talk," she said, her gaze shifting to the hall, and then to Jack, whose eyes were round disks, his mouth agape. The hair stood up on the back of her neck as an electrical charge traveled down her body. There was a subtle drop in temperature as the atmosphere changed.

"Do you feel that? Jess, it's in the air. Do you feel it? It's different, heavier. Can you smell it?" She sniffed the air. The smell of ozone was light but evident.

Just then, the soft chime rang out: PERSON NOT IDENTIFIED, PLEASE REMOVE YOUR SHOES.

James glanced at the small speaker in the upper right corner of the kitchen, then looked quickly around the room. His gaze landed on each member of the family, all staring at each other as they realized something weird was happening. He stood and with two strides was in the hallway. He looked left, hesitating, then went to the front door and checked the deadbolt. The smell of ozone was thicker in the front hallway, and the air seemed cold and heavy where he stood. The alarm was set to AT HOME mode, and the light was steady and green.

He glanced at the living room, but it was empty. He began to run censoriously through his analytical brain as he turned back toward the kitchen, glancing up the stairs toward the dark second-floor landing, knowing the entrance was safe from this end of the house.

He heard his wife and sister-in-law murmuring, then saw Jessica as she poked her head around the doorjamb. "Jimmy, what is going on?" She didn't seem scared, but there was a strained quality in her voice he knew too well. It was the what-the-fuck quality he ran into when she was in momma-bear mode.

He walked back to her, glancing at the small ceiling-mounted camera at the end of the hall, occasionally cocking his head as if to listen for any additional noise that was out of place. Reaching her, he patted her shoulder.

"Must be another damn glitch," he answered as he kissed her forehead. "I'll check the monitor; can you double-check the mud-room door?"

She gave him an apprehensive glance, then looked to the mud-room door, then to the kids, then to her sister at the table.

"OK, sure," she answered with a shake of the head.

His footsteps seemed louder and heavier in the moment, echoed by the kitchen clock. He was only gone a few minutes, but it seemed much longer. He returned to the kitchen and placed his hands on his hips as he lifted his chin, listening, then closed his eyes, as if checking again for any new sounds since his departure.

"Everything is secure, and the system shows no intruder. It was an appearance of another rogue PNI," he said, his words tinged with frustration. "It's just very strange, since everyone is entered in the system." He pulled up a chair, taking off his glasses and running his hands over his face. "We've had several PNI indications over the past month, well. at least the ones I've found. The latest was the other night, right after the perimeter setting was activated to AT HOME, and no sensors were tripped. It was as if the figure just appeared."

He shook his head and glanced around, then up at the IR camera, then continued, "Somewhere there must be an issue with a camera, or in the code, or in the scanning software. "Something isn't right." He ran his hands through his hair, then let them fall to his lap, closing his eyes. A distant squeak, followed by a thump, and then another thump caught his attention, and his eyes opened wide.

"Shit." The word escaped him, followed by a weary sigh.

"Did you hear that?" Tracy said, just above a whisper.

They all heard what sounded like footsteps crossing the ceiling above them. Alena's expression turned from wonder to fear, while Jack sprinted from his seat to the doorway to listen.

"I don't hear anything now, Dad," Jack said, leaning into the hallway with both hands grasping the doorframe to peer out as far as possible without actually leaving the kitchen.

"Old houses make strange noises, and this one tells a story every day. A creak here and a shift there. Let's not get worked up, OK?" James ruffled the curls on Jack's head before scooping Alena in his arms. "OK, baby girl, all is well."

With a kiss on the nose, she snuggled into her father's arms.

"Time for bed, I think." James patted Jack's arm, indicating the need to follow, then glanced at Jessica, who was not moving as she listened to the sounds of the house.

"On the way back down, check the security settings again and then turn up the heat, please," Jessica said, glaring up at him as she wrapped her arms around her shoulders and shivered to make a point.

"It's on seventy, Jess, and, yes, I'll check everything again." James, exasperated, turned to the thermostat on the wall by the hallway door. "I think I need to have the heating system looked at. I wonder how much that's gonna cost us?" He turned up the heat and, with Alena, was gone.

"It's your time for bed, Mr. Man," Jessica said, glancing at her son, who was shifting from foot to foot—something he did when stressed or nervous.

"But, Mom, Dad heard someone upstairs." He paused on one foot to plead with his mother. "Can you check my room?" He looked up at the ceiling.

"Yes, Mr. Man, I'll go with you to check every corner."

"Even under the bed?" he asked.

"Yes, even under the bed. C'mon, let's go," Jessica said, rising from her chair and taking Jack's hand. She glanced back at Tracy, mouthing silently the word *wine* with a nod in the direction of the plain, brown paper bag sitting on the counter next to the stove.

Upon inspection, Tracy thought the 1997 Shiraz from the Columbia Valley would be just the thing to lubricate the sobering conversation they both needed to have. Something was happening; she could feel it. *This isn't good,* she thought, *not good at all.*

Pulling down a glass for Jessica, Tracy uncorked the bottle and placed the newly freed cork on the edge of the sink. She desperately wanted to finish at least one glass before her sister descended the stairs, but one glass wouldn't make that much of a difference. She decided instead to transfer the contents to a carafe she found above the wine rack, letting it breathe. Facing the window, the old red maple tree mesmerized her as it swayed in the evening breeze. The light from the streetlamp gave the bright red and gold of the remaining leaves the appearance of fire.

"I would have expected the bottle to be half gone by now." Jessica stood in the doorway, arms around her shoulders, the chill still clinging to the room.

Tracy jumped, almost knocking over the carafe. "Jesus, Mary, and Joseph! Damn it, sis, don't sneak up on me!"

Snorting, Jessica elbowed her sister, picked up the carafe and empty wine glass, and with a nod moved in the direction of the kitchen table. "Ah, hell, you know I like to keep you on your toes. In fact, I've never seen you so jumpy."

"How are the kids?" Tracy asked, taking a seat opposite her sister, pouring the fragrant and much-needed nectar, then picking up her glass, tipping her head, and smiling wearily.

"Well, you know James. He's firm but loving. They're fine, I think. He said it may be a raccoon, which made Alena happy." She laughed, then took a long sip. "So, what did you want to talk about?" Jessica leaned on one elbow, resting her head in the palm of her hand while tracing the rim of the glass with the other. After a long day, exhaustion found a home in her bones.

Exhaling through pressed lips, Tracy tapped the side of the carafe as if to take assessment of how many glasses of wine she had left to drink before going down the paranormal rabbit hole with her sister.

"The long and the short of it is, sis...your house is haunted," Tracy said, her voice tinged with humor. She'd thought she would simply lay it out cheerily, but it sounded better in her head. She took a deep breath. Jessica's blank expression indicated that this would not be easy. "OK, look, you know...well, I sense things...I know things." With laser intent she made eye contact with Jessica. "Did you feel what happened this evening? The sounds, the smell of ozone, the weight of the air? Well, I also felt it last night. Your house is abso-fucking-lutely haunted, Jess."

With that, she drained her wine, setting the empty glass down firmly on the table. The wine lubricated her resolve. With a subdued chuckle, Tracy poured another large glass, waiting for a response.

Jessica, who had been practically lying on the table, sat up, shaking her head with purpose. "No, no, back up. You really think Casper is living here? C'mon, Tracy, I know you believe in different things, hell, strange things, but I've not seen anything or felt anything in this house."

There was a subtle creek of floorboards.

"Can I join you, ladies?" James asked, standing at the doorway. Jessica became a little taller in her chair as she sat upright with a jolt of surprise.

"Sorry if I startled you." James took a few steps into the room, pulling up a chair. He straightened his shoulders, vigorously rubbing his hands together for warmth. "I checked everything again, and I'm stumped. Maybe a few adjustments are needed in the sensitivity sensors or the motion-tracking camera? I'll temporarily uninstall the front hallway camera, taking it to the Geek Shed to see what can be done to avoid false positives. Maybe there's a loose wire, which could explain the electrical smell."

He wasn't sure if they were following his ramblings or not, but the blank expressions on Jessica's and Tracy's faces told him that geek-speak at this late hour should be placed on the back burner. He added, "Or, could be a raccoon making noise. Or an animal like a squirrel that made it into the house somehow."

That answer elicited hopeful agreement from Jessica, but Tracy knew in her gut that it was a long shot, and so did James, but it took the spook factor down a notch.

They sat in silence. The unease was palpable. There was more to the situation, and he knew it. Even though he was a numbers guy—a science guy—he could feel it. The home he loved, the home his great-grandfather crafted with pride, was suddenly unfamiliar.

Is it true, he wondered, *that some locations hold memories within the walls? Can wood, brick, and nails become a time capsule of love, laughter, and tragedy?*

"Look, I'm not jumping to conclusions, and neither should you," he said, responding to their gazes with a shrug. "I'll know more once I examine everything." Looking at the wine glasses, he sighed, then rubbed his eyes. "My head is splitting, so I think you two should finish your wine and I will call it a night."

Standing, he leaned in, kissing Jessica on the forehead. "I'll keep your side of the bed warm." He gave her a strained, tired smile.

Both Jessica and Tracy listened as James climbed the stairs, his footfalls fading toward the back of the house.

With her husband gone, Jessica's focus shifted back to her sister, who was now wringing her hands, unease showing. "OK, so why do you think the house is haunted? I mean, I felt something, but it could be simply my imagination, or, like James said, maybe a glitch in the security system. After all, there are bound to be some adjustments needed."

Tracy finished the last of her wine, feeling its effect, letting it slip down her throat. She set her glass down and directed her focus to answer with as much authority as she could muster. "Look, I know the signs. I sense it, Jess. I feel it when there is, I don't know how to explain it, well, when things are off, not right. I guess you could say otherworldly. It's when their plane of existence bumps into ours. I believe there is an energetic flow that is very real in their world and is very real in ours. In simple terms…when worlds collide, the result resembles the wave behind a boat as it cuts through water."

With her normal dramatic style, Tracy placed her hand on her chest and batted her eyelashes. "I call it a wake, and I feel them more than most and have since I was little, but I didn't understand what I was experiencing until much later."

"A wake? So why can't I feel it?" Rising, Jessica walked around the room, tilting her head and sniffing the air. "Is it here now? This wake? Where is it?"

Turning to her sister, exasperated, Jessica lifted her shoulders, palms turned up, questioning. A wide-eyed stare accompanied her hushed but urgent plea. "Sis, the kids are freaked out about this.

What do we do? Hell, I'm now freaked out, and how do you know so much about all this?" She waved her hand in the air above her head, looking around, as if a ghostly apparition would appear.

"I've studied spirits and higher dimensional existence for years. Hmm, I guess 'studied' may not be the right word. Think about it, Jess, you can read a thousand books, but how can we really understand what comes next? I've also experienced, you know— different things. Unexplainable things," Tracy said, a strained note in her voice as she closed her eyes, remembering. "You were so connected to Jimmy the moment you met him in high school that you never noticed I was seriously trying to figure out why I am the way I am." Pulling down her hair from its bun, she ran her fingers through the tangles and massaged her temples as fatigue drained what energy she had, evident by the darkness which framed her normally bright eyes. "So, after years of experience and hours of self-reflection, I find myself here, being my sensitive, woo-woo self. So much so that I feel like I've been hit by a bus."

Tracy mustered a tired smile as she reached out to pat her sister's hand in reassurance. "Don't worry, their world kind of bumping into our own may be a fluke."

Jessica locked eyes with her sister through strands of fallen hair that made her look young and frazzled.

A thin sound like air escaping a balloon came from Tracy. "I'm exhausted, and so are you. The best thing we can do is keep cool and not freak out in front of the kids if it happens again," Tracy said. She stood and took her sister's hands, pulling her to her feet, then turned her toward the hallway, and, with a gentle push, moved her forward. "Let's get some sleep, shall we?" She turned off the kitchen light.

They were silent as they climbed the stairs side by side. Tracy reached her room first, and, with an absent nod, murmured, "Night, sis." She slipped into the darkened room, closing the door behind her.

Jessica's exhaustion felt like a heavy winter coat. She reached her closed bedroom door and turned the knob slowly, hoping the usual metal squeak of the old hinges wouldn't waken James. The door gave a small protest before edging open. The dim light from the hallway spilled into the shadowy room, revealing the partial outline of her husband, sleeping on his side, a book still resting on the pillow beside him.

She closed the door behind her. The room fell back into darkness, and she moved blindly in the direction of the bed, unbuttoning her clothes as she went, tossing them to the side, too tired to care. She held her hands out in front of her but hit the edge of the bed railing with her shin and made a muffled, pain-filled noise in her throat. Fumbling under her pillow, she found her pajamas and slipped them on. Turning back the blanket, she crawled in, looking for sanctuary as she rubbed her leg.

Thoughts filtered through her mind as she grasped at the events of the evening, looking for solid fragments on which to ground herself. As she began to drift to sleep, she heard the click of the bedside table lamp, the light finding a way in around the edges of her lashes. Opening one eye, she saw the outline of James as he sat upright in bed. She closed her eyes tight, hoping he would wait to share his deductions until the morning.

"I've been thinking," he said in a quiet, serious voice. Patience was rarely his virtue. "It may be an EMF leak with the wiring, or it could be something, well, different, like what minerals are in the ground our home is built on. One is an issue with old homes—God knows this house has some years under its belt—and the other is a bit more complicated. I've been thinking, the anomalies began when I introduced graphene." He sighed as possibilities ticked in one by one. "Oh, hell, this is why I love my job. I mean, I want the system to work, not start picking up things that aren't there."

James leaned over to Jessica, nose to nose to see if she was still sleeping. He laughed. "Am I that boring, honey?"

Giving up, she sat up on her elbows, lids half closed, and looked at him. "What on earth is EMF and graphene? I think you told me once, and, ugh, all the rest is foggy. She rubbed between her eyes with her thumb and forefinger and tried to focus on what he was saying. "Could it be from those?" She pointed to the small round camera perched in the far corner, the tiny red light feeling like a one-eyed creature watching its prey.

"Um, no, I don't think the cameras could give enough EMF to make a difference. Also, it stands for electromagnetic field. It can make you feel, well, weird if the levels are too high. It can happen with old, bad, or exposed wiring, and graphene is a new, single-atom lattice that has highly conductive properties; it's used in the process of building sensors and can be doped either positive or negative, based on the desired effect." James slipped back down beneath the covers, turning off the light once more. He rolled on his side, facing his wife.

Jessica, following his lead, also settled back in, patting him on his side. "OK, OK, well, at least you might know the problem, even if I have no flipping idea what you're talking about. Just figure it out, would ya? The kids are freaked out, and, I must admit, I am, too." With her hand still on his side, Jessica turned her body to mirror his and drifted to sleep.

Chapter 11
Unexpected Gifts

Morning pooled near the windows, filling the room with dappled light. Jessica opened her eyes, thinking of the day ahead while staring at the ceiling. She closed her eyes again, deciding there was no real hurry, and listened to the silence of the house, the stillness of the air lending a false sense of peace. Reaching out, she slid her hand over to find James's side of the bed empty, the sheets cool to the touch. She propped herself up on her elbows, opened her eyes, and surveyed the room. The dim illumination of the digital clock read six a.m. and added a soft glow to the darkness. It was Saturday and the only day she gave herself to sleep until seven a.m. *He's at it early,* she thought.

With a sigh, she let her body fall back to the mattress, the heaviness of her lids pulling down, and, closing them once again, a smile pulled at the corners of her lips, knowing James was hard at work figuring everything out. She rolled over to face the door, nuzzling her pillow and squirming deeper under the blanket to enjoy the warmth of the bed for just a bit longer before chaos and breakfast.

I have an hour in bed by myself, she thought as she spread out her arms and legs, flopping and turning. She was restless and knew it was pointless to remain in bed. Sitting up, she gathered her energy to face the day. With half-opened lids, it took a minute for her eyes to adjust to the still dimly lit room. She yawned and stretched one arm at a time over her head, gently pulling at the elbows, feeling a slight release from the stiffness that seemed more present now that she was in her forties.

She swung her legs over the edge of the bed and placed one foot at a time into her slippers. She shuffled across the room, dragging her feet to the window to open the drapes, preferring natural light to fill the room as she woke up. It was like a slow charge before Mom Mode kicked in. She turned and noticed something on the oak table in the corner, something that wasn't there last night.

Treasured, framed photos of family adventures were lovingly displayed there, as they had been for years. A shiver running through her, yet, strangely, she didn't feel cold.

"What the hell is this?" She picked up a baseball that was foreign to her and out of place on the table. With one hand, she felt for the drape cord and pulled the curtains fully open. The cold morning cast a gray light into the room, yet the patina on the baseball was warm, a mottled beige and brown, the laces almost disappearing into the leather.

Upon closer inspection, the name *Rawlings* was still visible on the top of the ball, with *OFFICIAL* just below a row of faded, red stitching. On the bottom of the ball, she could make out *THE FINEST IN THE FIELD*. Turning it slowly, she discovered a faint, handwritten *H* and half of what looked to be an *A*.

"It would definitely hurt to be hit by this," she murmured as she tossed the ball between her hands. "Huh." *It must have come from one of the boxes they found in the Geek Shed*, she thought, placing it back on the table. She left the room and went downstairs.

Before undertaking breakfast duty, she walked past the kitchen to the back of the house to see if James was in his office. Eager to talk with him, she hoped he had already figured out the cause of the mysterious events from the night before. James wasn't there, but on his desk a lone screwdriver, a few unidentifiable items, and bits of wire indicated he had been working. *He must be in the Geek Shed,* she thought as she turned back to the kitchen to start breakfast.

James had been up early, working in his office for hours, and was now in the Geek Shed. It was cold in the late fall and winter, with no built-in heating system. James had worked out how to make the space more comfortable by plugging in a 1970s Marvin Portable space heater he had found in a box in a corner of the shed. With the heater turned on high, the garage for the most part was warm, as long as the temperature outside wasn't in the single digits. On the table before him lay one IR camera, two motion sensors—one new and one pulled from the office—and a professional-grade EMF detector. He had designed much of the security system, but he had adapted and revised the facial recognition software currently in use by his company, and those adjustments needed to be tested and reviewed. So far, everything was in working order, with no apparent system issues.

In the kitchen, Jessica worked on creating normalcy. The small television displayed a cartoon fish being chased by a whale, one of the kids' favorite shows, as she mixed waffle batter. Veggie sausage sizzled, and the smell of maple filled the room. Except for the occasional pepperoni pizza, the family had embraced vegetarianism when Alena refused to eat meat, crying that people were eating her friends. The first morning Jessica had cooked the new veggie sausage, she discussed it with Alena prior to breakfast, making it their secret. When the rest of the family cleaned their plates and said the sausage was delicious, it led them to embrace this new lifestyle and try other vegetarian options.

The smells that filled the house worked better than any alarm clock. Jessica had just finished making a stack of crisp, fluffy waffles when the scrape of chair legs on the tile floor prompted her to turn.

Jack and Alena were there, taking their normal places at the table. Both appeared as though they'd had a rough time sleeping. Alena's locks were standing on end, as if she had been riding in a convertible for hours, and the curls on Jack's head stood a few inches taller than usual.

"Good morning, my little loves!" Even with her hands full, Jessica moved gracefully, placing both plates simultaneously on the table in front of them. Without missing a beat, she followed with two glasses of orange juice.

Normally, waffles brought smiles in comparison to the boring cereal routine. This morning was different. Jack and Alena looked solemnly up from the plates laid before them.

"Momma, is there a ghost living with us?" Alena asked, barely above a whisper. Her eyes were large and pleading, giving the feeling of overwhelming bewilderment. "Jack said he saw him. And so did I, Momma." Tears shimmered in her eyes.

The back door opened and closed. A gush of cold air reached the kitchen with wintery fingers that fluttered the curtains. James stood just inside the mudroom, cheeks rosy as he unzipped his jacket.

"Waffles!" he said, hanging his coat on the back of the chair as he took his place at the head of the table. "What's with the sad faces?" He took two waffles off the top of the stack Jessica had placed in the center of the table after serving her kids.

"Alena thinks we have a ghost living with us," Jessica said as she sat down, picking up her plate and adding a waffle. Glancing at James, she lifted her chin in the direction of Jack. "He also told his sister he saw one."

"What? A ghost?" James looked at Jack, whose eyes were fixed on his meal, not wanting to be the focus.

Jack looked up. "I saw one upstairs…you know, a ghost," he answered. "I saw him, Dad. He went up to the playroom! He must play with the stuff there."

Jack's voice held conviction, prompting Alena to squeal, "No, no, no!"

"Now what?" Tracy's voice came from the hallway as she slowly entered the room. She stood in the doorway, looking in wonder as subtle chaos took over the kitchen table.

Alena was in full meltdown mode as Jack kicked his chair. His voice grew louder as he clamored to be heard over Alena's cries. "I think he's in the playroom in the attic, Dad," Jack yelled in one final effort to be heard. "Alena has seen him, too!"

"He?" Tracy looked from Jessica to James.

"Yeah, well, I think Jack's imagination is in full gear," James said, looking lovingly at his son and then at Jessica.

"No, I saw his shoes when I was in the hallway by the bathroom. He had on boy sneakers, Dad, not *girl shoes*." He widened his eyes in emphasis, as if girl shoes were a bad thing. "The door to the attic was open, and I could see his shoes." Jack glanced at his dad and played with his food, moving a square of his waffle to one side of the plate and back again, making a path with the extra butter smashed into the depths of each square.

"OK, buddy, I'll check out the attic playroom." James tried to calm Jack and shifted his attention to Jessica, who was comforting Alena, now sitting in her mother's lap, sniffling loudly. Alena's small hand held one square of waffle, dripping syrup down her arm.

"Did you hear that? Daddy is going to make sure there are no ghosts in the house." Jessica's soft, cooing tone poured over Alena as they rocked gently back and forth together.

Tracy entered the kitchen and poured herself a cup of coffee. *It's better that they get emotions under control before I offer my two cents on the situation*, she thought. Turning toward the table, steaming mug in hand, she grabbed the one remaining waffle before pouring a puddle of syrup in the middle of a plate.

Dipping one corner of the waffle in the syrup, Tracy chewed in silence, looking from Jessica to James for guidance, not wanting to upset the calm that was making its way back to the table.

Jessica glanced out the window. The morning gray was fading, and the sun was appearing between the shifting clouds. Jessica asked, "What adventure should we have today so Daddy can work on the house?"

Jack and Alena sat upright, eyebrows raised in happy surprise. "Green Lake!" Alena yelled. She always enjoyed seeing the ducks and squirrels.

"Let's go to the movies!" Jack shouted. Jack always chose to see a superhero fill the silver screen, triumphing over evil, their fantastic adventure temporarily becoming his own.

"Well, let's see if we have time for both," Jessica said. She asked James, "How much time will you need to get things straightened out here?"

James scratched his chin in thought. "Can you give me six or seven hours? I need to review the entire setup, which means no kids running through the house." He gave an affectionate bop on Alena's nose. "I've not wanted to dismantle the entire system, but I think I might have to. I also need to consider adding the staircase that leads to both attic rooms to the mix. It means extending additional wiring, and that will take time I don't have today. I'm now concerned that those areas, along with the few closets that are currently not part of the system, should now be." Leaning in, he whispered to Jessica," If we do have someone coming to pay us a visit, we can't give them a place to hide, now, can we?"

Overhearing this, Tracy laughed, adding, "Only nobody is getting in via conventional doors or windows, and walls don't really matter."

A stern look from Jessica made Tracy fall silent.

***

James spent the day checking and double checking all connections, IR motion-sensitive cameras, and sensors. He would need to order additional equipment to include the two attic rooms and the upper staircase, but for now he would work on getting things ready, and he felt confident that nobody could enter and move about the house totally unseen.

With the new alarm system, James quickly became aware of its repetitive nature and worked on streamlining the voice announcement settings. One of the big changes would be to limit how often the WELCOME message played, thus saving the nerves of everyone who heard WELCOME, JAMES every time he walked by the front or back door. He wanted to include the option of turning off the voice announcement system altogether or removing various household members.

Tracy spent most of the day catching up on work and sleep and sent a few emails to those friends and colleagues she trusted in the paranormal field. She felt it was important to inquire about their thoughts, knowledge of interdimensional wakes, and potential long-term physical effects. Most of her experience consisted of abandoned hospitals, sanatoriums, commercial locations with a tragic history, and an occasional haunted luxury liner. The fact that she had experienced something so profound twice in two days was extremely rare and had her buzzing. Throughout the day, the melodic chime and harpsichord notes rang out commands as the system was put through its paces, keeping her on her toes.

Moving through the house mid-afternoon, Tracy found herself in front of the refrigerator, pulling out leftover Spikes pizza and a beer. Sniffing under the tinfoil, she thought it may not be too bad if she heated it up. Placing two slices on a small plate, she set the microwave for thirty seconds.

"That pizza is a few days old but should be OK," said James, standing in the doorway with tools in hand. "Got a minute?" he asked.

Grabbing her pizza and can of microbrew, she followed him back to his office. "You may find this interesting. I still don't know what to think," James said as he reached the desk, turning the computer display in her direction.

On both the security and computer monitors was a green outline of each floor of the house. Upon clicking Play, a screen with FIRST FLOOR listed on the bottom right corner came to life. On the screen, they could see five figures in the area marked KITCHEN. Four were facing each other and one was standing off to the left. Each figure was identified with a name: TRACY, JACK, ALENA, JESSICA, and JAMES.

"See, there you are, that blue one there," James said, pointing to Tracy's pulsing blue avatar on the screen. "You exist" He laughed and waggled his eyebrows.

Tracy glared at him. "Ha-ha. Um, aren't all the avatars blue?" She tapped the screen.

"Yep, but your blue is special." He snorted, his finger on the keyboard's Forward button. "OK, wait, it's coming up." James watched intently, shifting his eyes from the screen to Tracy. He instructed, "Watch the entry hall."

Tracy stared at the screen, looking at the five figures and then the entry hall. There was a pulse of light, much like a bubble expanding on the screen, and then a small figure appeared.

"This is when we heard the 'person not identified,'" Tracy noted. It was in the same place as when she first saw the figure pop onto the monitor the night before. The figure moved slightly right and then left before disappearing.

James paused, then replayed, then fast-forwarded to skip ahead. "No perimeter trip in the sensors." He pointed to the system outline of the house. "Even with no sensor alarm, I've checked and double checked all entry points. Now, watch the second-floor landing at the top of the stairs." He resumed the playback.

On the screen, Tracy saw the small figure marked PNI appear

and then disappear in the front hall. A small pop of light moved from the center of the screen, then the figure reappeared at the top of the stairs, followed by two figures on the screen identified as JAMES and ALENA. The figure then moved down the hall, stopping at James's and Jessica's bedroom. Stepping into the bedroom, the PNI turned and disappeared into the closet.

"Did you see it disappear into our closet? We don't have any closets included in the system." James, excited, again paused the playback. "Now, watch. You will see Jack, followed by Jessica, move upstairs to his room. I was in the room with Alena." He pointed to her room on the screen and tapped on the Play button. "OK, here it is. Now you can see on the screen Jessica heading back downstairs." He pointed to the figure marked JESSICA. "But, when Jack heads to the bathroom right here…" James paused, then restarted the playback, but this time the system captured a small figure marked PNI at the far side of the landing. The PNI was standing at the door of the stairs leading to the attic. "Now, watch the PNI disappear again at the stairs, heading up to the third floor." A combination of excitement mixed with curiosity radiated from James. "But here, you clearly see Jack standing in the hallway behind whoever the PNI is. This is where Jack said he saw someone. My boy is telling the truth." Sitting back in his chair, James removed his eyeglasses, rubbing the spot at the top of his nose, and turned to Tracy.

"Do you think we have a ghost?" he asked. "I mean, really, truly, a ghost?"

Tracy reached out toward the monitor, as if to conjure and transfer to her fingertips a magical understanding held within the technology. "Yes, Jimmy, I think you have…something. Not sure what, but something." Her words were faraway and distant as she looked up at the ceiling, as if waiting for whatever it was to make itself known.

"Huh," she said, sliding her eyes to the doorway and back to

James. "I think you really fucking truly do have a ghost. This hasn't happened before?" She met his eyes, a small attempt at a smile pulling at the corners of her mouth. She turned back to the monitor.

"Nope." He rose from his chair, then leaned against the desk corner, squinting at the tree outside, his mind on the predicament he now was facing. "Well, at least I don't think so. I've never felt anything. Jess and the kids would have told me if anything was even a little off." Weariness and stress set in as he realized he was facing unknown factors outside his control.

"I saw the same thing two nights ago after you and Jess went to bed, and I was sitting here after we talked," she said. "The figure appears in the entry hall, looks around, then disappears. All I felt after that was this heaviness in the hallway, a whirling energy that almost knocked me off my feet."

Tracy closed her eyes, placing her hands wide on the desk as if to ground herself. The memory was close and vivid. "It was like being in a riptide. I was pulled in different directions all at once. It was definitely what I refer to as the wake. I explained it to Jessica, too. You know, science has proven that time is not linear. Imagine if the fabric of this time, this reality, is merged with another time, another reality..." Shaking her head, as if to clear her vision, she turned to James. "Put it this way, you don't want to be in the wake when this world comes back together again. You don't want to get caught in between."

"I guess I need to wrap my head around this," James said as he waved at the monitor. He gave her a look, his expression twisted and comical as he searched for the right thing to say. "It's not that I don't believe you. How do I say this? I'm trying to believe you, and I know you're aware of woo-woo things, but, Tracy, this is beyond woo-woo." He ran his hands back and forth through his hair, giving it a tug as if to confirm his own existence, his shoulders slumped in resignation. "Ah, hell. I'm lost, simply lost with all the this-world and that-world stuff."

"C'mon, my woo-woo world, as you call it, brother dear, is sort of scientific. I know with the right equipment, paranormal events can be measured, calculated, and recorded. It just isn't the science you feel has weight, because it's harder to prove, but they absolutely will one day. It's all about energy, if you really think about it." She chuckled as she followed his gaze. He was staring out the window again. She peered into the yard but saw nothing special.

James shuddered, and he blinked, coming back into his body and the room as he put his eyeglasses back on. "Yeah, well, there is no definitive proof of anything past this life that I know of, or at least that I would agree with." He met her eyes. "This really throws a monkey wrench into my test schedule. I mean, any glitch needs to be fixed before I take it to the powers that be."

He opened his mouth to speak but hesitated, giving Tracy a serious look, then continued in a slow, measured way. "I'm not sure if we should share too much of this with others, OK?" There was a sincere pleading in his eyes, and behind them was fear.

"Hey, I'm just a guest in this house. But I would say you have a visitor who didn't receive an invitation." Tracy stood and gave him a wink. "Never a worry, brother dear, never a worry."

Chapter 12
Out of Place

Jessica's trip to the park with the kids was brief, with just enough time to visit the resident ducks before heading to the local movie theater to watch the latest larger-than-life superhero fight evil and save the world. Jack lived with the characters in his books but enjoyed the magic of the theater. He needed nothing but the center seat about twenty rows up from the screen.

Alena, on the other hand, was content with her fill of concession food, which included a large bucket of popcorn, a package of licorice, and a large root beer. *Where does she put it?* her mother wondered. Her children were bookends on different ends of the spectrum—one lost in his head, while the other wanted to immerse herself in the world.

***

Tracy, a true extrovert, found her fountain of energy by going out and being surrounded by friends and music. A few calls resulted in an impromptu reunion of WSU classmates. Beer, food, and Irish folk music rounded out the evening, shaking the residual headache that nagged and pulled at her brain.

***

For dinner at the Allen home that night, Jessica picked up takeout from Snappy Dragon, their favorite Chinese restaurant, and, from the video store, a Disneyesque comedy about a talking bird. The goal was to keep the focus on anything but what might be going on in the house. Arriving home, Jessica turned on every light while James built a fire.

"Light dispels dark," she said to herself over and over as she flicked and clicked every light switch.

James and Jessica took the couch, while Jack and Alena made their space on the floor, using the extra decorative pillows and a blanket kept in a chest by the fireplace. It didn't take long before both Jack and Alena faded, slumped on the floor, snoozing away in front of the couch like sleeping garden gnomes.

Pointing silently at the sleeping forms, Jessica quietly said, "I'll take Alena." She tilted her head in the direction of Jack. "You grab Mr. Man, and I'll meet you back here."

James nodded. Scooping the bundle from the floor, he followed close behind Jessica.

Coming back downstairs, James stopped in the living room doorway, chuckling at the *Golden Girls*, where Estelle Getty as Ma was reminiscing about 1930s Italy. He continued down the hall to the kitchen to pour a much-needed drink. Rummaging around, he managed to find the only chilled bottle of wine, hidden in the back of the fridge. James was a beer guy, but Jessica loved wine. Tonight was a white wine kind of night, he figured, since that's all there was. Glasses in one hand, chilled bottle in the other, he headed back to the living room, where he found Jessica flipping through channels.

"Hello, Mrs. Allen. May I join you?" He placed the glasses and bottle on the coffee table. He nuzzled her ear as he settled in next to her, whispering, "It's date night."

She knew she couldn't avoid the subject of what was going on in the house.

"James." She turned to him. "Tell me you found nothing," she whispered, then added, "Well, nothing bad."

He poured the wine, not looking at her. "Clean as a whistle. I would say the house has been given a thorough checkup." Turning, he handed her a glass and touched his to hers in a celebratory toast. "We are all good. Now can we let it go? No boogeyman, I promise," he said in an effort to calm his wife.

With a sigh, Jessica sat back, moving close to him. "That's good."

They needed no other words, only mindless television, and lots of wine. It was almost midnight when they climbed the stairs, stopping at each of the kids' bedrooms for a quick check before heading to their own.

"All snug as a bug," Jessica said as they entered their room. Crawling into bed, she set the alarm clock on the bedside table before nestling in. "Remind me to leave a note for Tracy to turn on the system when she's leaving after us. I don't want to worry about security." She pulled the covers around her shoulders, suddenly chilled.

"Uh-huh, Jess." James settled in beside her, his response distant and disconnected, guilt pulling at him after lying to his wife about his findings. He arranged his eyeglasses neatly on the bridge of his nose, the morning sports section in hand. As he began to read, something caught his attention out of the corner of his eye. Tipping the right corner of the paper down to get a better look, he peered over at the table and at a round object.

"What's that?" he asked, motioning to the table, paper rustling with dramatic emphasis.

"What?" Jessica said, almost asleep. She opened one eye to get a better view, wearily lifting her head. "You mean...the baseball?"

"Yes, the baseball. Where did it come from?"

"I thought you put it there. Didn't it come from the box of things we found in the Geek Shed?"

"Nope, Jack must have set it there. He needs to keep track of his treasures. Next thing he'll be asking where it is." James shifted, bringing the newspaper back into focus as he continued to read the latest Seahawks injury report and upcoming game predictions. No response came from Jessica's side of the bed. Instead, her soft, steady breathing mixed with the wind that hit the west side of the house and occasionally rattled the windows. Normally, the sound of the wind was a type of white noise that helped him fall asleep, but not tonight.

"Night, Mrs. Allen," he said and turned over, placing his newspaper and eyeglasses on the nightstand and turning out the light.

Chapter 13
Last Call

Tracy let time get away from her that night, enjoying the much-needed laughter, sauntering down memory lane with friends that knew her well—friends who loved who she was in all her eccentricities. Last call came and went amid the chatter, with little notice that the bar was closing. Finally, it was time to get a cab and make her way home.

Because of the narrow street, the Yellow Top cab dropped her off at the corner half a block from the house's front entrance. It was only half a block, but it seemed like a mile that late at night. Walking up the sidewalk, she saw the upper floor just above the tree line. The dark windows gave her a sense of someone or something watching her from inside. Past the front hedge, she stopped, looking around the yard and to the house, which seemed larger than when she had left earlier that evening.

She felt a vibration in the sole of her shoes. Placing a foot on the first step, she hesitated. A strange tingling sensation poured over her, like a warm rain as it moved down her body. Her legs felt heavy as she climbed the handful of stairs leading to the porch. The beveled glass panes on each side of the large door offered no clear view inside the house, but she thought she saw movement as shadows shifted within. Climbing the remaining stairs, she used her key to open the door, but only enough to slip her hand in, feeling for the light switch and flipping it on.

She stepped in quietly, taking a deep breath. The entry felt strangely devoid of air. A chime softly rang out HELLO, TRACY, followed by a quiet beeping from the security panel near the door. Not used to having an alarm system, Tracy blinked, moving quickly to the alarm display as it began counting down from sixty. Her hands shook a little as she entered the code, disarming the alarm, followed by a soft chime. She set the alarm to AT HOME.

She was still unsteady, the tingling getting worse as a dark uneasy feeling enveloped her. Her arms felt strange, like they were floating in a warm pool of water, weightless. The hair on her neck prickled, causing her to take another long, deep breath.

"Not again," she whispered. She could feel the pressure, and, just as the vibration increased, she was knocked off balance and fell back against the door with a muffled thud.

"Shit," she muttered as she fought for breath. The wind, which had been temporarily knocked out of her, came back in a rush, inflating her lungs. Shaking her head, she tried to clear her ears, but the hammering of her heart made it difficult.

Another vibration and a shimmer of light bloomed from the back of the house, like the light of an approaching train. It spun down the hall to where she sat, legs splayed.

"Holy fuck." The words escaped her lips as she threw her arms up to protect herself. As the shadows fell away, a flurry of wind filled the space around her, and then, nothing.

***

Consciousness felt far away at first but moved closer as Tracy opened her eyes. Her blurred vision was jagged at the edges as she tried to focus on a figure of a boy standing in profile in front of her. She blinked, then blinked again, breath caught in her throat as she came back to herself.

Then the chime sounded, followed by the announcement: PERSON NOT IDENTIFIED, PLEASE REMOVE YOUR SHOES.

There was no response. The boy didn't seem to hear it; he didn't move. Tracy was frozen, as if encased in ice. *He's amazingly clear,* she thought.

In fact, the ghost was solid from head to toe, an unusual characteristic for a spirit. Most documented encounters described a ghost as having no legs or missing an arm or even a head. The classic transparency of form made it difficult to report details of ghosts, but this boy was solid. She saw the details of his hands; the wrinkles in his green, plaid shirt; even a loose thread that hung from the back pocket of his dark blue jeans; the rolled cuff at the ankle; and the hole in the right heel of his sneaker. His hair was a soft brown in a classic, flat-top haircut. It was if a life-size, three-dimensional, colored photo was dropped out of thin air and propped up like a display.

She thought she heard a click as the ghost suddenly lifted his head. It was as if someone had plugged him in. He turned, looking right and then left, not seeming to see her sitting on the floor. He had a spray of freckles on one cheek. He opened and closed his hands, making fists. He seemed agitated, looking for something or someone.

Does he see the house as it stands now, or is he seeing another time, another place? she wondered. There was something else; she thought she heard him say something. It was very low and hard to hear, but she heard him.

He was calling for Mr. and Mrs. Allen.

He hesitated as he looked up and seemed to hear something. Then, so did she, as footsteps were coming from above, headed in their direction. The ghost moved quickly as he ran to the stairs.

Tracy heard his footsteps when his sneakers hit the wood floor, but he vanished before reaching the first landing.

"Tracy?" The voice of her sister cut through the heaviness. Jessica grasped the banister with one hand, her other hand skimming the wall as she made her way down the stairs.

Tracy was up on her hands and knees, mentally urging her limbs to comply so she could stand. Head down, she looked at her tingling fingers splayed on the hallway rug and wondered how long it would take to fully feel them again. Jessica had reached her, kneeling as she gently lifted Tracy to a sitting position, telling her not to move.

"Are you OK?" Jessica asked. "Look at me." Two fingers gently touched Tracy's chin, directing her to face her sister. "How many fingers, sis?" She held up three fingers.

Tracy swayed. "Three."

For a long moment, the sisters stared at each other.

"Tell me you saw him?" Tracy asked, slurring slightly while still attempting to focus. "Please, tell me you saw him," she said again, this time sounding less inebriated.

Jessica fell to one side, settling on her butt with her legs curled beside her. She was staring at the hallway in the direction of the staircase. Her hair was pulled back, revealing her pale face in the dim light of the hallway. A shimmer flickered in her eyes as she held back tears. Tipping her head back, she looked at the ceiling, then closed her eyes.

"Yes," Jessica answered, just above a whisper. She covered her eyes and let out a long pain-filled sigh, then let her hands fall to her lap. "I did. I saw him. He was at the base of the staircase…" She paused, seemingly lost in thought, before continuing. "Our eyes met. Oh, God, Tracy, he saw me too." The tears she'd held back now slipped down her cheeks.

The tingling in Tracy's hands and feet was slowly abating as she worked her fingers. She moved one at a time as if playing an imaginary piano, while she pointed her toes and arched her feet like a ballet dancer warming up for a performance.

They sat together, the silence in the house reassuring. Tracy noticed her sister had placed her hand in hers. They were both looking around the hallway, then to the ceiling, then to the staircase as if something or someone would manifest at any moment.

I should check on the children, Jessica thought, hearing a bump and thud from above. A creek of a door, the sound of fast, heavy footsteps, and James appeared, almost leaping from the upper landing.

"I felt the bed shake. It took me a moment to realize because I took some allergy meds before bed, and you know how that makes me…" He lost focus, trailing off. "Anyway, then you were gone." He looked from his wife to Tracy. "What? Was there an earthquake and I missed it?" He glanced at the security panel by the door, making sure the perimeter was secured, then back to the women.

Jessica stood, shaking her head. "No, no earthquake." She bent down and gently lifted one of Tracy's elbows, encouraging her to stand.

"What were you two doing on the floor?" James asked.

"I saw the ghost this time," Jessica answered, clasping her hands to her chest with a terrified look. One step and she was in his arms, shaking like a leaf.

James drew her to him as he placed his chin on the top of her head. "Shh, it's OK, honey, saw who?" His stomach turned as he wondered how it would be OK. He knew he had no power over whatever was going on. He held Jessica tight, looking to Tracy, who was up and leaning against the wall. She looked frightened, and that scared him. His glance was pleading. He felt helpless.

"This, this is bigger than anything I've witnessed, bigger than anything I've experienced," Tracy said as she shifted her weight from one foot to the other. Her palms were painful as she turned her hands over, looking for damage. It was as if she had held a lightning rod when it accomplished its mission, bringing ten million volts home.

A sound from the upper floor turned the attention of all three to the two small figures at the top of the stairs, standing side by side, their faces in shadow.

"Hey, kids, go back to your room. We'll be up to tuck you back in. Everything is fine." Jessica hesitated, her voice shaking, as she didn't like to lie, but she didn't want to scare them.

"Yeah, your auntie is clumsy," Tracy said, chiming in. "I fell right down on my butt." She rubbed her posterior with great emphasis, making the kids giggle.

"You mean your bum, Aunt Tracy?" Alena asked, holding Mrs. Kelly tight in her arms with her nose resting on the squirrel's cheek.

"Yep, you are right. On my big old bum," she said in reassurance. "Thank goodness your mom and dad were here to help me up. Clumsy old Aunt Tracy."

Again, a snicker from the top of the stairs. Jack, still giggling, repeated the word. "Bum," he said, erupting into another fit of laughter.

The laughter lifted the tension. Jack and Alena, convinced there was no danger, turned and were out of sight, their soft steps receding.

Jessica, grateful, turned back to Tracy. She mouthed, *thank you*, pulling away from James and standing up to her full height. Tracy thought of it as her sister's warrior stance. Her sister was kind, sweet, and loving, but when it came to her family, she would fight to protect them.

With the children tucked back in bed, the three of them sat in the living room. The only light was from the hallway. The glow behind them in the darkened room gave a sinister feel to the gathering. Both Tracy and Jessica shared the events as they came flooding back, piece by piece, frame by frame. James listened intently, only asking a few questions as he worked to understand everything he could. Reaching out, he placed his hand over Jessica's, which was comforting. With a sigh, he again removed his eye glasses, rubbing his eyes, and appeared to be deep in thought.

"I need to wrap my head around this." He waved his hand dismayingly in the air, glasses swinging back and forth for emphasis.

"Jimmy," Jessica said, turning to him. "This..." Her hand waved in the air as she mimicked his motion. "I mean, all of this, started not long after you installed the prototype security system." It wasn't a question as much as an observation. Jessica and Tracy, weary to the bone, looked for a response.

"One more thing, guys..." Tracy, who was sitting quietly, hands clasped between her knees as if to warm them, hesitated, wanting to continue but seeming to lose her strength as she blew air out her lips and sighed.

"What?" Jessica knew her hesitation meant something. "What, Tracy?"

"The boy I saw..." Tracy looked at her sister again, hesitating. "The boy you saw. Well, he did say something, he was calling out to both of you...umm, he was looking for you."

A look of shock passed between them. Covering his face with his hands, James splayed his fingers, peeking through, like a child playing hide-and-seek.

"How does he know us?" Jessica asked as she looked to James. "My God, he knows who we are?" A waver in her voice told him all he needed to know. She was at a breaking point.

Lowering his hands, he focused on his sister-in-law. "What did he say exactly?" James asked, reaching out again, gently squeezing Jessica's hand in reassurance.

"Well, he looked around and then called out for Mr. Allen." Tracy looked at her sister. *There's something in her eyes, anguish maybe,* she thought. "And then he called out, 'Mrs. Allen.'" Tracy stood up and rubbed the space between her brows. She paced, a hum of energy rising off her, like summer heat on pavement. "Yes, that's it. He asked for both of you, and then he was gone. What is in front of me that I'm not seeing? Think Tracy, think." She sat back down, feeling like an empty sack, drained from the event as she tried to pinpoint what was missing, massaging her head with the palms of her hands on her temples.

"I don't know him. James," Jessica said in a tired voice, each word tinged with shock, cold and hollow. "I've never seen him before."

"I'll tell you, I've looked at the system several times. I have noticed these anomalies...is that the word I should use?" He paused as if questioning his statement and Tracy nodded in answer to his question. "I did note that these anomalies started after I closed the perimeter using Wi-Fi. Up until a month ago, the software had entry point detection, which is similar to most standard alarm profiles. You cover the front door, the back door, windows, etcetera. Homes of this size usually will have a few points not included on the upper floors, from cost and access standpoints. You target the most vulnerable areas of the house. With the introduction of Wi-Fi, I have been able to create a better system using several routers, something I believe will be the standard in the future. With my system, there is a difference, no breaks, no blind spots, no vulnerability—such as an attic window or basement-window well. It was the utilization of this new system that this..." James again waved his hands above his head if to indicate the event was created in the air.

Hands on her knees, Tracy no longer felt empty; she stood, feeling like sand filled her from head to toe. *A side effect of being caught between two worlds,* she thought. Weariness took residence in her bones as she looked from her sister to James, then back to the hallway beyond the living room. "I think we should all try and get some sleep. I can make some calls in the morning to people that may understand what is going on." Both Jessica and Tracy nodded in agreement, and then, as if they were highly synchronized automatons, turned, moving slowly to the stairs in perfect unison.

Chapter 14
The Veil

"The multiverse is a group of universes that exist within the entirety of space, time, matter, energy, and physical laws." James was reading out loud to himself at the kitchen table when he heard his wife enter the room. "Well, hello, lovely wife of mine. Sorry, I sort of took over, as there's more room." He nodded at the pile of books and journals. "Bigger table and all." He looked at Jessica over the top of his laptop, a piece of toast in hand. Peering over his glasses, his hair disheveled and standing on end, he looked like an eccentric professor.

"It's about physics." He scratched his nose. "I don't know, Jess. I've been researching, and there are lots of theories. Again, maybe it's the location of the house. I mean, we could be built on granite, which is known to conduct energy, or maybe it's the Wi-Fi. Maybe it's the equipment, the graphene, or the perimeter ICG software. I just need more information." He shook his head and exhaled, shifting his focus to a book that was in a pile he had made in the center of the table.

"I don't think there's anything that can harm us going on here." He met Jessica's eyes. "You and this family are the most important things in my life. That's also why this new system is so important for us. It's a way of making my mark in this world." His concern permeated the air. He had been up early, and it showed. The creases in his face seemed deeper, his eyes set in dark hollows that weren't apparent the day before.

"What time did you get up?" Jessica asked, concerned. She leaned across the table to inspect his face.

His eyes remained focused on his computer. "Early, baby, early. I wanted to get a start before the kids got up. Morning Dad can't be *that guy* unless he gets some things off his plate. Besides, there's a lot riding on what's happening here. So, I'm getting stuff out of my head." He looked over his shoulder, avoiding eye contact with Jessica. "Did you brew a new pot of coffee?" he asked, noticing the aroma filling the room. He scooted his chair back to rise, but Jessica placed a hand on his shoulder, stopping him.

"I'm getting myself a huge cup, so let me get yours." She paused with her hand still on his shoulder before patting him again with a gentle squeeze. Turning toward the counter, she grabbed the pink and white World's Best Mom cup that dwarfed all the other cups on the shelf.

"Yeah, I'm the best," she said, shrugging one shoulder as she pulled down another cup, filling them both.

"Somewhere there is an answer. I'm a determined kind of guy, so I *will* find the answer based on logic and science. Or at least I hope to God I can." James looked up, as if appealing to God himself as he brought both hands together, feigning a prayer.

"C'mon, Jimmy. Don't mock God. We need him, I think." Jessica set a cup down as she settled in next to him, ruffling his curls. The darkness under her eyes was testimony to her own lack of sleep mirroring his. "I wonder when Tracy will be up?" She closed her eyes as she sat with the mug between her hands, breathing deeply. Opening one eye, she looked at the clock: eight a.m.

Picking up a book, James skimmed the text with one finger.

Flipping from the front to the back, placing pieces of paper between the pages, he made notes.

"Here, it says an astral plane is an existence somewhere between earth and heaven." A small laugh escaped him. "That's rich, um, so where is heaven exactly? It seems you can't pinpoint the location of one without the other?" Shaking his head, he took a long sip of coffee.

He then looked at Jessica, who was still breathing the steam from her cup. "Thank you, baby." Setting the book down, he reached out to touch her arm. "I think we're in unknown waters here. I know physics; I also know physical atoms of energy can't be destroyed; their vibration will only change and shift, and that's my science brain talking. So, what is my brain saying now? Hell, I don't know, but I plan on finding out."

He was talking more to himself as he turned the page, making notes in his journal. "But what happened last night..." James didn't want to continue his thought, hoping his wife understood.

She met his eyes, then turned her attention to his pile of books. She picked her way through them, as if she could absorb knowledge from the titles. There were tears in her eyes as she looked out the window, then to the clock, before focusing back on James.

"You know, I don't scare easily, and I'm up for any challenge," she said, wanting to sound brave but coming off scared. "But, hell, I need to make sure the kids are safe."

"So, I hear someone is reading about the astral plane?" Tracy said, entering the room, disheveled, scanning James and Jessica with a narrowed look. "I heard you as I was coming down the stairs and listened for a bit." She grabbed a cup of coffee before joining them at the table.

"Look, astral plane, interdimensional existence, multiverse theory, parallel universes, are all good theories," Tracy said. "I think you're right, brother dear. I think it has something to do with this house and your new system. There is no such thing as coincidence.

And you are absolutely correct. Energy can never be destroyed, but it can be amplified, and last night was a whole bunch of amplification." Amused, she glanced at Jessica, who shot her a sobering look.

"Don't be frightened, Jessica. I don't get that it's anything malevolent. Well, not yet, anyway," she said under her breath. She took a long sip of coffee and closed her eyes as if to access information stored in a far-off place. "I don't know, guys. I feel things normal people can't. The subtle vibrations that are unseen, the layers in this existence." She tilted her head at the stack of literature on the table. "These are good books and give substance to the pieces of a very large universal puzzle…but when you add the knowledge and theories contained within them to the experience we're having, well, let's just say it's a whole different ballgame, and we now have more practical experience than most of these authors."

Tracy reached for a book on the top of one stack, *The Theory of Everything* by Stephen W. Hawking, smiled, and continued. "To try and simplify all of these," she said, returning the book to the stack, "well, that's a hard one. There are multiple realities happening at any one time. Our reality in this life may be different from a reality that is happening simultaneously in another existence, and, moreover, when one life ends, it continues elsewhere. Heaven may be a simple shift to another reality or dimension. I'm not ruling out streets of gold if that's your thing. Oh, and let us not overlook reincarnation for another layer of mind-numbing intrigue." She tapped her finger on the table. "We don't usually see glimpses of these realities, but when we bump into them or cross paths with them, it's what we call déjà vu. You feel you've done something or been somewhere before, and, of course, the answer is that you have."

"So, you're saying we have all simply experienced déjà vu?" Jessica inquired, closing one eye while sizing up her sister.

"Not exactly. I think we bumped into another plane of existence, but the law of physics says there can be but one reality at a time." Tracy raised a finger to emphasize her point. "This house either is unable to coexist with this other parallel dimension; and/or souls from there, wherever 'there' is, can't exist here without serious problems. When we get caught between dimensions, that's the wake, and the wake is nothing we can ignore. That's my two cents in a nutshell."

Jessica lifted one brow, questioning her sister's ability to reason. Then she shrugged, accepting Tracy's logic. "Can those souls, you know the ones that travel back and forth, hurt the kids?"

Tracy shot her a direct and unwavering gaze. "I don't think there's any danger. However, there are other things…" She paused, choosing her words carefully. "You know, the dark entities that are a part of *all* dimensions are always around us. This time, I hope, hell, I pray I'm wrong." Tracy believed what came out of her mouth, but there was always doubt in the back of her mind.

Chapter 15
Jeffrey

Standing in the front entry hall, the staircase appeared before him. *Why am I here,* he wondered as he looked right and left, squinting as his eyes adjusted to the light.

"Mr. Allen? Mrs. Allen?" Hesitating, Jeffrey took a step and stopped. *Something's wrong,* he thought as he looked for anything familiar to anchor him. He remembered the walls of bright yellow, always light and airy, but now they were beige, lacking color, unfamiliar. The pink and white flowered bowl was gone, replaced with a set of coat hooks, and to the right a square, white box with numbers and a small green light.

PERSON NOT IDENTIFIED, PLEASE REMOVE YOUR SHOES. A voice he didn't recognize echoed around him.

"Harold? Mrs. Allen?" His face twisted with questions, urgency moving through him as panic engulfed the air like a fire with no known source. He needed something, but what? *Home is safe. I should just go home,* he thought, but there was no reprieve from the unknown force that pulled him in. No control, his unknown quest propelling him. As he approached the foot of the stairs, he focused on the small pillar of light, which seemed to guide him to the floors above.

As he reached the top, a distant noise floated up from below. Ignoring it, he continued. Harold's room was the second door on the right, a dim rectangle in the shadows. The door was open just a few inches, just enough. He peered into the room, eyes adjusting quickly in the gloom as black and gray shadows moved to the corners, unfamiliar objects revealing their true nature. Rectangular shapes, stacked in groups, glimpses of color mixed in with toys and furniture. Silently, he backed up and turned, hesitating as he reached the foot of the second set of stairs and began to climb. As he looked up through the open doorway, he saw the source of the light. The familiar attic window came into view, comforting, urging him on.

Stumbling, he tightened his grip on the railing and climbed the remaining stairs. The first room contained stacks of boxes, furniture, and other remnants of a forgotten life. As he passed under the archway, he was relieved to see light from the second window illuminating the figure-eight racetrack that had been a gift to Harold for his eleventh birthday. His chest expanded, the pull in his stomach fading. *I'm in the right place,* he thought. *But where did the day go? Wasn't it morning?* He looked out window: the light spilling into the room came from a streetlamp, the darkness beyond a backdrop of stars.

He turned in place as he tried to make out the items that lay in the shadows, but nothing else was recognizable. The urgency pulled at him again. Not knowing what to do, he returned to the top of the staircase. A soft reverberation of voices rose from below—an inaudible rhythm that moved through the house. The door at the bottom of the attic stairs was partially open, giving him a small view of the hallway. He could feel a vibration of footsteps, along with formless words he couldn't make out. Then, from the shadows, a tall man, followed by a much smaller woman, flickered into view before disappearing into a room. As they disappeared, a bloom of light revealed a chair next to a pair of red shoes. "Harold," he whispered, desperate to find someone familiar. He would wait until it was safe to leave, he decided.

"Momma," he choked out in a whisper as he sat on the stairs and lowered his head into his lap, resting on his knees.

With a rush of pressure, he found himself on the sidewalk in front of his house. Columns of dappled sunlight streamed through the leaves of the large maple tree, casting gold and bright green on the lawn. Everything was bright, as if all shadows were suddenly nonexistent. The white of the house seemed new somehow, the purple and yellow flowers at the edges amplifying its electrified hue. Rubbing his eyes, he blinked, turning in place. The street was empty, and the row of homes stood with lawns mowed and shrubs manicured in perfect symmetry. The rich green from the foliage framed the houses, painted in muted colors, seemingly empty as they stood like ghostly sentinels in this world.

His eyes drifted to the street, where a single baseball, dirt clinging to it, sat alone as if calling to the children hiding in their homes to come play and relieve its lonesome state. In the driveway, the family's Chevy Bel Air gleamed a pale-yellow and white, the chrome twinkling in the bright sun. *Where are the others?* he wondered, listening intently.

He noticed his bicycle, a hand-me-down from his cousin, was still on the front lawn where he remembered leaving it. *When was that?* he thought. Panic ran up his spine as he remembered his father's warning not to leave it in the yard again.

His father was angry all the time, it seemed, so giving him a reason for punishment wasn't a good idea. Staring up the driveway, he noticed the baseball mitt he was carrying just moments before. It was a good, solid mitt, even though it was used. It was a birthday gift from his parents—well, his mother, really, since his dad was against wasting money on trivial things like baseball—but he was happy to receive it.

Today was his birthday. His mother had surprised him when she pulled the mitt from the top shelf of the closet.

"It's our secret," she whispered, putting one finger to her lips. She instructed him to tell his father that it belonged to a neighbor boy who had gone away to school and didn't use it anymore.

This was often that way with his mother; they kept secrets about a lot of things.

Picking up his bicycle, he rolled it to the side of the house. *Dad could be home soon,* he thought. Running up the back stairs onto the porch, he noticed Sammy's food bowl was empty. This was another one of his responsibilities. He loved Sammy, their black and white cocker spaniel and poodle mix, who was a gift from his aunt in Spokane after her dog had puppies. Jeffrey had so many responsibilities, but it had always been that way. His father traveled for business, so Jeffrey was the man of the house when his dad was on the road.

Jeffrey longed to live a normal life, but his had not afforded him much normality these past eleven years. He wanted family dinners, catch with dad, and baseball with friends. He dreamed of a life that belonged on the cover of the *Saturday Evening Post,* a magazine known for a Norman Rockwell portrayal of American life, but, sadly, this wasn't the case for him.

His mom said that the war stuck to his father like a raindrop on a leaf after a storm, and that he was broken with the weight of it. Jeffrey was young when his dad went to fight in Korea, so he didn't remember him any other way.

The war affected more than just his dad, though. Jeffrey's mom needed what she called her "special juice" to face the responsibilities of the day. It wasn't until he could reach the cupboard above the refrigerator and found the bottle of vodka that he understood. His mom would sometimes sleep the morning away, and, depending on how much fortification she would have in her coffee, sometimes the day. Fueled by alcohol and anger, his parents' fights were constant and explosive. It was all Jeffrey could do to stay invisible.

With his dad on the road, it had been a quiet morning. He hoped this day would be the day the boys from the Tigers would let him play. *Maybe when they see my new baseball mitt. I know they need a catcher,* he thought. *Don't they?* The last thing he remembered was running out the door with his new mitt tucked under his elbow, but where were the boys now? They had just been in the street in front of the house. Harold was playing catch with Timmy Douglas, the boy from one block over. He remembered Sam, Walter, Freddie, and Kenneth being there just moments ago. There was no warmth as he stood in the sun, and the air was void of the earthy smells of fresh cut grass, apple blossoms, and warm pavement. A silent, whirling expansion of air pulled blackness tight around him. Suddenly, light and sound reemerged, and he found himself standing on Harold's porch with his hand on the door handle. He stared at his hand. How did he get here? Finding his voice, he called out.

"Harold," he said as the door swung in. "It's me, it's Jeffrey."

Chapter 16
Ghosts of the Past

James was dreaming. An old record player from his high school days was spinning words and fragmented notes, as if someone was turning the sound on and off. In the dream, a familiar chime kept time with the rotating turntable. A shifting movement pulled at him from the depths of sleep as something nuzzled and dug into his side. A puff of air on his arm, close and warm, woke him up. He lay still, listening to the room as he pulled himself up from his dream.

Lifting his eyelids ever so slightly, he noticed it was still night. A noise at his left shoulder, light and muffled, startled him. Sitting up with a rustle of sheets and blankets, he looked at his wife, expecting to find her murmuring—a nightmare or dream coming to life. However, her silhouette was still as she lay asleep, blanket pulled close under her chin, a dark cascade of chestnut hair spilling onto her pillow.

Movement came again but from the middle of the bed, a small form under the rumpled blanket. One small, delicate hand protruded as if seeking air. James tossed back the cover and revealed a cloud of curls floating—as if in water—just above his daughter's face, one arm over her head as she twitched and moved in her co-coon. The pressure James felt must have been her foot as she tried to get comfortable.

"Daddy." Her young voice floated up and seemed to hover there.

"Yes, baby, Daddy is here. What are you doing out of bed?" he asked in a round, soothing tone.

"There was someone in my room," Alena answered, an edge of tears waiting in her voice as it wavered.

"Is he there now?" James asked, urgency rumbling through him as he pulled Alena higher in the bed. He put her head on the pillow between them, his eyes adjusting to the darkness in the room.

He felt her shake her head as she turned to him. "No," she whispered. "He left."

A hand came from the right side of the bed, gently landing on her daughter's head. Jessica shifted, rubbing her eyes. "You must have had a dream," Jessica mumbled with a groggy yawn as she propped herself up on one elbow. Her eyes narrowed to focus on her daughter, then she gave her husband a flick of her head in the direction of the bedroom door.

"I'll check to make sure." James was up and to the door.

A minute later, he crawled back into bed, pulling Alena close, sharing his pillow as he brushed the curls from her face. He gently tucked Mrs. Kelly between them, pulling up the blanket for both.

"Nobody was there," he said as he settled back into his pillow, "but Mrs. Kelly was lonely. You go to sleep, baby girl."

Looking to Jessica for a response, he noticed she'd already lowered herself back down, curling in as she reached out to touch her daughter reassuringly before falling back to sleep.

James mirrored Jessica. He closed his eyes, hoping to find sleep. Yet his heart still pounded as the fear of an unwanted visitor receded back into a dream.

Chapter 17
Morning Intruder

The chirps and calls of birds were distant as the light made its way into the room. There was a sense of awareness, a shifting of floorboards, and a shadow temporarily blocked the light as the air moved to accommodate a new visitor.

"Why is Alena in bed with you?" Jack asked, standing at the edge of the bed, inches from his father's face.

"Shh." James sat up, lifted one finger to his lips as he twisted to look over his shoulder at the two sleeping forms. Rising from bed, he moved gingerly, his knees popping, leading Jack by the elbow out the door and down the hall. Jack's head wobbled as he kept pace with his father's long stride.

"C'mon," James said. "Let's make breakfast for the women of the house, shall we?"

They heard the soft clatter of dishes in the distance, muffled by the furnace as it rushed warm air from the floor vents. James placed a hand on Jack's chest, stopping him mid-step halfway down the stairs.

"Dad what's—"

"Shh." James again raised a finger to his lips, then slowly covered Jack's mouth with his other hand.

They stood there, the morning stillness broken as the clinking of metal and glass cut the air. Jack widened his eyes, lifting his eyebrows high as he looked to his dad in panic.

"Stay here," James said, sitting his son down on the stair, then continuing to the hallway below, stopping briefly to check the security panel. The green light was steady and bright. Any trip in the system sensors and the light would be blinking red and the alarm sounding. Into the hall, James moved with caution toward the sounds at the back of the house.

His heart knocked loudly in his chest, the blood rushing in his ears, muffling the sounds in the house as he walked slowly down the hallway. He approached the kitchen doorway. The dim light from above the stove pushed back against the morning tones of blue and gray. Sounds danced in musical tones as movement and objects found each other.

The smell of ozone reached him; it had a quality much like oil floating on water, a separate density from the rest of the house. He inched closer and stopped, closing his eyes and slowing his breath to listen. A quiet void popped into place like a change in cabin pressure. The only sounds he could hear were the ticking of the kitchen clock, followed by a stuttered knock and the whoosh of the heating system.

Pulling himself up to his full height, he opened his eyes and stepped into the kitchen to face the unknown intruder. The stillness of the room felt strange and electrified. On the kitchen counter stood a ceramic blue mixing bowl that was not there the night before. Next to it was a large wooden spoon. Moving slowly into the room, he saw a medium-size cooking pot on the front burner, the kids' step stool in front of the stove. He reached out gingerly, tapping the edge of the pot, which was empty and cold. He noticed the pantry door was partially open; an unfamiliar box of Cream of Wheat and what appeared to be a retro orange can of Ovaltine sat on the counter next to the sink. He turned in place, taking in the scene, refocusing on the strangeness of the Ovaltine, which seemed decades out of place.

Picking up the can, he held it at arm's length, trying to make out the writing, looking for an expiration date, or any date for that matter. "Where did I leave my glasses?" The metal can was tall and round with an inset lid, like the old coffee cans from days gone by. *Strange,* he thought. *Did they still make this stuff?* But this one looked brand new. He didn't remember ever buying Ovaltine.

"Pfssssss." He pushed air through his closed lips and scratched his head. A chill came over him, followed by a rush of extremely warm air. His skin prickled as he turned in place, the empty room still heavy, and, for the first time, there was an eeriness that seemed to curl up in the corners, a darkness he had never noticed before. This thought snapped him back to reality, reminding him that he needed to get Jack.

"I don't like Cream of Wheat," came a whisper behind James. Jack's voice wavered, questioning his choice as he leveled a look at the box, then at the can of Ovaltine. "I didn't like sitting alone on the stairs," Jack confessed, eyes downcast as he focused on his feet, attempting to be small in a world that somehow had become too large.

"Um, OK, buddy. I was thinking of making pancakes. That would be easier than waffles, since we have a mix. We just need a bowl, some water, and—voilà—we are chefs." He was still holding the Ovaltine, which felt suddenly weighty and warm in his hand.

"What's in the can?" Jack asked as he peered closer, scrunching up his nose, freckles now looking like a large spot of dirt in the dim light.

"Oh, this? Ah, I think your mom may have picked it up," James replied, mirroring Jack's look of horror as he placed it back on the pantry shelf. "We'll stick with chocolate milk, OK?" He grabbed the pancake mix and walked to the counter, pulling out the griddle from its hiding place in the oven.

Jack turned on the television, cartoons jumping into view with small explosions of sound as he pulled out a chair, turning it toward the small screen. Elbows on the table, his hands supported his chin as he stared, expressionless, at the animated figures. His eyes shifted from his cartoons to his dad, who was mixing batter with the fervor of an animated chef.

"Dad, is Harold staying with us, or just, I don't know, just visiting sometimes?"

The large wooden spoon that moments before was whipping pancake mix into submission, stopped. James set down the bowl, letting go of the spoon handle and inhaling deeply. He wished he could take all the concerns of the morning, roll them up, and shove them down, keeping them from becoming visible, to somehow protect his family from the fear and panic that had the potential to spread like a virus. He turned to Jack, removing the griddle from the heat of the stove.

"Harold?" James questioned, focusing on his son, who now seemed so young.

Jack felt his father's intense gaze. Lifting his chin from his hands, he fidgeted with a corner of the previous day's newspaper. "Yeah, Harold. You know, the boy who lets me wear the green Tigers coat." He lifted his shoulders to his ears, shrugging, as if questioning his father's memory. "He lets me wear it."

"You mean the coat we found in the Geek Shed?" James pulled a chair up to the table and sat down across from his son. James folded his hands on the table, a weary attempt to appear calm.

"Yes," Jack answered, swinging his legs nervously, not understanding the sudden change in tone from his father, fingers tapping the table as chuckling laughter and exaggerated clangs and rattles bounced from the television.

James stared back at Jack, bewildered. "What are you talking about? Have you seen him, buddy?" James folded and unfolded his hands before finally resting them in his lap.

"Uh-huh. Upstairs in the playroom mostly." He closed an eye in concentration. "And once in my room, but he doesn't talk much."

James didn't want to scare his son, so he grabbed at anything to say. The morning was just becoming full with the rhythm of the neighborhood. Sitting at the table, he realized he was clenching his jaw so tightly it was making his back teeth ache. He held his words, forming them in his mind before rolling them into friendly, round tones as he tried desperately to remove the edge from his voice. "Well, he lives far away and doesn't visit much. When did you see him, buddy?"

Concern creased his brow as his son met his eyes. *What does he know?* James wondered. *What does he remember about his great-uncle?* The kids were so happy with their treasures that sunny day when they helped clean out the Geek Shed that they weren't interested in the details of the family that had packed them away. *Why would they? They're just kids,* he thought. The fact that Jack's new friend had been dead for a little less than fifty years was terrifying and gave pause to his normal happy Morning Dad routine.

"Pancakes!" The chorus broke the tension. Bed-worn, crumpled pajamas draped the two figures of Jessica and Alena, standing in the doorway with sleepy expressions glazing their faces, hair fuzzy, curls reaching to escape in every direction. Alena shuffled forward, taking a seat next to her brother. With lazy, dreamlike attention, she smiled at the TV, where a duck was escaping the clutches of a villain who licked his lips, intent on duck soup.

"You let us sleep in," Jessica said with a forced smile that lit her face at the sight of the griddle and bowl of pancake batter. "Oh, and breakfast all by yourself. I'm impressed with the effort, but you didn't make it too far. Don't worry, I got this." Jessica was off kilter as she grabbed the coffee pot, filling it with water, measuring out the coffee, and hitting the brew button.

"Coffee, coffee, coffee," she mumbled as she placed the griddle on the burner with a force that drew everyone's attention. "Sorry,

I'm in need of sustenance, primarily coffee." She pulled down two mugs.

Hilarity and commotion continued to roll out from the television, yet silence held court at the table. "Hey," Jessica said as she looked over her shoulder as batter sizzled on the griddle. She faced the table, one hand on her hip, spatula twitching, dripping batter on the floor as she scanned their faces. James met her eyes, lifting his chin and motioning her in the direction of the hallway. With a flick of the spatula, she flipped the first of several pancakes onto a plate. Moving the griddle off the burner, she walked toward the doorway.

James was already out of his seat, two steps ahead. Reaching the hallway, he gently took her hand, leading her to the living room for privacy. They moved in unison, both intuitively knowing their destination as they eased onto the couch and glanced at the door to make sure the kids didn't follow.

"Hold on." James jumped up and headed down the hallway, returning a few minutes later.

"What is going on?" she whispered to him, concern washing over her like a giant wave on the beach.

"I disengaged the voice announcement system. I don't want to hear any chimes for a bit. I'll add it back later. I just need a break." James rubbed his hand over days of beard stubble, massaging his jaw. "Jack's been seeing Harold in the house." He said it quickly, like ripping off a Band-Aid.

"Jack, too? Last night with Alena and, my God, now Jack..." She trailed off as anger rose up from the pit of her stomach. She was turning pink around the edges; the tip of one ear was now scarlet. Jessica gestured at the ceiling and shook her head, trying to refocus. "Harold is also showing up in our daughter's room. She told me this morning, Jimmy. She told me why she was in our room. Why, she was scared and, dammit...I am, too. I'm scared." She leaned in and met his eyes, hands trembling as she grabbed both of his.

"I know." He looked down, noticing a hole in his sock, then

back to the doorway, making sure the hallway was still clear. His nerves gripped him like a vice, settling at his temples as he rubbed her hands between his own and let go. "I know. She told me about the boy in her room, and I thought, well, that could just be a little girl having a dream, but this morning Jack asked if Harold was visiting. He actually wanted to know if his great-uncle, who has been dead for almost fifty years, is staying here." Urgency created a detached cadence of words just loud enough to be heard. James felt out of control and helpless, a bad combination for a man who prided himself on knowing all the answers, or at least how to find the answers. Now he was reaching blindly for any explanation.

"What the fuck?" Jessica's voice was low and filled with sharp glass, able to cut deep, depending on how you approached her words. The revelations of the morning pushed her to barely contained rage.

James continued as if he didn't hear her, filling the space as he rambled, spewing different theories, trying to make sense. "Where is Tracy?" James asked, bewilderment in his voice. "Where is your sister? She didn't come home last night. I have so many questions for her right now."

He ran one hand through his hair, wearing a small grin that seemed dangerously out of place. "Wow, yeah. Well, she's going to make me pay for all the times I've called her woo-woo, all the times I laughed at all her crazy stories of things that go bump in the night." James let out a maniacal laugh. "We are now in the land of fucking woo-woo right here, and I don't know what to do about it." He set his jaw as he took a sharp, deep breath, filling his lungs.

The rage that filled Jessica was subsiding, the razor's edge of her thoughts being pulled back in and pushed down, a skill many moms knew well. Rubbing her eyes, she let out a long, deep breath. "I think Tracy's with friends in the San Juans, maybe Friday Harbor, or maybe Roche Harbor?" Most of her anger was gone, yet irritation still underscored her words. She rubbed her temples.

"She'll be here later. Damn you, Jimmy, don't change the subject. What the hell is happening here? I mean, Jesus, Mary, and Joseph. If I had known we were moving into a house where your dead uncle still lived, well, maybe I would have passed, please and thank you." She stopped rubbing her head. Her eyes were red, exhaustion shadowing her features.

A light thump came from upstairs. Jessica looked up, narrowing her eyes. "Did you hear that?" She cocked her head in the direction of the noise. "Jimmy, Tracy isn't here, and the kids are in the kitchen; I can hear their chatter." Her voice was now back to a whisper as her eyes moved from the hall to ceiling.

James stood, patting her shoulder. "Stay here," he said as he headed toward the stairs.

"Ah, hell, no." She was up and close on his heels.

He stopped at the edge of the stairs and turned, grabbing her by the shoulders. "Jess…" She looked past him up the stairs. "Jess, listen."

He shook her gently, trying to get her attention. "Check on the kids. Make some more pancakes, and I'll be right back." He looked at the wall. "The alarm is still secure." With that, he was gone, taking two stairs at a time.

The hallway was shadowed with the gray hues of the morning, and, other than the faint noise from the kitchen below, was very, very still. James stopped to check each room, intent on finding the source of the noise. Nothing seemed out of place in the first three rooms. His attention was scattered as he entered their bedroom, banging into a chair near the door, pain radiating up his shin.

"Jesus, that will leave a mark," he said as he scanned the room, looking for anything amiss.

The curtains were halfway drawn, a stream of natural light filling the space in front of the closet door. "There you are," he whispered, still rubbing his leg as he limped to the bedside table, grabbing his eyeglasses and setting them on the top of his head. As he turned, he noticed a dark rectangle edged in silver lying on the floor next to the round table in the corner. He picked up the silver frame. The glass was broken, but the black-and-white photo, yellowed at the edges, didn't appear damaged. He tipped it upright, shards of glass hitting the floor.

Looking out from the frame, a world frozen in a celluloid moment, was his grandmother. She was wearing a flowered house dress. She was young in the photo, her smile as warm as he remembered, one hand resting on the head of James's father, who was maybe three or four years old. He was holding a toy airplane as he sat on the ground, leaning against her. His grandfather stood next to his grandmother, beaming in a toothy ear-to-ear grin; clothes meticulous, his dress shirt buttoned to the collar; his hair still thick and dark, combed straight back. He had one arm around his wife and one hand resting on Harold's shoulder. Harold's dark curls stood on end, his eyes narrowed in the brightness of the day.

"Shit," James muttered as he cut his finger on a piece of glass sticking out of the frame. He picked up the broken pieces of glass and wrapped them in a magazine from the bedside table. Carefully setting the frame back, he checked the rest of the house. It was empty.

Back in the kitchen, Jessica had cooked up a large stack of pancakes, and both Jack and Alena were immersed in syrup, remnants of pancake carnage scattered on their plates, and globs of stickiness everywhere. As he walked in, all three looked up, momentarily breaking from their mindless maple-drenched gastronomy.

"Mmm, smells good, where's my stack?" James asked, dumping the magazine and shards of glass in the garbage before pulling up a chair as his wife slid a plate in front of him. Jessica gave him a sideways glance as she handed him the butter and syrup, noticing the cut on his finger. An inconspicuous shake of his head calmed her fears. With a deep breath, she closed her eyes and exhaled as she sank into her chair.

Chapter 18
The Return

The evening was busy. Jack had a book report to complete, and Alena was learning new math with the help of her fingers and toes. The usual flow of family activities dulled the nervous edge from the night before. James spent time running over stored security data, which included an unidentified visitor. He tried to shake off the unnerving footage, focusing on answers, keeping his head down as he moved between his office and the Geek Shed, only coming up for air, coffee, and leftover lasagna.

A pile of clean laundry filled one end of the kitchen table. Jessica folded, sorted, and stacked the linens and clothing into piles, keeping her hands busy. On TV, the latest reality show was a mindless distraction. Her new cell phone on the counter buzzed and moved, indicating she had a message, startling her. She'd turned the ringer off, preferring it on vibrate.

"Friday Harbor is beautiful," Tracy said, "but I can't shake the feeling I have. Is everything OK? Call me." Her sister's voice was wavering but direct. Jessica assumed Tracy had left the message on her cell instead of the home answering machine to avoid questions from James if he picked up the messages first.

Not wanting to ruin Tracy's much-needed escape with her friends, Jessica thought she'd call her back later, yet the phone was heavy in her hand. If she didn't call back, Tracy might worry. Jessica let her thumb hover over the number before deciding to return her call.

The phone rang once, then went to voice mail. She knew the cell reception up in Friday Harbor was sketchy. Her sister's voice message was pleasant and friendly, followed by a beep.

"All is well, sis," Jessica said. "When are you coming home? I think you said tomorrow, so hopefully we'll see you then." She paused, not quite knowing what else to say, then hit the End button.

The remainder of the evening was uneventful. James purposefully avoided discussing his security system findings and the strange new pantry items until he had a rational explanation. After all, ignorance was bliss, or, at least for the rest of the family, maybe it was a good idea.

Chapter 19
A Pompadour

Monday morning arrived, as all Mondays did. This Northwest day was stormy, and the bluster and song of the wind were whipping the remaining leaves from their final hold on the trees. The *tick, tick, tick* of rain hit the side of the house. Small streams of water flowed over the windows, interwoven with the cacophony of sudden gusts—all of which were normal for the homes on the top of the hill.

Alena dressed herself, layering two distinct sweaters. The first had polar bears on a sea of pale blue, and the other was pink with kittens playing with balls of yarn. To complete the bright ensemble, she wore jeans and her glossy red rain boots. Jack came downstairs late, and the reason was apparent. His hair, which was usually worn with comb-free curls—their untamed nature part of his charm—was slicked at the sides and tucked behind his ears, the curls arranged with care. He was wearing a faded blue T-shirt and jeans, and in his right hand he clutched a worn green jacket with the head and neck of a shabby Tiger partially in view.

Jessica shot a questioning glance at James. Coffee cup to her lips, she caught his attention, then glanced at Jack. "Looking good!

Is that hair gel?" Jessica asked as she moved to the sink to rinse her cup.

James glanced at Jack, who was pulling up a chair at the table. "Good morning, buddy. Wearing your hair different today I see." He turned back to packing the kids' lunches.

Jack lifted his shoulders, palms up, gesturing. He then touched the top of his head, checking on his handiwork as second thoughts registered on his face.

"Well, I think it's great," Jessica chimed in. She was relieved there had been no mention of visitors in the night, no sign of distress in their demeanor. She could live with a few interesting fashion and hair choices, regardless of the danger that might lie ahead at school. As a teacher, she knew all too well that there were ruthless children when conformity and status were challenged.

James was overly enthusiastic as he embraced his Morning Dad routine, adding an extra cookie in each lunch. He was compensating, and Jessica knew it. *Those are guilt cookies,* she thought, but the squeal of happiness that came from both Jack and Alena made it OK.

"Honey, new glasses?" Jessica asked James as she settled her hands around his waist. She leaned back as she stood on her tiptoes, squinting at the top of his head.

He reached up, moving them into position on the bridge of his nose. The glasses sat askew, tilting to one side. James blinked, pulling them off his face and holding them at an arm's length over her shoulder, one arm still around his wife. The glasses were a heavy dark brown tortoiseshell frame with a well-worn gold side accent. The manufacturer logo had fallen off on one side.

Letting go of Jessica, he stepped toward the kitchen window. "Huh." He squinted at them in the light. "They resemble my own glasses, but they're not. These are, I believe…well, I'm not sure." He turned back to face her, confused, holding the glasses out as if they were dangerous.

"Jimmy, what is going on? You look like you've seen a ghost." She was half joking, a nervous noise coming from her throat as she stepped forward to touch eyeglasses.

"Hold on," he said, and he was gone, disappearing into the hallway, his footsteps receding into the house. He returned moments later with an old black-and-white photo of his grandparents. Holding the photo in one hand, he held the glasses, looking from one to the other.

"I think these are my grandfather's glasses," he said. "They were on my bedside table this morning." He was flustered, which didn't happen often, making Jessica nervous.

"Strange thing is, I remember these," James continued. "I played with them long ago, when my grandpa would take naps in his favorite armchair." A measured stillness hung in the air as he sorted through memories, calculating possibilities. "But I was so young." He moved them every which way, inspecting every detail. Shrugging, he sat them on the counter just as Jessica handed him his own eyeglasses.

"Here's the extra pair from your desk," she said, fitting them in place.

"Thanks, babe. I'll sort this out later. I have a meeting and will be back this afternoon," he said, kissing her gently. He ran his thumb over the curve of her cheek, and she felt his disquiet.

Jessica arrived at school, unable to shed her concerns from home, which wouldn't be helpful. Jack worried her. Hell, the whole family worried her, which made her jumpy. She found herself searching the faces of each student as they gathered before class. The highs and lows, the animated chatter were the white noise of the hallways and classrooms. Twice she thought she caught a flash of a green jacket or a bob of brown curls among a sea of faces.

A warm movement of air touched her neck. *Harold,* a hushed voice brushed her ear as she closed the door to her classroom. She walked to her desk, backing against the wall as she looked left and right for the source of the voice. She was alone at the front of the classroom. She gave the morning summary, her students looking at her quizzically.

Her sixth-grade class was in the middle of reading *The Hobbit* by J. R. R. Tolkien, one of Jessica's favorite books. She immersed herself in her teaching. The journey of her students into the world filled with dwarves and wizards relit her own memories of Bilbo Baggins, Gollum, and a golden ring—a classic tale of good versus evil. *It's always about good and evil,* she thought, *always.*

The echo of children brought her back. "OK, my people, where is Bilbo today?" She lifted the book as her day began.

Chapter 20
It's Me

There was an otherworldly stillness in the house, like a terrarium that had been sealed for a long, long time. The notes and sounds of life pulled from the outer edges toward the middle, remote, strange, and frightfully foreign. At the top of the attic stairs sat Little Harold, wearing dark blue jeans and a white T-shirt. In one hand, he held his favorite green metal car, the number eight visible on the door, mindlessly spinning its wheels. His treasured car felt reassuring as he struggled for understanding. Thoughts of his father kept him company as he listened for the strangers who occupied the familiar and at the same time unfamiliar place.

"Harold." A deep voice struggled to reach him. It was separate from the others in the house. "Harold, where are you?"

Suddenly he recognized the voice that had found its way to him from downstairs. His hand skimmed the wall as he descended the stairs, pausing just before the doorway to the second floor. More inaudible voices came from the room to his right. His eyes narrowed, and he saw a strange chair and a pair of red shoes. The green and gold carpet was gone, and the yellow walls were now beige and unfamiliar.

A small flash of light reached him from the far end of the dark hall. Swirling dust moved, shifted, and then expanded, gaining fullness and shape intertwined with colorful, reflective particles. A fragmented form rolled in on itself and grew, the layers stacking from the floor, revealing the figure of what looked like a tall man, the outline of him clear and solid. He was a dark, unrecognizable silhouette against a dimly lit backdrop. He stood as if on alert, only making small movements. He then appeared to be sniffing the air with his head tilted back, and, at the same time, listening for something as he looked around at the ceiling and walls. Then, standing perfectly still, he shifted his focus, as if sensing Harold's presence behind him.

Turning toward the attic stairs, the man stepped out of the shadows. He wore eyeglasses and what might have been his Sunday best: a beige button-down shirt and flat-front dark brown pants. Joy and relief surrounded Little Harold like a soap bubble. The man standing in the hall was his father.

As if rehearsed, they moved toward each other, recognition lifting them both as they met at the base of the stairs. Harold Sr. lifted a finger to his lips, signaling to be quiet while turning his head in the direction of the second-floor landing. Taking his son by the arm, he moved him up to the third floor.

At the top of the stairs, Little Harold spoke with hushed urgency, "Dad, I don't know this place." The words fell from him in a flurry. "Gosh, I mean, what happened to our house?" He looked up at his father as they crossed the first room, avoiding boxes and furniture. Harold Sr. silently lifted his chin in the direction of the second attic room. His hand, now on his son's shoulder, gently ushered him forward.

Little Harold continued, "Where is James? Where is Momma, Grandma, and Grandpa? Why do things look so different? Who are these people?" The questions continued to roll out of him as he whispered to his father in the shadows.

Meeting his son's eyes, Harold Sr. looked in the direction of the room beyond and the stairs. He knew they were in their home, but it was not the home of their time. He didn't know where his parents or Lillian or James were, but he'd found Little Harold in the cosmic web of all-knowing. They'd moved from their realm of existence to a world of ever-shifting reality.

Little Harold had passed away so young, so tragically. On the day of his death, his grandfather Philip and his grandmother Rose had greeted him. His favorite cookies were fresh out of the oven, waiting. He came to exist in the house of his youth before the accident—a house that was familiar and safe.

Every home was a vessel, a dimensional space that accommodated all who remembered it. One by one, they furnished their world with memories, all while molding their appearance to fit a portrait in their viewer's mind's eye. In time, all sentient beings came to know this. Some just held onto the physical plane longer than others or got lost in time. Wiser, elevated souls were shepherds and guides in both worlds. Little Harold knew these things down deep, as all souls did, but in his current realm that knowledge became lost in the linear thread of existence.

There was a burst of noise followed by the sound of air escaping. Harold Sr. stood firm as the room shimmered and vibrated.

Little Harold, feeling comforted by his father's presence, moved back into the attic playroom and to his toy racetrack, his questions displaced with the childish distraction of his favorite toy car. He placed Racer 8 at the top of the straightaway and, without the aid of electricity, set it in motion.

From the entry hall below, came: PERSON NOT IDENTIFIED, PLEASE REMOVE YOUR SHOES.

Then a voice called out: "Mrs. Allen? Mr. Allen?"

***

Jeffrey stood in the door, looking around before proceeding to the stairs and climbing to the familiar place. As he approached, he heard voices. He entered the attic room, where the green metal car was taking the second loop, speeding down the straightaway on its infinity-shaped track. The room was empty.

Disappointment sat like a rock in the pit of Jeffrey's stomach, followed by a tingling, pulling sensation that started from his feet and moved its way up to the top of his head. He blinked, the vibration flowing through him. It was followed by a momentary darkness, and then he stood on the street once again, his quest to find his friend Harold never-ending.

Chapter 21
Objects of Another Realm

James sat in his office, his grandfather's tortoiseshell glasses on the desk, the frames staring back at him. He held their empty gaze. They were very real and seemed to magnify his ignorance of things that he had at one time rejected as the stuff of ghost stories. He didn't even remember seeing the glasses in the house before, yet they were there, solid, scratched, and worn, the care and use in life showing. Pulling the computer screen into better view, he looked at his schematics and data. His pride and joy rested in the code he had written, the technology and science of it verifiable. *Somewhere there is a reason for all the strange events,* he thought. Could it be tied to his work? Or perhaps it was just a coincidence.

He tried hard to make himself feel better. He'd carried the weight of the events over the past few weeks, and it was taking a toll on his confidence.

There are a lot of fucking unknowns, he thought. The evidence of what's seen and what's not seen. Empty spaces hiding somewhere at the bottom of the ripples, but this was more than he could wrap his head around. He needed more time. Notes and books covered his desk. Pulling off his glasses, he laid them next to his grandfather's; the similarities made the hair on the back of his neck stand up.

"Any luck?" Tracy asked, standing in the doorway.

"Eh." He waved his hand over the sea of papers, picking up a corner of a book as if something dangerous lay hidden beneath the cover. Putting his glasses back on, he leaned back, hand outstretched in the direction of the chair opposite the desk.

"How was your visit to Friday Harbor?" he asked, fidgeting, his thoughts wrapped up in his theories and questions, anxious for answers.

Stepping in, she held on to one side of the doorjamb, as if an unseen force was pulling her in. She didn't want to bother him, but they were drawn together by their desperate need to find answers. She let go and fell into the room, settling herself into the chair, draping her arms as she tried to relax. Being back in the house set her teeth on edge.

"I'm thinking of buying a horse," she said, tilting her head and leaning in to look at his face. His eyes were fixed on a point somewhere in the distance. He'd gone from welcoming to distant and lost in less than a minute. "Hey!" She snapped her fingers.

"Yes," he answered, his focus now back in the room. His thoughts were dragging him away, and a headache was moving in fast. He shook his head to try and clear it. "I'm sorry, what did you ask me?" Weariness lined his face. A flitter of pain caused one eye to close, his thumb pressed the space between his brows, his teeth clenching, the muscles in his jawline tightening.

"Are those your grandfather's glasses?" Tracy reached over for them but hesitated, her hand hovering. "May I?"

"Oh, yeah, yeah. Help yourself."

She examined them, turning them over in her hand, working the hinges. Her eyes became slits, eyebrows pulled together, as she studied the writing, faded and, for the most part, worn away with time. "How do you know they're his?" she asked. "They could have been left by anyone." She set them back on the desk. "Jess said she'd never seen them, and she never met your grandfather, so there's that."

A thin, wry smile softened his face and the dark ashen circles under his eyes. He turned the framed photo that was facing him toward Tracy. "This is my grandfather, Harold James Allen Sr." The photo was old and yellowed, one corner bent and disintegrating. Harold Sr. had his arm around his wife, Lillian. They were young, appearing to be in their late twenties or early thirties. No children were present. It was one of those nostalgic, posed photos where the couple looked adoringly at each other. Harold Sr. was wearing glasses, though she couldn't tell their color, but the metallic oval that likely contained the manufacturer's logo on the extension was visible. They were the mirror image of the glasses now sitting on the desk before her. Picking them back up, she held them next to the photo.

"Well, I will admit they look like the ones in the photo and, hmm, they do look old." She glanced at him through the lenses as she continued to inspect them. "If they are his glasses, maybe the kids found them somewhere. Maybe they were tucked away in the attic and the kids were playing with them?"

"My grandfather's things weren't left sitting around. Heck, I talked with my Aunt Sandra, and she said she thought they were buried with him. I mean, who else would wear them?" Lifting his shoulders, he exhaled, blowing a strand of hair from his eye.

"Buried with him, you say." She chuckled, leaning back and lifting the front chair legs off the floor. "This is very interesting. The dead are moving back in, it seems." She threw herself forward as her weight shifted.

"Funny. Jess doesn't find it so interesting," he replied with an edge in his voice as he lifted one eyebrow, questioning her sense of humor.

"Sorry, you're right," she said with a flat note in her voice. "I shouldn't make light of everything. When I'm stressed, I cope with humor."

"Did she tell you what happened?" he asked.

"Yeah, she started but was only able to tell me about the glasses. The kids were fighting about who got to pick a movie, so I told her I would catch up with you while she sorted things out."

"Maybe we should wait until the kids go to bed." He looked at his watch. "They'll be up for another hour at the most."

She sighed. "OK. Agreed, but it's killing me." Standing, she grabbed the duffle bag she had placed next to the door. "I'll dump my things upstairs, change, and then we can catch up in a bit." She gave a forced smile before disappearing into the hall. "Oh, and I bought sage, dear brother. Lots and lots of it," she added in a high, triumphant tone, her voice fading as she moved down the hall.

Chapter 22
Energy

"I checked all the doors and windows, and, trust me, they are all shut tight," Jessica proclaimed while stepping around her husband. He sat, long legs pulled in, leaning back, as if he was trying to disappear into the big armchair that faced the center of the room.

"Shut tight?" Tracy asked.

"Yes. Well, there's a reason for it, not that it will do any good," Jessica said.

James had built a fire, stacking the wood in such a way that ensured hours of warmth. As the fire grew, the light danced around the room, the heat of the flames fighting the unearthly chill in the air. The color on the walls shifted around them as each log surrendered to the flames. The flicker, frightening as it danced, came to life with a preternatural movement.

Tracy went to the kitchen and returned with an open bottle of wine tucked neatly in the crook of her arm, glasses in both hands.

"Ah, you read my mind, girl." Jessica sat down on the edge of the couch, leaning forward, her mood fortified by the uncorked bottle now sitting on the coffee table. "So, do you want to start,

Jimmy, or should I?" Jessica poured the fragrant Shiraz, then set the bottle back down.

"That does look good," James said, getting up from his chair with a grunt of effort. "But I'm getting a beer. Start with the visit to Alena." He then disappeared into the hall.

"Alena?" Tracy questioned.

Jessica recounted the events of the last few days and nights: Little Harold in Alena's bedroom, his things being left around the house, and Jack emulating and building a strange relationship with his dead great-uncle.

"Have you asked the kids anything? What does Little Harold say to them?" Tracy asked, eyebrows knitted with concern framing her eyes. She looked to Jessica and then James, who had settled back into his chair with a can of beer now resting on one knee.

"We don't want to scare them," Jessica explained in firm, hushed tones. "How do you think they'll react if we tell them they are playing with…? Oh, hell, they can't know he doesn't exist. They would freak if they knew he was a ghost, spirit, whatever you call him." She drained her glass, hoping to calm her raw nerves.

"Oh, good God, I know, sis, but there needs to be a way to communicate it to them," Tracy said as she finished her own wine. "Maybe they can tell him to come and talk with us? After all, we've not been a threat, have we? Have you asked the kids to identify his picture? It would be good to confirm, I think."

James tapped his forefinger on the rim of the beer can. Cold and heavy silence blanketed the room. After a moment of thought, he finally said, "I agree, we shouldn't frighten the kids. I also agree that we need to confirm that it is, in fact, Harold that is visiting." He took a long pull on his beer, draining half the can before setting it down on the side table next to him. "We need to bring it up in a subtle way."

He rubbed his jaw and then the back of his neck. The tension waned as the beer and fire warmed him. With a deep breath, he continued, connecting thoughts by stacking them one on top of the other. "I've been looking at the new system. And this is just a theory, my woo-woo contribution, so to speak. The glitches with the system started when…well, how do I simplify this?" He took a deep breath, letting it out slowly. "The strange anomalies started when I built a filter pack with a lattice matrix of graphene and added the IR low-level motion-tracking cameras. I did it to have more flexibility and so I can change the matrix or add additional filters when necessary. Hell, it could also be the use of Wi-Fi. So maybe a combination of numerous things? Hell, I'm not sure of anything."

Jessica looked at him blankly. "Jimmy, what the hell did you just say? I mean, I know you are my tech guy, but can't you simplify things just a little?"

"Hmm," James groaned, clasping his hands together and tapping his forefingers on his chin. There was a silence among them for some time. Then, rubbing his hands together, he continued. "I think I changed the energy of the house. The system alters some kind of dimensional barrier, messing with space and time…" He chuckled, "Dear God, listen to me. I've never been one for sci-fi, but here I am." Looking at Jessica, his mouth twisted in a smirk. There was a new understanding forming between them.

"OK, there you go again with things I can't wrap my head around," Jessica said with a sigh. "The long and short of it is, maybe we should go back to the old system?" She knew her words would cut him even as they fell out of her mouth.

A wall met her spoken regret with the force of a linebacker on the ten-yard line. The sarcastic smile he had shared moments before was gone as he gazed at the fire, the golden light the only warmth in his eyes.

"Not sure that will make a difference," he said. "Everything that has happened so far seems to be when the system is turned on. I can keep it turned off while I try and figure things out." His eyes softened as he met Jessica's.

"Oh, Jimmy," Jessica said. "I know it's your work and that you put your soul into this new system. Can we just figure it out as soon as possible?"

She stood, moving to the side of his chair, one hand resting on the back of his head, her fingers twined in his curls. She turned his head to meet her eyes. "I believe in you Jimmy, but I don't want us to all start sleeping in the living room just to keep me from losing it." She smiled, her eyes worried as she spoke her truth.

He returned her smile. "I'm working on it, Jess." He directed his attention to Tracy. "So, any idea? Have you heard of this sort of thing happening before?"

Tracy was lost in the information shared and received. Years of experience and knowledge sifted through a filter of what she dared to risk sharing. Clasping her hands, she considered her words, the weight of them, and the potential damage they carried.

"I believe..." she started before a soft creaking of the floorboards upstairs drew her attention to the ceiling. Holding her breath, she searched the corners of the room before continuing. "I believe we have something special happening here. I think I read that there are six..." Tracy stopped again. Her mouth moved as she counted to herself. "No, not six. Sorry, seven planes of existence. Each plane is subject to its own vibrational laws and conditions. Others believe in multidimensional reality or parallel realities." She became more animated. "Take the mysterious items that are showing up from seemingly nowhere. Jesus, folks, my head is about to explode just thinking about it. I've read and heard so many theories over the years, and I know the crazy stories. I'm not sure if great Aunt Betsy's diamond brooch or Uncle Charlies's favorite necktie ending up here are on purpose or by accident, but these types of strange, unexplainable cases have been documented. If I remember correctly, the term for this is apport. A very good friend of mine, who is a parapsychologist, investigated a case in New York where coins fell from a ceiling; hundreds of them fell out of thin air, from absolutely nothing." Smiling, she held her palms up, wiggling her fingers, imagining the spectacle.

She paced in front of the fire. "I'm now thinking these things may happen when a parallel world bumps into us, even if only for an instant. After the two worlds separate, some of the objects from that other world are left behind. It's fucking surreal if you think about it." Shivering, even though the room was now warm, she stopped pacing and walked over to James. "May I?" Tracy reached toward James's breast pocket, where the edge of his grandfather's glasses could be seen peeking out.

He looked down, forgetting he had tucked them away there. "Yeah, OK." He handed them to Tracy.

She took them gently, as if they were a rare artifact, opening them and looking at the hinges, the little details. She lifted them in the firelight, inspecting the clarity of each lens as if checking their authenticity. "These hold memories. They are personal. They were important to your grandfather. These glasses were identified with the life that he lived here. They were a literal window to his life, his vision, his sight, and how he saw the world." She folded them gingerly as she handed them back. "Then there are the other items, the old softball on the table, and don't forget the can of 1950s Ovaltine you found sitting on the counter; I'd still like to mix some up and see how it tastes. But the most amazing display of interdimensional movement is the boy I saw in the front entry hall. For a ghost, he was clear and solid." She was waving and gesturing with every word, a jumble of excitement and wonder. "From his first appearance on the security monitor, then materializing in front of me. It was, for lack of a better word, amazing. I mean fucking amazing!"

"Why now?" James asked. "Why are these things happening now?"

"Remember, I'll say it again: Energy can't be destroyed. We are energy. These body suits are temporary." Tracy patted her arms and legs for effect. She was excited to share her ideas. The paranormal realm was her passion, and that passion was now overflowing, like a teakettle releasing steam.

"No matter what you think, time is an illusion, and so is this reality. With some intelligent hauntings, there may be a tragedy that propels a supernatural event, or there may be an attachment to a location, in which case, a remodel or construction can anger a spirit. If it's a residual haunting, then it can be a loop of time, like an event that happens over and over again. Think of it like a video recording, only nobody knows how the play button gets pushed, or how to stop it. The veil between this world and the next is thinner in places. It's where a parallel dimension can be seen or bumps into our own." Tracy looked at her sister and brother-in-law, expecting the same level of enthusiasm.

She continued pacing. "There have been many documented encounters on battlefields around the world: soldiers repeating their last moments, their tragedy amplified, leaving an imprint on the fabric of time. There was one encounter in Gettysburg. A Japanese tour group was thrilled when they stopped to observe what they believed to be a Civil War reenactment, but little did they know, there were no reenactments that day. Soldiers were seen marching through the mist, accompanied by yelling and the sounds of battle. Come to find out, these same soldiers are seen on the same battlefield often and by many. It happens when a fog rolls in over the land, accompanied by a thunderstorm. The theory is that the energy created by these storms allows the spirits to manifest. Unfortunately, they are unaware of their actions or why the last moments of their life and their tragic death repeat.

"To be honest," Tracy continued, focusing again on answering the question, "I'm not sure which is going on here. We may have both types of hauntings happening at the same time, but we need to identify the players. So, can we look at those old photos again?" Tracy was in her element, and, for the first time, she felt like she wasn't "nutty, woo-woo, Tracy."

Overwhelmed by what she'd just heard, Jessica let this information sink in. "The photos are in the office where we left them."

James didn't take his eyes off Tracy. She had his full attention. "Energy?" he asked. "Now that's something I can look at. Something I can sink my teeth into." A small smile relaxed his jaw as he stood and followed his sister-in-law to his office.

Jessica jumped up. "I'm coming with you," she exclaimed, filing behind them into the darkened hall. "You're not leaving me here alone."

The photos sat on the floor in the corner of the office. Tracy moved the plastic containers to the desk. She placed an envelope that contained newspaper clippings to the side as she carefully pulled the photos out of the container labeled *Family*, stacking them on the desk. All three of them stood around the desk. They looked at the piles, then focused on the face-up clippings.

"I'm not sure what we're looking for, but I think when we find it, we will know." James pulled his office chair out, moving it to make room for Jessica, who was moving the small chair from the other side of the desk. Tracy left the room.

Soon, through the doorway came one of the oak kitchen chairs, as if being levitated. Tracy's head was barely a foot above the back of it, allowing her to see where she was going. She dropped it in place across from the desk and sat down with enthusiasm. This brightness put Jessica and James strangely at ease.

"Well, you seem happy with all this," Jessica said. "I wish I held your enthusiasm."

"Don't you get it?" Tracy asked with an air of girlish glee, a smile from ear to ear crinkling her nose. She reached for the hair band on her wrist as she pulled her curls up and out of her face. It was a messy top bun that meant business. "This is an amazing paranormal phenomenon. I must say, I'm thrilled the stars aligned so I can be here for this. This is the divine universe at work, folks.

Besides, you would be lost without me." She glanced from James to Jessica, then back to James with a wink.

The first photo on the stack was an old black-and-white, curled at one edge. There were sixteen people, some on blankets, others leaning against an evergreen tree that was still standing in the backyard to this day, though it was much smaller in this photo. Two children were in the lower branches, legs wrapped around the branch as they held on with one arm. Each of them had a smile of pure delight on their faces. On the blanket to the left of the tree was James's grandmother, Lillian. Next to her, a boy sat, smiling, petting a cat next to him.

"So, do you recognize everyone, Jimmy?" Tracy skimmed her finger over the faces that were looking out from the happy family gathering. James leaned in as she studied the photograph.

"I can't remember everyone's name," James said. "But, yeah. It looks like the annual Fourth of July picnic. See the flag in the corner of the picture? My grandfather was very patriotic, and that flag was important to him. He displayed it on Veterans Day and Memorial Day, but the Fourth is when the family would come from all over." He tapped the photo with the back of his pen. "This is Little Harold," he continued, pointing to the boy on the blanket. "And here is my grandpa." James's thumb traced the tall man in the photo as he searched his memory. A warmth filled him, reflecting the love for his family.

He shifted his attention back to Little Harold, pointing again to the small boy. "He was really young, around two, three here maybe. He's sitting at the feet of my great-grandmother, Rose." He gestured to the woman sitting to the right of his grandmother in the shade, next to a table full of food. His young uncle beamed, his dark curls making his head look too big atop his tiny overalls.

"So, who is missing?" Tracy asked.

"Um, I'm not sure. Everyone looks to be there. Or, should I say, the ones I remember are there. My dad wasn't born when this photo was taken, so he's missing, obviously." James started tapping each person in the photo, recalling each name.

"He's not here," Tracy declared and stood up, hands on her hips. She waved her hand at the photo. "The boy I saw isn't here, so someone must be missing."

James looked down at the photo again. "Maybe. I'm not remembering. It's obviously before my time." He looked over his glasses as he glanced back and forth from the photo to Jessica and then back to Tracy.

"The boy I saw had one of those flat-top haircuts, you know, from the fifties," Tracy said with certainty as she looked for confirmation from her sister. "Remember, sis, you saw him, too."

"Yes, I think so." Jessica took the photo from her husband, scanning the faces.

"Flat-top?" James started to shuffle through photos. "I wonder..." He trailed off, his eyebrows pulled together as he shuffled the piles. "Wait, wait."

He looked around, searching, then his eyes landed on the manila envelope with the newspaper clippings. Lifting the envelope upside down, the contents fluttered in slow motion onto the desk, like birds landing on the water. The article he was looking for strangely landed face up. He handed it to Tracy.

The recognition hit her immediately; her eyes narrowed as she read the small print. "I did read this, but I was more focused on Harold's name and photo. But from what I can tell, this may be the boy I saw that night in the entry hall. It says his name is Jeffrey Simmons." The paper was old, and the face of the other boy was creased where it had been folded. Turning *The Seattle Times* article over, she scanned it, as if some additional information would jump from the fragile clipping.

She handed it to Jessica. "Things may be making sense. I need to know about Jeffrey." Her words were flat as a chill ran down her spine.

"I don't know the entire story," James said quietly. He rubbed his knuckles, then clasped his hands. "Again, Dad was so young, and my grandfather didn't talk about the day Little Harold died. However, I do know someone who may know more." He shifted his gaze to Jessica.

"Time to visit Aunt Sandra?" Jessica asked, one eyebrow lifted in question.

"Now, have I met Aunt Sandra?" Tracy asked. She gently plucked the article from Jessica as she took another look.

"She's my grandmother's younger sister," James answered. "I think you may have met her once or twice over the years."

"OK, hmm, how do we talk with her?" Tracy asked, excitement and anticipation ruffling her edges. "Does she live close? Is she in good health? I mean, she must be getting up there in age." The questions came, one, then another, as her desire for answers took hold.

"She's around ninety-five," James explained. "No, wait, I think maybe older. Oh, but she is as sharp as she has always been. The question would be if she is willing to talk about it." James lifted the edges of photos as the pile began to expand on the desk. "She's in a retirement home in Olympia, which is about an hour's drive from here. But how do we even bring up the subject and not look, well, wonky?" He twisted his mouth and closed one eye as if to judge the distance in his mind.

"You mean woo-woo," Tracy said as she tossed the pen she was playing with at her brother-in-law.

"Yeah, woo-woo." He caught the pen effortlessly, laying it on the table. "But we can come up with something, and we do need to visit. When was the last time we were there?" He looked at Jessica, twirling a small photo between his thumb and forefinger.

"Uhm, probably for her birthday back in October when Sandra's daughter, Jill, brought her for a visit." Jessica began to stack the photos in a neat pile. "God, I feel horrible."

"Road trip! I'm calling it," Tracy shouted. She began stacking the newspaper clippings with care. "But what can we do with the kids? And I'll need to make sure there are no set events around my exhibit."

"The kids can hang out with…I don't know, someone." Jessica placed the photos back in the box as she milled over the options in her head. "Let me talk with some of the moms, or I can get a sitter for the day. The only thing is that Aunt Sandra will ask where they are. What do you think, Jimmy?"

"We'll make an excuse to my aunt," James replied, a lackluster smile moving across his face. "And the kids won't know any better. They hate the retirement home. They think it smells funny. In the meantime, maybe I shouldn't set the perimeter alarm. I think my wife would prefer to not hear Beethoven's harpsichord in the middle of the night. Right, honey?" With a wink, he drew her to him. He rested his cheek on her head for a second before kissing the top of her curls.

"Thanks, darlin', you know how to warm a girl's heart," Jessica said, frosting her response with sarcasm as she leaned back, waggling her eyebrows before hugging him. "Besides, I think we're safe enough on Queen Anne." She shrugged with a wink, patting his cheek.

Chapter 23
The Trip

The Colville Retirement facility's walls were surprisingly bright. The smell of disinfectant and baking bread permeated the halls as they headed to room 222. Each room had equipment to care for one person. A small kitchen, a twin or queen bed, and a handicapped bathroom created a cozy—some would say cramped—existence.

Aunt Sandra took great care in displaying her life in a room the size of a large bathroom. Photos looked out from any flat surface and every inch of wall space. They were her memories. A life of joy and family now rested in her memory, most passing away within recent years. The one piece of furniture the facility had allowed was her husband's favorite beige velvet easy chair. The arms, discolored with time, were two shades lighter than the rest of the chair. She could almost see where his hands rested day-to-day, and it's where she now spent hours watching HGTV, daydreaming. Memories of her home and rose garden were always close to the surface and kept her company.

"We should have stopped at the store for her," Jessica said as they approached the door.

"I asked her last night on the phone, and she said she needed nothing," James answered through clenched teeth, nodding a hello to a care provider as they passed by.

Jessica rapped her knuckles on the door, and it sprung open without delay. Aunt Sandra stood beaming, her hair set in tight, old-fashioned, beauty-salon curls, the dark pink lipstick she had worn her entire life thinly applied and in place, bringing color to her pale cheeks.

"My kids!" Her smile widened, revealing teeth yellowed with time and a daily cup of her favorite English breakfast tea.

James sat on the bed next to Jessica, while Tracy took a small foot stool next to Aunt Sandra's recliner as they all settled in for the visit.

"Well, Tracy, my dear," Sandra said, patting Tracy's arm. "It's been a long time. We met years ago at Jack's christening, but you were busy. Oh, and there were so many people that day. Anyone care for a cup of tea?"

Her warm smile persisted as she leaned on her cane, a distinct limp slowing her pace as she walked to the counter. Lifting a tea cozy to reveal an antique silver teapot, she picked up two lumps of sugar with silver tongs and dropped them into the hot, aromatic tea.

"Milk?" Sandra looked at each of them as she continued to pour.

"Aunt Sandra, let me do that." Jessica met her at the counter. "You sit and I'll finish here."

"Oh, all right, I'm too old to argue." She smiled, squeezing Jessica's hand before moving with care to the recliner. "You know, carrying anything hot is risky business now that my hip isn't co-operating and walking is difficult." She set her feet wide as she slowly lowered herself down.

"Auntie, we've missed you," James said. True affection for his aunt bubbled up. He wished they didn't live so far apart. He placed the plastic bin on a small table. "We were hoping you could help us with some family photos. You see, we found a bunch along with a few newspaper clippings, but we don't know all the faces." He reached into the box, picking out a chosen few. At the bottom was *The Seattle Times* article.

Arthritis had taken her strength. Her hands shook a little as she reached for the stack James passed to her. She laid them in her lap. "Oh, would you look at some of these? Aw, and there is Rose." Her fingers traced the faces as her eyes lit up with memory.

"We thought you would like to have some of these," James said, feeling guilty that their true purpose for being there wasn't quite that straightforward. "They need to be out of the box, don't you think?" There were a few duplicate photos of his grandparents, his father, and Aunt Sandra. He knew she would love them and, at the root of it all, they were giving her great joy in exchange for much-needed information.

"Oh, yes. Oh, yes, Jimmy. I've not seen some of these." Her face twinkled and she closed her eyes with dreams of youth and family.

"You know, we were hoping to know more about Harold Jr.," James said, slipping the topic smoothly into the conversation.

A shadow passed over her face, dimming the light in her eyes. "Little Harold? That's what everyone called him. He was such a sweet boy. My sister thought the sun rose and set with him." Sandra gave a regretful smile, her voice now soft as she picked up the news article.

"One of the most difficult days of your grandparents' lives you know." Pain creased the corners of her eyes. and her vision narrowed as she pulled at her memory to try and remember that day. "It was right after school had ended. The boys of the neighborhood were getting a softball game together, I believe. The neighbor boy, I think his name was Jeff or Jeffrey, had a birthday and wanted to play with them, something about a baseball glove, or is that mitt? Little Harold was a lovely boy, and he liked everyone. He wanted to let Jeffrey play, but those other boys didn't quite understand him, I guess. He was, by all accounts, a different boy."

A sad smile came and went from her face. "You know, he had a hard time playing with others. I guess the older he got, the stranger he became. He and Harold were neighbors, so they spent time together, as kids around the same age do." She chuckled. "God, they were so cute when they were babies..." She trailed off, then came back to herself, looking around the room.

"Do you remember anything about the accident?" Tracy asked. At Sandra's knee, she felt like a small child, looking up, encouraging her to continue.

"Oh, oh, yes, where was I? Hmm?" Sandra looked down at Tracy. "Oh, yes, the accident. Well, my sister told me his mother, you know, Jeffrey's, well, she was a terrible alcoholic, and his father was just plain mean." She shook her head as if to eject the bad memories. "There were times when I was visiting your parents that, if the windows were open, you could hear him yelling at that poor boy. You could hear things."

She dropped her eyes then looked up. "It sounded like he hit him, but we never knew for sure." She picked up her cup, blowing over it before taking a sip. She stirred and set it back on the saucer. "Boys can be mean, you know, when someone is different. My sister told me that he would not meet your eyes when you talked to him. I don't think you were ever mean, Jimmy." She smiled at her nephew.

"Well, anyway, one of the boys from the other block, hmm, what was his name? Let me see. Well, I don't remember, but, anyway, he threw a ball hard and fast at Jeffrey. I guess he thought he would drop it or duck, I don't know. They said it bounced off his baseball glove and rolled onto your grandparents' porch. It was said Little Harold ran to get it, and Jeffrey ran after him, as he wanted a second chance. Things get a little cloudy after that. Some say Little Harold wanted to pitch to him—I'm sure he wanted it to be a fair pitch. Others said Jeffrey fought him for the ball." She paused and looked down at her hands.

"Somehow, they ended up in the street. I guess they just tumbled end-over-end into the path of an oncoming car. Little Harold died instantly. He was gone by the time your Grandma Lillian made it to him. Jeffrey was transported to the hospital and died shortly after." She touched the article, finger tapping the picture. "My sister was never the same, and neither was your grandfather. Is that what you wanted to know?" She moved the pile of memories to the table next to her chair, picked up her cup, and took another sip of tea.

"Do you know what happened to Jeffrey's parents?" Jessica asked.

"You can imagine, as it was their only boy, they had a difficult time of it," Sandra said, her voice quiet with the fatigue of her memories. "The heartache forced them to move back to somewhere. I can't remember. I think it was in Ohio, or was it Illinois? Lillian told me that his death had a great impact. His mother stopped drinking, and his father found God, or at least that was the rumor." She leaned forward. "Your grandparents closed away the pain, sealed up memories, and treated his space as if it were sacred."

"When did they move away, do you know?" Tracy asked.

"Around twelve years ago, right before Lillian died," Sandra said. "She had received a letter from Jeffrey's father—now let me think, what was his name? Oh, shoot, my memory isn't what it used to be." Sandra gave a flick of her hand as her mind cleared. "Anyway, he was looking for forgiveness, and his pastor thought a letter would do some good, but they are still alive, as far as I know. They were very young when they got married. Rumor was she was only seventeen when she got pregnant."

The clink of porcelain and the rattling of spoons were music in the air as they reminisced for the remainder of their visit. With that, they left Aunt Sandra, leaving a few of the family photos behind and another surface covered with memories.

Chapter 24
Tracking Souls

"I have an idea," James said in a quiet, gravelly voice as he carried a bowl of Toasti O's to the kitchen table. It was pre-dawn and what Jessica referred to as their Picasso time together, the gray-blue hues void of the sun's warm tones.

"Oh, really? What kind of idea?" She was reading the news on her school laptop, the illumination of her face contrasting with the ghostly room, a warm cup of coffee at her elbow, a sleepy smile curled up at the corners of her mouth.

"If I can upload images of a living, breathing human into the security system, why can't I scan old photos? Work a little magic and bring them to life, so to speak? My system is pretty darn slick." He shot her a smug look and spooned a mouthful of cereal, one eyebrow raised, feeling clever.

"Scan who, exactly?" She closed her laptop, picked up her coffee, and leaned back, a tangle of curls falling in her face.

Hugging his bowl of cereal against his chest, his spoon hovering midair, his eyes narrowed in decision. "I'm thinking of uploading Harold and Jeffrey. I don't have a side profile of Jeffrey, but my software can develop one based on uploaded facial schematics.

I can make a darn good guess, I think." Setting the bowl down, James waited, looking at Jessica as the clock ticked on the wall.

Her ring finger tapped the side of her cup, eyes drawn down as if looking at something at the far end of the table. Finally, she tilted her head as if calculating his seriousness.

"Jess…" He tilted his head, mirroring her response. "Hear me out. We will be able to track who is here, when they show up, and hopefully where they go." He set his cereal bowl down and folded his arms in front of him.

Her direct stare was cool, verging on outright frosty. "OK, so you want to scan photos of two dead boys into your system. A system, mind you, that somehow has the ability to bring their world here, and for what, exactly? We wait to see where they go. So, I can worry and track it? Play it back if there's nothing good on TV?" Her crystalline words were underlined by fear.

He was calm as he met her stare. "We are talking about two boys, not a couple of demons, Jess. Well, not that I believe in demons. Tracy is right, if technology is creating pathways from another parallel dimension to our own, then I have a responsibility to take a look at it, document it, and understand it." His voice rose with determination.

"Shh. Don't wake the house." She leaned closer, her sharpness landing between them like a chiseled stone. "What do you think you will discover? Damn it, Jimmy, it's our home." She turned her attention to the window and the mist that blurred the view.

"Good morning, my village." Tracy shuffled from the hallway into the kitchen, her hard, rubber-sole slippers clicking on the tile floor. Disheveled, eyes half closed, she made her way to the counter, sighing with gratitude as she reached for a coffee cup. "Thank you, Jesus, for coffee."

"Your brother-in-law wants to upload photos of Harold and Jeffrey so he can try and track their movements," Jessica informed her as she turned away from the window.

Tracy shifted her weight and closed her eyes. Placing her hands wide on the counter, she looked as if she were holding up the world as she took a long audible breath. Her shoulders lifted as she turned to look at her sister, and a subtle popping noise came as she let her head loll from side to side, releasing tension.

Picking up the coffee pot, she held it up, looking at the grounds swimming at the bottom. "How old is this?" she asked as she poured what remained and moved to the table. She swung a chair around and joined them. All three sat quietly in the cold gray morning light. Even the bright cornflower blue of the tile seemed dull and dark.

"OK." Tracy wrapped her fingers around her cup, both eyes narrowed in question as she looked at her sister.

"I hate it when you crack your neck, by the way," Jessica said, looking as if she smelled something bad, and snickering, lifting the mood of the room. "It gives me the creeps."

"Ah, well, I slept wrong," Tracy said, waving a hand in dismissal. "Now, if we are to figure out what they are doing here, we need to devise a way to communicate. We need to help them." She took a sip of coffee. The sound of birds grew as shafts of pale-yellow filtered through the clouds, staking a claim on the day.

"Worst case, Jess, I can dismantle the system," James added, looking for approval from his wife, who was running her fingers through her curls, her eyes closed in thought.

Jessica pulled one long curl as she let her hand fall, opening her eyes. "I trust you," she agreed. "But I will jump out of my skin every time I hear that damn chime."

Getting up from the table, Jessica opened a drawer, pulling out a loaf of egg bread, then moved to the fridge. "I better get the kids' breakfast ready. C'mon, Morning Dad, help me make French toast, would ya? I need to pack the kids' papers."

He met her eyes, warmth restored, in sync with the sunshine. "If Tracy will make a new pot of coffee, I think Morning Dad will make a tired appearance." The stiffness in his shoulders was gone as he put the griddle on the stove.

"How have the last few nights been for the kids?" Tracy asked as she scooped coffee into the metal filter.

"Well, we left the system off the last few days, and all has been quiet, thank God," Jessica said as she set the table.

"Hmm, I would leave it off, then, or at least until Jimmy can get the boys' photos uploaded." Tracy's eyes were on the coffee as it started to drip, spluttering as it hit the bottom of the pot.

James nodded in agreement as he dipped a piece of bread in the mixed batter, which included a dash of ground cloves and cinnamon. "I'm working from home today, so I'll go through the photos and see what I can find. Hopefully, there will be some of Harold that are close in age. I also want to take the film canisters in to be restored to see if there's anything that can be salvaged."

He rattled off his daily to-do list and began to hum as he twirled the spatula in his hand, peering close at two pieces of bread as they sizzled. "I'm excited to see if the egg substitute I found works well with the cashew milk. Heck, if this tastes as good as it smells, I'll add it to the vegan cookbook I'll write one day." He laughed, proud of himself as the edges started to brown, spices filling the air, tempeh bacon with a touch of maple adding to the delicious aroma.

"OK, I'm off to shower and will see you this evening," Tracy said, filling her coffee cup. She disappeared into the hall, her slippers clicking up the stairs with an occasional squeak of floorboards.

Chapter 25
Little Harold

The day that had started with sunshine was now raining sideways. Oh, how James loved weather in Seattle. In his office, four photos lay side by side. The green glow from the table lamp gave them a sickly hue. Familiar curls topped a young, freckled face, his uncle's smiling eyes peering out from the old black-and-white photos. The photos were taken within a few years of each other. The first was a straight-on shot with Harold Sr. standing behind him on the left, a baseball bat over his right shoulder. It was the most promising of the photos, as he was neither smiling nor frowning. In the next photo, Little Harold was in the backyard playing with his cousin. It was a background shot, as the primary focus was his Aunt Sandra and her husband with a new baby cradled in her arms. The other two photos were grainy, not the best quality, but he could use them in a pinch.

Uploading the first two photos, James adjusted the size and removed the background. The one problem was that he had only a right-side profile picture; the left would need to be mirrored and wouldn't be exact. He couldn't find any additional photos of Jeffrey, and the picture in the newspaper was degraded, so it would be difficult to clean up. The next option would be to check with *The Seattle Times* office to see if microfiche existed, but it would be easier to adjust and play with the needed parameters. *I'll make a call later,* he thought before attempting to clean up what he had.

He worked for an hour, adjusting the tone and clarity, his efforts producing what he thought were fairly decent subjects that he uploaded into the security system. A swirling ring of red popped up on the monitor as the information finalized the facial recognition data. The ring turned to green, and a message flashed at the bottom of the screen: UPLOAD COMPLETE.

The little boy with the free-thinking curls stared back at James as he typed in HAROLD. Hesitating, he then amended the name to LITTLE HAROLD. The voice modulator chosen sounded much like his own voice, but kinder, and that was important, as he wanted the message to be welcoming. James then entered several messages for his dead uncle. Each message varied, based on his location in the home. He sat back as goosebumps rose on his forearms, his little office seeming to grow dark at the thought of addressing the dead.

"OK, Allen, snap out of your self-induced spineless mode," he grumbled, embarrassed at how a picture could set his heart pounding.

Now what? He tipped his head back in thought. "Hmm, I think I'll try a little something," he said under his breath as he engaged the system. The green light lit up as the alarm was secured. Standing up slowly, his hands splayed on the desk, he watched the monitor intently.

James appeared on the screen, smack in the middle of the room marked OFFICE.

"Hey, Harold," he called out hesitantly, looking up at the ceiling. "I *really* would love to meet you!"

Sarcasm may not be the best path, he thought, *but it keeps fear at bay.*

"OK, Uncle Harold, what items hold your memory?" An airbag epiphany hit him with the force of a speeding train. The excitement of the unknown propelled him as he went looking for items of importance.

Returning to his office, he held two objects. In one hand he held the old baseball that he'd discovered on the bedroom table. In the other he held the green metal Racer 8. Setting them on the desk, he rolled the car back and forth as he contemplated what to do. He felt fear and uncertainty envelop him, magnifying his actions. He returned to the entry hall, leaving both items in the middle of the floor about two feet from the front door, and then he walked back to his office to watch the monitor.

An hour passed, the light of the day fading, shifting the shadows within the room. James busied himself returning company emails. As he set up various meetings, the eerie silence was only broken by the wind and rain outside, echoed by the distant *tick, tick, tick* of the kitchen clock mimicking a metronome. He would occasionally break from what he was doing and stare at his name as it glowed on the security monitor.

"Jimmy, what were you thinking would happen?" He shook his head, shifting his attention back to his work.

A rush of wind, this time from within the house, jolted his attention away from his computer screen. The items on his desk were vibrating like insects ready to take flight. The small room brightened, a hum of energy running up his arms as he held on, expecting the desk to rise up like in a horror movie and fly around the room. A distant chime caused him to let go of the desk, whirling his chair around to face the open door.

PERSON NOT IDENTIFIED, PLEASE REMOVE YOUR SHOES.

He looked at the monitor. The small familiar figure pulsed in the front entry hall, the perimeter security sensors glowing green and showing secure.

Jumping up, he hit his knee on the corner of the desk. "Fuck," he grumbled under his breath. The air had become thick and tinged with a hot burnt smell, much like a lightning strike, filling his nostrils. He didn't remember crossing the room or how he made it to the front entry hall, but he was there, his hands and legs tingling, the floor seeming to move beneath him, making him reach for the wall to steady himself.

Even with a surge of adrenaline, he wasn't fast enough to see the figure fully, but he did catch a glimpse of sneakered feet through the balusters running up the stairs. Gaining his balance, he grabbed the newel post and propelled himself forward, landing on the bottom step. He took the remaining stairs two at a time, heart pounding.

The hall was dark and empty except for a small sliver of light coming from Jack's room. James took a deep breath as he approached the open door, cautiously peering in. The room was empty. He stood rigid; a chill came from the floor like cold water filling a pool.

Another chime, this time coming from the direction of the attic stairs, echoed in the second-floor hallway: WELCOME, LITTLE HAROLD.

James narrowed his eyes, looking for movement. "Harold," he called out, wanting to be heard but not wanting to scare him. "I'm your nephew, your nephew James." He took in a slow, deep breath as he tried to calm himself, not wanting to sound frantic. Cold sweat ran down his back, settling between his shoulder blades as he listened to the house.

Approaching the third-floor stairs, he stood, staring up at the light coming from the attic windows. He saw only a part of the landing, the small space seeming much darker than normal, darker than the storm brewing outside. Something that sounded like footsteps echoed overhead; the sound was fleeting so he wasn't positive, unable to pinpoint their location.

"Harold?" he called again. Goosebumps broke out all over his body, raising the hair on his head as he continued upward, pausing between each step to listen. Reaching the top, his eyes swept the boxes of familiar family objects measuring—up until now—normal life. He took each step with care, his sinuses protesting as dust bloomed up from the floor. Pulling his shoulders back, he passed through the second doorway, entering the playroom with a false sense of security wrapped in machismo, a costume energized with excitement concealing his fear.

The thought of facing a ghost was terrifying to him. He wondered if Little Harold would look dead: shades of gray or green or covered in blood, the injury that carried him into the next life apparent. *Nah,* he thought. *That's all Hollywood special effects.*

His overwhelming need for flight was growing and taking shape in the darkness as he fumbled for the light switch. The brightness filled the room as shadows fled to the corners, illuminating items stored there for decades. However, one new object stood out. Sitting in the middle of the floor was a catcher's mitt.

His hands were still tingling as he bent to pick up the out-of-place mitt. *It's strangely warm,* he thought. He held it up, turning it over, examining the details with wonder.

"Huh, now who do you belong to?" he whispered. "Jeffrey." Sadness touched the name when spoken out loud and was as real as the leather he held in his hands.

Tucking the mitt under his arm, he returned to the main floor, checking each room on his way as he struggled to calm himself, an action designed to restore his peace of mind, which was on shaky ground. Reaching the entry at the bottom, he froze. The floor was now empty. The baseball and Racer 8 were gone.

"What the hell!" His agitation was growing with each strange and unexplained event.

Jack will be upset that I lost his toy car, he thought.

"Shit, shit, shit."

He was reaching a boiling point and he knew it.

Chapter 26
Lost and Found

In his office, James inspected the catcher's mitt. It looked used, but with no major signs of damage. A little digging identified it as a Paul Richards-signature, eleven-inch catcher's mitt by Wilson, a popular mitt dating from the 1950s. *It's in amazing condition,* he thought. It would have looked new if it weren't for the slight patina where it had been oiled. Was this the glove Jeffrey received on his birthday? How are items lost from a parallel world ending up in his home? How did Racer 8 and the baseball disappear?

That was the answer to the million-dollar question. *What draws them here,* he wondered, *and what does my new security system have to do with it all?* With a pencil, he found himself doodling on the edge of one of the aged newspaper clippings.

"Why? Where? How?" He repeated the words aloud, underlying each. *Where are the answers? Is it our connection through thought, or is it the home itself?*

No matter how many questions he wrote down, he doubted the answers would follow easily. They were experiencing a phenomenon, after all, a glimpse into the existence of life after death. What would people think if any of the happenings within the house slipped out into the small but tight-knit community of Queen Anne? Would they become the crackpots on the block? Would their children be left off the party list and sleepover invites? Would his job be secure? Hell, would he ever hold a job if the technology community felt he were wearing a tinfoil hat? All the questioning tore at his seams and weighed down his heart. He would never want to endanger or hurt his family, yet that was exactly what he was doing, and he needed to apply damage control. *Keep this close and do not speak of it to anyone,* he thought. Yet he knew the kids would talk. He and Jessica would and could simply laugh it off as kids and their imaginations or kids making up invisible friends.

James was a skilled critical thinker. Finding truth hidden within the noise was something he was good at, and he hoped it wouldn't take long to piece things together. Maybe the key was the accident?

He made a few calls and was told he could scan a clearer version of the article that detailed the accident at the Seattle Public Library. Afterward he'd drop off the film canisters with his friend Fred Hobbs, who was one of the top restoration experts in Washington.

Chapter 27
Movie Night

The smell of curry, rich and spicy, filled the house. James was an excellent cook and loved to express his culinary creativity, especially when the universe hit him with a curve ball and, as of late, he'd been given too many to count. It was a way for him to escape his brain and feed his soul when caught in a loop of unanswered questions.

His favorite chef, London-born Graham Kerr—also known as *The Galloping Gourmet,* a television program popular in the late '60s, '70s, and '80s—inspired tonight's dinner menu. Thanks to the internet, Graham flooded the room with his refined British flair and gregarious, over-the-top love of food and wine. James's mother had been a big fan and never missed a show, always dreaming she would be the one Graham would pull from the studio audience at the end to enjoy the lovingly cultivated meal on the air. *The Graham Kerr Cookbook* that his mother purchased back in 1974 was an integral part of the kitchen and was open tonight to pineapple curry.

Jessica and the kids arrived in a whirl of chatter, their arms full of homework, projects, and books. Jack received an A on his book report, and Alena had built a bird house out of popsicle sticks.

She'd painted the new addition to the backyard a bright green and red with a yellow and white daisy painted on the roof. She'd gone above and beyond by adding a special touch of grass and leaves so the birds would be cozy.

"It is important they are warm," she said.

The sun was setting, the smells of dinner and laughter adding to the energy and buzz of much-needed normalcy in the Allen home. James didn't know how to break it to his wife that his experiment was a partial success. How could he tell his partner that the home now recognized those who were not of flesh and bone? He listened to the evening banter, his sense of care and love of family close to the surface, the warmth of it welcome as he shoved his encounter with his uncle down beneath the need of knowledge in all things woo-woo and unknown.

Jessica hummed—something she hadn't done in weeks—as she set the table. The choice to leave the alarm system off was bringing her a sense of calm and, with it, her sense of peace. *How long will it last?* he thought. He would rip the joy from her if he told her about his experiment and that the system was able to recognize his late Uncle Harold. *Again, it can wait,* he thought. He just wanted to enjoy the night and his family.

With dinner finished, the kids hurried to complete their homework. Their motivation was the new Pixar movie released on Netflix and a bowl of popcorn with extra butter.

"Let me see your homework, then take your clean clothes up to your room," Jessica said, peering over a pile of student book reports that needed grading.

Jack picked up his backpack, grasping the strap with both hands. "Will you turn on the alarm tonight?" he asked his dad. He was swinging the bag between his legs, nervously awaiting a response.

Jessica looked up from her grading, sliding a sharp look at James, who was leaning back in his chair, watching Alena as she finished her homework.

"No, Buddy. It will be off tonight." James looked to his son, who had stopped swinging the backpack. "Come here. Do you not feel safe?"

Jack's hair was starting to spring up after a day of quiet submission under layers of gel. He hesitated before responding, "No, I mean, yes, I feel safe. Just wondering." He looked at his shoes as he kicked a spot of dirt on the floor.

Jessica moved the papers aside, giving her full attention to Jack as he moved closer to the table. It was obvious he had something on his mind.

Jack rolled his eyes to the ceiling and then back to his parents. James noticed he had Harold's green coat in the crook of his arm. It was never far, always there within reach.

"I was just wondering." Jack turned on his heel, disappearing into the hall. "Don't start the movie without me," he yelled over his shoulder. His footsteps faded as a faint click of a door could be heard overhead.

Alena, her wrist bent and tucked in under her chin, had finished her homework and was doodling circles, swirls, and what looked like Mrs. Kelly. She cocked her head, looking to her parents, waiting for a signal that she was excused.

"Is that it for today?" Jessica asked, holding out her hand to inspect the homework.

Alena nodded. "Can we hang my birdhouse tonight?"

"No, not tonight. Maybe tomorrow," James answered softly, a smile lit when he looked at her.

"OK, take your laundry upstairs and change into your pajamas," Jessica said, placing Alena's homework on top of her pink, flowered backpack. Alena was off like a shot, a blur of curls as she flew up the stairs, followed closely by her mother.

***

"Hey, husband," a voice said from behind James, still at the table. He was lost in thought, thinking of his day. He turned in his seat and looked at her. Jessica was smiling at him, the type of smile that made him feel everything would be OK, and he needed it more than ever. She pulled out a chair and sat across from him.

It's so creepy the way she knows everything, he thought.

"So, how was your day?" She nudged him with her foot, since he was out of arm's reach.

"Hello, wife." He returned the smile as he reached under the table and grabbed her foot, making her yelp in surprise. "Brr, we need to get you some socks or your slippers," he said, holding her foot in both hands.

"Yeah, well, I was too lazy and forgot them upstairs. I'll live." She smiled blissfully, not taking her eyes off his face as he continued to rub her foot while looking out the window, now avoiding her gaze. He wanted to take in the night and wait, but she knew him too well.

"I found out I can get a copy of the article," he said. "So hopefully I'll have a better picture of Jeffrey tomorrow. The article we have is too faded and blurred."

"Is that what The Times said?" She closed her eyes, enjoying her foot rub.

"Yep, and I dropped off the mystery film canisters, so hopefully we'll know what's on them or, should I say, if anything can be salvaged." He released her foot as he stood. "I'll go grab your slippers. Continue your grading, and I'll be back."

The evening was uneventful, the movie lulling the kids into a dreamlike stupor for bedtime. Jessica and James were enjoying the simple, childlike animation, which required very little thought or focus, giving them a break from needing to think about anything and everything.

James elbowed Jessica, lifting his chin first to Alena and then Jack. Curled up in the couch pillows that were now on the floor, a half empty bowl of popcorn between them, both had their eyes closed. "I'll get them tucked in," he said with a motion in their direction.

***

"So, now that the kids are in bed, want to tell me what's going on with you?" Jessica was curled up in the corner of the couch, the remote in her hand as she scanned the TV programs with a continuous *click, click, click.* She kept her eyes on the television, perusing the late-night programming and only occasionally glancing at James, who was looming quietly.

He stood next to her, the corner of his mouth pulled up in a smirk. "How do you always know? It's kind of creepy, Jess. Do you also have these abilities like your sister?" He sat down close, pulling her into him, his arm encircling her shoulders.

"Are you asking if I'm woo-woo?" She turned her head, sliding her eyes toward him.

"Well, how else would you know everything I'm thinking?" He gave her a squeeze.

"How about two decades of marriage? That will do it, I think." A sly smile touched her lips as she focused on the television.

James stretched out his feet, resting them on the top of the coffee table, and pretended to care about the shows that flashed over and over as she turned the channel from one program to the next. With a click, the television went dark. Jessica pulled away, setting the remote on the table. "OK." Her back was straight as her focused narrowed, intent on answers.

One word was all it took. James knew he couldn't hold off any longer and that the evening bliss would end. The house grew silent, the normal sounds shoved down below the surface, shadows lurking in the corners getting closer as he contemplated how to begin.

"I managed to upload Little Harold's photos this morning," he said, meeting her sharp gaze. "I also set the alarm and used a few of his things, like the baseball and his toy car to, well, maybe get his attention." She didn't move, and he gave her a nervous smile as he poked her leg, wanting the trancelike stare to end.

"Anything else you think I should know?" she asked, softer now, but still on edge. "What happened when you turned on the system?"

He gave a long, exhaustive sigh as he ran his hands over his face several times, then scratched the beard stubble that had taken over his usually smooth face. "Well, the system picked him up and someone else, but I don't know who." He began to rub the spot between his eyebrows, his headache moving in again, fogging his vision. "He took the toy car and ball I left for him in the hallway."

"He? Who is he?" she asked, her skepticism hiding under layers of sincerity, wanting desperately to believe what he was about to tell her. She looked around the room and then back to her husband.

"I'm not sure if it was Little Harold or maybe Jeffrey. I went up the stairs, and, when I returned, they were gone." He shrugged as he glanced at her with an air of helplessness and, he slumped back into the couch. "I'm hopeful now that I know it works. I just need to figure out why they're here one minute and gone the next. Oh, and I'm only guessing the other unidentified visitor is Jeffrey."

"Wow, so it works," she said, leaning back next to him as the stress ebbed out, moving just a little.

"Don't worry, I'm not planning on turning on the system when you and the kids are home. My theory is that the technology and equipment setup releases energy in a way that allows them to visit or become visible to us. I'm not sure exactly, but, again, I'm working on it. When does your sister get home?" He grabbed her legs under her knees so that she could stretch out, her feet resting in his lap, and she picked up the remote, turning on the television.

"Tracy said she would be home late," Jessica said. "They have their first viewing of the exhibit tonight. I must admit, I like having her here, with all of the craziness going on."

James agreed; she was a wealth of knowledge, filling in the blanks on so many levels.

"Maybe she can tell me how to get that damn toy car back," he said, tipping his head back, closing his tired eyes for a moment. "It's only a matter of time before Jack realizes it's gone." He got up and chose one of his favorite DVDs, placing it in the Blu-ray DVD player and hitting Play. The opening music settled him in for the night.

Jessica laughed as the beginning credits popped on the screen. The movie was *Defending Your Life*, filmed in the early '90s and starring Meryl Streep and Albert Brooks. It was about a man who was hit by a bus and how he spent his time in limbo between worlds.

"Well, how apropos." She nudged him with her foot as he laughed, shifting his eyes to her, the moment's lightness a joy for both of them.

"I thought it was perfect for the evening," he said, crossing his feet and getting comfortable.

Chapter 28
Who's There?

Tracy's night was late, and she was still exhausted. She felt the light of day even with the blankets pulled over her head. She heard the distant noise of the morning, a gentle tug at the edge of wakefulness, urging her to be part of it. Pulling the pillow from under her head, she hid beneath it in a sad attempt to block out the world. The birds, however, were in on the conspiracy, their chirps and chatter filling the air with pockets of sound, giving her no reprieve from nature's alarm clock.

"Aaargh! OK, OK, I'm getting up!" she yelled. There was a flurry of sheets and blankets as she kicked them free of her feet, her pillow somehow becoming airborne and landing on the other side of the room. Eyes closed, she propped herself up on her elbows, taking stock as she gathered her strength to rise and become one with the living.

Groggy, she pondered her museum checklist for the day. Their exhibit featured a few new Abstract and Kinetic artists, and some art pieces had moving parts that needed constant support. Looking for her phone, she saw the baseball James found nights before sitting on the corner of her bedside table.

"Huh." She reached for the well-worn baseball. It was warm in her hand, and she thought about Little Harold, wondering if he missed it.

She heard her family, the normal morning sounds working their way up the stairs. Then silence as the back door closed. The kids were off to school; her sister would have left half an hour before to ready her classroom, as it was Thursday, when her class started at eight a.m. James would be back home after he dropped the kids off at school. Tracy looked forward to an update on his progress uploading Jeffrey and Little Harold.

In the kitchen she tapped the side of the glass coffee pot: still warm, just enough remaining coffee to start her day. She placed the baseball on the counter, making sure it wouldn't roll off, then reached for an empty cup and began to pour. A loud *rap, tap, tap* echoed through the room, making her jump and spill the coffee. She turned to the window and saw that a large robin had landed on the exterior windowsill.

"Ha! Pfft, OK, little one, you had me going for a minute. Just a little jumpy this morning, and, no, you can't come in." She looked past the bird. "But it is ugly out there," She sighed, as if commiserating with her feathered voyeur.

A chill came from behind her. The mudroom door stood open; James was home, rain dripping from him as he closed the door, his dark green Gore-Tex raincoat making noise with each movement.

"You know the saying, it's raining cats and dogs?" he asked, smiling. "Did I scare you?"

"No, I was having a discussion with a bird, so you just startled me a little. I'm going to need more coffee; want some?" She took the empty coffee pot to the sink, rinsing it out.

"Yes, and thank you. I'll be in my office. Why don't you join me there?" He removed his coat and wiped off the raindrops clinging to his lashes and nose. Turning to retreat to his office, he noticed the baseball on the counter. "Where did that come from?"

"I found it on my nightstand this morning." She walked over to pick it up. "I'm not sure. I think Jack left it there."

James met her at the counter, holding out his hand to take the ball. "I lost this yesterday." He looked down, forehead creased, trying to work out the puzzle. "Now I hope Jack's favorite car finds its way back. Poor kid doesn't know I lost it with this baseball." He shook his head as he turned, motioning for her to follow while tossing the ball in the air and catching it.

In the tiny office, the dreariness of the rainy day added to the atmospheric gloom, much like a ship caught in a storm, the sound of rain hitting the deck outside. James sat behind his desk, placing the baseball in the middle as Tracy tilted her head, peering inquisitively at it as if seeing it for the first time.

"So," James said, "you said objects have been known to apport. Do you think they move back and forth, from one parallel dimension to another on purpose? You know, like a young boy wanting to keep his prized baseball close?"

"Sheesh, not sure," Tracy answered with a smug *I-know-more-than-you* smile. "If Jack or Alena didn't move this, then, yes, maybe." She rolled the baseball a few inches, like a fidgeting child. She stopped playing with it, looking around the room as if reminding herself where she was, then, giving James a direct look, she continued in hushed conspiratorial tones, as if she were about to share the hidden mysteries of the universe. "One case I read was that an item appeared after it had been destroyed in a fire. It was a carved pipe owned by a famous sea captain and was on display at a museum in a glass case and," she held up one finger to make a point, her tone a bit louder, "under lock and key, in a small town outside of Boston. It was purported that old, faulty wiring started the devastating fire, bringing much heartache to the small community and its seafaring heritage. When the fire was safely out, they tried to save what they could, but water had destroyed what the flames did not. They sadly gave what remained of the pipe to the great-grandson of the captain."

She tapped her finger once, twice, then continued, again in the hushed conspiratorial tone. "Now, this is what is interesting: the pipe was, in fact, destroyed, though some of the carving and art remained, and it was given a place on the mantel, along with a small painted portrait of the captain. One morning, the great-grandson was building a fire when he noticed the pipe was perfect, without a flaw or hint of the fire or age. So, you must ask yourself, was the pipe moved from another place and time? It has been documented that when an item crosses from their time to our own, the object reflects the condition of the dimension from which it came. However, I'm not sure if our things can move to their space and dimension."

She was still focused on the baseball as she stood up straight, then looked at her brother-in-law. "Anything of yours missing?" She tossed the ball back and forth between her hands before placing it back on the desk.

James glanced at the baseball and then to Tracy, his wet shoes squeaking as he turned back toward the computer screen, shaking his head. "I'm not aware of anything missing, but this house is so big, how would I know for sure?" He shrugged. "Have a seat. I've been wanting to do this."

He pulled the scanned photo of Jeffrey he'd found at the library from *The Seattle Times* article. Manipulating a side profile, he waited to see if the system would accept the upload, the red circle spinning for what seemed to be forever. With a beep, a message appeared on the screen that the upload was successfully complete. He typed in the name JEFFREY.

Tracy, now sitting in the chair across from him, watched with fascination as James reviewed his data files and his journal notes while filling her in on the events from the day before.

"Hmm, tell me, will communicating with the dead be a feature of the new system?" She covered her mouth, trying not to laugh.

"Kidding, brother. I'm sure that isn't a feature you want to advertise."

He laughed, lacing his fingers, hands clasped in front of him. "I've been stalling my team. They want updates and data on how things are going and, well…to buy time, I've told them there are some small coding glitches. I can see the tagline now: We Can Monitor Your Family, Alive or Dead." Another laugh escaped him as he rubbed his neck. "I'll keep feeding them the information they need to know for now. If I can't figure out why this is happening… well, it will be a career disappointment, to say the least."

Tracy pointed to the picture of Jeffrey. "What message should you give Jeffrey?" Her eyes took in his features, finger tracing his outline.

"We need to let him know he's OK here, I guess," James said, looking for guidance. "Do you think he even knows where he is?"

"He seems lost," Tracy said. "I think it's a loop. If you notice, he comes in and does the same thing every time. He looks right and then left before he runs up the stairs. He may not know he's doing the same thing over and over again, so it's a loop. Ask him to stop, hell, anything that breaks the cycle. Maybe we can snap him out of it."

She continued, watching James as he entered messages into the system, "Think about it. What if you had the same dream night after night and at the end of it you fell off a cliff? You may even come to expect it, not understanding why. Then one night someone steps out of the trees and breaks the pattern, keeping you from falling." She lifted her shoulders and sighed. "We need to step out of the trees, so to speak."

"OK, so, Hello, Jeffrey?" He typed in the first message for the entry hall, followed by another for the back door mudroom. "Maybe keep it simple, after all, nothing like a kind hello to greet you." James chuckled. "I still can't believe I'm adding the dead neighbor boy."

With the data input completed, he set the keyboard aside. "I'll make some calls and get some work done."

"Want to meet me back here in a few hours?" Tracy asked.

James lifted his chin at the security monitor, and a nervous smile filled his face, knowing in his gut that it would work: they would come. "Nobody I would rather go down this rabbit hole with. We just need to be gentle with Jessica. I've never kept anything from her, never in all the years we've been married. I just need to know more of how this works to reassure her that all will be OK."

He looked at the framed photo of his grandfather on the desk corner and then back to Tracy, now standing in the doorway. "Do you think there's any danger?" he asked, concern and stress radiating from him and apparent with the dark ashen circles under his eyes. He wasn't sure if he wanted to know the answer.

Tracy looked at the empty hallway, then back at James. "Knowing you are alone and feeling you are alone are different, you know," she said, looking up into the corners of the room. "No, I don't believe so. Nothing seems dark to me."

An *I-know-what-I'm-talking-about* look from her allayed his fears. Tracy glanced out the window, squinting into the day and then to her watch as she calculated time and their next move. "Let me get showered and changed. You're right, we need to figure all of this out or Jess may disown both of us. So, two hours, then?" She turned into the hallway and was gone.

Chapter 29
Reunion

When Tracy entered the office, James was on the phone. He held up a hand, indicating for her to pause, then turned to the printer. "OK, I thank you for your time. I appreciate it. Just let me know when you find them." He finished the call and turned to Tracy.

"I found Jeffrey's parents' information based on his birth certificate," James said. "Or at least I think I found them. This is from an old neighbor who is retired from the SPD. He was in homicide but said he can track them down for me." He handed her the pages from the printer. "It gives their name and place of birth for each. I think Aunt Sandra said they moved to his hometown. She also said my grandfather received a letter from Michael Simmons, Jeffrey's dad. There were stacks of envelopes and letters in one of the boxes we found in the Geek Shed. I'm going to look after dinner." He was swiveling his chair left and right in a nervous, rhythmic way.

"Michael and Carolyn?" Tracy said, reading their names twice, committing them to memory. "And remind me of your grandparents' names? Lillian and Harold?" She looked up from the printout. James had turned back to his computer, fingers flying on his keyboard. "James, hey, are those their names?" She raised her voice as she wrapped her knuckles on the desk.

"Oh, what? Yes, sorry." He finished his manic typing, then swiveled back in her direction. "I also left a message for a neighbor who lived here when the accident happened; he now lives in Nevada. It took some work tracking him down. His brother lives on the next street over. Anyway, he moved away ages ago, sold out like most on the block."

Tracy held up a hand, motioning James to slow down. "So, have you thought about it? I mean, think about it, Jimmy. What will you say when you come face-to-face with your long-dead uncle?"

There's a directness about her that's comforting, he thought. *Woo-woo as hell, but comforting, nonetheless.*

"I thought I would start with a hello," he said, one eyebrow raised in jest. "Then, maybe ask how he managed to be here, being dead and all. Hell, I've not had many conversations with the dead before." Nervous tension filled the space as he tried to make light of it all.

They stood side by side as he engaged the alarm. Then they moved to the front of the house, taking a seat just inside the living room, their line of sight the entry hall.

Neither one spoke. An understanding of sorts loomed between them. Was it fear, anxiety, or anticipation? Something had taken up space and was keeping them company; the size and weight of it was large, dense, and growing darker by the minute.

An hour went by, and tensions eased. Tracy looked at James, who was staring at the alarm control panel in the front hall.

"There's something missing," she said. "What did you do yesterday that was different?"

"Nothing as far as I know. I turned it on and waited. No, wait. How could I miss this piece of it?" he asked, sighing. "Grandpa's glasses, the catcher's mitt, the baseball, you know, their personal things, that's what's missing. I'm embarrassed that the simple connections escaped me."

"Hell, that's it." Tracy was out of her seat, disappearing into the hallway. She returned a minute later with the baseball, the catcher's mitt, and a pair of tortoiseshell eyeglasses. She calculated their location and placed them gently in the middle of the floor, directly across from the living room.

"Now," she said, "think about your uncle. Think about Jeffrey and your grandfather. Remember each time someone thinks of them, our connection becomes stronger. These objects are a reminder of their time on Earth and are a part of who they once were." She contemplated the importance of the items on the hallway floor. "Or, maybe these things, these trinkets from the past, keep us hopeful that our loved ones are close and feel the invisible cord that connects us." Optimism bounced off her, the wheels now in motion as they moved toward finding answers.

They sat, looking at the three objects. Tracy focused with intensity, her lips moving as if chanting a spell, calling their names under her breath, while James sat with his eyes closed, as the wind and rain muffled the world outside.

Tracy felt it first. The familiar vibration was ever so subtle as it moved up from the floor. She looked to James, his eyes popping open with the sensation. Then a light came from the back of the house, accompanied by a swirling warmth of air that moved around them like water filling a glass. Their hands reflexively covered their eyes as the smell of ozone wafted around them, stronger than before. Their hair whipped in different directions as if in a strong invisible wind. Tracy was on the floor, not remembering how she got there, her hands and feet tingling as she tried to focus, the room spinning. She blinked, and the walls wavered like curtains in a light breeze. Sounds seemed to disappear, as if they were being pulled down beneath the surface of the water. The only noise to reach them was distorted and distant.

James stood, swaying, his arms stretched out, reaching for something, anything, to steady himself as he opened and closed his hands, occasionally shaking them as if they were covered in something.

A muffled chime: Person not identified, please remove your shoes.

Up on her knees now, Tracy grabbed the couch's arm, looking to her brother-in-law, who stood turned away only a few feet from her. He appeared large from her vantage point on the floor. He looked down over his shoulder at her. Their eyes met, acknowledging the situation. He turned back to the hall, his steps slow and calculated as he swayed.

"What can you see?" Tracy asked. Her voice seemed small inside her head, ears ringing with a high-pitched buzz.

James shook his head, hair still standing on end, jagged movements making him look robotic and rusty as he moved to get a better view to the back of the house. The objects were still in the middle of the floor, the hallway empty. He turned, moving back into the living room to help Tracy up, not letting go until she seemed steady. He held her by the arms just under her shoulders. She felt like a puppet on a string, weak and unstable. Grabbing his forearm, she dug her fingers into him as she held her breath, trying to clear the buzzing in her ears.

"Hey." He winced at Tracy's nails digging deeper. Tracy didn't let go, her eyes widening, mouth agape as she looked past his shoulder.

"Jimmy, look!" She lifted her chin in the direction of the hall behind him. They held on tight, supporting each other as they rotated a few steps, allowing him to follow her gaze.

Not far from where they stood, there was movement in the dappled light as all sound disappeared, including the wind and rain outside. In the space before them, swirling, small fragments of color stretched, elongating in a disjointed rhythm, filling the hall from the direction of the staircase. The world around the unnatural dust storm revolved in slow motion as the walls on either side moved like liquid, flickered, then solidified, revealing random splashes of bright yellow on the walls. From within the strange silence, noises began bubbling up, as if the volume of life was suddenly turned back on.

Defying any sense of possibility, in the center of the entry hall stood a tall man, his dark hair slicked back, framing his open and kind face, sharp strong nose, and dark expressive eyes. The man's eyes shifted quickly between James and Tracy. He wore a plain beige button-up shirt, dark brown flat-front trousers, and gray suede shoes, looking exactly like a television dad from the '50s.

The familiar chime rang out again, yet the sound now had an underwater, sinister quality to it: PERSON NOT IDENTIFIED, PLEASE REMOVE YOUR SHOES.

In one fluid movement, the dark-haired man bent down and picked up the glasses. He unfolded them as he pulled a handkerchief from his pocket, gently cleaning one lens and then the other before settling them on the bridge of his nose.

"I've been looking for these," he said, his voice calm and friendly as he locked eyes with James. "Hello, Jimmy." A smile slowly grew into a grin, creasing his cheeks.

James turned to Tracy, his eyes flashing concern and fear as he searched her face. "Are you OK?" he asked. The question seemed disconnected from reality, considering the circumstance. He felt a stab of pain and glanced down at her white knuckles; she trembled with effort as she held on.

She followed his eyes. "Oh, God, sorry." She let go and stepped back. A strange synchronicity possessed them as they shifted in unison to face the man who stood less than five feet away.

Rolling his shoulders back and standing straight, James hesitated, his lips moving silently as if he were counting. Then he took a shaky, hesitant step closer to the preternatural visitor. His mouth hung open; the words stuck in his throat. He closed his eyes, hoping that when he opened them, the man would be gone, or at least that he would have mustered his courage. Opening his eyes, the stranger remained, still smiling, hands now clasped in front of him.

"Hello," James responded, just above a whisper. It was only one word, an accepted greeting worldwide, yet the essence of it in this instance seemed weak and pathetic.

The visitor responded with a slight tip of his head, as if any sudden movement would break the spell. James looked the man over, taking in every detail as questions raced through his mind. *How can this be? Is he real?* A bolt of understanding hit him as doubt cracked, then fell away.

"Dear Jesus," James said, the words cutting the silence like a prayer as he instinctively reached to shake the hand of the man who appeared to be his grandfather. A vibration ran up his arm, tingling his shoulder, causing James to look at the connection where their hands joined.

"Yes, Jimmy, I'm real." Harold James Allen Sr. made this statement as if he could read James's mind. In that moment, their existence merged, sharing time, space, and the home they both loved. They held on for what seemed like forever.

"Look at how tall you've gotten," his grandfather said, his eyes moving over his grandson as if taking inventory. There was a twinkle behind the glasses, the soul of his grandfather looking out through the eyes of a thirty-something-year-old man. There was recognition in his mannerisms, the smirk that pulled at his upper lip, the familiar nod of the head; all were window dressing in an ageless world, free from the physical constraint of growing old.

"And look at you," James exclaimed, the observation a little unnerving. "God, Grandpa, you look younger than me." Overcome with emotion, he hesitated for only a moment before stepping forward and throwing his arms around his grandfather.

When alive, his grandfather often smelled of Vitalis, cherry pipe tobacco, and Borax soap. The man he was hugging, however, had no perceptible smell at all. He looked like the man in the old family photos that hung on the wall and peered out from the frames scattered throughout the home, but there was a strange, warm undercurrent, a movement of energy just below the surface where they made contact. He'd felt it when they shook hands, but the embrace amplified the unnatural feeling, causing James to pull back and let go.

Tracy gasped. The scene unfolding before her was a testament to her core beliefs, speculations, and theories, all bouncing through her brain, challenging the framework of her life.

"Holy fucking shit," she said, her eyes wide open with astonishment as she looked at both men, who turned their attention in her direction. Slow realization running up her spine, she repeated with a flourish, "Holy mother fucking shit!"

Harold Sr. smiled at her with a laugh of amusement, then turned his attention back to James.

It's uncanny, she thought. *He looks just like his picture—the same photo he took with his family in the backyard on that sunny day decades before.*

Looking over James's shoulder, Harold Sr. turned his attention back to Tracy. "I've seen you before," he said. "You are Jessica's sister." His voice was friendly as he shifted one step to the right, extending his hand in greeting.

Her legs were wobbly. She needed a moment, so she held on to the arm of a chair before taking a step. Shaking, she reached out; their hands met; his, much larger, thrummed as it wrapped around her own.

"You are warm," she said, shocked, her hand and fingers tingling from his touch.

"And so are you," he said with a cock of his head. "Interesting, isn't it?" Releasing her hand, he turned, stepping back so he could view them both.

"Have you seen Little Harold?" Harold Sr. addressed his grandson in a matter-of-fact tone, as if they were simply catching up after a long time apart.

"Um, no, not today," James replied. "I think my son runs into him more often." His heart swelled at the mention of Jack.

"Yes, Jack," Harold Sr. said, sharing the nostalgic reunion and pride of fatherhood. "Harold has told me much about him. I think your son views Little Harold as a dream."

"Grandpa, where's Dad?" James asked, peering into the hallway, hoping he was on his way or would magically appear. "Is he with you?" He slid his eyes back to his grandfather, then looked around at the walls and ceiling, marveling at the merging worlds, colors melting into each other.

With a nod of understanding, the question moved over his grandfather's face. His head tilted up as if the answer would come to him from above. "Your dad is somewhere, perhaps with your mother. You will see them both again. Time is a facade with no walls or boundaries. Our time…who we are while on Earth is just a stopping point, a construct made of flesh and bone."

Harold Sr. paused, turning his head as if listening to someone behind him and then giving his attention back to James. He gestured, waving to the ceiling and then the floor. "You live in this reality. Until forever comes. And it comes for every one of us." He stepped to the window as if he saw something hidden from view.

Tracy cleared her throat. She shook her hands and rubbed them together, giving both the men a grin. "Um, I hate to break up the family reunion, but there are so many questions, and well, do we have any idea how this works or how long we have? Time, my friends, we have so little time. But, damn, this is so cool. I'll sit with this the rest of my life." Her smile faded as a serious note came back to her voice. "Mr. Allen, Harold, any idea what is happening here?"

A shadow darkened his features, then his smile returned as he tilted his head once again as if waiting for an answer. "I don't know how long we have." He looked around as if just now realizing where he was. "There are times when I see you from where

I am, but you can't see me. Becoming visible in this place is difficult and takes a great deal of energy. I'm really not sure how I'm doing it now. I recently crossed into your world when Harold, my son, needed me." He seemed to stand a little taller at the mention of his name.

"So, I found him here, calmed him, and, with great effort, we found our way back home, but I left these behind," Harold Sr. continued, tapping the frame of his glasses and taking another look around, this time turning in place. "Our home has yellow walls, you know. You know your grandmother loves yellow. She is going to wonder where I am." His eyes were soulful as he talked of Lillian. He shifted on his feet, looking back as if hearing something or someone behind him.

"I'm right here," Harold Sr. called out. He was responding to a voice only he was able to hear, his face suddenly very animated as he looked at his grandson and then back to the hallway. "I'm with Jimmy," he said, hand cupping his mouth, giving strength to his voice, which seemed to bounce off an invisible barrier before falling flat and muffled.

Bewildered, James took a step forward. The hallway behind his grandfather was rippling like rain hitting the surface of a pond, the liquid-like atmosphere only feet from where they stood.

"OK, Lily," Harold Sr. answered. Then, suddenly, the walls glimmered and changed, shifting the view. Harold Sr. was calling to his wife Lillian, who appeared to be standing at the end of the hallway, but she was in a house of a different time—the house with yellow walls.

Turning his head, he looked at James. "Your grandmother will be so happy to see you."

Without another word, Harold Sr. walked into the wavering hall. There was a shimmer that seemed to gather him in, the yellow walls expanding and retracting in response as he walked. James saw a shadowy figure surrounded by light at the end of the hall outside the kitchen doorway. The details were blurry at first, moving in and out of focus: the vision was his grandmother.

"Grandma!" James called, bellowing at the top of his lungs to be heard, but his greeting bounced back as it hit the flickering scene. He stood on his toes, his hands held above his head, waving—the memories of childhood, of cookies, of love and family flooding back. The yellow walls, just feet away, continued to move, pulsing like a living thing. He could see her. She was young like his grandfather, and, in that moment, she saw him, too. No sound made it to him as she waved back.

"Grandma!" he called to her again. *Is any of this real?* he wondered.

There was a sound like air escaping a long-sealed jar. The light grew, then a popping noise changed the pressure as the walls straightened, becoming solid and still. The hallway, a familiar and comforting beige, was empty once again.

Tracy, still light-headed, stepped slowly over to James, who was rigid, as if it would keep him upright, tears filling his eyes as he stared into the hallway. She placed her hand gently on his arm, the muscles tense under the fabric of his shirt.

"Wow," she said. "Just wow." *It's the only word that seems to fit,* she thought.

James looked down at her, his face lit with wonder as he met her eyes, his body relaxing as he dropped his shoulders.

"Grandma Lily," he murmured as he shifted his gaze back to the hall where she had stood just seconds before. He turned to Tracy, looking for a sense of understanding, struggling with his words. "My grandpa, he, he looked so young. Not old, not like he did. Didn't he? I never knew him like that. And my grandma, did you see her? She also was so young."

He rambled on, taking two steps toward the kitchen, then stopped, placing his hands on his hips and standing silent for a good, long while. Tracy stood with him in the silence. She knew the moment shared between them would change their lives forever.

"Hey, the trigger objects are gone," she said with realization, looking around at the floor.

"Huh, I wonder where they went?" He, too, looked at the floor, then he shifted his weight as if he wasn't sure where to go or how to proceed. He stilled his fidgeting, narrowing his eyes at Tracy. "I'm not sure if this new security system will make people feel safe. Man, I thought this is my time. I thought this project would make a difference. Shit, shit, shit." He wiped at his mouth, then moved his glasses to the top of his head before rubbing his eyes. He shook his head and looked back into the hallway as if waiting for something or someone to appear.

Tracy passed behind him, giving his elbow a light squeeze before she turned off the alarm system. "I think we've had enough for today."

James said nothing, just stood there.

"Well, I need to get this shit down," she said with a little more volume. "I need my laptop to document this."

James simply looked at her.

The air was still electrified, the smell of ozone lingering, irritating her lungs with each breath. She needed to move, feeling light-headed and unsteady. On the way to her room, she stumbled halfway up the staircase. Luckily, she caught the banister, which kept her from falling. Dark spots floated in front of her, so she decided to sit until her vision cleared. She closed her eyes, listening to the house. Nothing could be heard but the familiar far-off ticking of the kitchen clock, which was strangely comforting. The rain was much lighter as the wind died down to a gentle breeze.

While pulling herself up, she looked through the balusters at the hall below. James was still standing there. He hadn't moved.

***

Returning downstairs with her laptop, Tracy expected to find James in his office, fervently documenting his experience, but the room was empty. Setting her laptop on the desk, she peeked out the window, looking to the Geek Shed for signs of occupancy. No light was visible; only darkness filled the small casement window.

"Hmm." She bit her lower lip. A soft thump on the ceiling moved her to the hallway. "James?" she called. Footsteps, muffled and heavy, came from overhead. "Jimmy, are you up there?"

She slowly walked the hallway, taking in the photos on the time-travel wall, thinking how the events of the day gave the wall a whole new meaning. She arrived at the staircase and began to climb, stopping halfway up. She leaned on the banister, looking to the floor above, listening.

"Tracy? I'm up in the attic." The distant response from James cut through the silent house.

She hurried to the attic staircase. "Jimmy?"

There were steps and a rustle of movement from above as James stepped into view, the catcher's mitt in one hand, baseball in the other. "I found them here." He tossed the baseball into the mitt as he turned, a flick of his head in the direction of the playroom requesting her presence.

A rectangle of light guided Tracy up to where James stood, waiting.

"All these things," she said, looking around the room, the toe of her shoe tapping on the racetrack. "Goodness, some of these things are old. Well, hello, you are lovely, well, you were once anyway." She picked up an old doll with a delicate hand -painted face. She was wearing a yellow and white checkered dress with frayed lace trim, her hair a mop of matted brown curls topped with a matching white lace cap that had seen better days. Tracy brushed at the doll's dress before setting her down on the blue duck-cloth steamer trunk in the corner.

"Do any of these things belong to Jack or Alena?" she asked, rubbing her fingers together and noticing the dirt that covered her hands from picking up the doll. "They all look, well, from another time."

"No. Most of this stuff was left here. Ya know, the funny thing about this track…it was in the Geek Shed in a box for years, then Jack found the box and took it to his room, um, and now it's here and Jack swears he didn't move it, let alone put it together." He put down the ball and catcher's mitt and picked up a red, gray, and blue airplane with the words *Sky Cruiser* printed in red on the top.

"This," he said, moving the plane in a fluid motion like a child, "this belonged to my father, and it's been gone for decades." He placed the plane on the ground and turned to her. "The question I have now is, should I let the world in on what's going on? Did I create this? What in the hell have I done?" He leveled a pain-filled glance as he surveyed the room.

"Good question, but I think you need to figure out how to break it to Jess first." She rubbed her temples and sighed. "I'm glad I got to meet him."

"Who, Grandpa? Yeah, he was—or should I say he is—a good man." He held a faraway look, toward a place Tracy couldn't see.

Chapter 30
The Note

James and Tracy sat at the kitchen table that evening, reflecting on the day. Every moment held up in memory as they discussed their collective experience. James was methodical as he wrote in his journal. He cataloged everything, to study and understand, his need for logic and science coloring his version of events. Tracy was much more animated and passionate. Her life, feelings, and theories now unfolded outward. To her, it was solid and real, in spite of the mitigating woo-woo factor.

Jessica stood at the kitchen window, silent, hands resting on the counter, fingers drumming as she thought. "So, we are a petri dish for the paranormal?" she asked. There was a far-off note in her voice, tinged with anger, like a storm was about to roll in. "Have we figured out how it's happening yet?" Turning, she looked at her husband and sister, strain showing, the darkened circles under her eyes looking like deep hollows as she tried to wrap her head around their words. Words that seemed unreal and impossible.

"Like I said before," James answered carefully, not wanting to anger his wife, but needing to understand the heart of her question, "it may be that it's the energy dispersal, but you don't really care, do you? Whatever is happening may be a scientific anomaly. You might call it a miracle." He glanced sideways at Tracy.

That struck a chord. "Ha! A miracle? Well, maybe, just maybe." Jessica pulled a chair out, joining them. "So, what should we do?" She placed her hands on the table, bringing forth her inner strength to the team, planning their next move.

"We need to turn on the system again," Tracy said. "But I think it would be wise to do it when the kids aren't home. I also think we should be cautious in the entry hall. It seems that the front of the house is the epicenter when the two worlds bump into each other. It just about knocked me across the room, but not you, Jimmy." A quizzical look passed over Tracy's face as the wheels spun in plain view. She looked to her brother-in-law, who was making notes, focusing on gathering and documenting every point of his experience.

He looked up. "What? Who? Me? Oh, I felt it. My hands still feel fuzzy." He lifted one hand and wiggled his fingers. "How do you like that for a scientific description?" A rueful, crooked smile filled his face.

"Dad." A small voice came from the hallway. Jack stood in his rocket-ship pajamas, his hair sticking up on one side.

"Buddy, you should be in bed," James said. "It's late." He moved to the hall, the light from the kitchen painting a glow across Jack's face. Jack looked down at his closed fist, then raised his hand, opening it slowly, revealing a small piece of paper.

Immediately at his side, Jessica knelt on one knee and took the paper, which was lined, torn, folded twice, rolled, and creased, as if someone had been holding it tight for a long time. The color was yellowed with what looked to be water stains—small droplets touching the edges, blurring the bottom of the note.

"I found it next to my pillow," Jack said as he looked to his mom, then his dad, concern pinching his brow, his lower lip pulled in between his teeth. "I think he's in trouble or sad or something." His eyes drifted back to the note now in his mother's hands.

Jessica's mouth moved as she read the note, but no sound came. She handed the note to James, still standing, his hand on his son's shoulder, reassuring him.

Tracy stood in the doorway, leaning against the doorjamb. "What does it say?"

James turned to her, lifting one shoulder, handing her the note, then looked back to Jessica.

Tracy read the note silently, her brow furrowed. She read the note out loud: "I'm sorry." *The words are short and to the point,* she thought. "So, who exactly is sorry?" She held the note at arm's length, as if a different angle would reveal the answer.

"How do you know he's in trouble?" Jessica asked her son.

"I don't know." Jack shrugged. "I see…" He trailed off, as if concealing something. Still biting his lip, he looked down at his hands. "But," he continued, looking up, "he doesn't talk to me, just goes upstairs, followed by his shadow."

"Have you seen him lately?" Tracy set the note on the table.

Jack shook his head. "Just his shadow."

"His shadow?" Jessica now looked concerned. Her eyebrows drawn together as lines of worry were set deep, making her look much older than she was.

"I thought our shadow was with us in the sunshine?" Jack asked.

"Yes, it is with us in any kind of light," Jessica responded, her brow softening, a smile pulling at the corner of her mouth.

"OK, buddy. You think can you go back to sleep?" James asked in a caring voice as he patted his son on the back.

"Yeah," Jack said. "I just wanted to make sure you knew he was looking for Uncle Harold." He had stopped biting his lip, his tension lifted as he turned back toward the stairs.

All three of them stood and watched Jack climb the stairs, listening as his footsteps faded. Looking from one to the other, they turned, returning to the kitchen table where the note sat, curling at the edges.

"It looks old, doesn't it?" Tracy was the first to address the elephant in the room. James reached across the table, spreading the piece of paper flat, smoothing it over and over, trying to keep it from rolling in on itself, holding the edges down.

Jessica snatched the note up, holding it first to the light and then her nose. "It even smells old. You know that musty smell that comes with the years and storage?"

There was an audible intake of air as James rubbed the back of his neck. "He must have left it when we turned on the system today. I'll check the security footage." James tapped his fingers on the table, thinking. "But we didn't pay any attention with Grandpa here." He looked to Tracy, eyebrows raised in question. "But Jack knows who Harold is, so maybe Jeffrey?"

"I was so blown away at the full body materialization of Harold Sr. that I didn't check for anyone else," Tracy said, nodding. She picked up the note. "Do you think he's in trouble like Jack says? I'm pretty sure ghosts don't have a shadow. Maybe the item moved from his dimension to our own; maybe he didn't bring it this time. Or maybe it has always been here, and Jack just found it?"

"Another million-dollar question," James said, his shoulders slumped as fatigue set in. "I won't turn on the system until I think things through." He smiled wearily at Jessica, reaching out to give her arm a reassuring squeeze. "Time for bed."

"I'm concerned about the shadow," Tracy said. Fatigue and concern cut lines in her face, her worry now apparent. She was thinking out loud, answering herself. "OK, that's a question for another day. I must be up early tomorrow and will be back late." Tracy didn't wait for a response and was gone into the darkness, her steps moving away from them.

Crawling into bed, James placed several books on quantum physics on the nightstand and opened his laptop, scrolling through various online resources, unable to turn off his mind.

Jessica turned to him, her eyes half closed and sleepy, forehead creased in concern, and sighed. "You need to turn your brain off for the night." She closed his laptop slowly, using one finger, the light from the screen fading like someone pulling down a window shade on a sunny day.

Looking over the top of his glasses, he smiled another weary smile. "OK, I can take a hint, and you are right. This was a big day. This life will never be the same." He stared into the room; an imaginary view of an unknown world lay before him. "I can't wrap my head around it. The realization that there is an existence, a home parallel to our own and as real as you and me." He motioned to the air in front of him. "It's out there right now. People we love and thought we lost are existing."

He took off his glasses, running his hand over his face and rubbing his eyes, the events of the day becoming part of his soul as the stress of it rolled away, making room for much needed sleep. "Oh, Jess, I saw my grandmother today, and she's been gone for almost twenty years. Hell, she smiled and waved at me." Placing his laptop on the bedside table, he turned to her and leaned in so that their noses were touching. "To know we will always be together is a beautiful thing." He kissed her nose, the glow of the table light catching the warmth of her curls and framing her face.

"I wasn't there," she said. Moving in closer, she pulled the blanket up under her chin and shuddered. "I believe you, but every time something happens, I'm more concerned for the kids. Have you noticed Jack seems detached? He hasn't read a book in weeks. Thank goodness Alena has the attention span of about a minute."

"Grandpa said he believed Jack thinks of Little Harold as a dream," James said. "But dreams don't leave notes, baseballs, or a catcher's mitt."

He reached over and turned off the light, settling back in close, the light from the streetlamp outside illuminating the room in shades of blue. "I don't think I should turn on the system while the kids are home." A sleepy tone, just above a whisper, hung in the air between them. He felt her hand reach for his as his body relaxed.

Chapter 31
An Intruder

A heaviness moved over Jessica. There was a pressure, first on her arms, then her chest. She opened her eyes but couldn't make out any objects in the room she knew well. *I must be dreaming,* she thought. A pool of blackness was moving around her as she tried to find the surface. Her shoulders were pinned, and her chest constricted as terror replaced confusion. Panic washed over her, each breath becoming more strained. There was a burning in her throat as bile rose from her stomach, choking her scream.

Scream, damn it! she thought, but she couldn't make a sound. Her eyes were rolling around, looking for an anchor to release her from the nightmare, yet she couldn't find a way out from the darkness. Tears rolled down her cheek as she closed her eyes and began to pray. *It is just a dream. Dear Jesus, please help me.*

Then, a release of pressure, the sound of the room flooding in again. Jessica's body was suddenly light, the heaviness on her chest gone. She sat up, bathing herself in the familiar things that grounded her as she reached out, searching the bedside table, her hand landing on reading glasses as she fumbled for the light switch.

The light was comforting. James didn't move, which panicked

her, then she saw the subtle rise and fall of his chest as he slept. She reached out to him, needing to hear his voice.

She placed a hand on his shoulder, gently shaking him. Opening his eyes, he tried to focus, her face just inches from his. His vision pulled to the outline of her hair, a halo framing a featureless face as sleep fell away.

"Shh. There is someone in the house," Jessica whispered as her fingers dug into his shoulder, each word measured like an iceberg.

The unseen danger was in front of him but hidden from view. He kicked back the covers, patting her hand in reassurance, adrenaline signaling to his body that it was time to fight for everything he held dear as his world was being dismantled. His long-held logical view of life now mocked him, dropping his heart into the pit of his stomach as a cold sheen of sweat prickled his brow.

The door to the hallway was open. He stood, looking over his shoulder at Jessica, who sat up and swung her legs over the side of the bed. In a blink, he felt her touch on his elbow, her panicked energy joining his.

"I'm going with you," she said, barely audible, but direct.

"What did you see?" he asked. As he turned to her, the light from the hallway sparked the green of her eyes, which were wide and frightened.

"I saw someone in our room. At first, I thought I was seeing things. I thought I was having a nightmare. There was no real shape, and then, dear God, the darkness *moved*, Jimmy. It fucking moved, blocking the light from the door." There was a tremble in her voice he had never heard before, and it was more terrifying to him than any darkness.

They moved together, their determination as one, the night-light near the floor in the hallway casting sinister shadows. A collision of sound came from downstairs. They grabbed at one another in reflex as they edged to peer over the banister. The stairs were empty, the glow in the hall fading into darkness as the light ebbed away, the ability of the small light to illuminate going only so far.

Suddenly, a scream from behind cut through the hallway, filling the space around them. James instinctually grabbed Jessica, one hand forcing her behind him as they turned to confront the source of the high-pitched shrieks. At the end of the hallway stood Alena, Mrs. Kelly held upside down at her side, a glimmer of tears streaming down her face as she gulped the air. Her chest and shoulders were moving with the effort, followed by a noise they had never heard from her before. It was the sound of pure hysteria.

Moving around her husband, Jessica ran toward Alena, who was spilling out fragmented words punctuated by hiccups and sobs. Falling to her knees, Jessica drew her daughter into her arms, cooing words of reassurance. "Baby girl, what happened? Shh, you are OK. Mom and Dad are here."

"The blanket…" A gasp of air. "Tried…" Another gasp. "To eat me." Another supply of tears filled her eyes. "The blanket was over my head…" Another gulp of air. "I couldn't pull it down. It tried to eat me."

"The blanket tried to eat you?" Jessica asked as calmly as possible, rubbing her daughter's shoulders.

Alena's tears kept flowing. She nodded her head yes and then burst again into tears.

"I'll have daddy look in your room." Jessica looked up to James, who was standing by her side.

He hesitated, not wanting to leave them, before proceeding into Alena's room. A *click,* then a rectangle of yellow spilled into the hallway. James reemerged, a pink and white bunny blanket in his hand. "This one, honey?"

Alena squealed, burying her head in her mother's shoulder. "Yes, Daddy. Yes."

James shrugged, feeling helpless. "Are you hurt?" he asked Alena.

Jessica's eyes were moving over Alena. Checking hands, arms, neck, head, and legs as she systematically patted and ran her hands over her daughter, looking for any sign of injury. Looking up through her lashes at James, she gave a quick shake of the head, continuing to calm her daughter, who was now breathing a little more calmly.

"There is nothing now, baby girl," he said. "We'll get another blanket for you." He moved past both of them, whispering to Jessica, "I need to check the rest of the house. Take her into our room." He paused to kiss the top of his daughter's head and then he was gone.

Stopping midway, he listened for any unfamiliar noise. The reassuring green light of the alarm was now dark, setting him on edge. For the first time, he felt he might have made the wrong decision to keep the alarm off, leaving the house open to intruders.

There was movement, yet he saw no one. Shadows within shadows shifted at the edges in the corners and along the wall. He blinked and blinked again, the cool, black tones of the hall seeming to undulate and move, but it was empty, making him feel foolish.

He grabbed the baseball bat leaning against the wall near the front door, pausing to check that the door was locked. His eyes flicked back and forth. He could feel a vibration all around him. The hairs stood on his neck as he turned from one side of the hall, then back again, expecting to be face-to-face with a preternatural intruder.

He entered the living room, hitting the light switch and lifting the bat high, ready to swing. The light extinguished any apparent threat, leaving him standing alone in an empty room. An icy burst of air against his back caused him to spin around in reflex.

"Fuck," he muttered. He crept back to the hallway—the bat still held high, straining his muscles—then noticed something was wrong.

His mind tried to grasp what was out of place. The photos on the time-travel wall were askew, all tipped, as if a great force had tried to blow them down, giving him the feeling of a funhouse, throwing him off. At the end of the hall, just on the other side of the kitchen, he saw there was an empty spot where the last family photo had been hanging, a small gold hook the only evidence of its disappearance.

"OK, calm the fuck down Jimmy, old boy," he said as he widened his stance. The floors were cold, prompting him to look down. His feet were bare. Both hands tightened on the bat. His palms felt slippery with sweat, his chest tight as he prepared to swing.

Moving ever so slowly toward the back of the house, he stopped just before the kitchen doorway. He studied the light that reached him from above the kitchen stove. There was no movement; anyone within the kitchen would pass in front of the dim light, casting shadows and revealing their presence. He stood as tall as he could muster and turned the corner, bat held high. In the center of the kitchen floor was the missing photo, his family smiling up from a broken frame, glass fragments spilling out from the center.

He lowered the bat—looking into the room, but not daring to enter—as his mind calculated the distance the photo had traveled to end up there. Small shards of glass shimmered on the floor, prompting him to look down again at his bare feet. He squinted at the mudroom door. Light from the outside porch spilled through the small glass window. The deadbolt appeared locked, but he couldn't tell for sure.

James took cautious, measured steps to his office, turning on the light. The catcher's mitt sat in the center of his desk, rocking slightly. Seeing this, he placed his hand flat against the wall and felt for movement.

There was another clatter of sound, followed by a crash in the hallway behind him. He turned, moving quickly into the hall. Several more framed photos lay broken on the floor. A pain ran up his right arm as he realized he was gripping the bat with such force that his hands ached.

"Damn it," he whispered, glancing down at the glittering shards of glass. Hugging the wall, he moved carefully, edging his way—at times on tiptoe—using the bat as support like an old man's cane, hoping to avoid cutting his feet with a wrong move.

"James?" Jessica called to him from the top of the staircase.

Tracy stood near the front door, her mouth open as she pointed to the photos on the floor. "Did you see it?" she asked, focused on the hallway just beyond the kitchen. "It came from your office, bounced off the wall, knocking off the photos, and then it came at me. It fucking came at me." There was astonishment in her voice as she looked to James, then up the stairs to Jessica as she stood leaning over the banister at the top of the landing.

Jessica held a finger to her lips, whispering, "I just got Alena settled. She is still upset. We need to keep our voices down."

Tracy nodded with understanding, then turned her focus to James. "The system isn't on," she said, glancing over her shoulder at the security panel, then back to her brother-in-law. "It's not fucking on."

"Yeah, we know," James said with a sideways glance at his wife, who had come down to the bottom of the stairs. There was defeat in his voice with this new and terrifying revelation. "Who or what doesn't seem to need the system anymore. This time it went after Alena." As the words tumbled out of his mouth, the meaning fell like an anchor.

"Oh, God, the children," Tracy muttered, her eyes moving between them. "What is going on? Are they OK?"

Jessica met her eyes, fear and anger moving over her, causing her to ignore the chaos in the hallway and focus on the children. "Yes, Alena is in our bed, and Jack didn't wake up until I went to check on him." She looked at James, still holding the bat, his brow furrowed, jaw set. "I don't think that bat is going to help or protect us from whatever was in Alena's room, and I don't believe it was some little boy or one of your grandparents."

She looked down at her hands, where she gripped the banister, then lifted one hand, slamming it down as if punctuating her thoughts. "Maybe we should turn the security system back on," she said, glaring at the security panel on the opposite wall, as if questioning her desire for safety versus possibly making things worse. "I don't want anyone or anything else sneaking up on us. At least with the chime, we will know they are here. I want to go to sleep if I can. I'm exhausted, and I have school in the morning, but I'm afraid to close my eyes." She gave a long sigh, shoulders dropping as she let go of the banister.

James leaned the bat against the wall, his fingers stiff. "Until I know what is going on, the system should stay off." A look of pain and concern crossed his face. He didn't want his wife to be frightened. He wanted to protect his family, but, either way, the system off or on, their life was turning a corner on a road James wasn't prepared to travel. Honey, go to bed. I'll check all the doors and windows and be up in a minute." He shook his hands. "Oh, and peek in on Alena, and I'll stop by and talk to Jack if he's awake." He touched her cheek, giving the best reassuring smile he could muster. She turned, wrapped her arms around her shoulders as if cold, and reluctantly moved up the stairs.

"I'll grab my old work boots and clean up the glass."

"This is what I've been afraid of," Tracy said. She caught James by the arm as he walked past her to check the door. "With light, there is always darkness, and that is in any realm of existence, not just this one." She let out her breath and, with it, the fear she kept close. "I didn't want to say anything in front of my sister, but this could be…"

She stopped, searching for the right words, hesitating for a good long minute. Finally, in a flurry, she let them escape like a balloon releasing its air. "This is bad, Jimmy." She let go of him and began pacing in a circle. "I'm not sure what we're dealing with, but it's not sweet Uncle Harold, Jeffrey, or your grandparents or any other relative." She stopped pacing and lifted one finger in the air. "Yes, I need to sage the house." She began to pace again, set and determined, shaking her hands as if dispelling her fear through her fingertips. She had a plan.

"Sage? Like the spice you use in the turkey dressing and on chicken?" James grabbed his work boots from the front closet, stepping into them without lacing up. "Huh, strange." He picked up the baseball bat and set off to check the upper floors of the house, first checking on his son, who was somehow still asleep.

He returned to the first floor to clean up the glass and debris when he smelled something strange. He then saw a haze drifting toward him. From around the kitchen corner, Tracy held a plate with a burning clump of something in the center. With her other hand, she held a magazine and was waving the smoke like an offering as it rose in front of her.

"Only light and love may remain," she said quietly as she took a few steps, stopping to fan the burning sage. "Only light and love." She repeated it, barely glancing at her brother-in-law as she walked past.

"Don't wake up Jack," James said quietly before she disappeared from view. He continued to focus on his task, occasionally stopping to listen, the only noise coming from the heating system as it moved air through the house.

James followed the smell that lingered in the front hallway, up the stairs to the second-floor landing, and paused. A barley imperceptible whisp of smoke floated near the ceiling. "Huh," he said under his breath, then moved to the attic, where the air was thick with the smell of sage. He heard Tracy's intent murmuring, only catching words here and there. Moving slowly, the trail of smoke showed him the path she had taken to the second attic room. Standing in the middle of the playroom, Tracy was turning in a circle, her words connecting, the meaning clear.

"You must leave this house," she repeated, raising her voice.

She caught sight of James and stopped, lowering the magazine in her hand, allowing the smoke of the smoldering sage to dwindle.

"I felt it when I came into the attic," she said as she glanced back at the window behind her.

"Was it in the shadows?" James asked, looking around the room and then following her gaze to the window and the night beyond.

"No, it wasn't in the shadows." There was a detached cadence to her voice. "It *was* the shadow." She shot a direct look to her brother-in-law. "It is the darkness or was the darkness. When I turned on the light, it went out the window." Her eyes followed the path in her memory.

"Do you understand what's going on?" He joined her as she stared out into the darkness. "Because I'm lost. Hell, a few months ago I would have said you were just my crazy sister-in-law. I would have said the idea of heaven was a nice thought meant only to comfort those who are afraid of dying."

He gave a sideways glance down at Tracy and then back out the window. "I would have said that I think when we die, we return to the dust, you know, the big sleep, a dirt nap. The whole dust to dust thing." A noise escaped his throat. "I would have also told you that when our physical body breaks down, we simply become debris, and most people simply plant that debris with lots of other former live humans in a place where we can visit. But, I would have never in my wildest dreams thought we move to another plane of existence, even though quantum physics tells me energy can't be destroyed."

Pain shadowed his face, followed by a weak smile. "And, I would have never thought I would ever see my grandparents again." He shrugged in acceptance. "But I'm not the man I was then. So, tell me, what do you think actually flew out the window? I can take it."

Tracy looked down to her plate, the sage almost out. Only a small clump remained. "I'm not one-hundred percent sure. It could be an elemental."

"OK," he said. "What's an elemental? Do you think it was what scared Alena? I mean, how does a blanket eat a little girl? Figuratively, that is, as she is still here in one piece."

"I'm not sure what was in her room. It could be, maybe." Tracy took her time, wanting to find the right words. "Well, if that is what we are dealing with, then it is a spirit that has never walked the Earth as a human. Some think of them as nature spirits. They attach themselves to things, trees, plants, and places. They are everywhere and low on the totem pole, so to speak. The higher-level entities, such as those with an elevated vibration or from the angelic realm, are much more powerful." There was a question in her voice, which dropped as she looked back into the night, which suddenly felt much darker.

He shot her a look. "Wait a minute, angelic realm? We are now talking about magical beings with wings. And how in the hell do you know about these things? I mean, are there really experts on angels and shadowy woodland spirits? How can you be an expert on things that can't be proven?" There was a smile in his voice, yet a serious note underscored every word.

"Lots of questions, but let's start with, yes, there are those who believe themselves to be in touch with various entities and spirits. Hell, there are books on almost every subject out there, but you know this, dear brother. The rest comes from people I know, experiences they've had, and, well, my own experiences. I've just filled in the blanks here and there, I guess. And as for magical beings, elementals have no wings, or at least none that I know of." She looked up at him, her face conveying pain and fear as she tossed the magazine on the floor, the sage now completely out.

"There are other things, truly scary things, that exist." She paused. "But let's not go there, shall we?" A look of concern touched her features briefly and then disappeared.

She chewed on her lower lip. "I may need to call a few friends to help. Don't mention any of this to Jessica, OK? Let me talk with her. I know how to deal with my sister, after all, I've always been, as you would say, woo-woo. God, hopefully she was able to go back to sleep, poor sis." Looking for acknowledgment, she met his eyes. "OK, Jimmy? Mum is the word. She may just freak out if we tell her any of this tonight, and she needs her sleep."

"OK, I'll tell her to talk to you about it," he said, exhaustion hitting him. "I think that is best. I need to check back in on Jack and get some sleep of my own. I have a report to write up tomorrow on the new security system. Do you think whatever it is, is gone? I mean, does that stuff work?" He pointed to the lump of ashes on her plate.

"Let's hope so," she said as she picked at the remaining sage with one finger and then turned to leave. "I should sage your room and Jack's, but it can wait until tomorrow. Thank God I purchased a case of this stuff. Ugh, I know the things that go bump in the night, but this…" She waved her free hand, gesturing around the room. "This, today, hell, everything is new territory for me." She turned to go, stopping at the doorway.

"Good night, Jimmy," she said without turning back, and she was gone.

Chapter 32
Visions of the Past

Morning evolved, as it did most days, with a cartoon, a *beep-beep* followed by the *plunk* and *screech* of a desperate coyote and distant roadrunner, the volume turned down to background noise. Jack and Alena entered the room in a silent haze, still in their pajamas. Alena's normal brightness was dimmed by lack of sleep. The typical gray day, a constant in Seattle, matched the mood in the heart of the house.

Tracy was up and dressed when they came down for breakfast. Pancakes with chocolate chips were on the menu, piled in a tall stack in the center of the table. The cocoa with extra marshmallows sat in cups ready for hot water. Jessica, up early, had snuggled with the kids before leaving for a teacher's meeting, relying on James and Tracy to navigate the dark emotional mood of breakfast.

"Good morning, little ones." Tracy greeted them with the largest smile she could muster, her Morning Auntie—a much more subdued version of Morning Dad—on full display. Jack dropped his backpack against the wall and pulled out a chair, followed by Alena, who was clutching Mrs. Kelly around the neck. Their eyes moved over the table, resting first on the stack of pancakes and then the television. Their favorite cartoon was in full comedic motion.

Tracy placed each cup in front of the kids and smiled. "Hot cocoa on a drizzly morning," she said, followed by a wink.

Alena inspected her cup and counted the marshmallows. "I have seven." Her lower lip protruded slightly, soft brows pulled together, as she looked at her brother, who was sinking his marshmallows with a spoon.

"I have nine," he said with a mischievous grin and waggle of eyebrows, intent on upsetting his sister.

"Aunt Tracy!" Alena's lower lip took over the lower half of her face.

"OK, let me see." Tracy proceeded to even out the score for Alena, whose pout receded, and a smile took over, followed by smirk directed at her brother. "Now you two finish your breakfast. Is your homework finished?" she asked, turning to the sink with a bowl and dirty utensils in hand.

"Yep," they said in unison, both staring at the television as they picked at their plates.

A cold gust came from behind as the door swung open. James stood in the mudroom doorway with no jacket, his laptop tucked under one arm, books under the other, and a forced smile as he greeted them. Morning Dad was tired.

"Good morning, family." He gave Tracy a sideways glance on his way to the table. He grabbed a plate and stacked four pancakes in the middle. "Mmm, this looks good. Did you thank your auntie for breakfast?" He leaned in to catch the attention of Jack and Alena, who were far away, engrossed in an animated bunny looking for his next meal.

Tracy finished placing the dishes in the dishwasher. "I think they're just tired. We'll have an early night tonight, and all will be well tomorrow."

"I received a call from my buddy, Fred," he said. "He's been working on the film inside those old canisters. I need to pick them up. He transferred what they were able to save onto a hard drive. Maybe we'll have family movie night." He raised one eyebrow, as if questioning such a move.

"Hmm, well, wait for me. I'll be home around eight." Tracy smiled at Jack, ruffling the curls on his head, the hair gel missing, but Harold's green baseball jacket was on the seat next to him. "I'll take them to school on my way to the museum."

***

During meetings at the office, James kept the setbacks of his system quiet. When picking up the film canisters on the way home, his friend informed him that over fifty percent was unsalvageable.

Sitting at his desk, James realized the events of the last few days had affected him more than he had admitted. Turning on every light in the house in the middle of the day wasn't normal, but he couldn't help himself. He was jumpy. He couldn't stop looking into the shadows, waiting for movement and hesitating before entering a room. He was equally amazed that night that the kids seemed unfazed, other than wanting their night-lights on and Alena wanting her door open a little wider.

He powered up his computer, connecting the LaCie hard drive. At first, fragmented faces flashed and moved across the computer screen. Then, his grandma, Lillian, under the backyard tree, came into focus. A small boy was on her lap, waving with small bursts of sound but nothing audible. The apparent family home movie for the most part was silent. He hit Pause, focusing in on the boy in her lap. The face of his father was half hidden, turned to her shoulder, not wanting to be part of the activities. He looked around three or four years old. He hit Play. Coming into view from the right was Little Harold. He was tossing a baseball as he it hammed it up in front of the camera, his wide smile filling his face from ear to ear, his eyes narrowed, crinkling in the bright sunlight.

A noise broke the silence, a distant clang and rattle coming from the kitchen. Pausing the home movie, James was up and into the hall. The normal *pop* and *whoosh* of the heating system kicked in, startling him. *No more Mr. Nice Guy,* he thought, steeling himself before rushing into the kitchen.

He was met with silence. Nothing was out of place. He turned, walking to the mudroom door, checking the lock. He repeated this, checking doors and windows before returning to his office. These safety rituals were becoming a part of his strange, daily life.

Stepping through the office doorway, a low mechanical whirring noise caught his attention, and it took a second for him to realize the movie was mysteriously playing again. Movement in flashes filled the screen, then Little Harold came into view, smiling into the camera. In the background a group of boys were celebrating on what looked like a baseball field. Cheers moved in and out as the scenes delayed and stuttered. James hit Pause, his hand shaking, his nerves shot as he tried to calm his fingers. Sitting back down, he pulled his chair up to the desk, took a deep breath, and hit Play.

The screen went black. Several clicks, then shades of sepia and gray popped in and out, rolling into vivid forms that came into focus. Harold Sr. took center screen, this time animated, a rag in hand as he polished the bumper of what must have been a new car, laughing it up for the camera. He stepped back, waving invitingly as he opened the door, showing off the interior. James hit Pause.

In the background, standing almost out of view, was Jeffrey, a hand above his eyes, watching from his yard next door. James's heart dropped as he watched both boys, who would be gone not long after these scenes were filmed.

"Jeffrey," he said, glancing at the desk. At the corner, half hidden behind the monitor, was a baseball. He reached and rolled the ball toward him. It stopped a few inches from his keyboard, the faded *H* and part of an *A* visible.

"Huh. How did you get there? I left you in the attic." James tossed it between his hands.

The video started again. James hadn't touched the keyboard. Swiveling in his chair, he hit Pause. Frozen on the screen was his grandfather standing in front of the car he'd just been lovingly polishing. Peeking out from behind the corner of the house was a man James had never seen before.

"Now who are you?" James asked himself. This man's features were angular and half in shadow. James grabbed a screenshot and hit Play again. The man was gone. Staring at the screen, James shrugged, stopping the playback and disconnecting the hard drive. "I'll finish the home movies later and figure out who you are." He swiveled and took a step up and out of the chair in one fluid movement.

2005

Chapter 33
A Catcher's Mitt

Weeks passed without incident, giving a tenuous sense of security wrapped in what they now considered to be their new version of normal. James continued to work on reconfiguring his prototype security system on paper—nothing operational, of course. At the same time, he was dealing with the day-to-day needs of his company and their inventory of current security systems. Jessica looked forward to a much-needed spring break, which was right around the corner. Tracy, wanting to be there for the family, took an opportunity to extend her exhibit while working on additional projects with the Seattle Art Museum, which made her sister extremely happy.

Sunshine was beginning to warm the air. Seattle was always beautiful when the crisp winter turned toward spring. The bright wisps of green in numerous shades expanded and filled in the gray, lonely trees. The leaves unfurled from the trees, seemingly from nowhere, as closed tulips, hiding in flower beds, broke the soil, promising bold colors and a bluer sky. The Emerald City was coming to life.

Jack and Alena had pulled out their bicycles. They were back to their old selves. Their whoops and giggles mixed well as nature flipped its switch, urging humans to join in. The smell of charcoal grilling was in the air even though the temperature was only fifty-five degrees—those who lived in Seattle were a hardy group, and, to them, it was the beginning of the best half of the year. The sound of laughter and of lawnmowers added to the spring serenade. Jack continuously rang the old-fashioned bicycle bell attached to his handlebar as he chased Alena in continuous loops around the Geek Shed, up the drive and back, giving their parents much-needed time alone.

The new security system had been in the house for months, and the various progress reports to corporate were intentionally vague and misleading. Watercooler talk included every executive office, hallways, and even the bathroom. With excitement growing about the new system, a handpicked marketing team amplified the whispers.

James knew how to manage expectations by sharing his constant refinements, usage clips, and interactions. He even included the neighbor's dog, a nine-year-old cocker spaniel named Max, who stole the hearts of all the animal lovers on the admin staff. Constant testing gave him more time to try and figure out the real dangers of his technology. Currently the number one concern was the darkened corners and what was moving within them. The new reality of events, happening whether the system was on or off, terrified Jessica and unnerved James, adding to the sense of helplessness.

***

The aroma of apples and cinnamon permeated the house. Fragrant spices and the smell of pastry drifted up, pulled into the heating system, the sweetness finding its way throughout each level. Alena had signed up for her school's bake sale, and apple pie was an exciting contribution in lieu of the standard chocolate chip cookies. Any remnants of the baking would find its way to her backyard battalion. Alena wasn't sure if Matilda, the neighbor's cat, was a fan of pie, but Alena would make sure there were no leftovers. Jessica's baking skills were famous, bringing a high demand and price, helping with the class's wish list of supplies.

Down the hall from the kitchen, James closed his eyes, breathing deeply, his mouth watering. The smell of the baking pie lifted his mood and painted the walls a shade brighter, though the clouds were thick and gray. Determined to solve the scattered and seemingly disconnected collection of events, he tried to fit them together so he could have an idea of what he was up against. Each one of his family held a piece of a much larger puzzle, yet there was a missing piece somewhere.

Jack and Alena were open, innocent, and his focused concern. Alena lived in an imaginary world, believing in the magic of it all. Friendships hidden in fur and feathers had their limitations, so new playmates were always welcome. Jack, his nose in books, sensitive and introverted, had difficulty cultivating friends, and Harold was, after all, family. In Jack's mind, he was a cool new friend.

Laying out the puzzle in his mind, James focused on the neighbor's boy Jeffrey. Rumors and hearsay did not equal facts, making any information important. Armed with a computer and critical thinking skills, James moved through the mountain of dead ends and weak possibilities, finally tracking down Jeffrey's two living and breathing long-ago neighbors.

"Michael and Carolyn Simmons, Jeffrey's parents, currently of Dayton, Ohio, are very much alive, but I'm not sure how well they are," James said to Jessica. A toss of a hand and two sheets of paper came down in the middle of the kitchen table, where Jessica sat peeling apples for the next round of pies. "I think this is Michael." He set down a picture of the man hiding in the shadows, a screenshot from the old, converted film.

"Ohio? Good God, they must be ancient now." Jessica held the picture at arm's length and squinted. "God, I need my glasses." She pushed wayward apple peels into a pile with her free hand. Jessica knew they had to dig to connect the dots, and her husband was the perfect person to find the links, find a pattern.

"Michael and Carolyn must be old as the hills, but by God they are alive. Can you believe it? They're alive," he said, rubbing his forehead, puzzlement passing over his face. "I was able to track them down once I knew where they had moved to." James pulled up a chair, peering over her shoulder as she read. "God, that smells good. Can we have a pie for us? I'll be glad to contribute to the school." He patted his stomach and reached for the pile of apples with his thumb and forefinger, a small corner of apple disappearing into his mouth with a crunch.

"This is the letter your Aunt Sandra mentioned," Jessica said as she scanned the lines. "Wow, there's a lot of guilt going on here. I wonder if he received the peace and forgiveness he was looking for?" She looked up over the edge of the paper, one corner torn. Her eyes shimmered as she blinked back tears.

"I know my grandfather was a kind man. I believe he would have forgiven him. So, yes, I think so. I wonder if I'll get to see him again?" James was off somewhere. Thoughts of his grandfather floated in front of him, the memory of the last encounter close enough to touch. He reached out, pulling the corner of the letter down to make eye contact with Jessica.

Placing the letter down gently, she held his gaze. "Well, if you turn that damn system on, then there's a good chance you will. It sounds like something from a science fiction movie." She shuddered. "Maybe we can turn it on when I'm here. I don't know what I would do or say, but I think I need to experience it for myself."

"Yeah, I think he would like to see you again," James said, a smile touching his face, lines of fatigue making him look much older. Letting his head drop, he pressed his palms into his temples.

The pollen count was high, and he felt another headache coming on. "Jack keeps asking when the system is going to be turned back on. He's a smart kid. I think he has a strange bond with Little Harold." He sucked air through his teeth, jaw clenched. "We need to think about the kids." Lifting his head, he squeezed the light from the corners of his vision, his head aching from the haze of allergy overload and stress.

"I want to talk with Jeffrey's parents. Maybe let them know I found their letter and their son's old catcher's mitt," he said. "I don't know. There is something I feel we need to do for him." His chest expanded as he rolled his shoulders back, letting out a long sigh.

"Him who?" she asked, her palm up under her chin.

"Him. Jeffrey," he said as he dreamily looked out the window, the day growing rounder and richer by the minute. "It's going to be beautiful today. The buds are just peeking out on the Japanese maple."

She stared at him, snapping her fingers next to his ear. "Hello, anyone home?"

"What?"

"So, what do you want to do for him?" she asked. "I mean, he's been gone for how long? I don't want his friend that lives in the shadows to feel too comfortable, do you?"

"I'm not sure. Just a feeling." Placing his hands wide on the table, he pushed his chair back and paused. "There is this sadness that lingers in the room when he's been there. From what Aunt Sandra said, the reports from witnesses make him the bad guy in this tragedy. His parents, I guess, were shunned in the neighborhood jury. I mean, Jesus, how can a ten-year-old be a bad guy? He was just a kid." James rapped his knuckles on the table.

Acknowledging him, Jessica picked up the letter, gently tapping it against the envelope on the table, laying them both within arm's reach. "Can you ask your friend Barry, with Seattle PD, if he can help you with the accident details if you can't find anything on the internet?" She held the letter out to him.

"That is my plan," James said, a tired grin filling his face. He squinted as he gave a slight chuckle. He took the pages of the letter and stood, glancing out the window once again. "I'm glad the weather is changing; it will keep the kids outside. Maybe Tracy would consider babysitting tonight so I can take you out for a dinner away from all this?" He turned back to Jessica and saw her focused on her pie making, fervently peeling an apple.

She stopped, a long red strip of peel curling around her hand, and smiled. "Ya know, I was dreaming of Lebanese food the other night." She looked up at him, resting her arms on the table. "I know Tracy has been at the museum since zero-dark-thirty, so maybe we'll see her at a decent hour. I'll call her." A breeze of normalcy swirled with the thought of getting out into the world.

"OK, you can find me in the Geek Shed working on my stuff and figuring out how to keep my job." With a few large strides, he was out the mudroom door.

Chapter 34
Movie Night

The house seemed darker, even with spring growing rich and tall all around them. Tracy handed off her duties at the museum after a week of odd and extremely long hours. The exhibit was a success, which gave her some wiggle room in setting her time off.

Her relationship with the kids had always been special. Without children of her own, she treasured her time in Seattle with the family, and giving her sister and brother-in-law time away from their parental duties was a gift to all of them.

The temperature always dipped low at night, giving an excuse for a warm fire. Tracy picked up dinner from her favorite pho noodle restaurant on the way home. With a transition from VHS to DVD, the Allens had a collection of both, with most of the old favorites on VHS. After a quick review, they settled on what Jack called an old-timer movie.

"OK, you guys have fun and behave for your aunt," Jessica said, kissing the top of Jack's and Alena's heads.

"Hey, guys, stay out as late as you want. I'm looking forward to doing nothing." Tracy smiled and wrapped her arm around Alena, who was pulling on Mrs. Kelly's ear as she danced in place, looking like a windup toy with nowhere to go.

Chitty Chitty Bang Bang was one of Tracy's favorite old-timer movies and, to both Jack and Alena's delight, they all had a great time singing along.

"Oh, you, itty bitty baby, I love you," Alena sang an impromptu tune after the movie, in keeping with the musical theme of the evening as she held up Mrs. Kelly. She hopped from one foot to the other, shaking her hips. Jack seemed unimpressed, pulling the couch pillow over his head and sighing dramatically.

"My sister is weird," he said, and he tossed the pillow, a direct hit to her back, knocking her off balance and into the armchair.

"Hey!" she squealed, turning on him with her most formidable elfin glare.

"Goofy kids, it's late, and I've had a long day." Tracy stood, the light from the hallway illuminating her from behind, casting her face in shadow. Picking up the remote, she turned off the television, then tossed it back on the coffee table.

"Head on up," she said, turning the still-dancing Alena toward the stairs and giving a loving little shove. She turned back to Jack, still on the couch, now throwing the other couch pillow up, catching it, then tossing it up again.

"When will Mom and Dad be home?" he asked as he sat up, staring at the now-dark television.

"I don't know, and it doesn't matter," Tracy said, hands on her hips. "Time for bed, Mister Man."

There was a defiant moan from Jack, but he was tired and relinquished the fight. He peeled himself up off the cushions and shambled away, dragging his feet.

She listened as he climbed the stairs, the creak of his footsteps fading into the distance. She proceeded to methodically check all the doors and windows, wearily turning off lights and glancing at the corners and behind furniture, looking for movement.

She stopped at the security system control panel. The glow of the screen indicated the system status. She knew James and Jessica had left it turned off in a hopeful effort to avoid any unwelcome visitations.

Tracy intuitively understood the connection the living had with the dead. They were always connected, but this was different. The system was giving them a level of existence she had never thought possible until now. Her hand wavered over the keypad, holding it there for what seemed forever. After a deep breath, she lowered her hand. The system was still off. Turning, she lifted and dropped her shoulders, knowing the simple act of setting the alarm brought consequences. *Thank God the sage seemed to work,* she thought as she continued to check and recheck the windows and doors for a second time, knowing the insanity of it.

Leaving one light on in the living room, she headed up to check on the kids, then to her room for a little reading and hopefully a good night's sleep.

Chapter 35
Dinner for Two

The restaurant was small, tucked in a middle-class neighborhood not far from their home. Candles and small arrangements of wildflowers adorned each table. Exotic spices filled and drew in the senses the moment they stepped in the door. James had donned his best suit, a little tight around the middle and a little dusty at the shoulders, but still fitting. Jessica embraced the rare opportunity to get out of the house and had decided to wear a dark red dress she had purchased years before for a Christmas benefit. The soft scooped neck, trimmed in a cascade of ruffles, enhanced her figure and clung to her curves. A much-needed night free from the strange and paranormal was also on the menu, and Jessica was excited to be alone with her husband. They spent hours delighting in each other's company, lingering over baba ghanoush, besara, and bright skewers of vegetables with tahini sauce.

"Have I told you how beautiful you look this evening, Mrs. Allen?" James said. His eyes were soft as he held up his glass of wine, candlelight dancing off the crystal.

"We needed this. Thank you, my love." She met his glass with her own, the dark red liquid twinkling as she lifted it. Her smile faded, then brightened again.

"What?" he asked at the shadow of question in her eyes.

"Do you think we should leave the kids alone in that house?" she asked, setting her glass down, her wine untouched.

"There is nothing wrong with the house, Jess, and your sister is with them. If anyone can deal, it's your sister." He set his jaw, his glass still held tight. "It is the house of my family..." He corrected himself. "The house of *our* family. There is a lot of love there." His eyes softened again.

"I know," Jessica said, a long sigh escaping her. "Let's not think about it anymore tonight. Want to head to Jazz Alley?" Reaching out, she touched his hand, her smile radiant in the candlelight from the one small votive on the table.

***

The hour was late when they arrived home. They had closed the club, the music filling them. As they walked through the back door, a warning beep from the security system surprised them, the engaged light burning bright green. James had disengaged their personal chime notifications some time ago but they were still startled. He raised an eyebrow, giving a sideways glance to his wife as he entered the alarm code, disengaging the system.

"Tracy must have forgotten," he said, turning off the light.

The kitchen had its normal glow, the ticking of the clock strangely comforting, the rhythm familiar. Jessica reached for the light switch, the bright overhead light bringing an additional sense of security as she slowly removed her coat, head tilting, listening for anything out of place.

James stopped in the hall, looking at the empty spot where the photo had been before being ripped off the wall. "I need to get that photo reframed." He was two steps ahead, turning the lights on in the hallway, guiding their path to the front of the house. No flutter of movement in the corners, nothing out of place, all as it should be.

Ascending the stairs to the second floor, he stopped, looking back at Jessica, each step questioning what lay before them. *The system was supposed to be off,* he thought, which should mean no ghostly visitations. As he reached the top of the stairs, he felt a touch at his elbow. His wife's hand now rested in the crook of his arm. Jessica tipped her head in the direction of Jack's bedroom, where a soft sliver of light spilled into the hallway.

Placing his hand on top of hers, they walked slowly to the doorway, inching the door back a few inches for a better view. The light from the bedside table glowed dim, shapes casting shadows throughout the room. Jack's bed was empty.

With a single push, James opened the door, turning on the overhead light. The room blazed into view. They picked up blankets and opened the closet, a quick check, their concern growing.

Understanding moved between them as they looked up at the ceiling. Moving quickly, they were at the door and up the stairs to the attic. The first room was dark, the rectangle of light gray and blue, spilling in the spaces between the furniture and boxes. The second room also lay in shadow. It was a cloudy evening and the light from the window only traveled so far. A small dark figure curled in the corner caught their eye as they stepped into the space. Jessica found the light switch, and, with a flick of her wrist, the shadows dissolved.

Jack sat upright, hair flat on one side of his head where he had been sleeping on his forearm. Next to him was the missing Racer 8 and two ceramic cups. Jessica bent and picked up a cup; inside were the remnants of what looked like cocoa, a brown ring halfway up the inside and a lone marshmallow clinging at the bottom, mindlessly setting it back down as if not wanting to disturb a crime scene.

"Jack, buddy, what are you doing here?" Jessica reached for his arms, helping her sleepy son sit up. "It's way past your bedtime. Were you playing with Alena up here?" She pushed back the curls as she stroked his brow.

"No, just...just me." He rubbed at his eyes and, without assistance, rose to his feet and moved toward the doorway, shuffling and swaying from side to side as his head wobbled with the movement.

"Climb in bed, and I'll be there in a minute to tuck you in." She spoke above a whisper, just loud enough to be heard.

James looked at the toys scattered in the corners—Racer 8 at his feet—as he held both cups. He looked at Jessica and exhaled, shrugging his shoulders. "I'm glad you're back with us," James whispered to the car, one toe nudging it as he shook his head, not understanding its return, but relief like a warm blanket wrapped around him anyway.

"What do you think of this?" he asked Jessica, lifting both cups, sniffing what little remained, a puzzled look crinkling his brow.

She'd been standing in the doorway, watching her son make his way down the stairs. She moved back into the room. She took a cup from him, examining it. "I don't like this. The system was on, and I don't like his strange obsession with his great-uncle." Her mood shifted into question, her night of freedom from concerns wilting at the edges.

"Yeah, on the strange-o-meter scale, this is just one more item on a long list of the strange and not yet explainable happenings in this house." James released a breath as he tried to brush off any indication of danger in tonight's events. "So, what's the worst thing? He had a cup of cocoa with his dead great-uncle?" His words had a comedic edge, intending to lighten the mood, but Jessica was not up for it, not tonight.

She turned toward the stairs, not bothering to answer. The mood had shifted quickly. The wine and music that had filled them both was gone.

Chapter 36
Forgiveness

Jessica was up with the dawn, the events from the night keeping her from any truly restful sleep. She opened Tracy's door quietly, just a crack at first, only enough to see the form of her sister, her back to the door, lying still on the bed. The narrow column of light from the hall cut through the middle of the room, shades of gray and black on each side, making her weary. Ever since she witnessed the darkness moving in the house, Jessica kept the doors open, light always within reach. She stepped in, shutting the door and moving to the bed, where she gently sat down on the edge. She let her eyes adjust to the gloom and studied her sister, listening to Tracy breathing steadily, calmly, and peacefully.

"I need to know," Jessica said, her thoughts tumbling into one another, anxiety painting colors of vivid, angry red. Tracy gave an involuntary twitch, making Jessica catch her breath, the hand that was hesitant to wake her sister pulled back against her chest. Tracy moved, turning on her back. Jessica reached out again, slowly touching Tracy's leg. No response. A second attempt, this time a stronger hand, the pressure of movement waking her sister.

"What the hell! You scared the shit out of me!" Tracy yelled.

She pulled herself up, her back leaning against the headboard.

"Did you turn on the alarm last night?" Jessica asked.

Tracy had pulled the curtains and blackout shades the night before, hoping to sleep in, so Jessica's face was in darkness. Tracy leaned to the right, fumbling with the small bedside table lamp. With a click, the soft, yellow light bounced off the walls, giving them both a jaundiced pallor.

"Look, sis. I didn't turn on the security system…" Tracy hesitated, sudden concern making her heart skip a beat. "Why? Was it on?" Her tone turned to questioning frustration as she struggled to adjust her eyes, rubbing at them, waking slowly.

"Yes, it was on, and Jack was curled up in the attic playroom," Jessica responded, her anger settling like a weight around her shoulders. "He didn't look like he was alone. There were two cups. He made cocoa for someone."

Jessica took a deep breath as she realized the obvious. "Well, then, Jack must have gotten up and turned it on," she said quietly.

"What time is it anyway?" Tracy grabbed the small digital clock on the bedside table and turned it so she could see its face. For a split second, the red glowing numbers gave her face a warm, orange hue.

"It's early. I'm sorry," Jessica said as she stood up. "I couldn't sleep. I guess I was hoping you would tell me that you forgot or thought it was OK. Shit, anything to give me hope that my son hasn't figured out how to make his little playmate appear."

Now awake, Tracy let her head loll back with a thud on the headboard before searching her sister's face. "Sit down," she said. She motioned Jessica back to the bed. "If Jack turned on the system, then I'm sure you're right, and he believes that he gets to see his friend when that happens. He gave an indication of understanding what was going on in the kitchen the other night." She readjusted her position, bending her knees. "He looks at him as family. That bond doesn't understand the wall that life sets up between them at death. I mean, it could be worse." She gave a small snort. Thoughts of communicating with the dead had always shared a space in her life and didn't frighten her, but now her sister would have to understand.

Jessica's head turned sharply. "I would rather my son become friends with my daughter's stuffed squirrel." Anger made a home between them, the warmth of the sisters cooling with misdirected humor and misunderstanding.

"Look, Jess. I know this is scary, but it will be OK." Tracy took the round tones reserved for the kids and made them softer in an attempt to soothe the frayed edges.

"I don't know, I just don't know," Jessica said, feeling panicked, the weight of understanding that her son had turned on the system overwhelming. "Go back to sleep. We can talk later this morning. The day is supposed to be sunny, so we can send the kids outside." With a pat on Tracy's leg, Jessica stood, arching her back with a yawn as she scratched her head.

Chapter 37
Visit at Will

The morning was cool, but the atmosphere in the house was colder. Frustration took refuge in the walls of their beloved home on the hill. It had been a home that, until a few months before, was full of love and laughter. Now, the bright notes in the heart of the house no longer beat with a steady rhythm.

The Geek Shed, with all its moving parts, was in full force. James needed the time and privacy, his brain swirling with unfamiliar paranormal theories offered from his enthusiastic and well-meaning sister-in-law.

On his worktable, the odds and ends of his innovation lay open to the world, making him feel disconnected and a bit sad as he reviewed and questioned everything. Multiple windows glowed with promise on his laptop. Stacked books—some open, others used as shelving—were scattered about the room. The hum of the HEPA filtration system was soothing in the coolness as yellow pollen clung to the windows.

Bubble universes, parallel universes, mathematical universes: there were so many theories, so many possibilities. His reading choice this morning—*The Fabric of Reality* by physicist David

Deutsch—explored the multiverse, quantum theory, and time travel.

If his security system created a pathway to and from an alternate universe, then it would reason that when the system was off, these events should end. But the moving shadow took refuge in the darkness even with the system disconnected from its power supply.

James sat, his brain tired, examining the remains of his morning coffee cup. Grounds clung to the sides, but he took a large mouthful, draining the last few cold sips, his head lolling from side to side as he rubbed his eyes, his back stiff from his position over his worktable. Rubbing his neck, he let his eyes fall on a single branch of a small maple tree outside. He saw a single bright green leaf, a stark contrast to the gray landscape as it emerged from winter.

There was a resistant groan and stutter of the old garage door, stuck a foot from the ground. James frowned. He needed a new door and a better way of protecting the items inside. Currently his Geek Shed security consisted of a large, heavy-duty Master Lock padlock, which he was aware any bolt cutter could conquer. He hoped the sorry state of the small garage wouldn't be appealing, with all the large homes and high-end vehicles to attract thieves.

From under the door's edge, red Converse sneakers moved as a small hand gripped the bottom of the door, trying to maneuver it upward. James grabbed the handle, easily lifting it another few feet. A head of dark curls bent and moved under the door, then Jack stood, book in hand, wearing Harold's green baseball jacket.

"Hey, buddy." James was happy to have a break. His research was making his brain feel scrambled. Returning to his desk and pushing his work journal aside, he smiled. "Whatcha reading?"

"Ah, this?" Jack hesitated. He looked down at the cover and then back to his dad. "Just a book. *Huckleberry Finn*. It's Harold's favorite." He held it up, his free hand flipping through the pages.

James sat back, hands folded in his lap, legs wide and feet firmly planted, a smile gently emerging, along with his curiosity. "Hmm, Harold's favorite?"

Jack didn't make eye contact. "He loves books, like me." Jack took a step forward, pretending he was interested in the stacks of literature on the table. "I told him I can predict what happens in books and that I win lots." He lifted his head, a mischievous smile crinkling his nose.

"Yeah, you do win a bunch," James said, tilting his head as he looked into the face of his son. He didn't want to concern Jack, so he spoke with a quiet calmness, but his heartbeat was loud in his ears. "When did you have this discussion with your great-uncle?"

"Last night. We talked about a bunch of stuff, and he saw his old book." Jack walked around the shed, looking up and down and out the window at a squirrel sitting on the branch outside. His eyes met his father's for a brief moment. Jack knew his father was concerned.

"Where does Harold go after you're with him? Do you talk about it?" Still calm, James folded and unfolded his hands, turning in his swivel chair, keeping up with his son as he circled the room.

"He just, I don't know, goes," Jack said, shrugging his shoulders, his back still to his dad. "But he said he can come back: I just need to think about him." He looked over his shoulder, making brief eye contact again with his father, the concern pulling at him, his shoulders slumping.

"Son, did you turn on the system last night?" The words rolled out, monotone and cool.

Jack turned to his father, placing the book on the table. There was a momentary recognition of the questions, then his eyes moved, looking for a distraction and settling on a jar of nails on the shelf. He was calculating his response, biting his lower lip. "No," he said, sending his father a direct look as he stood straight. "Harold did." He turned back to the shelves.

"How did Harold turn on the system?" James remained cool, believing his son was simply avoiding responsibility.

A shrug again from Jack, who picked up his book, fluttering the pages nervously, sensing his father was tense and unsettled. "He says it helps him to be here." There was a thoughtful pause as Jack knit his brow, then continued, "But he can come if he wants. They all can visit; we just can't see them until the light is green." He closed the book, standing tall once again.

The hair on James's arms stood and his scalp prickled, an all too familiar feeling as of late, he thought as the words registered. "They can all visit; we just can't see them," he repeated. "Who turned on the system, Jack?" Annoyance tinged his words as the tips of his ears turned red.

"I told you, Harold turned on the system." Jack looked up at his father. "So, I can see him."

The words fell with great weight, the reality hitting James.

A sudden breeze from the half-lifted garage door fluttered the pages of the open books scattered on the worktable—some closing as if by invisible hands—startling them both.

Jack's eyes flickered around the room, then back to his father. "Are you angry?" Jack looked up from under his young, furrowed brow. "I didn't turn it on." He looked down, kicking a pebble on the floor, avoiding his father's gaze.

James felt jumpy. He removed his glasses, rubbing the space between his eyes, "Jack, come here." He reached one hand out, motioning him to move closer, his words round and tender.

Setting the book down, Jack stepped forward. "I didn't do it," he added again.

"I believe you," James said, placing his hands on Jack's shoulders as he exhaled, the tension and anger leaving him. A smile and a nod of understanding between them. "I do. Next time he visits, can you let him know I would like to speak with him?"

"He said he knows who we are." Jack raised his shoulders to his ears and dropped them, as if questioning his father.

James nodded as he ruffled Jack's curls. "Hey, run and ask your mom about lunch. I can run and pick up takeout, I'm thinking Chinese." James turned his son toward the garage door opening and gave him a gentle push. "Tell her I'm craving dim sum."

Jack disappeared under the edge of the garage door. James sat motionless. He was aware of his chest expanding, the rise and fall of breath, the rhythm of it filling the room.

"What the hell?" James said, tension moving behind his eyes. Now, day by day, there were new layers of concern piling on top of him, leaving him with more questions and less understanding, while the lines of reality took unnatural turns.

"Yoo-hoo!"

There was a high whistle call and a tap at the door, followed by a stutter and a groan as the door was raised farther, giving a few extra feet of clearance. Jessica held a fresh hot cup of coffee in one hand.

"How long have you been out here?" she asked, looking around at the literary carnage strewn over his worktable, eyes landing on the dismantled equipment. She handed off the fresh cup of coffee. "Jack said you were craving dim sum. He seemed a little upset." She picked up the papers that had fallen to the ground. "Did you talk with him about last night?"

James sighed, rubbing the back of his neck again. "Yeah, I did. He said Harold turned on the alarm so he could be seen."

Jessica pivoted, her mouth open. "Fuck," she said, her eyebrows pulled together, anger flashing, settling into concern. "I mean what? Do you believe him?" She turned in place because there was no room to pace. She gave her husband a sharp look—direct and cold—as he sat motionless, hands clasped between his legs, watching her.

"Jess." He reached out, catching her by the arm, pulling her close. She smelled of lemon furniture polish and her favorite spearmint gum. He held her hands in his; they were cold. Their eyes met. A sadness rolled off her like the wind outside.

"Jimmy, now what are we going to do?" she asked, placing her hands on his shoulders, leaning into him as she buried her face in his chest.

He held her close, resting his head on hers. "I'm not sure. I just feel we need to know more before I tear my work apart. It's my career. It's our future." He could feel her nod as she pressed farther into his arms. She turned her head and began to cry.

"Shh, it will be OK," he said, holding her tight. "What's there to be afraid of? After all, they are family, for the most part." He was thinking of Jeffrey and the shadowy specter terrorizing his family. He pulled back, looking at her, wanting to calm her fears as well as his own. "And my grandparents always loved you."

She resisted the smile that tugged at the corner of her mouth as he dried her tears with the sleeve of his shirt.

"Yeah, well, your family knows I'm good for you. And, may I add, I'm the one that will put up with you." She rubbed her nose, stepping back, and he let go.

"Well, I never said it would be a picnic, but I'll talk with my dead uncle and see if I can cut the visits down to a minimum." His lighthearted attempt at humor received a frosty glare, followed by a snap of the head toward the house.

"I confronted Tracy this morning, and she didn't turn on the system either," she said with defeat in her voice. "God, I believe both of them. C'mon, mister, you said you were buying lunch." She wiped at her eyes again, pushing back the curls that stuck to her cheek.

"Looks like I need to review the footage from last night," he said, resignation in his voice. "Especially the attic and who was drinking cocoa while we were out. But I have a feeling there will be two on the monitor, Jess. God, I wonder how many visits I've missed that have been recorded? We need to wrap our heads around all this craziness but not give in to fear if possible."

He gave her a long squeeze, pulling back as he met her eyes. "I got you and, remember, we have amazing, smart kids who are resilient, and they will be just fine." A weary smile came and went, and he kissed her forehead.

Chapter 38
Popcorn

The sun set as another night of uncertainty loomed. In the living room, a princess sang, dreaming of her prince. Her high melodic voice was sweet and hopeful. Jack and Alena lay on their stomachs, feet crossed at the ankles, chins resting in their hands, with a large bowl of popcorn between them.

Jessica was at the sink in the kitchen. The ritual of washing dishes was an escape from her thoughts, as she found the hot water hypnotic and soothing. She didn't join in the conversation Tracy and James were having, just shook her head, little signs that let them know she was listening.

"OK, so let me get this straight. Jack said Harold turned on the system?" Tracy asked in a hushed and low voice as she sat next to the kitchen window, patches of coastal blue glowing as evening dusted the sky.

"Well, that's what he said," James said.

The room was getting darker by the minute. The glow from the light above the stove didn't seem bright enough, so James got up and flipped the light switch. "No shadows tonight," he said, smiling as Jessica looked over her shoulder.

"There is intent in his actions," Tracy said, pulling her knees up, wrapping her arms around them, resting her chin. "An intelligent haunting gives the spirit purpose of being. I'm still curious about the other boy, Jeffrey. His actions repeat over and over again." She lifted her chin, looking from James to her sister, who was working on the pots and pans. "You know, sis, you have a dishwasher for that," Tracy snorted, a friendly jab to lighten the mood.

"Washing dishes calms me. It always has," Jessica said. The steam rising from the sink wove through her curls, giving them additional volume, some standing on end in tight corkscrews. Setting a pan on the counter, she stopped and turned to face them, picking up a towel to dry the pan.

"If you turn on the system," she said, wiping her hands on the dish towel and folding it, turning it over and over, a nervous habit, "have a damn plan. And tell them hello for me and that I miss them. God, now we all are woo-woo." Her words sounded silly to her, the color in her cheeks flushing pink.

"I was actually thinking of layering an additional graphene matrix to support and perhaps extend the range of the cameras within the house." James pulled back on his words, but it was too late. The balled-up towel flew, missing James and landing on the floor behind him.

The ticking of the kitchen clock emphasized their hesitation. All three sat there looking to each other, the tension growing, moving up the walls. Taking off his glasses, James pressed the familiar spot between his eyes, the epicenter of his headaches. He was buying time, thinking of what to say and wishing he could take back the idea, bottling it up for the morning after a good night's sleep.

Letting his hand drop, eyes squinting to focus, he said in a staccato and strained voice, "I need more time. I believe the system gives them clarity and substance, makes them visible to us, and Jack's statement supports that theory." He let his shoulders slump. The fear of his work being dismissed as a dangerous adventure was growing, turning in the pit of his stomach. "I spent the day reviewing the research of some of the brightest minds in science." He let out a noise that resembled a chuckle as he realized how crazy he was sounding. He was talking as if the authors of the books were old personal friends. "They concur in some way or fashion that interdimensional or multiple dimensions exist. There are, of course, different views as to how many exist, but many believe there are more dimensions or parallel dimensions than this one." He motioned to the room. "This is big, and I know it's scary, but how can I walk away? It's an opportunity to find a place in my world. In the science world."

He returned to the table, taking a seat and leaning forward, placing his hands in front of him and splaying his fingers. He looked to his wife, who had joined them at the table, and then to his sister-in-law. The color was fading from Jessica's cheeks, emphasizing the tired lines that were becoming visible with lack of sleep. Tracy sat silent, facing her sister, feet now firmly planted on the floor.

A flash of light moved fast through the room, followed by a hollow popping sound, a burst of air, and the smell of electricity and ozone. Tracy was up and so was James, who had jumped up so fast his chair toppled over and was now rocking back and forth on the tile floor. Jessica moved with a slow effort, defeat in the set of her shoulders.

All three stood motionless, staring into the hallway, the sound of distant singing coming from the living room. The kids' animated voices filled the air, along with bursts of giggles and punctuated by the noisy crunch of popcorn being devoured, the sudden noise and electrical smell not fazing them.

Jessica took labored steps to the doorway, her hand on the doorjamb, tilting her head in the direction of the kids. "Thank God, no chime," she said, looking back at her husband, who was standing as still as a statue, his eyes moving from Jessica to Tracy and then back to Jessica.

"Jess, I turned off the voice announcement system and the chime, so it's silent, well, for all of us, anyway." His eyes told the story. There was a vibration moving around them and through the house. The low rumble felt like that of an underground train passing beneath them.

A soft but audible gasp came from Jessica. Confusion filled her eyes as James moved past her, his finger to his lips, a silent effort with each step. Tracy patted her sister's shoulder as she mouthed, *It will be OK.*

Following James past the staircase, Jessica tapped on his shoulder, pointing to the wall and the security control pad. Acknowledging her concern with a nod of his head, he gently elbowed Tracy, who turned to him. He pointed to the control pad: the activation light was glowing green. All three stared at the small—and now terrifying—pinpoint of light, then up at the motion-tracking camera in the corner just above them.

Tracy was at the panel quickly, punching the alarm code, intent on turning off the system. She turned to Jessica and James, who acknowledged her actions with simultaneous nods of their heads.

All three turned their attention to the living room doorway a few feet from where they stood. The glow of the television reached out with shadowy fingers, animating the walls as the delight of a prince holding court enchanted a would-be princess. Alena was chattering on about the castle design and of the animals of her court living within the walls of her kingdom. Jack's voice, lively, chimed in, exclaiming that romance was icky and stupid.

They were followed by a third, unfamiliar voice who agreed with Jack.

Jessica's head snapped up with a sharp inhalation of air. Her eyes were wide as she grabbed her husband's arm.

"Fuuuuuck," Tracy's response came with a low, drawn-out, terror-filled whisper. Her hand reflexively moved to cover her mouth; she simultaneously squeezed her eyes shut as she backed against the wall.

James moved slowly, every cell in his body on high alert, adrenaline bathing him in sweat as he peeked around the edge of the doorway. At first, he saw Alena, sitting forward, legs crossed, the bowl of popcorn in her lap, eyes focused on the movie. Jack was just out of sight. His hand came in and out of James's view as the boy plucked handfuls from the bowl.

Moving closer, James broadened his view of the living room. Jack was sitting with his legs crossed in front of him, throwing popcorn in the air, catching each piece in his open mouth. James gave a quick intake of breath—the electric smell filling his nostrils—loud enough to catch Alena's attention.

"Hey, Daddy," she said, shoving a handful of popcorn to her mouth.

Jack stopped tossing popcorn, his eyes sliding to his sister, then to the empty space beside him as his half-seen father edged into view.

"I heard another voice?" James asked as he walked into the room, bending to take a handful of popcorn, trying to look casual even as the hairs prickled on the back of his neck.

"He thinks you'll be mad if he's here," Jack answered, his voice hesitant as he looked up under thick lashes before shifting his gaze at the television, not wanting to make eye contact with his father, his sudden laser interest now on the fairy-tale princess who filled the television screen.

Not expecting an honest answer from his son, James chewed the popcorn much longer than needed as he formulated his response. "It's fine if he's here. He's family," James said, working on keeping his voice calm.

Around the corner, out of sight, Jessica held Tracy's hand as they listened intently, not wanting to overwhelm the situation by bursting into the room.

Jessica thought, *It's best that Jimmy talk with the kids alone.*

"So, I'll ask again, where did he go?" With an effort, James sat in the empty space next to Jack on the floor, his long legs bent at his knees in front of him as he squeezed in.

Jack shrugged again, his eyes rolling up at the ceiling.

"Is he upstairs?" James followed his son's gaze.

Jack tilted his head, twisting his face in thought. "Or maybe he left," Jack said. He looked straight ahead again, avoiding his father. "Don't know." His eyes slid to his sister, who was still watching the video.

Calculating their entrance into the conversation, Tracy and Jessica met each other's eyes and, with a subtle squeeze of Jessica's hand, Tracy nodded. The electrified feeling in the air floated around them, dense and warm. Suddenly, a noise caught their attention, a footfall hiding within the layers of noise, coming from behind the base of the stairs.

Tracy heard it first, automatically turning her head, heightened awareness prickling her scalp, her ears suddenly warm. From the corner of her eye, she caught movement, forcing her to rotate her body, her gut turning over as her sixth sense blazed awake. Just feet away, a small silhouette stood, the night-light from the hall illuminating only half a boy. The other half was swallowed by darkness.

Jessica couldn't catch her breath. Her chest constricted as she struggled for air, releasing her sister's hand. Her palms were sweating; she could feel the vibration that filled the hallway. This time it smelled like melting tires and was stronger than the usual ozone that hung in the air during an event.

"Jeffrey," Tracy said. Not wanting to scare him, her voice was low. She could feel Jessica's distress as she reached out, gripping her arm above the wrist, their beating hearts thumping together in the darkness. He moved just enough to confirm his existence before them, the slope of his upturned nose temporarily visible as he turned his head. They couldn't see his eyes, a swath of darkness creating a void where his face should be, which Tracy found odd, as there was light coming from the living room and hallway. She looked down at her hand, moving it back and forth, confirming visibility in the shadowed gray spectrum of the dimly lit house.

At first he appeared motionless, his face a dark oval. Then his right hand opened and closed, twitching. To his left, the density of shadow shifted, pulling away slowly as it separated from him. There was no sound, only a movement of wind as the black shape floated up, appearing to cling to the ceiling, rolling like a storm cloud within the confined space. Jeffrey looked around. He seemed puzzled by their presence, as if suddenly awakened from a dream. He was wearing the same plaid button-down shirt and rolled-up jeans as the first time Tracy had encountered him months before in the front entry hall.

His eyes, now visible, glimmered, meeting hers as he moved and shifted nervously from one foot to the other. Tracy felt a hand on her right shoulder. It was big, heavy, and warm. She looked up at her brother-in-law, who gave her a sideways glance, nodding his head, acknowledging the unearthly specter that stood in the hall, moving his gaze to the inky darkness that clung to the ceiling. They watched the black undulating mass expand, roll, and collapse into itself, anger and hate radiating from it.

"Hey, Jeffrey," James said, refocusing his attention as he struggled to keep his tone friendly, non-threatening, casual, and, as he called it, neighborly.

They stood, all three side by side, looking into the face of a little boy who had been dead for decades, while the moving mass of darkness hung in the air above him like an evil rain cloud. The burned electrical smell that had floated in the air seemed to expand just before a muffled, tearing noise drew their eyes to the black mass, which flew toward the back of the house, disappearing down the hallway.

Jeffrey didn't register the movement behind him, his eyes never leaving the three strangers who stood before him, searching each face, confusion mixed with caution and fear taking over.

"Hi." A small voice came from behind them. Jack was leaning against the wall, giving him a partial view, peeking around his father. From around the other side, Alena stood, a handful of popcorn in her hand.

Jeffrey's eyes flickered with recognition, landing on Jack. He shifted on his foot, leaning to the left, looking at Alena.

"Hello," Alena chirped, smiling.

"I'm looking for Harold," Jeffrey said. He was unsure and hesitant. The script had changed. He'd broken his normal pattern of searching for his friend as he directed his question to Jack.

"He's in the playroom." Jack, popcorn butter smearing one cheek, was matter-of-fact as he lifted his chin in the direction of the stairs.

Alena chimed in, rolling her eyes to the ceiling and then adding a firm, "Yep, upstairs." The curls of her ponytail bobbed up and down as she nodded.

Edging back into the hallway, Jeffrey's eyes focused on Jack, his stare unsettled and pleading as he turned, disappearing, as if into thin air, toward the staircase.

Jessica was the first to move, running past the doorway, turning toward the staircase. James and Tracy, two steps behind, reached her side. All three froze, heads tilted up, listening to the footsteps, the weight of them floating out of earshot. In the distance, a quiet interaction, a muted cadence, two voices, followed by unearthly silence.

They exchanged glances. Jessica looked over her shoulder toward the living room, where the sound of singing could be heard. The music was a sharp contrast to the haunting that brewed like a hurricane moving over the sea, heading to shore.

"What should we do?" James looked to Tracy, then Jessica, who was shaking her head, hands on her hips, looking stunned.

"I'm checking on the kids," she said, brushing by her husband, who was still looking up at where the black mass had been. "I have real children to protect."

"I'll go upstairs," Tracy said, catching her sister by the arm, stopping her. "I am, after all, Little Harold's nephew's sister-in-law." She flashed a pained, crooked smile and reached out to James, patting his shoulder. "Or maybe a woman will be less scary. Go check on your family." She inhaled, forcing her shoulders back as she took the first step.

Remember, Tracy, this is what you've waited for your entire life, she thought. "Time for my big-girl panties," she whispered as she climbed the stairs, eyes darting back and forth, looking into the shadows that filled the nooks and corners.

Reaching the top of the stairs, she stopped. She was tingling, excitement moving under her skin. The hallway was dimly lit. Jack had left a light on in his room, with the door ajar, the crack of light creating a dim yellow stripe across the hallway. The air felt like it had substance. *Like a trail behind a snail.* She chuckled at the thought, stepping quietly, looking from room to room as she moved down the hall.

The door to the attic stairway was closed. She turned the handle. It was eerily cold, but her imagination could simply be in overdrive. She reached the top of the stairs. Light from the streetlamp spilled into the room through the first attic window, producing shadows and eerie outlines of obstacles littering the floor.

Nothing moved, yet a noise filled the space, a steady, buzzing, rhythmic hum coming from the second room. She sidestepped past a tower of boxes, hugging the wall, her version of being stealthy. At the edge of the doorway, the noise was stronger. *It's more of a whizzing sound,* she thought, *the strength of it rising, falling, and moving.*

Standing to the right of the doorway, she slowly tilted her head to peek into the playroom, eyes squinting in the shadows, searching for the source of the noise. The room appeared to be empty, yet the sound continued. She reached, sliding a hand up the wall until she found the light switch: a soft *click,* and the overhead light filled the small room, causing her to squeeze her eyes shut for a moment as she adjusted to the brightness.

Her eyelids felt heavy, the thickness of the air laying on her skin and clinging to her lashes as she blinked, looking down, the whirring sound that filled the room slowing, the noise of it softening. The toy racetrack was alive with movement: the beloved cast-metal car with the number eight painted on its side was circling the track, slowing at the corners, buzzing down the short straightaway. She watched the consistent movement as the car lost momentum, slowing by degrees until it came to a complete stop at the top of the curve farthest from where she stood.

From behind her, she heard a rustle. A cascade of thumps followed by an icy crunch of glass. She took one nervous step into the darkness, her eyes scanning for the source of the noise. The tower of boxes she had passed earlier was now missing the top two, which both lay on the floor. As light from the playroom cut through the blue of the room, she saw the words *Christmas decorations* written in black marker on one.

"Well, there will be a few less ornaments on the tree," she said under her breath. "Next time, Tracy, grab a flashlight." She made a nervous sound just shy of a chuckle. Finding humor in her situation had always served her nerves well.

She maneuvered the two fallen boxes back into place and heard the shards of glass rattle freely, which made her wince. *Jessica will not be happy,* she thought.

A creak of floorboards, followed by movement at the far side of the room. Momentarily, the darkness moved from left to right, interrupting the light from the window. A tall box marked *toys* swayed and rocked before falling still. Struggling to catch her breath, she edged slowly toward the doorway at the top of the stairs. The light switch was around the corner and hard to reach. An old highboy dresser stood a few inches back from the wall, blocking easy access. Closing her eyes in anticipation of the light, she slid her hand between the wall and the dresser. Using two fingers, she flipped the switch to the on position.

Light filled the room, dispelling the remaining shadows that clung to the boxes and furniture. Moving with purpose, she was careful as she made her way around obstacles. When she reached the far side, she stood on her tiptoes, peering carefully over two old, stacked chairs. There was nothing there. Tracy was able to reach the box marked *toys*, pushing it with her fingertips. It was solid and heavy, her efforts only moving the box an inch.

Whatever had caused the box to sway had strength, she thought. *Yep, whatever was happening had energy and power.*

Leaving the lights on, she made her way down to the second floor, stopping at Jack's room. The door was now closed. Tracy stood, wondering if she should go in, then thought better of it and continued down the final flight of stairs. She saw the light from the kitchen spilling to the front of the house and heard murmuring voices.

"The kids in bed?" Tracy asked after rounding the corner. James and Jessica were sitting, elbows on the table, leaning in nose to nose. They both looked up. Jessica had been crying, her cheeks damp, her eyes red and puffy.

"Alena is in our bed, sleeping, and Jack is in his room," James answered wearily. "They seem to think nothing of their great-uncle and his friend popping in and out."

"We've been talking about what to do," Jessica said, her voice matching his weariness as she rubbed her eyes, a delicate strand of pearls dangling from her hand, swaying with movement as she talked.

James hadn't noticed the pearls until that moment. He looked quizzical as he reached out, touching the necklace.

"They're just kids," Tracy said. She swung a chair around, her legs straddling the back as she joined them. "I mean, for the most part, we are talking about family, those who share this house, whether you are able to see them or not. I don't think there is much to be frightened of when it comes to Jeffrey or Little Harold." She reached out, plucking the pearl necklace from her sister and holding them up to the light as they draped over the back of her hand. She looked them up and down as she turned them over, letting them dangle, then gave her sister a purposeful, serious look.

"Not much to be frightened of huh?" Jessica returned her gaze, reaching out, taking back the pearls. "The kids don't seem to get what is really going on." She tossed the necklace from one hand to the other, then wrapped her fingers around them, concealing their opalescent gleam.

"How long have you had those?" Tracy poked at Jessica's hand that was still closed tightly.

"I've never owned pearls. Well, at least not real ones. I had a cheap strand when I was younger, but they're in Alena's room somewhere." Jessica looked at James, then set the pearls on the kitchen table, arranging them as if on display.

James reached across the table, poking at the necklace, examining the strand carefully. "These look like my mother's," he said, his eyes moving quickly between them, looking for a reaction.

"Your mother's?" Tracy picked them up again, looking closer. "When and where did you find them? I think they're real." She held one of the pearls between her thumb and forefinger, scratching gently at the surface, then moved them to her mouth to assess their authenticity.

Jessica looked out the window. "I found them when I put Alena in our bed tonight. They were on the corner table, exactly where I found the baseball."

Concern etched Tracy's face, wrinkling her brow.

"My mom wore these to church every week and to every family event," James said. "See the clasp? Those are real garnets and there's one missing. That happened one summer when our dog

Chip got ahold of them." James pointed to the clasp, the delicate gold filigree slightly bent where the stone had been. He smiled at the thought of his faithful but sometimes naughty dog. "The thing is…these pearls are with my mother, now six feet under at the Mission Hills Cemetery."

Revulsion contorted Tracy's mouth, pulling down at the corners as if she'd been sucking on a lemon. She placed them with care in middle of the table, looking at her hands and then wiping her mouth with the back of her hand.

James grabbed the necklace, rolling the smooth, round pearls between his fingers. He concentrated, as if weighty life decisions rested in his hand, a decision hidden within a strand of pearls. "That's it. I'm dismantling the security system in the morning. It's not worth this. My family is in the middle of a bad horror movie, where Casper the ghost wants to become a real fucking boy…" James hung his head, groaning, the pearls spilling from his clutched fist. "Sorry, I'm tired."

A low moan came from across the table. Sleep-deprived, Tracy covered her face with one hand, fingers splayed, one eye looking at James and her sister, who sat in curious disbelief.

"So, your mom was here?" Tracy asked James.

He sat back in his chair. "She must have been," he answered slowly, his words wrapped in melancholy, as the necklace, solid and real, represented so many memories. "How else do you explain it? And, yes, that sounds crazy, I know." He sighed. "Part of me wishes I could have seen her. I mean, wouldn't you want to see your mom just one more time? I'm sure when I review the security footage, there will be PNIs all over the place. What can I do about it? I mean, we turned off the system, but they were still here." He lifted his shoulders as if defeated, looking to Tracy, hoping for some explanation.

Jessica nodded in agreement. "I would," she said, her voice was far away, imagining.

"OK, then, hell, we must try again." Tracy slapped her hand on the table for effect. "As a man of science and technology, are you willing to let an opportunity like this slip through your fingers? What would Stephen Hawking or Carl Sagan do?" Tracy kept her voice low, enthusiasm radiating off her like heat.

"Well, I'm not sure what either of those great men would do." James smiled at her. "However, I would think some critical documentation is warranted before turning it off for good. But answer me this, what do I do with this information? Simply document it, then hide it away? How do I let the world know about something they shouldn't mess with?"

James tapped on the table, thinking as he spoke. Then he looked at Tracy. "I'm assuming you found nothing upstairs." He rubbed his chin, the wheels spinning.

"No, nothing. Nothing I could see anyway, and I definitely didn't bump into your *mom*." She raised one eyebrow as she used her fingers to air-quote *mom* in her best Dr. Evil voice, trying to lighten the mood. "I'll call work tomorrow and tell them I can't come in. Do you both need to work?"

"I have an important meeting in the morning about the progress of the system and when it may be ready to launch." James laughed. "God, if only they knew. I'll tell them again there is a problem with some coding, and it might take a few weeks. Maybe it will buy me some additional time to change the filter pack. I think the additional energy created by the graphene has amplified the optics of the motion-tracking system. When uninvited visitors or spirits or whatever they are move into the dead space, or out of the line of the cameras, they disappear. I think that's why they come and go when the system is on. Maybe I can figure something out." He shook his head, as if talking to himself.

Clutching the pearls in his one hand, James opened and closed his fingers, tossing them and catching them again before handing them to Jessica. "I hope I can sleep tonight. The woo-woo factor just went up a notch."

Jessica and Tracy stared at each other as the details of his thoughts supplied more questions than answers, the engineering and technical jargon far out of their reach. Jessica knew it was his way of working things out. He often walked about the house, talking to himself. At times when she brought snacks to the Geek Shed, she would hear his one-sided diatribes, broken technology bearing the brunt of it all.

Chapter 39
Toys of the Past

It was the early blue of the morning before the world came to life. James moved quickly through the semi-dark hallway and down the stairs. Jessica had set up the coffee maker the night before, and, with a flip of the switch, he set the morning in motion. Its sputter and gurgle, the familiar daily rituals, were now treasured for their normality. The quiet before last-minute schoolwork, filling backpacks, and breakfast squabbles was usually a relaxing time, but now the silence had him on edge as he found his senses on continuous high alert, waiting for another shoe to drop. Every dimly lit corner and shadow made him anxious. He pulled a loaf of potato bread from a drawer, popping two pieces in the toaster. The smell of the toast mixed beautifully with the Colombian roast, making his stomach grumble.

A popping sound—far away, brief, and sharp in contrast to the silence of the morning—caught his attention. He had been taking the top off a jar of strawberry preserves but now froze. He listened, the hair on his arms standing at attention. The strange popping came again: disconnected fragments stuttered, then stopped, as muffled words drifted from the back of the house.

Setting the jar down quietly, he walked down the hallway. The door to his office stood open, and there was movement on the wall just inside the doorway—a dark, muddled light flickering. Inching closer, he saw the edge of his desk; the small chair opposite was at an angle, leaning against the wall. The desk lamp was off, the familiar glow missing, jerking his attention to the security system monitor. From his vantage point he had only a partial view; no green light meant the system was disengaged. He was standing just to the left of the door, hands sweating as he gripped the door frame. He wanted to stay out of view, well, as far out of view as possible, considering his height. The room appeared to be empty as far as he could see.

Thank God, he thought as air escaped him through clenched teeth. Then a *click*, followed by a *rumble* and *hum* caught his attention. *What the hell?* His mouth was suddenly dry. Words emerged, not all of them immediately recognizable as they rolled from the depths of the tiny room.

"It's simple, Jimmy old boy," he said under his breath, half hoping that if anyone hiding heard him, they would run. "Take two steps and see who is in your damn office." He shook his head, thinking of how his life, now upside-down, would never be free of the things that went bump in the night or, in this case, the morning, real or otherwise.

Innocent ignorance weaved a sense of safety in most average middle-class lives. Oh, how lucky they were and didn't even know it. Fear had forever torn the Allen home, never to be mended. The darkness burned the threads of certainty at the edges. He paused, turning to look down the hallway behind him, afraid of ambush. The baseball bat was leaning up against the wall near the front door. To his right, the photos of his family, which were usually comforting as he walked this part of the house; his family members seemed to stare out from their frames, years of time travel now askew, the markers of time diminished with uncertainty. He contemplated how many steps it would take to retrieve the bat, then ruled against it. If there was anything to fear, a baseball bat wouldn't do him any good.

Behind him, the floorboard lightly creaked, turning his attention back to his office. He leaned toward the open doorway, his view still limited, and listened. Again, the faintest shuffle of movement caught his ear. He took the last-needed step and brought himself fully into the room, bracing himself as a rush of blood filled his ears, muffling all other sound. It was as if he was diving far beneath the sea.

His computer had been turned on, but by whom? The glow of the monitor made the small room feel claustrophobic, like the light in a tunnel from an oncoming train looming in the distance. He couldn't see the details on the screen from his position. Touching the top of his head, James then remembered he had left his glasses on the kitchen table. He squinted, trying to bring his vision into focus on the distorted face of a man in the middle of the screen. From behind him, what looked like a woman was just stepping into frame.

James was so focused on the frozen image on the computer screen that he missed the top of a small head sticking up a few inches above the desk chair. The subtle movement caught him by surprise, causing a chill of gooseflesh to spring up all over his body. His legs turned to cement as his brain registered the tiny figure, triggering a fight or flight response in his body, which was unlike him.

He willed himself to move deeper into the room, stopping at the corner of the desk, giving him a clear view of the visitor.

James stammered clumsily, taking a sharp intake of breath, not knowing what to do or say. "Jesus." That was the only coherent word he could utter.

Jeffrey stood, hands fisted at his side, not moving. There was a delay in his response, like waking a long-sleeping child. He turned his head slowly away from the computer screen and looked up at James. He'd been watching the old Allen home movies, a sadness emanating from him in waves, the sorrow as real as the objects in the room. He turned back to the faces frozen on the screen.

"Momma?" The words seemed to come from him, yet his lips didn't move, giving a word synonymous with love a sinister tone. "Momma?"

He lifted his small, clenched fist, index finger rising to point at the image caught in mid-motion, grainy and blurred.

James looked at the faces captured in mid-motion. He didn't recognize them. He hadn't watched all the film saved from the canisters and didn't know who they were. They must have, at one time, been close to his grandparents to be on the film.

"Jeffrey," James said, speaking his name quietly. He then hesitated, not knowing what to say next.

Puzzlement passed over Jeffrey's face as he shifted position, peering around the chair, looking above at the ceiling, and then back to the doorway. He was calculating something, most likely an escape, and James was prepared for him to disappear, as ghosts do, but Jeffrey did neither. He just stood, looking around, then back to the computer, then again to James. If they'd been cowboys, this would have resembled a showdown.

Then, out of the blue, Jeffrey turned, walking around the desk, moving as if in a dream, around James. He left the room, a light smell of ozone trailing behind him, the depths of the hall swallowing him whole as he disappeared.

James found himself in the doorway of his office with no recollection of how he got there, when a *click* and *hum* behind him drew his attention back. The frozen screen was now back to life, the sounds jolting him back into his body. He returned to the desk, shutting down the computer, nervously arranging the scattered papers and newspaper clippings, all while thinking to himself that he needed everything organized and normal. He paused to examine the floor where, only just moments before, Jeffrey stood.

"Jeffrey," he said, as if trying to convince himself that what he'd experienced was real.

"Jeffrey?" Jessica was standing in the doorway. She was wearing her light-blue pajamas and a matching velour robe, a mug of coffee in each hand. She stepped forward, eyes anchored on his face as she handed him his morning fuel, her nose wrinkled like a bunny's as she sniffed the air.

"Thanks," he said, taking the cup. He was so engrossed in thought he hadn't even heard Jessica approach. "This smells like heaven to me. Mmm, dark and strong." Trying to draw attention away from the remnant of ozone still floating in the air, he took a sip with a weary smile. Their eyes were still fixed as if in a staring contest.

"What, Jimmy?" She wasn't budging as she sniffed the air again. With her free hand she grabbed the small chair from against the wall, turning it toward the desk, and sat down. A nod of her head told him to get comfortable; he wasn't going anywhere.

He sat on the corner of the desk, crossing his legs at the ankles and resting the cup between both hands, grateful for the coffee and for not being alone. "When I came down this morning, I heard a noise coming from in here. That's when I saw the computer was on. It was playing part of one of those home movies my grandfather filmed. Jeffrey was watching. I can't imagine what he thinks, or, hell, how he even turned on the computer. It was starting and stopping by itself. The screen then froze on what must be his parents, at least I think that's who they are. Hell, I didn't recognize them. Anyway, he was calling one of them Momma, so that would be the obvious conclusion, I think."

Jessica's eyes moved to the now-dark computer screen, then back to her husband, who was taking a calculated, long, cautious sip of his coffee.

"The system isn't on," she said, looking over her shoulder at the security monitor, verifying for herself, then turning back. "It isn't on. Was it on?"

"No, it was not on when I came in," James said. The silence between them matched the cold Seattle morning outside. "I know. Shit, I know, you don't need to say it. Another glitch in my theory. I mean, well, shit. I have no idea how he is here." Exhaustion was showing, aging him, draining what remained of his youth as he slumped in his own skin. He ran one hand through his hair, his body suit feeling much too small. He floated his attention away, out the window into the day that was just rising from the blues of night to the warm golden tones of what would turn out to be a beautiful spring day.

"Did I screw us up, our family and all that we've worked for?" James asked. The discomfort in his unease caused him to focus on the dark moss growing on the trunk of the large evergreen tree outside the window. The colors changed with each minute, as if an invisible hand was painting the world as it awoke.

"No. Look at me." Her answer was short, meant to get his attention, the edge in her voice purposeful. She wanted answers.

Her words snapped his attention back into the room. He turned to her. "I know…" His voice trailed off as he set the cup on the desk corner and rubbed his neck, a move he hoped would disguise his trembling hands. "I need to get to work. I also need to figure out a new configuration or different power supply." He bent to kiss her cheek. He wanted to ramble and fill the silence with logical words and thoughts. He wanted to remember who they were before he brought his work home and into their lives. He felt the need to move and do something, anything, to create normalcy and forget the dead boy who had just called for his mother.

She was silent, closing her eyes with his touch, remembering who they were together. Jessica grabbed his hand, stopping him, drawing his attention to her as she met his eyes. "Jimmy," she said, squeezing his hand.

Just hearing her speak his name warmed him. Looking down at her, he remembered just how lucky he was. She was beautiful even when she was angry with him. "Yeah, I know," he said, kissing her forehead. "And I love you, too."

"I love you, too," he repeated, stepping out of the room.

Jessica followed her husband into the hallway, stopping at the kitchen, where she stood in the doorway, looking into the room, the cornflower blue tiles jumping out, seeming brighter than usual in the morning light. On the table, the pile of student papers seemed to have grown before her eyes, amplifying her need to finish grading them and start on the morning chores before chaos trickled down from the bedrooms upstairs.

***

James continued quietly checking every possible hiding place, looking for Jeffrey—a task he knew was futile—while Jessica focused on her schoolwork. The boy had vanished, but that wasn't surprising, as he came and went with ease.

Where did he go? James thought as he walked the halls, looking at the motion-tracking cameras and sensors, rethinking his work as he moved to the third floor. The attic wasn't on the grid, no coverage, no cameras. *Maybe that explains why they play in the space.*

He sat on the floor of the playroom, hand tracing a long length of racetrack, his thumb feeling the groove where the car hugged the line. The metal airplane his father played with as a boy sat on the blue canvas trunk, gleaming like new, which was strange, as it was over a half a century old.

He heard the animated voices of the kids and felt the uptick of energy as the house moved into the day around him, but his energy was draining away. He was no longer certain of the future, no longer the chief protector of the family and its legacy. The overwhelming feeling of failure was taking his strength by inches. He was trying to get his bearings and feel the floor beneath him, but questions flew at him when he allowed his mind to still. Would there be another report of a malevolent bunny blanket trying to swallow one of his children today? His worries were getting the best of him, and, for the first time, he actually wanted to run away from his life.

Reaching past the racetrack, he grabbed the toy plane, examining it. The paint was perfect, no scratches, no signs of any child ever touching it, which was strange. Even stranger was how it felt in his hands; it was toasty warm. He rolled it over, looking at the bottom. The metal wheels, painted black, were perfect, and there was no manufacturing logo or stamp anywhere.

"You spend as much time up here as the kids," said a voice behind him. The smell of coffee filled his nostrils.

He had his back to the doorway. He turned, picking up his feet, rotating his body, and spinning like a rusty top.

Tracy stood in her WSU sweatpants and a white T-shirt, a cup of coffee in hand. "Sis told me you had a chat with Jeffrey early this morning," she said, walking to the far side of the small room where she lowered herself to the floor, crossing her legs, and placing her coffee mug next to the track. She held out her hand, palm up, moving her fingers in a *give me* motion. James handed over the toy plane, shrugging. She turned it over in both hands, looking at it carefully.

He pointed to the plane. "That toy plane is over fifty years old. Completely void of any dust, it looks new, not a nick or scratch on it. And I can't find a manufacturing stamp or label either, which is strange. And then there is that mysterious note that looks like it's old as the hills." He rubbed his hands together as if he could feel the time and imaginary dirt on his palms.

Tracy looked at the plane, squinting at the seams and feeling the weight of it. "So, could it be an off-market replica of an old toy? Huh, it's hot." She transferred it from one hand to the other.

There's an unearthly feeling, a vibration, she thought as she continued to search for clues.

A laugh escaped him. "Maybe, but where did it come from?" He leaned in, taking it from her hands and looking closely, as if one more inspection would make a difference. "It just showed up, and it's the exact same toy plane, or a mirror image, of the one my dad played with. Heck, there are multiple photos of him with it. He carried it with him for a few years until he grew tired of it, as children do." He gently placed it back on the steamer trunk, then looked at Tracy. "Do you think my father dropped it off, like the pearls from my mother?"

She took a sip, looking out the window. The clouds were moving with the wind, giving way to sunshine, which lit the room with columns of bright light. "Remember, I talked about items appearing out of nowhere," Tracy answered. "How they can apport or move from one dimension to another…" She waited, letting words sink in. "It could be that your dad still plays with that plane in this house. Jimmy, I believe someone still plays in the dimension where this home has yellow walls." She pointed to the plane, then the walls, rolling her eyes to the ceiling, and then took another sip.

A questioning, guttural sound escaped his throat. "The crazy thing is that I'm actually following you now," he said, scratching his head. "But how? Where do they go? I mean, Jeffrey walked out of my office and then, poof, he was gone." He laughed. "I'm sounding like a bad country western song. Wasn't there a song on that old TV show *Hee Haw* about poof and things being gone?"

Tracy chuckled. "Let's stay focused, shall we?" She cleared her throat. "With some hauntings, spirits have the strength to manifest at will, but they are rarely solid and whole. They will steal energy from anywhere they can to materialize and be seen in this world. They will drain things like batteries. Hell, they'll even steal heat from the air to gain what they need. Your grandfather, Harold, and Jeffrey, they are different; they appear solid. Your grandfather's hand was warm when I shook it. He seemed just as real as you and me." She adjusted her position, sitting up on her knees. "And their personal things, the items that had meaning to them, the glasses, the baseball, the catcher's mitt, your mother's pearls. It's as if they leave a little piece of themselves behind. As if the fabric of time and this dimension are all screwed up, and the things that go bump in the night, well, let's just say they are riding on the coattails of our interdimensional visitors, feeding off them and, my guess is, the main course is Jeffrey's guilt and sadness. I just hope we aren't on the menu."

"The darkness feeds off sadness?" Irritation and frustration distorted James's features into a grimace. "Feeding off my family is not an option." The feeling of helplessness turned to anger, digging at him, making him feel hollow.

"Oh, dear brother, the term feeding is a figure of speech." She let out a long breath. "I guess you could say that some darker spirits, well, they feast on sadness and fear to remain viable, to give them strength and energy. Kind of like a boogeyman smorgasbord. With all that is good in the world, these entities exist, but we just don't see them. This house is different. Sis also told me the security system was off. Is that right?" There was concern in her voice, but James wasn't sure who the concern was for.

"Yep, the system was off. I made sure and double checked. So, that is a glitch in the matrix, don't you think? I mean, I thought it was my system that created this mess." Resignation tinged with some relief in his questions gave Tracy a sense of how to respond.

She shrugged. "Well, maybe their batteries are all charged up? I know some spirits, when strong enough, can come and go as they please." Her answer was simple and sincere.

With a flick of his finger, he hit the propeller of his father's toy plane. "Maybe you're right." He got up, rubbing his knee, stiff from sitting so long. "Nothing is normal in this house, and, yes, maybe their batteries are full. My brain is tired, and I have a meeting at the office. Will you be here later in the afternoon?" He of-fered her his hand, pulling her to her feet.

"Yeah, I need to get down to the SAM to talk with them about the possibility of extending the exhibit another few weeks." Tracy looked up, not sure how he would feel about extending her stay.

He reached for her, picking her off her feet in a big bear hug and spinning her. His mood had changed quickly, his energy lift-ing. "Thank God," he said, shocking her. "We need you here. You know what is happening on levels I can't comprehend. Jess will be happy and relieved, I think." The sharp edge of the unknown that faced them was now somewhat softened with the news.

Chapter 40
Trigger Objects

Jeffrey had been on James's mind all morning. Through the various meetings and discussions, his thoughts would wander to the small lost boy, his freckles clear, his eyes searching, making it hard to ignore the unearthly abilities of his new, prized security system.

Company executives were hopeful that a large rollout was around the corner. They discussed the benefits and positive tests with the next-door neighbor's dog, the desire to include the family pet in their sights and in their bottom-line budget. Pet owners would spend big money on their furry family members, and the identification abilities of the IOS—or Identified Occupant System—was very promising, with some simple adjustments to the body-scan and facial-recognition software.

James had a sense of accomplishment with the responsiveness of the system, even with the obvious unearthly glitches. He pushed the positive attributes, while proposing the need for additional time and his desire to adjust the positioning of the motion-tracking cameras for Fido and Fluffy. Upper management gave their blessings and additional time needed to create a flawless pet-friendly system, and he was relieved that he could temporarily redirect the focus. The company would direct focused efforts aimed at the large demographic of animal lovers, who would predictably love to program messages throughout the day, giving them peace of mind with the ability to check on their four-legged friends' movements with accuracy.

As he was packing up for home, his cell phone buzzed, moving like an upended insect on his desk. The stored number on the screen indicated he had a message from his friend at the Seattle Police Department. The message was brief, giving the details of Jeffrey's parents, along with their last known phone number. It was the information James had been wanting to track down, but the strange events at home had kept him preoccupied and scattered. *The timing is eerie,* he thought, *with the latest appearance of my new house guest.* Maybe Jeffrey was looking for help, and the universe was telling James it was time to step up? James admitted that he wanted to help move Jeffrey back to where he came from, as it was getting a little too crowded in the Allen house.

Later, walking through the mudroom door, he found Tracy at the kitchen table, her back to him, her laptop open, papers strewn everywhere. *The Seattle Times* lay open on the table to an article on her exhibit, two paragraphs highlighted in yellow. She twisted in her seat to look at him over her shoulder, one hand lifted in a screw-in-the-lightbulb wave.

"Hello, my brother," she said.

James settled in, dropping his messenger bag on the far end of the table, not wanting to disturb her work, and pulling his chair away from the table so he could sit and stretch his legs. He folded his hands across his stomach and gave her a laser-focus stare.

"So..." He paused, waiting for her attention. "I now have the phone number for Jeffrey's parents. Do you believe that spirits hear us when we talk about them?" His question was matter of fact and direct, and his eyes didn't leave her. He wanted to do something, hell, anything, to help his family and maybe a lost soul.

Tracy took in his words. For the first time, she believed that they truly were beginning to understand each other. She shut her computer and gave him her full attention, her gaze as direct as his. "Yes, I believe they hear us. If it is our intent to communicate, it's much like a vibration through a spiderweb, our thoughts traveling up and down invisible connections to find them. In my humble opinion, anyway."

He nodded his head slowly in agreement, tapping on the table, his habit when deep in thought. James unbuckled the messenger bag, pulling out notes and his cell phone. "Do you think we could, I don't know, do something that would ensure that he would hear or be present for a phone call to his parents?"

Tracy tilted her head like a dog questioning its master. "Now that is interesting. I wonder..." She, too, started to tap her fingers as she squinted, looking out the window. "If we had something he loved there with us, something that had his energy, an object of importance... You know where I'm going with this, don't you?"

With a nod, he was out of his chair and up the stairs. Tracy followed the echo of his footsteps overhead, then opened her laptop once again and began flipping through her paperwork.

He returned ten minutes later, pushing her paperwork to one side to make room and setting the baseball and catcher's mitt on the table. "Will these work?" His finger traced the lacing in the glove.

"What's your goal, Jimmy? So, let's say we get them on the phone, we place the objects of that tragic day there, and, what, tell them we have their son here and to say hello?" She poked at the baseball with the end of her pen, causing it to roll to the table edge. She knew where he was going with it but also knew he was asking for a family to take a look at a difficult, tragic day and possibly open up old wounds with no guaranteed outcome.

James ran his fingers through his hair, then pulled off his glasses. "I guess some thought is needed as to what we would say, and, yes, it could make things worse if they haven't found peace in the events of the past, but I really think they have. I read the letter to my grandfather." He used the palms of his hands to rub his eyes and looked at her. "I really think they are OK, and I want Jeffrey to know that. Don't you think part of the problem is the guilt of not only killing his best friend, but disappointing his parents?"

She was clicking her pen and chewing on her lower lip in thought. "It could make things worse, but, yes, it could also help with the haunting of Jeffrey." She nodded in agreement, touching the catcher's mitt. "I would turn on the system and use these," she nodded at the ball and mitt," and make that phone call. Just re-member, you need to move the conversation in the right direction."

James looked at the wall clock; it was a little after three p.m. Jessica and the kids would be home soon, and he needed to work. "Are you working at the museum tomorrow?" He leaned forward, glancing at her computer screen and notes.

Tracy sat back again, closing her laptop. "I have a morning meeting about possibly moving the exhibit to the main floor, due to its popularity, and then I'll be free. So, your woo-woo sister-in-law can be here, let's say around noon." She waggled her eye-brows and grinned. "With the system on, we can record anything that happens."

"I'll talk with Jess; she'll need to know." He scooped up the ball and mitt, tossing the ball in the air and catching it with the mitt.

Chapter 41
Time to Listen

Jessica had a long-standing beauty routine. She'd wash her face, apply serums and creams, and, after a rough and often frazzled day of teaching, she would use the brush given to her by her mother to brush her chestnut curls into smooth ringlets. As she stroked her hair, she would often float away in her head, thinking about the events of the day or her to-do list for the next morning, but tonight her mind was uneasy, eyes darting to the corners, looking for the slightest movement. She hoped the night would be quiet, her family safe.

The brush bristles felt good on her scalp, her rhythmic movement a moment of bliss, followed by thoughts of Jack and Alena and their friendship with children long dead, children with the ability to manipulate security systems and time. An unsettling feeling of dread suddenly came over her, prompting her to drop the brush in the sink. The need to check on the children was overwhelming.

Alena's room was closest, her door open six inches or so. Inside the room, the yellow and orange ferry night-light cast a year-round sunset glow, which warmed her room even on cold, winter nights. Jessica saw her small form, the new blue and white cloud-themed comforter tucked under her chin, Mrs. Kelly shared her pillow, one ear hanging off the edge. All was quiet.

She walked quietly over, gazing at her daughter, who was out cold after a long day of school and afternoon play. Jessica reached down to kiss her forehead, but hesitated, not wanting to wake her, instead bringing two fingers to her own lips and blowing a kiss before leaving.

Jack's room was on the other side of the hallway, near the attic stairs. His door cracked open just a few inches, the pale-yellow glow of his desk lamp reached her where she stood. Peering in, she saw his desk, books piled high. Draped on the back of his pulled-out desk chair was his great-uncle Harold's green baseball jacket. Pushing the door slowly, a loud creak startled her, and she stopped, her heart jumping.

Taking a deep breath, she pushed the door, allowing just enough room to squeeze in. The noise of her intrusion didn't wake him. She walked to the bedside table and smiled. On his chest was *Adventures of Huckleberry Finn*. Removing the book, she was careful to set it down open to where he'd left off. She wondered if she should turn off the lamp, ultimately deciding to leave it on so he wouldn't wake to darkness. As she was turning to leave, it registered that the chair, normally tucked in the kneehole beneath the desk, was facing the head of the bed, angled in as if he had an audience. She thought this was strange but figured maybe Alena had been in the room, though she preferred the company of Disney characters and Mrs. Kelly.

Returning to her bedroom, she saw James propped in bed, glasses sitting on the end of his nose, his laptop bathing him in a soft white light. He turned his head, hearing her, his eyes twinkling as she approached the bed. To Jessica he looked like an angel.

"Good evening, Mrs. Allen." He was smiling, but the shadows under his eyes gave away his exhaustion.

Pulling back the covers, she crawled in, fluffing the pillows and turning on the bedside table lamp. "Good evening, Mr. Allen," she answered, pulling the blanket under her chin, her arms on top, folding them across her stomach.

"How are the kids sleeping?" He turned away from his laptop to look at her.

"Sleeping so peacefully I must admit I'm jealous. I mean, they have no idea, do they? These strange events simply don't seem to faze them." Her tone was low, a hint of humor underlining her words. She shifted, pulling on the blanket and smoothing it against her.

He closed his laptop, set it on the bedside table, and rolled to his side to face her. "Well, kids seem to be a little more resilient, as they don't know what is normal in the world, I think. You hear about children with their invisible and imaginary friends, but how imaginary are they? Heck, I read about a seven-year-old boy who was visited by his dead grandmother at least once a week for almost a year. She would read to him. The kid never thought it was strange. After all, it was just his grandma. Maybe grownups should look at the unexplained through their eyes." He reached out, rubbing her shoulder.

"I'm not frightened by Harold or Jeffrey," Jessica said, puzzlement at her own statement flitting across her face. "Well, maybe at first, when I didn't know or understand. I think the darkness scares me the most, the shadow within the shadows. I'm tired of being on edge all the time. I'm tired of being afraid of everything." Her eyes shimmered as she blinked back tears. One escaped, running down her flushed cheek, and she quickly wiped it away.

Leaning over, his voice intimate and sincere, James placed a hand alongside her face and kissed her cheek. "You and the kids are the most important things in the world to me. I'm going to figure out why so many unwanted visitors are here, I promise. I'm getting up early to get my work done and out of the way." He took a deep breath. "Then I'm turning on the system when everyone is at school. I'm hoping someone will show up and help explain some things."

A tired smile came and went as he removed his glasses and rubbed the bridge of his nose. "I'm sure Mom is missing her pearls. My God, I never thought I would be trying to reach my dearly departed using my security system. Wow, I must sound nuts." He let his breath out slowly, closing his eyes.

"Am I losing it? I mean, I'm trying to sound logical, but I only sound crazy. If I can't figure it out, we can sell the house like everyone else and move." He looked at Jessica, sadness coloring his words at the possible defeat.

Jessica rolled on her side, mirroring him, her gaze now soft and full of love. She reached out, giving his hand a light squeeze, then met his weary smile with one of her own. "James Allen, you, my love, will figure it out. I'm just being a momma bear." A child-like giggle escaped her. "I went to Costco today and bought a few dozen lightbulbs so that we can keep the place nice and bright. No, this is our home." She looked into the corners of the room, the dark shadows unmoving, and sighed.

"So, does that mean that you're OK with me turning on the system tomorrow? I also want to call Jeffrey's parents, and I hope, well, I'm not sure why I want to contact them, but I feel I need to. Maybe if he knows they're OK, then he may be OK to move on, or at least your sister thinks so. Hell, I'm even beginning to believe in this crazy need-to-be-at-peace stuff." He looked in her eyes, trying desperately to read her thoughts.

Jessica released a long sigh; she was reading him, too. "So, can Tracy be here when that damn thing is on? And I'm not sure why you feel the need to contact that boy's parents, but if you must, then you must. It's quite touching that you care about a boy who has been dead for fifty years." Her particular form of humor seemed to place him at ease.

"Yeah, well, maybe there's a clue about why he is stuck or why he haunts us. Nobody seems to know all the details of the accident. And, yes, Tracy said she'll be home early in the afternoon, so I'll wait for her; she knows more than both of us."

James was relieved. *We're going to be OK,* he thought. He patted her knee and turned out the light.

Jessica rolled onto her back, turning her head to look at him, the shadows of the room enveloping his side of the bed. She then turned the other way, looking at the light coming from her nightstand. She tried to relax, exhaustion moving through her body, then glanced back at James, who had closed his eyes, his own exhaustion taking him away. She reached for the switch at the base of the lamp, hesitated, then drew her hand back, squinting into the sea of darkness around the room.

Stop this nonsense, she thought. *This is your room, and James is next to you.* She closed her eyes, wondering if she could sleep with the light on. It was as if her eyelids had become thin as paper, her lashes letting the dim glow slip in. Jessica scooted her way to a sitting position, pulling the blanket higher up, just under her chin, then over her head.

I used to do this when I was a child, she thought. The light was still taunting her, yet it created a comforting force-field of protection from the darkness she feared. Slowly, she slid down, returning to her back, the blanket still over her head, and fell asleep.

Chapter 42
Calm and Silence

To Jessica's relief, the night was uneventful. She awoke just before dawn, the sun still hiding beyond the morning horizon. Fatigue was holding on, her body aching from head to toe. She stared at the curtains, which hung open about a foot, allowing the light from the streetlamps to cast a deep blue rectangle of color near the window. Something caught her attention, drawing her eyes to the ceiling, where she noticed a small dark crack radiating from the edge of the wall behind the headboard.

"What's this now?" she said quietly as she propped herself up on her elbows. "Huh, that's new." Surveying the room, she noticed her bedside light was off, most likely by James when he got up before her. His side of the bed was empty.

She heard the kitchen in motion, a faraway rattle and clank of silverware, water being turned on and off, giving life to the stillness of the house. Sitting up, she swung her legs over the edge of the bed, slipping her feet into her slippers and glancing at the clock, the glow emphasizing just how early it was, 5:20 a.m. Standing, she wavered, still sleepy; getting her bearings, she pushed back one curl plastered to the side of her face and tickling her nose. Descending the stairs, she heard James's humming, which he sometimes did when he was Morning Dad. It was a song from his favorite movie, where a happy groundhog would do the twist in his hole on a golf course.

"Good morning." Her voice was low and gravelly. He was at the counter, making lunch for the kids, and he turned his head, acknowledging her.

"I smell peanut butter and jelly," she said. Her hand touched his back as she peered around his shoulder.

"Yep, I was just getting ready to make yours. Would you also like a cookie, Mrs. Allen?" His voice was quiet, matching hers. James stopped making sandwiches, lifting his arm so she could snuggle into him as he pulled her tight, kissing the top of her head.

He smells like linen and soap, she thought as she buried her face in his shirt, enjoying the quiet of the morning and the moment.

"You smell good. How did I not hear you shower?" Jessica smoothed her hands over his shirt and hugged him tighter. "I miss this." She turned her head as he held her; the view out the window was gray, with the newness of the morning sun moving into view at the top of the maple tree in the yard, turning the tips on the leaves electric green.

They stood for what seemed an eternity, taking in the calm silence. With a sigh, James looked down, his smile transforming his face into the young man from high school sneaking a kiss at his parents' house, the lines and years of middle-age disappearing into the face she first fell in love with long ago.

"You look like a teenager in this light," she whispered.

"Well, let's hope my parents don't catch us alone." He kissed her and then kissed her again.

Chapter 43
Understanding

James attended his morning marketing meeting via conference call. Normally he would want to be face-to-face with his team, but uncertainty and concern kept him close to home. He was great at giving them excuses. Today he was in the middle of installing additional motion-tracking cameras and planned on borrowing the neighbor's dog. He had mixed feelings. On one hand, he felt excited about expanding the system, and he studied the placement of the additional cameras, but, on the other hand, he was very aware that what he was creating could come tumbling down around him if he couldn't figure things out.

He warily moved ahead and decided to install the four additional IR cameras and equipment at different levels, settling on the less used second-floor hallway leading to the back of the house, the attic staircase, and both rooms on the third floor. He was nervous about turning on the system, but there was no way around it. He retrieved two additional mesh routers from the Geek Shed. In order to expand the system, he needed to use a graphene lattice to replace the CMOS element in the second floor and attic motion-tracking cameras, greatly improving the sensors. He settled on the standard pack for the test, adjusting the views and options on the security monitor. The tests were uneventful and ran smoothly, giving more depth with the additional views. He was nervous and jumpy, not knowing what to expect, leaving the system on for only an hour at a time.

Sitting at his desk, he reviewed the data, a sense of growing unease swirling around him like a cold arctic breeze. His eyes flickered from his work to the security monitor, expecting somehow that it would magically come to life. He pictured the lights blinking on as the system warned of an encroaching ghostly dimension. He chuckled at that thought and at how things had changed in his structured and uneventful life.

He imagined the ad he would create: "Hey, world, want to know when your spectral family comes to visit? Well, just sign up for my new multidimensional security system," he said, laughing at the sound of his voice. "You are officially crazy and now talking to yourself." Pushing back from the desk, he rocked his chair nervously back and forth. The movement was an attempt to soothe his agitated nerves as a prickle of electricity moved down his back, lifting the hairs all over his body. "What should we do Jimmy, old boy?" he said to the empty little room, letting his head fall back, looking up at the ceiling for answers.

"You know what they say when you start to answer yourself," Tracy said, standing in the doorway. She dropped her bag next to the chair against the wall and sat down, one eyebrow raised in question. "Was it a good conversation?" She waggled her eyebrows in an attempt at lifting the tension in the room.

"Actually, I'm quite funny and brilliant," he said as he rubbed his arms in an attempt to quell the involuntary goosebumps that had taken over.

"So, what's the plan?" She pulled off her jacket and then dug through her bag on the floor, dumping out random items: wallet, lipstick, numerous pens, a flashlight, a small journal, and multiple crumpled envelopes.

"Wow, you would have won on the show *Let's Make a Deal,* but that may be before your time. Good God, how many pens does one need?" he said with a laugh, matching her salty tone; their banter changed the focus for a minute, and he needed the break.

He wondered what exactly she was looking for as she shook her purse upside down—a few coins giving up their hiding place and clinking as they hit the floor—and he waited as she scoured her possessions before continuing. "I've added two additional cameras upstairs, re-installed the original power pack, and turned on the voice announcement system, so everything is ready to engage. I did a few trial runs, without any ghostly visits, so I guess that's good. But if their ectoplasmic batteries are charged by the system, well, then, it doesn't matter, right?" He shrugged, questioning, watching his frazzled sister-in-law as she continued to find items hiding in pockets and add them to the growing pile.

"Ah, there you are!" She held up something small that looked like a furry rubber band, sliding it over her hand to her wrist, then shoving the items strewn on the floor back into her bag. "Thank God for old hair ties. I think this one is at least ten years old." Pulling her hair into a top knot, she looked at him; he was obviously confused.

"Anyway, look, we're in uncharted territory, so, to answer your question, I have no idea," he said, then resumed moving nervously back and forth in his chair and glancing at the top of her head. "I'm sorry, all that for a hair doodad?" He pointed.

She shot him a dismissive look and then a smile. "I feel something will happen, and I'm usually not wrong." She stood and began to stretch, touching her toes.

"Are you going for a run?" He raised his eyebrows as he leaned to the right, tilting his head in order to view her bent-over, head-down position.

She popped up, standing straight, her face flushed. "Well, if things happen like they did last time, I want to be, well, ready, I guess." She nervously laughed, then took a seat across from him, the small room feeling suddenly much smaller. "I don't want my hair getting in my eyes." She tucked one stray curl behind her ear and shrugged, feeling silly. She then noticed the items on his desk. "Oh, I see you have the trigger objects. Do you have the home movie ready to play?"

He poked the catcher's mitt with his index finger. "Trigger objects? So, these are meant to trigger them? In what way?" He picked up the ball, rolling it between his hands.

She leaned in. "Yeah, that's what we call the items spirits are attached or drawn to. I also feel that having pictures of Jeffrey's mom and dad up on the screen, well, I think it may bring him out from wherever he is."

Leaning back in his chair, James pulled out his computer keyboard, tapping and clicking. The home movie began to play. He hit fast-forward, looking for the section where Jeffrey's mom and dad appeared. "And there they are." He clicked Pause, their faces frozen on the screen.

"So, you've thought about what you're going to say? You know he'll hear you. He just may not, you know, show up." She took the ball from him, tossing it between her hands. She had an air of authority, and it was comforting.

"I have no idea what to say. I was thinking of lying just a little." He stared at the faces on the computer screen and then the catcher's mitt. "Let's face it, the pain and loss of the accident has lived within these walls for far too long. My grandparents never really dealt with the death of their firstborn, and my dad lived with a gaping void caused by the tragedy. Their world was affected on every damn level."

His ears were turning pink, his emotions rising to the surface. "My father told me there was a dark cloud over the house; he could feel it but figured it was buried and wanted to leave it there. I used to think it was normal to grieve for those we've lost, but now I'm thinking he might have been feeling Jeffrey." He pushed back from his desk, hitting the wall, rubbing his forehead and temples. "I know you feel his sadness. I'm not a medium, but it's in the air when he's here. This loop of his, do you think it's been happening since his death?"

Tracy sighed, still holding the baseball, running her finger over the faded *H* and *A*. There was an edge in her voice, yet her walls were coming down. "I felt his sadness the first day I entered this house. At the time, my woo-woo, crazy sister status was a joke, so I never brought it up. I mean, would you have believed me? I believe Jeffrey has been stuck in an unfamiliar world. He's been in a place where his guilt keeps him searching for peace and searching for Harold. He may not even be aware of his predicament, the responsibility of the accident anchoring him, keeping the two boys separated." She narrowed her eyes in thought, then added "It's sort of like ending up in a room that looks familiar, but it's not right somehow, and he is alone."

She set the baseball down and leaned on the desk, her hands spread apart as if her arms needed the support and met his eyes. "I don't know why, but the activity is increasing. It may be because your security system is acting like a big paranormal battery, giving them the strength they need…" She trailed off, looking out the window, her wheels turning.

"Yep," she continued, "it's just a matter of time before they find each other now, with everyone focusing on them, and that's even with the system off." She looked up to the IR camera, then back at James.

Tracy knew this reality might be difficult to swallow, but it was important that he understand. She pulled herself up, squaring her shoulders, calculating where to begin her tale. "Last night, after the museum closed, a few of us decided to attend a get-together not far from here. A friend of a friend was throwing himself a birthday party, complete with an amazing karaoke system." She laughed, placing her hand on her head. "Oh, my God, he had a mini stage and everything, talk about over the top; all he was missing was a spotlight. Anyway, sorry I digress, we were there way too late, and I made it home around two a.m. When I walked in, I saw him. I saw Jeffrey at the top of the stairs."

She'd been looking at the baseball again, not wanting to make eye contact, and kept her head tilted down, looking up briefly through her lashes as she continued. "I was startled at first but knew he had to be close, as I could feel the vibe; you know that static electricity kinda feeling when the hairs stand on end? But it wasn't as strong as when the security system is on." She looked at James. He was sitting eerily still; she had his full attention. "I was about to call to him, when he, well, he just, fragmented like a statue breaking apart, disappearing in a whirling motion like dust falling from a ceiling fan after it's turned on. He was partly in shadow, but I know who I saw."

"What?" He sat forward, looking instinctively at the security system monitor.

Tracy followed his gaze, looking over her shoulder, confirming what she knew he was thinking. "No, the system wasn't on. I checked." She turned back, looking at him. His eyes slid back to her. They sat in silence.

"Well, don't keep me in suspense." He was trying to lift his tone, trying very hard to stay cool, yet sweat prickled his brow though the room was cool.

She rolled the baseball to James, who caught it as it left the edge of the desk. "I called out to him, and I believe—I really believe—he saw me. Jimmy, as I said, he may be lost in this dimension, which isn't bad, but it can't be good if he never makes it to where he should be." Tracy pulled back, standing again, her nervous energy almost bursting out of her. It was apparent she needed to move.

"So, what does that mean? People see ghosts all the time, well, at least they say they do." He lifted his forearm, rolled up his sleeve, and looked at the hairs that were standing on end, then he shook his wrist as if he could shake off whatever made him break out in goosebumps in the first place.

"Yes, he is very much a ghost, and that is why the alarm is never tripped. He doesn't break any sensor," she said as she started to pace in a small circle, then stopped, her desire to be understood rolling before her like a tidal wave propelled to shore. "I believe that, until recently, he held space in another dimension separate from this one and separate from Little Harold. When we see Jeffrey, it's like a video playing one specific moment over and over again in a loop. Kind of like purgatory, a temporary holding pattern, not permanent, and now with your system we may be able to help Jeffrey heal from the tragedy that took his life decades ago." Tracy grabbed a piece of paper from the printer, then scanned the desk. James knew what she was looking for and, opening the top desk drawer, he fished out a pen, handing it to her.

Tracy sat down again; she was like a jack-in-the-box and couldn't stay still. She moved the books and files that covered the desk in order to make room. Drawing multiple squares, she placed stick figures in each. "Within the house, there are many dimensions or realities that are happening all at once. In this square," she pointed to a square with four stick figures, "you, Jess, and the kids live. And in this dimension," she drew and pointed to the next square with five stick figures in it, "is where your parents, grandparents, and Harold exist...not exactly live, you know, as they have already lived once and now are in the reality or dimension with yellow walls. I'm sure others are there, your father, for instance, but we'll keep it simple."

Tracy continued to the next square with one stick figure. "This is the place where Jeffrey has existed since the accident. It's a duplicate reality and, yes, the house he visits every single day has yellow walls because that's what he remembers. But like a cruel cosmic form of self-punishment, he is alone." She paused, then started to fill in the last square with seven stick figures crammed together.

"This is what our reality looks like now." Using her pen, she pointed to each figure. "You, Jess, Jack, Alena, Little Harold, me, and over here in a room alone is Jeffrey. Oh, yes, and how can I forget the occasional visit from Grandpa?" Tracy then added a smiling stick figure on the edge of the square with glasses waving.

"The dimensions change and shift. They have substance, yet they are pure energy, and when these equally real dimensions bump into each other, the release is like a glass overflowing. and something is left behind." Reaching for the catcher's mitt, she held it up to illustrate her theory. "These objects weren't the only things left behind. The question is…" She hesitated, then placed the mitt back on the desk, clearing her throat. "The question is, how do we get them back where they belong and keep them there?" Her tone was low and serious, the angle and green glow of the table lamp making her features grim, much like a medieval storyteller predicting their fate, her theory foreboding. A chill fell over them as she looked to James and then over her shoulder to the security system monitor.

"Your graphene lattice matrix or whatever you call it, this system of yours, it gave them the energy to move or maybe the ability to be seen, creating this new reality." She waved her hand above her head for effect, rolling her eyes to the ceiling and then around the room.

He'd been rubbing his neck, listening. Her words felt like a lead weight being dropped in water, each ripple of understanding moving within his gut, making him queasy. With the final reveal he met her eyes.

"Shit. Just shit," he said.

He knew he had choices to make, and he had his family to think about. Releasing air slowly from between pursed lips, he sounded like someone letting the air out of a tire. "Well, I have the equipment available, so I think the sensors without the graphene lattice matrix is the smart choice for today." He began gathering his books and paperwork, creating a protective wall of knowledge, the words a link to what he had always believed in— and that was science. He was diligent as he documented his findings in his journal, keeping every thought, every written observation written on paper, then condensing it into outline form on his computer in a separate file. This gave him time to review and recount his findings, making sure absolutely nothing was left out.

"When did you change from the standard power supply to your super-charged invention?" Tracy asked. "And let's not forget all those pesky points of light that seek out, well, people, I guess." She was following his thoughts, watching him as he searched and then gathered items from around the room. She tilted her head, trying to read his journal upside down.

"I added in the graphene lattice matrix to the low-level IR motion tracking sensors, hoping it would give my system an edge. As I have said, it's new and I believe will be used in the future for its highly conductive properties. By replacing the CMOS element in the camera, it has improved the sensitivity. There I go again; I know you have no idea what I'm talking about." He looked down at his notes, then back, giving her a resigned look. "To simplify, I wanted to be a pioneer, since graphene hadn't been used with this type of equipment and technology. It's sort of like a turbocharging a car."

He went to the system monitor, pulling off the back panel, then clipping in a slender black column, attaching wires as he moved, and then with a click securing the cover plate back into place. "There may be just enough juice to start a conversation but not too much energy for them to stay." He continued to mumble to himself, the one-sided conversation incoherent at that point.

Tracy moved closer, looking at his handiwork. "Turbocharged, OK, that makes sense. They use energy to, you know, make things happen. Is this graphene difficult to work with?" Her eyes locked on the security monitor now as if it would start ticking like a bomb at any moment.

"Well, graphene is only one atom thick and not powerful on its own. Damn it, there I go again. Sorry. I won't bore you with the details. I work with it just fine."

Responding to his chuckle, perplexity moved over her face, making her look younger somehow, as she never seemed to be without focus or purpose. Here, she was lost, and it showed.

James's shoulders moved as if he were laughing silently, his smile widened, the pressure of the day finding an outlet in the busy work of this hopeful solution.

"Um, you lost me, anyway." She peered at the monitor's back panel.

"I can relate. Now you know how I feel when you talk about ghosts, interdimensional existence, manifestations, and people with one leg or no head," he said, smiling. "But, hey, I've learned some interesting hypotheses. Heck, I've even written some of your theories in my journal, which says something."

Tracy ignored the hint of sarcasm as she rattled everything off. "Lattice matrix, graphene, low-level motion tracking, scanning, soul capturing mother fucking cameras. I'm learning a great deal as well." With a very unladylike belch, she settled back in her chair, the green glow casting fewer shadows as the light shifted outside, the sun making an appearance from behind the clouds.

"Perfect. My technology creates a platform for spirits to manifest in this dimension, or until they can show up on their own without my help as long as their ectoplasm is charged up." He laughed heartily after this statement. "Maybe we'll write a book together. *Welcoming the Dead Through Technology* will be the title." He added, "*Without pissing off your spouse*. Yes, that would need to be the subtitle." He mused as he continued his work.

"Wow, ectoplasm? Someone's been doing their research." She laughed louder than normal at this statement, then snorted. "Haha, funny, Jimmy. So, are we ready? Oh, and did you turn up the volume on the voice thingymabobber?" She leaned in, inching her chair close, waiting.

"Yes, I turned on the voice thingamabobber, and I left everyone off the system but Jeffrey and Harold. Oh, and of course any new visitor will be recognized. I'm focusing on the main hallway. Have you noticed they show up somewhere near there?"

James focused as his fingers moved over the keyboard. A chime rang out. It was a test, yet even so it raised the hairs on his arms. Tracy jumped in her chair, eyes wide. Seeing her response, he gave her a reassuring smile. "Don't worry, I was just checking to make sure it's on." Now with the system back and fully functional for the first time in months, he questioned it. Hell, he questioned everything.

"How should we proceed?" James asked, sitting forward with one hand on his journal and notes. "Should we talk of Jeffrey, and you hold Harold's baseball and I hold the catcher's mitt while we call Mrs. and Mrs. Simmons?"

"Wow, yes, that would be ideal. Hopefully, if Jeffrey doesn't materialize, he may still hear you and hopefully hear them." Tracy picked up the baseball, cradling and rolling it between her hands.

James picked up the catcher's mitt, moving it closer to his computer, then he pulled out the piece of paper with the phone number to the retirement home. "Oh, wait," he said, jumping up and pushing his chair back so fast and hard that it rattled items on the desk. He moved quickly behind Tracy, turning on the security system, the light blinking bright green, then a floorplan filled the screen with their names appearing in the area marked OFFICE.

Back in his chair, he placed his hand on the catcher's mitt; warmth emanated from it even though the room was chilly. He looked at Tracy and called out, "Jeffrey, we are calling your mom and dad to say hello. If you want to hear them, come to the office."

He waited for a sound or indication that they were not alone—then shrugged, feeling a little silly. "From engineer to crazy guy calling out interdimensional travelers from another parallel world." He waved his fingers in the air while making a wooing noise like a boy playing trains. The wind outside was whining loudly through the trees, adding to the macabre feel of the day.

"Have you checked out the sky?" James pointed to the window. The intermittent patches of blue were gone, replaced with a dark gray stormy view.

Tracy stood, pressing her nose to the cold windowpane. "Hmm, we just need a crow or raven on the fence; after all, every official haunted house has at least one harbinger of death hanging out." A nervous, maniacal laugh escaped her, leaving a small foggy mark on the glass just as the house creaked loudly, as if embracing its new ghostly identity.

"Did you hear that?" She gasped.

Her gleeful enthusiasm was a bit unnerving, James thought, but her response confirmed why he knew she was the right person to help him navigate what was happening. He shrugged. "Old houses make noise," he said, shooting her a look over his glasses. He turned his attention to the phone. His hand didn't want to cooperate, punching wrong numbers and missing digits as he dialed the phone number at least three times. The ring seemed distant, with a tin-like quality, so James adjusted the speaker volume, causing the ringing sound to fill the tiny room. There was a clicking sound, then silence.

"Hello," answered a crackling, dry voice that sounded as if it resulted from many years of cigarette use. James looked at Tracy, who was leaning so far over the desk she was almost lying on top of it. James bent over as they strained to hear.

"Hello, is this Michael, Michael Simmons?" James paused. "Father of Jeffrey Simmons?"

No words, just a rustling noise, followed by a clank, as if the phone hit something hard, followed by more rustling. The faraway voice said, "Hello? Yes, this is Michael."

"Michael, my name is James Allen. My grandfather was your neighbor over fifty years or so ago." Silence. "Can you hear me?"

"Yes, I can hear you. You are Harold's grandson, you say?" There was a quality and frailty in his voice that made James want to clear his throat; it was tentative, quiet, almost fearful. "What can I do for you?"

"When I was cleaning out the garage, I found a letter you sent to my grandfather. I also found a catcher's mitt of your son's and didn't know if you wanted it back."

Silence. Then Michael stammered, "A catcher's mitt? Who is this?" His voice seemed to gain strength, perhaps with frustration.

"Yes, I found it in the garage. I'm Harold's grandson. My uncle was Harold Jr. He was friends with your son," James answered, looking to Tracy, who was looking around the room as if waiting for someone to appear.

As if on cue, a chime followed by a distant: HELLO, JEFFREY.

A subtle, familiar popping sound followed. James's eyes slid to the monitor. On the screen, he saw a blue pulsing figure in the hallway near the staircase.

The speaker on the phone buzzed as if the line was being muffled, then James heard detached words. "Seattle. Jeffrey. Catcher's mitt."

A female voice got on and asked, "Hello, who is this? James?"

His attention was on high alert as he looked back to the phone. Why was he calling? What would it achieve? Maybe this wasn't the best idea. He was questioning everything as guilt washed over him.

"Hello?" Mrs. Simmons's strained voice called out again. James hesitated, his hand hovering, then he picked up the receiver, disengaging the speaker.

"Yes, I'm James Jr. You may remember my father," James answered, eyes darting from the phone to the security monitor, watching the small figure as it stood still in the front of the house.

The smell of ozone had reached the small office. Tracy sat staring at the monitor and the blue pulsing figure on the screen approaching them. Her palms, then her fingers, began to tingle. The room was cold, but a strange warm vibration traveled up from the soles of her feet, twisting her stomach in knots, causing her to twitch, followed by a grunt, like someone had punched her.

He is just a boy, she thought. Yet, in her mind's eye, she feared the darkness, and her imagination was on overload. Her feet wouldn't move as the buzz in her ears grew louder. *Damn it, what's wrong with me?* She couldn't take her eyes off the name that pulsed like a flashing warning. He was just outside the office and, according to the system, just feet away. Closing her eyes, she blocked out the noise, attempting to squelch the sudden terror that kept her anchored. As she leaned back against the desk to steady herself, the static of the phone and the voice of Mrs. Simmons sounded as if it were in a long, faraway tunnel. James had set the phone receiver down and was staring at the monitor. His eyes slid away and caught her gaze, acknowledgment moving between them.

James snapped his attention back to the phone on the desk as the voice on the end of the line called out. "Hello?" Mrs. Simmons was still there.

Shakily, he lifted the receiver to his ear while he kept a laser-like focus on the monitor. "Yes, sorry," he said distractedly. "I just wanted to reach out, I mean, I know it's been a long time, decades, in fact." He paused, trying to pull his thoughts together. "Anyway, we found the letter and the catcher's mitt and wanted to see if you wanted them back. I think my dad would want us to, I don't know, say hello."

This wasn't going well, and he realized he was rambling.

"My dad talked of your son," he continued. "And, well, I thought you may want to know we found something of his."

There was a long silence as his attention was again pulled back to the monitor, where the pulsing figure was now moving back toward the front of the house. A burst of color, like a soap bubble popping, and another figure appeared at the other end of the second-floor hallway where PNI pulsed slowly.

"What the hell," he said under his breath.

He leaned across the desk and poked Tracy to get her attention. Tracy had seen the new figure pop onto the screen, causing her mind to race. She was unable to move as she speculated as to who or what it was.

She gave a sidelong glance to James and, with a tip of her head, hesitated before walking out of the office and into the darkened hall. James saw three figures now on the monitor screen: Tracy in the hallway on the way toward the front of the house, and the figure titled JEFFREY moving up the stairs and stopping just short of the second-floor landing, where the new visitor stood near the attic stairway.

Mrs. Simmons broke the silence as if talking to herself. "Jeffrey had a catcher's mitt. Yes." There was a strength in her that Mr. Simmons lacked. There was another long deafening silence. James was on his feet, not knowing what to do. Should he hang up and go to Tracy? He stared at the phone, wanting to shake it, sending his frustration to the woman who held the receiver thousands of miles away.

"The mitt," Mrs. Simmons said, her words purposeful and much clearer. "The catcher's mitt was buried with my son over fifty years ago."

"Fifty years ago." He murmured as if in a trance. The words hit him, drawing him back as he stared at that phone, which crackled from the weak connection.

Footsteps above moved quickly, faded, and then stopped. James stared at the ceiling. The shadows from the tree outside created dark fingers, reaching across the plaster when a gust of wind shifted the branches. His heart jumped, bringing his thoughts back to the room and the phone call.

"Hello?" the voice of Mrs. Simmons called again.

"Oh, sorry, bad connection." He reached for words, needing time to think. "I guess it was my father's. Sorry to bother you. If you are ever in Seattle, let us know." James didn't wait for an answer; he simply hung up and went to the door. He glanced one more time at the screen; the new visitor was still on the second floor.

"Dad? Grandpa?" he whispered. Hope bloomed within him at the thought of seeing someone he loved, forcing out the fear.

Tracy's figure pulsed brightly at the bottom of the stairs. She wasn't moving.

"Go, go, go!" he said under his breath. "What are you waiting for?"

Letting go of the door jamb, he stepped into the hallway. The air was thick; his movements were sluggish, like walking through a slow-moving river. Hearing nothing, he continued, stopping at the kitchen doorway. He glanced in; the light from the windows lit the cornflower blue in places, the rest of the kitchen disappearing into dim, colorless shadows, as if the painter of the scene had run out of pigment. It seemed like it took him forever to reach the staircase. Tracy was no longer there. He stood silent, listening for voices or footsteps.

He turned to the security alarm panel; the light was a steady green. In the living room, the only light, slipping in from around the edge of the drawn curtains, was a gray glow, giving shape to the objects in the room. James reached in, sliding his hand along the wall until he found the light switch; the brightness won over, allowing him to exhale.

Turning back to the stairs, he headed up with his back against the wall, taking each step slowly. At the top of the stairs, he took another deep breath in an attempt to quiet the internal noise. The doors were all closed but one. The attic door stood open slightly, the light making a pale thin rectangle at the end of the hall. With calculated, deliberate steps, he headed toward the open doorway. His heart stuttered in his chest when the space in front of him dimmed, as if someone or something was moving in the room above, blocking the light of the window.

"Tracy!" He gave a restrained shout, which disappeared into the void that stretched around him in all directions. Then, like when an airplane lands on the tarmac, there was a pop, and the release of pressure in his ears cleared his hearing. He pulled at an earlobe, cocking his head, listening for movement. Another distinct thud from above sounded like the shifting of something heavy, followed by a few steps and then silence.

As he stood, he realized he'd raised his arms a few inches at his sides, like a bird getting ready to take flight, protecting himself from the unseen to his right and left, ready to move. He lowered his arms and stood up tall, then walked up to Alena's door, opening it slowly. Mrs. Kelly was placed, as if sleeping, on the pillow of her made bed. He then moved to Jack's room, which was a bit more disheveled—the bed not made, his books open everywhere, with many piled at the door. This made him smile as he remembered back to his childhood room and the books he loved. *Like father, like son,* he thought.

He was leaving Jack's room when he heard steps in the hallway, causing a tingling sensation all over his body. Someone or something was just feet from him. His scalp prickled. James had a newfound appreciation for gut instinct, and his was now on high alert. He felt a vibration in the soles of his feet as he stood in front of the master bedroom door. A sense of foreboding moved through him as he placed his hand cautiously on the doorknob. A white lighting jolt moved through his hand and up his arm.

"Shit!"

At first, the flash of sensation registered as pain, but he realized it was ice cold. He pulled his T-shirt out of his pants and, using the corner of it, opened the door. It moved in slowly, as if someone was on the other side of it, pushing back. Determined, he leaned in with all his strength and opened it just enough to allow him to step into the room. The space was abnormally bright on the far side of the room, a sharp contrast of two worlds before him. It was like viewing two snapshots of the same space fifty years apart.

The side of the room closest to him was the familiar muted beige and shadowed tones of the present, the gray clouds outside the window offering very little light. The bed in the center of the room appeared to be split down the middle, a preternatural demarcation; the far side of it seemed to be electrified, as if someone had adjusted the colors to a setting of unearthly glow, giving the vision before him a strange, dreamlike contrast.

On the bright side of the bed sat a petite woman, her back to him. She appeared to be looking out the window. James inhaled deeply, his heart picking up the pace of his excitement, thumping against his breastbone as his fingers tingled.

A supernatural breeze stirred the curtains, but he felt no movement on his side of the room. The woman sitting on the bed didn't seem to know he was there. Her shoulder-length, mahogany-brown hair was styled in soft finger waves and moved in the phantom wind. The green flowered dress she wore had short sleeves ending a few inches above her elbow. Her hands rested at her side, as if she were preparing to rise.

His brain was on overload. The light was wrong. The room in all its details was wrong. He struggled to understand the scene playing out before him. On the far side of the room, he saw a cloudless, Tiffany-blue sky framed by delicate white and yellow flowered curtains. A white chenille bedspread with intermittent embroidered yellow flowers covered her side of the bed.

His muscles strained as he tried to move deeper within the room and closer to the figure on the bed, but he was held back, bouncing off air that felt impenetrable.

"Hello," he called, but it came out as a muffled whisper. The invisible wall absorbed his voice, keeping him out of a world where he didn't belong. He stood helpless, his hands caressing the air before him, trying to find a way past the supernatural barrier. As he did so, the word Jell-O came to mind.

It was like looking at a ship in a bottle. Stopping his effort, he stood mesmerized, taking in every nuance of the visitor on the bed. Her hands were beautifully sculpted, with long slim fingers, nails painted a bright ruby red, the skin flawless, void of the blemishes time and life would leave behind. Her arms were also clear, her elbows smooth. It was like someone had molded her into a vision from a dream or memory. Her dress seemed familiar; the green was the color of sage, the flowers small and white.

From behind him he heard a noise. James looked over his shoulder, the bedroom door still partially open, his view limited. He craned his head, yet, try as he might, he saw nothing.

When he turned back to the woman on the bed, she had changed position, moving ever so slightly, as if sensing his presence. Head turned, she was now in profile, her skin delicate and clear, her lips red and full, a few light brown freckles visible on her cheeks. James gave another shove against the invisible barrier, but to no avail. Then, an airbag epiphany as realization hit him. His world, already on full tilt, was now completely upside down.

"Mom," he whispered, the word disappearing into nothingness, resisting transmission.

Like an answer to his call, she rose to her feet, turning away from the window and meeting his eyes. She was wearing her pearls. A silent understanding, as if she could read his mind, passed between them. Smiling, she lifted her hand, touching the gleaming, delicate strand that hung an inch above her Peter Pan collar.

She then walked gracefully, almost as if she were floating,

around to the end of the bed, stopping at the edge of the chenille blanket and the end of her world. She looked down at where the rose-pattern carpet melded into the beige woven jute rug and then up to meet his eyes. The person he knew better than himself smiled out from a young woman's face. She nodded, as if acknowledging his thoughts, then shimmered, breaking apart into golden particles, and was gone, leaving the room engulfed in a sea of beige.

Chapter 44
Jeffrey

Jeffrey found himself in the entry hall. He felt as if he had forgotten something important, something he needed to do. The house was familiar, yet void of the bright yellow that usually greeted him.

"Mr. and Mrs. Allen," Jeffrey called out, his pattern set in the steel rhythm of his heartbreak and confusion. A melodic noise came from above him, like icicles falling to the ground, causing him to search for the source.

HELLO, JEFFREY. The security system scanned him on arrival. He was part of the framework and a recognized cast member of the household. He waited, hesitating, then the house pulled him in, tugged as if an invisible cord was wrapped around his middle, vibrating, illuminating his path.

"Harold?" The name of his friend was met with silence, the familiar emptiness comforting to him as he approached the stairs and stopped. A flurry of voices bounced off the walls to find him, his usual path to the second floor disrupted.

Turning away from the staircase and toward the source of the noise, he tiptoed toward the back of the house, pausing occasionally as he walked the long hallway, stopping at the framed photos of strangers that included a boy and girl he seemed to know but couldn't remember how.

As he approached the small room, voices tumbled out, all foreign to him except for one he knew well, separate from the others.

"Jeffrey?" The questioning voice of his father stiffened his spine as he flattened against the wall, trying desperately to become small. His father was talking, but the disjointed words were still unclear.

Jeffrey inched closer, peeking around the edge of the door, his father's voice like a beacon pulling him along. The door stood open; the tall, familiar man was talking to the pretty woman who always seemed to see him. Again, the familiar voice of his father filled the room.

The woman seemed to sense his presence; she snapped her head toward the doorway. Jeffrey needed to find Harold; his quest was always to find Harold, but his journey, like a dream, had included others of late, and that was confusing. Was he dreaming? *Do you dream of people you don't know,* he wondered? His father's voice continued to fill the air, but he could not see him. The woman turned; she was coming toward him.

Run! he told himself, but he hesitated as confusion enveloped him. *Run!* Invisible hands turned him, the panic lifting his feet back toward the front of the house.

Reaching the foot of the stairs, Jeffrey heard footsteps from the floor above. A vision of the attic playroom filled his head, just as the need to return to his usual route propelled him. Taking two steps at a time, his small legs stretching to accommodate his need, he made it to the top of the first set of stairs.

"Harold," he called out in a quiet, hesitant voice, but then stopped. The hallway was changing. Unrecognizable furniture lay in shadow against a beige wall on one side of the hall; the opposite side was bright as sunshine, the familiar cheery yellow comforting and familiar; a blurry line ran down the middle, like two different photos of the same scene, taken at different times, had been torn apart, and then different halves from each had been taped together.

The walls vibrated as they shifted and changed; a small table halfway down the hall rattled, coming into view, then disappearing. It reminded him of the funhouse his mother once took him to at the county fair. He was standing just a few steps from the second-floor landing when a noise from below drew his attention away for only a second. Someone was coming; they were coming.

"Mrs. Allen?" The quiver in his voice muffled his plea for help as he froze, his back against the wall, looking down the stairs. Movement at the corner of his eye snapped his gaze back to the second-floor hallway, where a brown-haired woman now stood on the yellow side of the hallway with her back to him. She was still, looking up the stairs to the attic, her dress gently swaying in a preternatural breeze, her hair lifting from her narrow shoulders. Her head turned slowly, as if she was listening; she seemed to be waiting for him. She knew he was there.

"Mrs. Allen?" he called again, the woman now in profile, recognition escaping him. This time there was more strength of purpose to his voice. The bright golden colors of the hallway were at war with the darkness that was moving in narrow tentacles up the walls and ceiling, devouring the luminescent pools of color that undulated like a dying animal in protest.

"Jeffrey," a voice called from below, rising with the stairs to find him. The tugging in his middle tingled, drawing him toward the dark-haired woman waiting there. He felt a shift beneath him, the carpet transforming from a mottled green and gold to an unfamiliar light brown.

"Jeffrey?" She spoke his name softly. He looked up from his feet as the dark-haired woman turned toward him. She was smiling, leaning toward him, the brightness of the yellow world radiating around her.

"He's upstairs," she said with a nod toward the attic door, the smooth melodic notes of her voice comforting.

She must be Harold's mother, he thought. But why did he have such a difficult time remembering? She looked different somehow.

"Mrs. Allen?" His voice was small and questioning.

She leaned in closer, her thoughts telepathically connecting with his own.

He's waiting in the playroom. Her message was clear as she touched his shoulder, guiding him toward the stairs. *Hurry.* She gave him a gentle push, which tingled much like the feeling that tugged at his middle.

The pulling sensation came again, the hand on his shoulder falling away as he stepped toward the open door. Squinting into the light coming in from the window above, Jeffrey continued up the attic staircase without thought or direction. As he reached the top, he noticed one side of the room lay in darkness, causing him to shrink back. There were scary things that filled the inky blackness, filling him with fear. He turned his attention to the bright side of the room and the welcoming warmth that spilled in. Much like the hallway below, there was movement in the walls and floor. Items rattled and shook as dark fingers reached out from the blackness, devouring all in their path, crawling toward the light. He stood watching as objects appeared from nowhere, absorbing the bright colors. The room was mutating before his eyes as the bright sunny day outside the window changed into a gray sullen sky.

A popping noise, followed by stillness.

"Hey!" a familiar voice called to him as the yellow walls disappeared like liquid being absorbed by a sponge into the beige, unfamiliar world. "I have the track together."

The voice came from a small shadowy figure who stood in the doorway of the playroom. The dark stormy day wrapped him in a pallet of blue and gray, hiding his identity.

As if on cue, the clouds parted for a moment, the pale light of the sun escaping to illuminate Little Harold, his clothing, freckles, and curls eternally unchanged from the day of the accident. He was holding his favorite green metal car, a soft whirring sound coming from the front wheels. He seemed at home as he rested against the doorjamb, the line between dimensions blurred and tossed aside.

A strange yet calm understanding came over Jeffrey and, without words, they both moved into the playroom, Little Harold leading the way.

As if scripted, they sat down together at the far end of the racetrack, legs crossed in front of them. Little Harold beamed at his friend, then gently placed Racer 8 on the downhill straightaway and let it go. The usually electrified track needed no assistance to propel the much-loved toy car.

It was as if no time had passed; the acceptance of circumstance and of their existence in this world was organic and natural. Jeffrey sat watching the car move in a calculated rhythm, slowing at the corner, then picking up speed, its journey set with no destination.

A dull thump from the next room broke the hypnotic susurration of wheels on plastic, followed by a shuffle of footsteps, interrupting the reunion. Their eyes shifted to look at each other. Jeffrey conveyed his panic to Harold without sound, in a world where words fell away, their use at times irrelevant. He was still fearful of the strangers he had encountered.

"We don't need to hide," Harold spoke aloud to get Jeffrey's attention as he stared at the doorway. Jeffrey turned back to Harold.

Just let go of where you believe yourself to be, Harold telepathically reiterated the message. *Focus on becoming invisible to them and not being, well, here. C'mon, focus, and they will not see you. It's always been that way here.* Little Harold's smile turned to a grin, then he refocused on the car, which was slowing. *You'll see. We can do a bunch of stuff. Quick, focus. She is here.*

With a click, light filled the space. With her hand still on the switch, Tracy surveyed the room from corner to corner, her eyes finally resting on the racetrack and the car that was still in motion.

"Jeffrey," she called into the now empty room. The familiar vibration was running up and down her arms and legs, and the hair on her scalp bristled. The smell of electricity and ozone floated in the air.

In the room, invisible to her, the boys sat watching, waiting for her to leave.

Chapter 45
Tracy's View

Tracy made it up to the second floor, then froze. The left side of the hallway was in the present. The contemporary neutral tones and small foyer table were familiar and in their place. The motion-tracking camera near the ceiling faded and appeared again as the walls warped and shifted. The other side of the hallway was a shocking bright yellow, the crown molding a luminous white. She instinctively moved to the guest bedroom she occupied and turned the knob, which tingled in her hand as she pushed the door open. It moved only slightly. She tried again, but it remained frozen in place. Peering through the crack, she saw a strange space painted a mint green, a comparably cool tone in the bright sunlit room. To the left she saw the edge of a maple dresser and to the right a patchwork quilt of blue, white, and pink on what looked to be a full-sized bed.

"Holy hell, shit balls, this fucking house," she said under her breath as she forced her hollow legs to move. Her feet were blocks of wood and the floor a moving river. She had a hard time standing, as if the world with yellow walls were pushing back, the dimensions of the second-floor corridor colliding, each fighting for existence. The safety of her contemporary monochromatic world was disappearing by the second, each step taking great effort as the thick sting of ozone floated up from the floor, filling her nostrils. She continued forward the best she could, staying on her side and in her time.

Something was building, she could feel it. Fear tugged like a whirlpool. Her heartbeat sped up, breaking its normal rhythm with an occasional pause so great that she wondered if she had met her end. Closing her eyes, she concentrated on blocking out the chaos. *Focus, girl, focus,* she thought. *Please, dear God, don't let me have a heart attack; I'm not ready to leave this world.*

"Tracy." A voice—vapor thin and sounding miles away—brought her back from the hole she was falling into. James was right behind her, pushing her to double her efforts, giving her strength for what lay ahead.

Maybe turbocharging wasn't such a good idea, Jimmy, she thought.

"God help me," she moaned as she reached the attic stairs and started to climb.

She navigated the attic, knocking over a box before turning on the light. The playroom was empty; just the slow, dying movement of Racer 8 remained. She picked up the metal car. It was very warm to the touch, and she turned it over in her hand as she scanned the room, her eyes landing on the toy plane, which rested on the blue duck-cloth trunk. She heard a noise coming from below. Pausing, she surveyed the room one last time before turning off the light and leaving to look for her brother-in-law.

Chapter 46
Friendship

Descending the stairs, Tracy emerged to find the walls solid, the familiar dull colors where they should be, the hallway table in its place. Just then, James emerged from the master bedroom, rubbing his hands together as if to generate heat.

"Did you see the walls?" Tracy asked.

A quizzical look came over James, followed by a grin. "Walls? No, I admit that when this shit happens, I get lost in what I'm focusing on, but I did see my mom. She was the other PNI in the system. When I made it up here, she was sitting on the bed in our room. God, she was so young, oh, and she has her pearls back." He looked back into his bedroom, his eyes glimmering.

He was like a boy on his birthday who has just opened the biggest present ever. The joy of his encounter gave him a lightness, a palpable air of happiness. Continuing, he spoke slowly as he recounted his experience, "Wow, she was beautiful. Now I know why Dad fell head over heels. I mean, she was always beautiful to me, but, let me tell you, Gene Tierney had nothing on my mom." He closed his eyes as if to capture the scene like a snapshot in his memory. His body swayed, and he opened his eyes.

Tracy beamed at him as he relived the encounter. "It's like they're bouncing back and forth from their world to ours, almost like it's nothing to them," she said. "But I worry as they grow stronger; I worry about the darkness that lives like a parasite off not only their energy, but ours, sucking away at our strength. Don't you feel drained?" She looked down at her hands, rubbing her palms together as she questioned her own well-being.

James ran his hand over his face; he indeed felt unusually exhausted. He could also smell the sour sweat that clung to him. "I don't think it's that easy. I think Mom is still in that world. I tried to get close to her, but her side of things, well…the room was not of this time or at least not her half of it. It's not like when Grandpa was here in our hallway."

He tallied the information in his head, intending to catalog it in his journal and study it. He had a strange, faraway look as he rattled off his observations, the reality of what he had just experienced sinking in. "It looks like they can enter our world." He shrugged. "But we can't enter theirs."

"I think that's because we still travel in a body suit. In other words…we're not dead yet."

"Hmm…" He scratched his head. "And, you know, it was as if she could read my thoughts. Well, let's add telepathy to the list." He mentally checked off the myriad of things he would need to investigate.

"Yeah, well, there are documented cases where the ghost or spirit responds to the thoughts of the living human in the room. It's just a theory, but I think spirits just choose to speak to us, so we don't freak out; they're keeping up appearances, so to speak." She returned his smile, his happiness contagious in spite of the fatigue, matching her own measured excitement.

James was silent, hands on his hips, as he gazed down the hallway. Feeling her stare, he snapped back to attention and looked down at Tracy, grinning up at him.

"Someone is a believer," she said and started to sing a tune mimicking an old Monkees' song as she poked him in the middle, teasing him. Overcoming her fear from earlier had her almost euphoric.

"Hey, now." He pushed her hand away and rubbed his stomach where she had jabbed him. "So did you find Jeffrey?"

"I saw him. He ran up the attic stairs, but when I got to the playroom, he was gone. That damn car was circling the track. I don't know, maybe…" She trailed off in thought as she continued thinking of Racer 8, now the focus in her mind.

"Maybe…" She shrugged, then rubbed the back of her neck. "It takes a great deal of energy to be seen, remember, and the fact that they seem solid, and for so long, tells me that something in this house is giving them abilities, like a huge battery."

She looked up at the IR motion-tracking camera, the red light reminding her of its presence in the dark ceiling corner. She waved at the corner. "So, give them some more juice, make them strong enough to show up on camera. Then they will not just be scanned but recognized and, voilà, you have created the largest paranormal experiment ever. Who would have thunk it, my brother-in-law?" Her shoulders moved in silent laughter. Then she stood straight and saluted.

"OK, yeah, it's ironic, haha. I know, but let's get back to how they turn invisible. You say they can disappear and still be here or they may have gone back to their plane of existence?"

"Well, I'm not sure you can rig your system to track them when they move to their dimension. But even when they can't be seen, there may be something there that can be tracked. Like a feeling or a smell in the room." She waved her hand above her head at both corner hallway cameras. "I mean, c'mon, you're the tech guy." She shrugged again, still staring at the camera, the red light suddenly giving her the creeps.

"Hmm, so how do I tell Jess that the number of family visitors is growing?" James was talking to the air, as if he knew what the answer would be. Excitement of discovery, pressure, responsibility, and fear were all byproducts of a system designed for safety, which now seemed to be exposing what lay on the other side of their world. He'd inadvertently created a large looking glass into a parallel dimension many suspected existed, capturing the evidence in treasured snapshots, video clips, and electronic voice phenomenon recordings. What he'd discounted as fantasy now fascinated James, moving him to spend hours voraciously reading and reviewing paranormal and theoretical data, trying desperately to wrap his head around the world his sister-in-law understood so very well.

"We'll talk with her tonight after a few glasses of wine," Tracy said. "No, make that a bottle or two, and after the kids are in bed. No reason to discuss things in front of the kids."

"Yes, we'll approach it delicately." His happy demeanor wilted just a little. "But I'm not sure we have enough wine." He made a dismissive noise in his throat. "I'm off to my office. I'll turn off the system and start reviewing data. I need to wrap my head around what the hell happened, see how much was captured." He shook his head in an attempt to rid himself of his tunnel vision.

"I'm sorry, are you OK?" he added, resting one hand on her shoulder, embarrassed that her well-being was an afterthought.

"I'm good, just drained." She lifted the shoulder of her shirt with her opposite hand, sniffing in the direction of her armpit. "Whew, and ripe." Her face twisted in a look of disgust. "Sheesh, I'm off to take a shower." She was in step with him, needing to document the events while fresh in her mind.

Chapter 47
Home Home Home

J essica had a late teachers' meeting and called to ask if there were anything needed while she and the kids were out and about after school finished. They needed to stop at the library and the grocery store before coming home. This gave James and Tracy time to make notes and review and replay the monitoring and motion-tracking system. It was important to give an air of normalcy, the calm before the storm that would be Jessica after the day's events.

The obnoxious smells they had come to expect with the ongoing strange phenomena took some time to retreat. Tracy opened the windows, allowing the windy Northwest day to cleanse the air. She had enough time to shower and transfer her findings to her laptop. A strong pot of coffee would help compensate for the extreme exhaustion that made her bones ache and muscles burn.

Her laptop, sitting on the kitchen table, had only thirty percent battery left. Her charging cable was in her room, but she could enter her notes and plug in when she retreated for the night. She was working out her thoughts, trying to formulate her experience, hoping it would make sense, but she was tired, scattered, and overwhelmed, with no path of clarity. If she didn't take her time, it would read like the ramblings of an insane person.

Opening her laptop, she stared at the blank page and the pulsing curser. Her right hand sat resting on the keyboard while the other lifted her coffee cup to her nose, letting the aroma drift up, filling her nostrils.

A sudden noise and gust of cold air came from behind her. The mudroom door hit the wall and the wind rushed in, scattering her notes so forcefully that it pushed her laptop six inches forward before stopping smack in the middle of the table, as if an invisible hand were trying to wipe the table clean.

"Are you done?" she asked, her words tinged with irritation and weariness as she turned, expecting to see James.

The kitchen was empty but for scattered brown leaves that tumbled in on the wind. The door bounced once, then twice, before slamming shut.

"Fuck!" Her hand began to tremble. Glancing down, she saw the coffee in her cup pitching from side to side like waves in a storm. She grabbed the cup in both hands, trying to steady her hold and keep the contents from spilling onto the floor.

A hot warmth swirled around her like a large industrial oven being opened, moving her hair and T-shirt. She stood still, and her heart raced, jumping in her chest and making her light-headed. The spirit realm never frightened her, not like this.

A sensation of breath on her left cheek caused her to drop her cup, spraying her legs, the floor, and the lower cupboard with coffee. For a moment it looked like dark blood in the dim light. Icy sweat pooled between her breasts as a sudden bone-chilling cold pushed the heat from the room. Her breath rolled out in clouds as gooseflesh rose all over her body.

A rasping inhalation followed by an exhalation of breath rose and fell through the kitchen. She instinctively covered her mouth, knowing she wasn't alone.

There was a strange pulsation in her feet, starting with her toes.

It was different from the vibration she'd feel right before some of the recent supernatural events. Accompanied by heat, the pulse slowly moved up her body. Then a darkness, like a curtain being dropped over her head, blinded her. She opened her eyes and saw nothing but small flashes of light, like exploding stars, appearing at the edges of her vision. Terror like she had never known took hold, overshadowed by an angry, red-hot rage that was not her own.

She began to wave her arms wildly, hoping to fend off the entity that shared the kitchen. The flashes in her vision connected as parts of her sight returned. The sound of breathing moved, retreating in the direction of the mudroom, filling the space with sound as it went. The back door flew open, rattling the glass in the door and stirring the curtains above the sink as if waving a white flag.

Then the rage that had filled her was gone.

"Shit!" she yelled, this time to be heard. "I mean what in the fucking hell?" Tracy stared at the open door. She looked down at the mix of leaves, glass, and coffee while rubbing her cold arms. Now she knew without a doubt that there was something to be fearful of, and it knew she was there sniffing it out.

"You don't scare me!" She threw her head back as if her words could penetrate the plaster and wood. "Nope, you don't scare me," she mumbled under her breath. It was more of a confirmation to herself than anything else as she bent down and began carefully picking up the larger pieces of the obliterated coffee cup.

Chapter 48
Child's Play

Dinner consisted of homemade pizza slightly burned around the edge. The small kitchen television tuned to the Hallmark Channel was showing a Christmas movie that was months out of season, irritating everyone but the kids, who thought Santa was cool every day of the year.

Homework complete, Jack asked to read in his room. That wasn't unusual for Jessica's young bookworm, yet it didn't escape her that he grabbed several additional cookies before she excused him for the night.

"I'll be up to tuck you in," she said as he disappeared from the kitchen, a new stack of library books bulging under his arm.

Alena seemed distracted, picking at her food. Even Mrs. Kelly didn't finish her dinner of a few almonds. "Sweetie, you OK?" James asked, patting his daughter on the head.

She shrugged. "Yeah, I guess." Her eyes focused on Jack as he left the kitchen.

"What is it, honey?" Jessica took the chair next to her daughter, watching as she picked at the lone remnant of the cheese and veggie pizza, pushing it little by little to the edge of her dish.

"The boys won't let me play with them."

"Boys? What boys, honey?" Jessica slid her eyes to James, who looked out of the kitchen and into the hallway.

Alena shrugged again, flicking the last bite of crust off her plate, where it tumbled to the floor. Her green eyes sharply glared at the empty plate, as if it was the reason for her anger.

James and Jessica's eyes met, their ability to read each other's thoughts a superpower when it came to the kids. In unison, they both looked at their daughter, still staring at her plate.

"Want to watch your favorite princess for a bit before bed?" Jessica asked quietly while tucking a curl that had gone rogue behind her daughter's ear.

Alena gave a quick enthusiastic nod of agreement, then pushed away from the table. Tucking Mrs. Kelly tightly under her arm, she navigated around her mother, heading intently to the living room.

James watched his daughter walk past him, concern about her well-being in the forefront of his mind. She was still waking up in the middle of the night and tossing off her blanket—believing it to be scary—which would then create an excuse to crawl in bed with Mom and Dad. He turned with a nod to Jessica, following Alena. "Be back in a minute," he said, disappearing into the hallway after his daughter.

She heard the television turn on, then the sound adjusting as music swelled in volume.

"Hey."

A voice from behind her made Jessica jump and place her hand over her heart. "What the fuck?" she hissed through clenched teeth.

"Calm down, just me, sis," Tracy said. "Where's Jimmy?" She'd slipped in while Jessica was at the sink rinsing dishes, a look of concern knitting her brow.

Jessica looked up from the dinner plate she was holding. "Um, what happened to one of my favorite coffee cups?" She nodded at the remnants of the stoneware cup in the garbage can.

"Yes, but not our room, and that's what I find fascinating. Up until now, they have been here, you know, in our time. As hard as I tried, I couldn't enter her side of the room." His enthusiasm turned to frustration, and he spun around, writing in his notebook again as if he couldn't wait to document some revelation.

"Oh, wait, wait, can you go back?" Tracy said, hitting buttons and stopping the playback. She turned to James, who had his nose in his journal. Jessica stood, stunned, looking back and forth between them.

James stopped writing, as both he and Jessica looked down at where Tracy was pointing. "How far back do you want to go?" he asked.

"Remember when I said I made it to the attic playroom, and it was empty?" She pointed at the word PLAYROOM that glowed on the screen.

"Uh-huh," he said.

"Hit Play," she said quietly, as if any loud noise could change the outcome.

The figures pulsed, moving slightly within the room. They saw Tracy on the attic stairs and then all three on the third floor. When Tracy entered the room, she, Jeffrey, and Harold were just feet from one another.

"Stop there." She hit his arm again, shaking her finger at the screen, her voice rising, intent on making her point. "We were all in the same room together. Don't you remember what I told you? I was alone in the room."

"Yeah, hell, so we now know the system picks them up." He met her eyes, defeat settling in the lines that looked deeper than the day before.

Tracy continued, a tinge of frustration lacing her words, "Your grandfather said they see us, but we don't always see them. Your system allows us to know they are there even when invisible to us, but your mom disappeared just like the walls. I find it very interesting, don't you?" She looked up into the corners of the room. "Better get that in your journal, buddy, that we still don't understand everything that is going on. And have you picked up evidence of the entities that hide in the dark, you know, those dark things that hide in the corners? Have they ever shown up here?" She wagged her finger at one of the pulsing figures.

James looked at the screen, then back to Tracy, his irritation growing. "Nope, I've looked for those things, and they don't show up anywhere. I guess I can review footage from the beginning, but I don't think they can be recorded." He shrugged in an attempt to let go of the things he couldn't control.

Jessica collapsed into a chair, looking up at them. "I'm not sure if understanding anything is making my family safer. Now Alena is upset that our son and his friends don't want to play with her. I mean, what the fuck?" She shook her head, a red angry flush working its way up her neck, looking like a flower blooming. Emotional exhaustion was taking over, the circles under her eyes giving her a look much older than her years.

"What? Alena said Jack is playing with who? Harold and Jeffrey? When did she say this?" Tracy shot a concerned glance at her sister, the excitement in her voice now gone.

James stopped the playback. Walking behind the desk, he moved his chair to face them. The lamp distinctly flickered twice, like ghostly morse code, making them all jump before silence filled the room.

"We don't know what all this means." James was now back in charge of his senses.

Jessica didn't have a response as she stood rigid. She looked at them both, then turned and walked out of the room. "The children are my priority," Jessica could be heard saying as she was halfway down the hall.

Tracy leaned forward, placing her head in her hands, elbows resting on the desk. She felt like a ball of yarn being fought over by two cats. "She is right." She sat up, letting her hands fall. "Are we risking the family?" She added this knowing what had happened in the kitchen, that what she encountered was as evil as it could be, and she let out a sigh as if the last of her energy reserve had been spent on the thought.

James also felt the drain and ache of his muscles and bones as he sat listening to the house for any unfamiliar noise. They looked at each other, now weary, the darkness outside the window seeming darker and colder.

Tracy wrapped her hands around her shoulders and stood looking small. "Tomorrow is another day," she said as she left the room.

Alone in the room, James let his shoulders slump with the weight of the world.

Chapter 49
Dark Waters

The cold water swirled around him, tugging at his limbs. He opened his eyes, the inky blackness endless, with no reflection of any surface light. His heart was racing as he kicked and struggled against the undercurrent, which was pulling him down.

I must get to the surface, his thoughts raced, his chest compressing from the depth of the water, an ache moving through him as he sank. He struggled, his clothing moving in rhythm as if in tune with the water. *Help!* A silent scream formed in his throat.

Jessica, help! His inner plea silent, he couldn't speak. Invisible hands now held on as he gave one last futile attempt to scream, his eyes searching the darkness.

A hissing sound came from above as the cold fell away, the sense of water disappearing. Phantom hands pressed down on his arms and legs as a flutter of something brushed his cheek. His brain scrambled to clear as questions flooded his brain. *Was it a feather, a bird?* He took a shallow breath. The pressure on his chest felt like a slab of concrete across his rib cage. A puff of air hot in his face, a stench of something rotten and foul. He tried to turn his head but couldn't. Within him, he raged against the dream, terror seizing him as fingers tightened, digging into his flesh. His thoughts turned to his wife just inches from him. *Oh, God, Jessica.* He stopped struggling.

A low, jagged, phonetic whisper spoke slowly and with purpose. *Jesssssssica.* An inhuman hiss from somewhere above.

His fear flooded back, filling him with adrenaline and a wave of determination to rise from the nightmare. Sweat slid down his face, falling into his hair as he tried to move his head to the left toward Jessica. His muscles strained beneath his pajamas and against the unknown thing that held him in a vice.

A high keening replaced the sound of his inner cries, but it wasn't a sound Jessica had ever made: it came from within the room.

Then...release. The pressure was suddenly gone, his chest lifting and heaving as he greedily took in air, gasping. He sat up, breathing fast and deep. Pools of darkness gathered at the edges of the windows, the nightmare that terrorized and clung to him moving into his waking world.

Jessica lay still. Turned away from him, her chestnut curls were barely visible above the blanket. He didn't want to touch or scare her, so he focused on the gentle movement of her breathing, which was difficult to see in the dim room, but it was there, soft and steady; she was obviously unaware of the terror he had just experienced.

His senses were on edge; he could smell the sweat that clung, chilling him. There was a shuffling noise to his right. Turning toward the sound, he looked past the nightstand, where the depth of the darkness seemed vast and endless, an inky black hole somehow separate from the rest of the room. He swore he smelled something again, but it was brief, making him question his reality. It was just the remnants of his nightmare, he reminded himself, yet he could not take his eyes off the corner and the darkness that loomed.

Desperate to ground himself, he scanned from left to right, starting with the bedroom door, open about a foot, the hallway night-light giving a comforting golden glow a few feet into the room. He let his eyes roam, stopping at the closet door, the darkness within the opening no longer innocent, but a sinister hiding place for the unknown malevolent creature now stalking him.

He squinted, taking in his grandfather's highboy dresser, which appeared larger than he remembered, with a glint of polished, brass-accented knobs forming eyes that watched his every move. Along the wall were his work boots and running shoes, vague shapes on the floor landscape. His eyes were becoming more accustomed to the room, the veil of the nightmare disintegrating, allowing his rational brain to take over. He reached for the nightstand light, his hand still tingling as he fumbled with the switch. A soft click illuminated the space between him and the wall. The darkness was gone, his baseball bat mocking him. To the right of the bat, something out of place caught his eye. A small, jagged crack had appeared a foot above the floor, radiating toward the ceiling like a vine in search of light.

Getting out of bed, his feet felt inert as he hobbled toward the wall. The crack was about two centimeters at its widest point and stopped three to four feet up from the floor. His fingers traced the damage, looking for any corresponding defect in the ceiling. The home had settled over the years, but never like this. He reached up, rubbing his neck; his hand returned slick and damp with the remnants of his nightmare.

Jessica stirred, rolling to her back. "Jimmy, you OK? What's going on?" she whispered.

"Yes," he said, his voice raspy as his chest expanded, the pressure slowly ebbing away. "Did you hear or feel anything?" he asked, still facing the wall, his eyes tracing additional smaller cracks that he hadn't noticed before. They ran a few inches from the bottom, along the baseboard.

A hand touched his back. He jumped, pulling away with a guttural cry.

"My God, Jimmy."

His reaction startled her as much as her loving gesture of reassurance took him by surprise.

"Oh, Jess, I'm sorry, baby." He took a step back and sat down on the bed, careful not to sit on her. "I just had a bad dream, that's all, and I'm not quite awake." He twisted to kiss the top of her head. She scooted on her stomach to his side of the bed, trying to get a better view of the damage he was looking at.

"So, when do dreams cause damage like that?" Her question was direct and drenched in sarcasm.

"We must have had some settling," he said, hoping to sound reassuring, "or maybe a small earthquake and we both slept through it."

"Sounds like you're trying to convince yourself." She gave him a poke to his ribs, humor falling away as she looked at the damage. She pointed to the cracks that looked like the shadow of a small leafless tree. "How in the hell could we sleep through an earthquake strong enough to cause that?"

He could feel movement in the bed behind him. "Jess," he said, still staring at the wall. There was no response, so he turned to look for his wife.

Jessica had gotten up and moved to the end of the bed. She was standing with her back to him.

"I think I may need to get a structural engineer to check to see if there is any issue with the house; this is a big crack," he said in a matter-of-fact tone. He ran his fingers through his hair, the dampness pushing his thick curls back in a slick pompadour. "I don't know, maybe I'll need a contractor to fix it." He turned to her. She was still turned away; she hadn't moved. He stared at her. There was something wrong. He could suddenly feel the blood moving through his body, keenly aware of his mortality in that moment. She wasn't moving.

"Jess, honey," he called to her again, taking two steps toward his wife. She didn't answer. He saw her head tipped up slightly, as if looking at something in the far corner of the room, her hands in fists at her side.

He was within arm's reach but hesitated to touch her, instead calling her name gently. "Jessica, Jess?"

There was no response.

"Honey?" This time he reached out, pushing her curls from her shoulder, then settled his hand on her upper back. He could feel her heart pounding fast, the vibration moving up his arm in sync with his own as fear again moved over him.

He stepped closer; he could smell her vanilla-bean soap. Some of her curls clung to the beads of sweat on her face, creating shadows, obscuring her features. He followed the tilt of her head; there were no discernible threats that he could see. He moved next to her, following her line of sight.

"Honey, what is it?"

Her mouth hung slack, open about a half an inch, her eyes unblinking as she stared at something unseen to him. Turning her gently, he called her name again, shaking her shoulders, trying to get her attention. Her expression didn't change. He shook a little harder, his grip tightening.

She blinked, her eyes shifting toward his face, the empty stare leveling him.

"James?" She was now looking at him, seemingly bewildered. "What are you doing?" She pulled away, rubbing her shoulders where he had gripped her.

"You wouldn't answer, and it scared the shit out of me. What were you looking at? What did you see?" James turned her toward the bed, sat down, then guided her to take a seat beside him.

"I don't know. I really don't remember. I was looking at the wall with you. Then you were shaking me." She shifted her position on the bed, causing the springs to squeak in protest.

James reached out his hand, looking for hers, the warmth moving through him, pushing the nightmare down. He lifted her hand and kissed it. "Maybe things aren't safe. Maybe I should dismantle the system." The defeat in his voice reached her.

"It was just a nightmare. Let's get some sleep and worry about the house tomorrow. There may have been an earthquake; we are due for another one." Jessica stood up slowly and took one hesitant step, as if questioning her next move, before walking around to her side of the bed, throwing back the covers, and crawling in.

James sat on the edge of the bed, rubbing his chest where the weight had pinned him down. He was numb and confused as he surveyed the room.

"Hey." She launched a pillow at his back.

His skin was still crawling with gooseflesh, but he was coming around. "OK, Jess," he sighed. "OK."

Chapter 50
Midnight Visitor

Sleep didn't come. The remnants of the dream clung to him like pajamas made of rough burlap. No matter which way he moved, he couldn't get comfortable. His mind raced and his body twitched as if to continuously check on its freedom. Jessica fell asleep without issue, which made him question his entire experience. If something was wrong, Jessica usually sensed it; she was always aware of changes in her "mom barometer."

Moving slowly, so not to disturb her, he swung his legs over the side of the bed and looked at the crack in the wall, which was large and very concerning. The new jagged lines radiating toward the ceiling drew on his logical mind. He knew something was wrong and that dreams don't usually move into your waking world in so many ways. Just the thought of it brought back the sick smell that made his gut surge and head swirl. He closed his eyes, running his hand over his face as cold sweat prickled between his shoulder blades. He tried to forget the sensation of the ice encasing him, pulling him down into the darkness.

Slipping his feet into his slippers, he stood, his back cracking with the effort, his muscles straining as if he had run a marathon.

Stopping at the end of the bed, he watched Jessica under a jumble of sheets and blankets. He listened for her breathing, watching her body move gently with each exhalation. The glow from the light in the hall cut through the room near the bed; it was comforting. His eyes shifted as he searched the blackness far from the reach of it, the glow now a symbol of goodness against the evil that hid like a parasite escaping detection.

He felt surprised by the change of atmosphere as he crossed the threshold into the hallway, prompting him to look over his shoulder at the sleeping form of his wife. He hesitated to close the door behind him; doing so would entomb her much like in his dream. He shivered. He pushed the door, opening it farther, allowing the light to spill farther into the room, a shield against the unknown.

Turning down the hall toward the stairs, he purposely forced his shoulders back, the need to reclaim his house taking over. He stopped at Alena's door, which was slightly ajar, giving a dark glimpse of the very pink fairy-tale world in which she lived. The top of her head on her pillow was visible, next to the tail of her beloved squirrel. A release of tension left his shoulders as he viewed his daughter safe in her room, a small dismantling effect of his nightmare.

He slowly closed her door and stood again listening, the faint ticking of the clock below in the heart of the house echoing his own heartbeat as if they were a part of each other.

The night-light in the hallway was not strong enough to illuminate the entire corridor, giving an illusion of a golden bubble in the middle that thinned at the edges in all directions. He squinted to make out the end of the hall and the closed door to his son's room about ten feet away, when footsteps came from behind him. He whirled in place, more an instinctual response than a calculated one. The hallway was empty, the end of it falling into blackness, framing the attic door, which was open, a gray glowing rectangle floating in midair, an optical illusion that greatly unsettled him.

He stared at the doorway, senses on high alert, his eyes reflexively looking to the dark motion-tracking camera at the end of the hall, staring at him like an evil black eye mocking the growing fear of his creation.

The need to check on his son was now overwhelming. He moved quickly; as a tall man it only took a few large strides to reach Jack's room. He stood on the other side of the door, anxiety coming over him as he reached out tentatively for the doorknob. A sharp, cold jolt of sensation moved up through his hand and wrist, causing him to pull back.

"No, no, no," he muttered under his breath, a rush of noise filling his head. The house seemed to move in response, and the vase on the hallway table rattled against the wood as if in agreement. His hands trembled as he used the bottom of his T-shirt to twist the handle and open the door. The room was in deep shadow, the dim hallway light only penetrating a few feet.

There was the now familiar but faint smell of ozone as it wafted around the room. Then a sense of something moving past his shoulder alerted him that they were not alone.

In the bed he made out the small figure of his son; to the right his desk was a square gray shape in the gloom, the topography of its surface covered with books. The desk chair, normally pushed within the kneehole, was against the wall opposite the bed. Navigating the room wasn't easy. He shuffled his feet slowly so as not to trip or bump into anything and injure his shins, not an easy task for a large man in a small, dark room. He stopped for a moment, letting his eyes adjust, hoping there would be no need to turn on the light.

He heard his son breathing. The faint but distinct smell of electricity reminded him of the danger and amplified the anxiety that wrapped around him like a cold blanket, remnants of his nightmare holding on. What was truly shocking was that the temperature of the room dropped dramatically after he entered. Even in the dark he saw a plume of air swirl as he exhaled.

The preternatural coldness touched his skin as he realized there was someone or something now occupying the chair facing him, the head and shoulders outlined by the dim light of a distant streetlamp as it made its way into the room through the small separation between the curtains.

Recoiling, he took two steps backward, his calves hitting the edge of the bed frame, the sharp pain making him yelp. He turned to look at his son, who lay unmoving. A shuffling noise drew his attention to the corner farthest from the window, his heart jumping once, then one more thump, erratic and skipping beats before returning to its natural rhythm. He wiped at his face with the back of his hand as beads of sweat tickled his brow. Then the fear fell away, replaced with anger and a deeply ingrained instinct to protect his son. He sidled to his son's desk in search of his small planet-themed lamp. His fingers were cold and numb as he fumbled in the dark.

Fuck, it's cold, he thought as he searched for the push button on the base, then found it. With a click, the soft light filled the space, erasing the dark sinister shape that had occupied the chair. Had he been imagining things? No, he could feel it. There was someone or something there in the room with them.

Jack, who'd been sleeping on his side, remarkably undisturbed with all the ruckus created by his father, rolled over, sleepily rubbing his eyes, then lifting himself up onto his elbows, curls standing on end as if charged by an invisible helium balloon.

"Is it time to get up?" he asked sleepily, wiping at his face as if to clear away the confusion.

"No, buddy, it's still nighttime."

Jack looked at the chair, then to a chocolate chip cookie sitting on a paper napkin on his desk. Next to it was an empty napkin that held the ghostly outline of grease and a few crumbs where a second cookie had been.

"Did you bring a cookie for your great-uncle?" James asked while trying to smile.

"Yes," Jack said in a voice just above a whisper and tinged with guilt as he sat up straight, folding his hands in front of him. "He says he likes cookies...but he never eats the ones I bring him." He glanced at the remaining cookie.

James inspected the contents in the small wooden wastepaper basket. The basket was empty but for a few gum wrappers.

"I sometimes eat them when he doesn't. I didn't have time to eat that one." Jack knew instinctively his father was looking for the remnants of discarded cookies.

James relaxed his shoulders, the thought of his dead uncle refusing to eat the cookies...well, it made him chuckle. Pulling up the small desk chair, he hesitated, then sat across from his son, placing his hands on his knees, knees that seemed a little weaker than they were the day before.

"Do you see him often, and, if so, where do you see him?" he asked, the question sounding like an interrogation, but he needed to get some answers. "I mean, it's OK." He tried to soften his approach, scooting the small wooden chair closer.

Jack gave his father a half smile, his brows pulling down in thought. "Um, well, I see him almost every day." The words were quiet, his eyes shifting from his father and then back to his hands, which were now picking at a loose thread in his bedspread.

"Every single day?" James felt his stomach tighten, the ball of tension and fear returning, seeming to double within. He felt his face flush with anger at himself for not keeping his kids safe, for not questioning Jack when he would see him sneak extra cookies, and for all the time his son seemed to be distant, spending much too much time alone in his room or upstairs in the attic.

"Sometimes up in the playroom," Jack said. "Then sometimes I wake up and he is sitting in my chair." He glanced at the chair his father was now sitting on. Jack fumbled for words while he worked the bedspread between his hands. "I've asked him to go outside and play ball, but he says he can't leave. There's now another boy who is with him sometimes…" He trailed off again, his eyes focused on something over his father's shoulder.

"Is his name Jeffrey?" James leaned closer, looking into his son's face, his fear masquerading as compassion. His voice registered just above a whisper.

Jack looked down, shifting his gaze, looking up from under his lashes as he gave a sharp nod. "Yes."

The words that fell from his son's mouth rang like a fire alarm in James's head. He feared there was a dangerous cliff that lay before his family, an abyss that might swallow them whole. Realizing he'd been holding his breath, he slowly let it out through his nose. He shifted his gaze, looking out the window as he calculated his next line of questioning. The chair he was occupying wobbled slightly beneath him, with an audible straining noise like a branch getting ready to give way, as he sat on a much too small seat and on way too thin legs. Feeling like Alice in Wonderland, he adjusted himself, wondering how long before he found himself on the floor atop fragments of wood. He looked back to his son, who now seemed even smaller to him.

"Can I say hello next time they're here?" James clasped his hands while resting his elbows on his knees, trying to look casual. *A sad attempt,* he thought, but he was desperate to remain in control.

Jack sat up a little taller, his shoulders lifting as he realized he wasn't in trouble. "They can't leave." His words hung in the air; he didn't realize the weight of them.

"They can't?" James responded as ice filled his veins.

Jack shrugged but heard the concern in his father's voice, again looking down at his hands as he picked at an invisible thread. "They don't know why they're here. They say they're stuck."

James warmed as he remembered that these were just kids. Simply kids. *How could they hurt anyone?* he thought.

There was an audible pop, a flapping of curtains followed by a subtle movement in the room. From the corner of his eye, he saw Jack's red sneakers next to the bed shifting slightly as if occupied. At the same time, the pencils on the desk rattled in their cup holder. It was as if the house was responding, acknowledging the needs of all who resided within: past, present, living, or dead.

Jack followed his father's gaze, shifting between the red sneakers and his desk. "What was that?" he asked.

"I think the house is settling a little, that's all," James said, attempting to be reassuring, but he knew his son saw the bewilderment that crossed his face. "Go to sleep, buddy. I'll make pancakes in the morning, OK?" James forced a smile. Morning Dad was making an early appearance, but he wasn't sure if it was to calm the fears of his son or himself.

Chapter 51
Morning Menu

James retreated to his office, his place to think. It had always been his ship in the storm of life, but for the first time he felt his vessel sinking. Opening his journal, he began to feverishly document the night's events while they were fresh in his mind. He was a measured man of numbers and common sense who found himself battling a supernatural-tinged nightmare even on paper. He was strongly aware that anyone reading his journal would conclude the unraveling of his sanity with each written page. He sat, pen in hand, not knowing how to proceed, how to sound rational in his now unstable and irrational world.

He woke with his head on his forearm, resting on his open journal. The morning sunshine streamed in, illuminating the green glass of the lamp, which glowed in sad competition.

Voices rolled in from the hallway. It was his children. Their normal banter and the squeaking of chair legs on the floor told him the world was in motion around him.

"OK, Jimmy, let's see how good of an actor you are," he said as he got up, pushing away from his desk. He smoothed his hair the best he could and wiped his hand over his face, dislodging a paperclip stuck to his cheek. Reaching deep, he focused hard, pulling from what energy reserves he had left, praying he would get through his next performance. Morning Dad stumbled a bit but made a grand entrance, considering he was running on gas fumes.

"Good morning, Allen family!"

The room was quiet.

"OK, tough crowd this morning," he said under his breath, looking at the faces of his children, who stared blankly at the television, which was on but with the sound off. Alena and Jack sat side by side, Mrs. Kelly occupying the empty chair next to her human. She was sitting on a stack of books, her nose and tail poking above the table.

James, dazed and sleep-deprived, his eyes burning, began looking for pancake mix in the lower cupboard. To his right he noticed the handle of a wooden spoon peeking out from the top of a large, orange, ceramic bowl. On the counter next to it was the box of Cream of Wheat and the can of Ovaltine that had mysteriously appeared weeks before.

"Hmm, what's this?" he asked, a cold shiver running up his back.

He turned to his kids, the can of Ovaltine in hand, to ask the obvious question, yet it was one he didn't want to know the answer to.

"Did you get these things out?" Holding up the can, he gestured to the box on the counter.

Jack and Alena looked at their father, then each other, and shrugged in unison.

"So, nobody knows how this stuff made it out of the cupboard and onto the counter?" This time Morning Dad was gone, replaced by Stressed Out and Weary Dad.

"They wanted us to try, well, that stuff." Jack pointed at the counter, not sure if he would upset his dad.

"Yuck, they like the icky stuff," Alena said, her nose crinkling as she looked at the box of Cream of Wheat. "We don't want it; we want pancakes and hot cocoa!" Her voice lifted at the end with hope.

"With marshmallows!" Jack chimed in, his curls standing on end. He furrowed his brow, eyes pleading as he looked across the table, hoping for support from his sister.

James chuckled despite himself, even as his head started to hurt. "So, that's why you have the gloomy faces this morning. You think you have to eat Cream of Wheat? How about pancakes and Cream of Wheat? I can make both. How about that?"

He thought better of it, not knowing if magical food from a parallel dimension would have any nutritional value or even be edible. He moved the bowl, searching for another, when the sound of feet on the staircase caught his attention. Jessica looked drained as she walked into the kitchen. Her face was pale from lack of sleep, yet her hair was styled—her chestnut curls catching the light from the kitchen window—and she was wearing her favorite periwinkle-blue velour sweats. *Even tired, she looks lovely,* he thought.

"Good morning, Mrs. Allen," he said. His strained smile met her own as he grabbed her, wrapping his arms around her waist, breathing her in.

Tilting her face up, she puckered her lips, waiting for a morning kiss. He pulled back, his hands falling to her waist, and looked into her eyes for any hint of the night before, wanting to see recognition in them.

"Well, now, did you brush your teeth? I mean, if you're looking for a kiss." He tickled her waist and pulled her back in—wrapping his arms tighter—and kissed her firmly while patting her backside.

"Well, at least I don't have lines on my face. Let me guess, you slept on your desk," Jessica said, running her hand over a crease on his face where the journal had left a mark.

"Ick, mushy stuff," Alena groaned as she played with Mrs. Kelly, moving her across the table. "I'm hungry and so is Mrs. Kelly."

"All right, all right," Morning Dad exclaimed, pulling open a drawer that contained the chocolate chips and pushing the Ovaltine and Cream of Wheat to the side. "I think we need some of these in the pancake batter, don't you?" He shook the chocolate chips above his head like a maraca.

"Yes, we do."

A voice from the hallway caught them all by surprise. Tracy stood barefoot in her sweats, yawning, her hair disheveled, curls wild.

"We all need extra chocolate chips this morning," Tracy said. "And I don't know about you, but I need marshmallows in my coffee since I'm not having cocoa. Right?" A sleepy smile lit her face as she rubbed the heads of both Jack and Alena, their giggles erupting as she kissed each of them on the cheek.

Jessica filled the metal coffee filter and hit the brew button, placing the teakettle on the back burner of the stove. The smell of coffee burst into the air as she turned the television volume up, the sound of cartoon babies infusing the morning with artificial laughter. Normalcy had its pluses, and they needed a big dose of it this morning.

Tracy picked out three large coffee cups, placing them on the counter next to two small ones and filling the smaller cups with a packet of cocoa each. She seemed distant and dazed as she watched the dark brew splash and gurgle. Noticing the Cream of Wheat and Ovaltine, she picked up the Ovaltine and she turned it over in her hand, looking for something.

"Is this a retro can? Gosh, our mother talked about this stuff like it was the elixir of life." She looked over her shoulder at Jessica, who was sitting expressionless, her eyes fixed on the can in Tracy's hand. James grabbed the can and put it in the cupboard without comment.

Turning in place, Tracy followed him with her eyes. She narrowed her gaze, with a nod toward the cupboard.

What's going on? she mouthed to him with her back turned to her sister.

"I'll tell you later," he said in a low hushed voice, glancing at the table. The boisterous cartoon engrossed the kids, while Jessica sat, staring blankly at the coffee cup Tracy had placed before her.

"Everyone looks a little worse for wear," Tracy mumbled as she reached for the plates.

"Hell, I didn't sleep well," James said. "I had a very strange dream where I was sinking in a lake or maybe it was the sea. I don't know. Maybe I watched an old episode of *The Undersea World of Jacques Cousteau*, and it's been sitting in my subconscious." He gave a quick shake as if he could dislodge the nightmare that still clung to him.

Tracy hesitated to respond, lost in thought, looking at the plates in her hands. "Now what was that...oh, yeah, remind me, Jimmy, to look up the meaning of water in my super woo-woo dream book." She gave him a sideways glance, rolling her eyes.

James ignored her, stirring the batter and adding copious amounts of chocolate chips, not thinking about the ramifications of too many and the mess it would create.

"Yeah, I had a rough night," James said, pondering out loud as he leaned toward Tracy, his back turned to the table so as not to be heard by the rest of the family. *In a haunted house,* he mouthed.

James smiled—a broad, forced smile—as Morning Dad was back on the stage, pouring the batter with an exaggerated motion, the batter sizzling on the hot griddle.

"I think we need whipped cream, don't you?" he asked in the best upbeat voice he could muster.

The response did not match his effort. Jack simply lifted his fork, waving it over his head, a small *uh-huh* coming from Alena.

Chapter 52
Off Switch

Two long meetings, one after the other, took their toll on James. He'd never danced around issues or out-and-out lied so much in his life, and it made him feel guilty, tired, and distant as he separated from his past views, cautiously and reluctantly accepting his new understanding of the world.

Telling them that he needed to dismantle the system came as a shock to them, but he told them some old knob-and-tube wiring in the home was to blame, even though he'd replaced it years ago. Most of his team understood the issues with turn-of-the-twentieth-century homes, so they understood. This bought him some much-needed time.

With Little Harold knowing how to turn the system off and on, James really had no choice if he wanted to keep his family safe. If Tracy was correct and the system was most likely to blame, he must make changes. He was still looking at other theories, wanting to explore every avenue for answers, scientific as well as other less conventional pathways.

He wasn't really going to dismantle the entire system, not completely, just the connection to the main power supply. He could easily fix this once he identified the supernatural source of the problem. He had no idea if there was any hope, but he was holding on with both hands, pushing logic to the side for a while and sleeping with the lights on.

Chapter 53
Nice to Meet You

Jack knew Little Harold was his friend from the moment they had met. The kinship was evident as their time together grew, their similarities of manner and personality comforting. He also knew his parents didn't understand how hard it was for him to make friends at school. Others often made fun of him. Kids called him names like Book Brain and Nerd Worm, which was a silly, uninventive version of bookworm, Jack thought, but painful just the same. The love of the written word bound Little Harold and Jack, providing them with a feeling of inclusion, trust, and understanding.

After the treasured box of Little Harold's things was found in the Geek Shed, the link between them magnified, the unseen universal cord vibrating much like a spider's web as thoughts traveled on unseen paths, merging the two of them together within the eternal cosmos. There was a longing for connection from the moment Jack put on the faded green baseball jacket, a need to belong to something, to leave a lonely world behind and to finally shed the nerd badge that followed him no matter how hard he tried.

The night he first met his great-uncle, Jack felt filled with excitement at the prospect of a summer backyard campout. While eating dinner that night, his much-loved Aunt Tracy promised she would devise the plan as the family reminisced of past adventures, which included a large tent and a movie night under the stars.

Jack carried his great-uncle's jacket around with him everywhere when he wasn't wearing it. While in his room, he would hang it on the back of his desk chair, giving him a clear view while reading the latest library book in bed. Occasionally, he'd daydream of baseball and of the family he never knew. A few weeks after the installation of the new security system, Jack had fallen asleep in his room, the book he'd been reading tumbling to the floor, the small clip-on book light dislodging, landing just under the edge of the bed. The pinpoint beam stretched only a foot, much like a strange miniature searchlight.

He awoke, not sure what had roused him from sleep, the weak glow on the floor giving an eerie, alien feel to the room. As with any child, there was a fear of not only things that go bump in the night but also the monster under the bed. Jack was no different and took this danger seriously.

He sat for a long moment, his head fuzzy with the cobwebs of sleep. He used the palms of his hands to rub his eyes, trying to clear his vision and adjust to the darkness. He leaned over on his stomach, hanging his upper body over the side of the bed, his hands gripping the bed frame as he lowered himself about six inches above the floor. Subtle movement within the room directed his attention away from the floor. He saw his breath roll into the space before him, becoming part of the darkness that now terrified him. Closing his eyes, he held his breath as he gathered his courage.

In one swift move he lifted the edge of the bedspread, opening his eyes wide with the expectation of ghostly horror. To his relief, he found one rumpled brown sock—somewhat dusty—a broken number two pencil, a book on birds of the Pacific Northwest, and his slowly dimming book light.

Sitting up, he repositioned himself, holding the small light in front of him like a glowing fishing pole, scanning just a short distance in an arching motion. He narrowed his vision back to the bed in front of him, moving his feet to verify what he was looking at and then past them to the end of the bed and the edge of safety, the dark abyss only feet away making his heart beat faster.

As he moved the light slowly, he could only see fragments of objects as it scanned the room. The sleeve of Little Harold's green jacket on the back of the chair, the book he dropped on the floor, and then the light caught the edge of one unfamiliar black and white sneaker a few feet from the bed.

His heartbeat felt like a trip hammer as fear pulsated through him. Gripping the light as steady as he could manage, he slowly moved the beam up from the floor, catching a brief glance of a rolled jeans cuff.

The unknown sneaker, visible in the wavering light, suddenly moved, taking a step, and then there were two sneakers, side by side. Jack's shaking grew worse, the beam of the light now moved wildly and catching a flash of white T-shirt and then an arm. He tried using both hands, desperate to keep the light steady as the figure stepped closer. Jack closed his eyes tight.

"Nobody is there," he said under his stuttering breath as the electrical smell reached his nose. "It's not real." He was almost pleading as he steadied himself, then let his eyes fly open.

A boy was standing there.

"Hi." The voice was friendly and his visage familiar, though the visitor was foreign to him and out of place. Any immediate connection with old photos escaped Jack's notice. The warmth of his greeting contrasted with the cold shadows that swallowed the room.

The small beam of the book light resembled a vibrating halo as it lit upon the head, neck, and shoulders of the visitor. The face appeared open and kind. His brown curls faded into the background where the light fell away. Jack suddenly knew who was standing just a few feet from the bed. He'd seen him around. Flashes of him, like snapshots in the hallway and on the attic stairs. Jack had spent time studying his face in the old, faded photographs throughout the house. It was a face he knew.

"Harold?" Jack's heart froze as he gazed upon his great-uncle, who was smiling a big toothy grin, freckles visible on the bridge of his crinkled nose.

"Hi," Little Harold said, again waving one hand. "Didn't mean to scare you." He took another step forward, bringing himself closer to the bed.

For some inexplicable reason, calm settled over Jack. The fear slipped away, the strangeness of the visit replaced with the magic of it. It was something special, a club not anyone could belong to. It was like a visit from Peter Pan, who took him to a wondrous world that only a child would embrace and adults could know nothing about.

They sat in the dead of night, Jack reading out loud, Harold sitting in the chair across from the bed next to the window, sharing favorites like *Captains Courageous* and, of course, *Peter Pan*. They talked of adventure and their preciously held secret—safe from those who would not understand, and from the red-eyed monster tucked in the upper corners throughout the house, tracking their every move.

Soon after they met, both he and Little Harold figured out how to turn on and off the security system to avoid detection. Before that, the interdimensional traveler's movements between worlds had been recorded. With so much footage, Jack's father was much too busy and wouldn't spend the time reviewing all the hours recorded and stored unless prompted by an event, research, or a very good reason to do so, thus hopefully missing the late-night visits altogether. The other issue was avoiding detection from his parents and sister in real time. Though they spoke quietly, keeping their voices just above a whisper, Jack took additional precautions after almost being discovered by his mother one night while reading *Huckleberry Finn.*

At first, he would lock the door, but then thought a pile of books strategically placed in front of the door would give Little Harold enough time to leave yet was easily explainable, as Jack often left piles around.

When Little Harold dematerialized, he would step into the nearest closet, making it easier for his nephew to deal with his fairytale-like departure. Other times, when in a pinch, he had no choice but to simply shimmer like sun on the water, breaking into small sparks of light before winking out.

Little Harold's visits grew in frequency, and he mainly spent time with Jack in his bedroom or the attic playroom. When not discussing or reading books, they would talk of television and the shows they both loved, especially *Bugs Bunny.* They found themselves doubling over with laughter when remembering the antics of the trouble-making bunny. Relishing the familiar was comforting to them both. Their ability to recollect together was as great of a bond as the title "family" gave them. A few times they would sneak to the kitchen early in the morning when the security system was off to watch the Cartoon Network, with Jack introducing Harold to one of his favorite shows, *Dexter's Laboratory.* At the end of their visits, Harold would always circle back around to the show *Father Knows Best,* saying his dad, Harold Sr., was very much like the dad on the show.

Months later, Little Harold introduced the neighbor boy, and Jack thought two friends were much better than one, though Jeffrey remained quiet and distant most of the time. Both boys would wake him in the middle of the night and spend hours playing old games his parents kept on the storage side of the attic.

All three agreed their favorite game was Monopoly, and they would play this the most. At times, Jack needed to deal the money and move the game pieces if his new friends couldn't. They said their ability would come and go, depending on their energy reserves. Harold was good at buying up property, while Jeffrey and Jack ended up in jail more often than not. Only a few times were they almost discovered, forcing Jack to become a master at the quick stash-and-dash—as he called it—where he would quickly bend the board in the middle, allowing all the game pieces and money to fall into the box without order. He'd throw the lid on, though it didn't fit quite right, and hide the game behind a box of Christmas ornaments. He'd then pretend to be playing by himself when anyone stepped into the room, casually watching Racer 8 whirl around the track.

Once he offered Little Harold some hot cocoa with marshmallows, which Harold graciously declined, so Jack gladly finished both cups. He made sure to never do that again, as it made his parents not only suspicious, but angry, like when they found him sleeping late one night in the attic.

Both Little Harold and Jeffrey realized their appearance and disappearance would be frowned upon, even scary, so they made it a game to leave the room and go invisible, keeping the process away from Jack. To Jack, they simply would leave the room quickly, and he didn't push or ask questions.

The biggest hurdle wasn't his parents, but his sister. In the beginning, like Jack, she would catch glimpses of the boys as their worlds wove and mixed with their own. One night, when Little Harold was exploring, he entered her room, but the event was written off as a nightmare or dream.

Months later, she caught Jack as he slipped past her room on the way to meet with Little Harold and Jeffrey in the attic, and she followed him. She stood just outside the playroom door, watching them for some time before stepping quietly into the room. All three leveled a panicked glance between them, and Little Harold stood up, nodding to Jeffrey. To disappear in front of her would terrify and frighten her, and they knew this. They agreed that they would allow her to play Yahtzee, but only after she was sworn to secrecy.

Jack figured it was easier to make her think she was part of the club, rather than on her own, where she would have nothing to lose if she snitched. At first, she thought it was fun, but she never got the hang of the game and bored quickly, leaving them on their own. To her they were as real as anyone she knew, and she no longer questioned the strangeness of their visits or the time of night. She was part of a secret club and that's all that mattered to her. Ghosts, after all, were scary white moaning things that floated out to get you in the dark, much like when her blanket came down over her head. Both boys didn't resemble anything scary and therefore couldn't be part of that creepy Halloween world.

What puzzled Jack the most was where the boys went when they weren't together. Why did the shadows frighten them, and, of course, why on earth would they prefer things like Ovaltine and Cream of Wheat over his mom's amazing pancakes and hot cocoa? Several times, Jack offered to make these things, but Little Harold said it was the memory of them they missed, and they couldn't actually eat in what he said was "in this world."

"This world?" Jack asked, confused by the comment.

Harold looked at Jeffrey, then back to Jack and shrugged. He told him he would understand one day, a look of longing passing between the two dead boys.

Chapter 54
Darkness Sets In

Jessica didn't feel well. A dull, foggy feeling had been in her brain for days. *Maybe something was going around the school,* she thought as she turned on the coffee maker, the *click* and *hum* music to her ears.

"Coffee, coffee, coffee," she said in the predawn light of the kitchen.

Closing her eyes, Jessica rested her hands on the counter, the strain and tension moving up her back and shoulders making her feel like a rubber band about to snap. The smell of coffee was just as provocative as champagne when it came to her well-being, and this morning it was heaven.

She stood up straight, rolling her head again, hoping to release the stiffness at the base of her neck. After a light *pop*, she felt a warm escape of pressure down to her toes. She opened her eyes, reaching for the cupboard and a coffee cup. Her favorite, given to her by the kids, was large and trimmed in yellow, with *Mom* written in bold blue letters, the *O* replaced with a big red heart. She smiled as she looked at the cup, remembering the burned toast that accompanied the Mother's Day breakfast. Alena, then four years old, had been in charge of that part of the feast, and she was proud that she'd buttered each piece all by herself.

As she set the cup down, the room changed, becoming cold and dark, like a cloud blocking the sun. The word *Mom* disappeared as a black veil engulfed her vision, a smell of decay moving past her. It lasted only a second, but the hate that accompanied the temporary blindness was terrifying, like a blindfold being pulled tight, then yanked away.

She was strangely out of breath, as if she had been running. She felt drained. Her knees were weak. *Something is wrong,* she thought; *maybe I'm ill.*

Flopping onto a kitchen chair, she closed her eyes and concentrated on her breathing. The rhythm of her exhalations reassured her as she warmed up, the only smell the Colombian coffee. She'd shake it off before the rest of the house woke up, but she threw a packet of Alka-Seltzer in her purse in case her stomach protested during the day that lay before her.

Chapter 55
Frosty Greetings

Jessica had only one class on Friday, and normally she'd spend the rest of her day reviewing student work, creating future assignments, and meeting with those who were struggling, but today she couldn't face anyone. With everything happening at home, she was afraid she wouldn't be able to keep up appearances, even if it were just small talk. Avoiding the typical chitchat in the teachers' lounge, she gave an excuse of the semiannual migraine, gathered up her papers, and quickly escaped out the side door.

Arriving home after her morning class, she was alone. James was at the office, and the kids wouldn't be home until after three p.m. It was her time to decompress. She looked forward to the much-needed solitude, a chance to recharge, soak in the tub, and watch mindless television free of cartoon characters, but the home that she lived in no longer gave her comfort. There was now a cloud of uncertainty, a type of energetic agitation that covered the bright colors of home and family.

She set her tote on the counter and looked around the empty kitchen, glancing up at the corners before opening the cupboard and pulling out the teakettle—she'd often change to herbal tea in the afternoon once her coffee quota was met for the day. The room seemed abnormally chilly considering the warm weather outside, so she checked the thermostat next to the kitchen doorway. It was set on sixty-eight, but it felt like forty-eight, so she moved the lever up to seventy-two degrees. She heard a whoosh of air as the heating system came on.

She stared mindlessly out the window as she filled the kettle. Small red and yellow tulip buds had sprung up in the flower beds next to the fence, which gave her a sense of well-being. The running sink water added to the pleasant scene, reminding her of sound machines that played ocean waves as well as rain. Splashing brought her attention back to the kettle, which was full and overflowing. Picking up the kettle, she turned toward the stove, but movement to her left caught her eye. The window above the sink appeared to be fogging up. Setting the kettle on the front burner, she leaned in, looking closely, one finger touching the misty pane of glass.

"What the hell?" she said, wiping her cold, damp finger on a kitchen towel.

It wasn't fog at all; the pattern was that of ice forming, crystals of varying geometric shapes being born from one another, moving in from the edges and corners, the clarity of the window disappearing before her eyes. She noticed her breath was rolling from her in small white plumes. The temperature had dropped drastically. Her teeth began clicking together, sounding like ice tinkling in a glass as she began to shake.

Rubbing her hands together, she crossed the room, double-checking the thermostat, making sure she hadn't turned it the wrong way, but it was firmly set at seventy-two. Just then, she heard a crackling sound from behind her and wheeled around on her heels.

The window above the sink was now completely frosted over. More noise, like ice cracking on a frozen pond, drew her attention to the mudroom door, where the small rectangle of glass was alive with swirling movements. She whirled around again, looking to the large window next to the kitchen table, and it, too, was icing over from the edges, moving in toward the middle—the cloudy, fragile-looking frost obscuring her view of the outside world.

"Jesus." She turned in a circle, freezing tremors running through her body as she puzzled over what to do.

Instinctively, she ran to the front entry hall to inspect the security panel. Her hands touched the numbers and then the darkened blank screen, which was void of life. The system was off. The thought that it, whatever *it* was, no longer needed James's security system was terrifying.

She found herself in the living room as tears began to fall. Throwing herself onto the couch, she pulled her knees up, resting her chin on her hands, and let go. It had been years since she'd cried without fear of appearing weak—something she hated in herself—or thought of discovery, yet wasn't the inability to be authentic also a symbol of weakness? She was tired and confused. She was not only a momma bear but a wife, sister, daughter, and teacher. Her nerves were wearing thin, which placed her on shaky ground.

Her family was the thread that kept the fabric of her soul together, but equally important was what she and James wove together. He was deeply intertwined with her existence and as vital as the blood that ran through her veins. How could she walk away from his dream and not create a hole in their life?

The tears turned to sobs as her vision blurred, then the sobs turned to screams of rage and frustration.

"Stay away from my family, you fuck!" She clenched her fists so tight that her knuckles were white as she pounded her knees.

As if answering her cry, a rumbling sound came from above.

The fear she had been carrying solidified in a defiant roar. "I'm not afraid of you!" She was off the couch, the blood rising in her as she felt her strength return. Yet at the same time, she had never felt so alone.

Tracy was always the strong one, the person who thought outside the box, but she was changing. The light that filled her sister seemed to be dimming. Jessica was deep within a well of the unknown, and her husband was afraid to move forward, give up, or let go of his coveted project. The only saving grace was that her children seemed to be blissfully unaware of most of the supernatural happenings.

James and the kids would be home soon, followed by Tracy, who was working late at the museum. Jessica had a small window of time to wipe her face, apply cold packs to her puffy eyes, and think about what to do.

Chapter 56
Momma Bear

Warmth returned to the kitchen. The windows were clear again, and a sense of something resembling normalcy embraced the house on the hill. Jessica kept dinner light and easy, pulling a jar of marinara sauce and a can of green beans from the cupboard. She buttered sourdough bread, sprinkling it lightly with garlic and coating it with Parmesan for the kids' favorite cheesy toast. The smell of Italian spices filled the heart of the house, which was her intent. She wanted the familiar comfort of dinner to greet her family upon arriving home.

Still unsteady from earlier, she moved hesitantly from room to room, making sure one or two lights illuminated the spaces without switching on every available light source. She felt that light created a mood, a way of decorating, so she also lit two large candles, moving one to the sofa table and the other to the middle of the kitchen table.

The evening was cool and dark by the time she heard the car doors close outside. James entered via the mudroom door, followed by the children, stooped under the weight of their backpacks loaded with books, art projects, and homework.

"Hey there, mister," Jessica said. Her smile was slow but purposeful as she met his eyes. There was a long moment where they held each other's gaze while trying to gauge each other's mood. A bang from behind James made them both stop, startled. Jack had dropped his backpack and, with the number of books it held, it made quite a sound when it hit the floor.

"Sorry," he said, the hand that was holding the strap to the backpack still outstretched. Alena rolled her eyes at his clumsiness and scooted past him, propping her backpack up against the wall under the window, her typical spot for doing her homework after the table was cleared of the evening dishes.

Jessica rubbed her arms, as if cold, and stared blankly and unfocused into the mudroom.

"Hey, Mrs. Allen." James immediately noticed his wife's faraway and lost look. Not wanting to startle her, he touched her arm—giving it a gentle rub—then pulled her in, hugging her.

"Sorry, the wind is cold," she said, looking up into his face as he held her.

"You OK?" He held her gaze, trying to read her mood, noticing the redness around her eyes.

"I'm well. I'm fine…" She broke eye contact and twisted from his arms. "I gotta check on the bread." She was trying to be brave, but fear colored her every word and move. There was no real way to be normal, no matter how hard she tried.

He turned to watch her. After decades together, he could read her like his own thoughts.

"Jess, how was school?" he asked, trying to match her normal.

"Oh, just one class today so it was an easy day," she said, not looking up as she flipped the bread, sprinkling more cheese on each piece.

We'll stumble through our version of life, but it's more and more obvious something needs to be done, James thought as he observed the waves of fear rolling off his wife. He could feel it. He knew her well.

Chapter 57
Time To Go

Saturday was easy for the most part, with no agenda, work, or classes to get to. After an early morning huddle around the coffee maker, James, Jessica, and Tracy felt it was time to do something. Everyone agreed the goal was to try to get things back to some semblance of normalcy.

"Well, as normal as possible," Tracy said, "considering a door to a parallel universe has been opened, then closed, and now there are two ghostly children seeming to hang out within the house."

Yet, even with all the questions and all the unknowns, they devised a plan.

Jessica still had reservations about reconnecting the system, but she understood that the darkness, the thing that preyed upon her family, was with them and might remain in their world, and that terrified her more than two unearthly lost boys. After much discussion, she reluctantly agreed to tuck the children away in their bedrooms that evening, with everyone always watching out for them and one adult stationed in the hallway to ensure their safety. They also talked about sending them to a friend's home overnight, but, in her gut, she knew the evil thing that fed on her family could follow them anywhere, and her kids being even a block away would be too far for her liking. She needed to have them close to defend them.

In his office, James sat at his desk, fingers moving quickly over the keyboard. Then he was up, making the additional adjustments to the system before engaging it. His face flushed with effort, and his glasses slipped to the end of his nose as he stooped.

Standing up, he looked at his wife, a weary smile bringing her the hope she desperately needed. One bright spot in the rollercoaster they found themselves on was the knowledge that they would exist past death and that those they loved were never far away.

James used his shirt sleeve to wipe his face, then pushed his glasses back into place. The previously disconnected and dark monitor, which had remained inactive for several weeks, was now glowing and pulsing like a living thing. SYSTEM ENGAGED jumped out on the screen like a human voice yelling, "Danger!" The outline of the second floor showed three pulsating blue figures: Tracy, Jack, and Alena. Together they watched, the additional IR cameras he had installed on the third floor picking up Harold and Jeffrey near the attic playroom.

Jessica bent over, tracing each figure as if they were the embodiment of a miracle. She read each name out loud.

"All present and accounted for!" she added, like some sad military drill. She stood, placing a hand on the small of her back, a light snapping sound making her grimace as she blew a lock of hair from her face. "Am I getting old?" she asked, rubbing her hip as she looked at James, giving him a shaky look.

James was tired but returned a smile, sliding his eyes to the pulsating figures on the screen, focused on where Jack and Alena were as they moved within their bedrooms. Tracy's blue figure pulsed as she held her position on the second floor. "Everyone is where they should be, yet I can't seem to move," he said as he met Jessica's gaze.

"I know. I keep thinking right now, well, if we could just get things back to the way they were, it will be OK." Jessica mirrored his thoughts, much like they had done throughout their marriage. She hesitated. "But we both know things can't remain as they are, and we can never go back. Everything will be forever changed."

James slowly nodded. "The thing that is infesting our home has found its way into the walls and feeds on us like a tick, then slithers back into our nightmares and waits..." He trailed off, seeing distress move across his wife's face. Reaching out, he touched her hand, giving it a light squeeze before finishing his thought. "It's a parasite, and we need to fucking exterminate it, and we will, Jess. We will."

"What if it doesn't work? I mean, Jimmy, what if all the extra whatever it is you have done..." She flapped her hand in the air. "You know, the extra souped-up graphene. Well, what if it leaves the door open for more of those things to come in? I know we think it came with Jeffrey, but how do we know for sure?" It was as if she had been holding her breath, the fear of the unknown releasing with that one thought as she sighed. She turned away from him, looking to the attic room on the monitor and the boys who waited there.

"I don't know, Jess. I mean, does anyone really know what is happening? Let's see what they will do and hope the boys go back to where they came from and, well, then let's pray that thing will follow, if in fact it came from there. So, let's hope my grandpa knows what we are doing, and they don't go invisible on us." He was trying to be convincing as his voice rose and his back straightened. He met her eyes one last time before he began gathering his tools, placing them in the utility box, then sliding them under his desk.

"They have no reason to go invisible," she said, tilting her head, more curious than afraid now. "They need to be where they need to be. Do you think family will come to help them? Your grandpa said he knows what is happening here. He will come, right?" She turned to him, her eyebrows furrowed, the concern of a mother and protector coming to the surface, ready to fight.

There was a sharp crack from within the house, like a great tree being split down the middle, a straining, tearing noise followed by a distant tremble through the walls. The sound had substance as it rolled from the front of the house, reaching them where they stood in the office. A look of fright came over Jessica as James reached for her, pulling her to his side, a resolute calm coming over him even as the hairs stood up on the back of his neck.

"C'mon, let's see if they come." He nodded at the monitor, then looked up at the ceiling as he thought of his family, both living and dead. Closing his eyes, his lips moved in a silent prayer even though he was not a religious man.

As they walked down the long hall toward the front of the house, the framed photos on the wall rattled against the paint and plaster. Jessica gripped James's his hand, letting out a small noise, trying to ignore the subtle movement that seemed to come from everywhere.

As Tracy rounded the newel post at the top of the stairs, she came into view on the second-floor landing. Upon making eye contact, she silently lifted her chin in acknowledgment, urging them forward.

James and Jessica climbed the stairs in unison, joining Tracy. James pointed to the end of the hallway and gestured up the next set of stairs, indicating the need to move to the third floor. Tracy nodded as another wave of vibration reverberated through the house, knocking her off-kilter, causing her to reach for the wall to steady herself.

They were halfway down the hall when a flash of white light stopped them, followed by rumbling in the floorboards under their feet, turning them back toward the front of the house.

"Shit." Tracy looked at them both with a mixture of fear and excitement. She attempted to hide a smile.

"Maybe this wasn't a good idea," Jessica said, frantically looking around for the source of the noise. Jessica met Tracy's eyes. "Do you hear that? It sounds like the beating of wings."

Tracy looked wildly around, then up at the ceiling. "Birds? Invisible ones?" she answered, pushing back a damp strand of hair out of her eyes. "And it sounds like it's coming from all around us. Hell, it's *all* around us."

"Mom? Dad?" Jack called from his room, his voice barely audible. "Everything is moving in my room." Despite his cries, he didn't sound panicked.

Jessica instinctively ran to his door, leaning in and trying to appear calm, not wanting to frighten him. "It's OK, honey," she said.

She didn't know where Jack would be safe and was now doubting their decision to turn on the system. Opening the door wide, she saw her son sitting in the middle of the bed, his hair ruffled, with small hairs standing on end as if rubbed by a balloon. The room fell still when she took a step inside.

"Everything will be OK; just stay in bed," she reassured him while trying to convince herself. He stared at his mother, shrugged, then looked back down at the book resting in his lap. She reached down and kissed his cheek, then noticed the catcher's mitt, baseball, and Racer 8 on the floor next to the bed. She was not surprised that he would surround himself with his friends' things and at his disconnected response, as he often became engrossed in whatever book he was reading. Turning, she looked back over her shoulder. Jack continued to read, not looking up, so she softly closed the door.

She gave a sideways glance at James. "Wow, the resiliency of kids," she said while wondering if telling Jack to stay put was the right thing to do.

He met her eyes and nodded, though in his gut he was unsure. "Yeah, I think he's actually sad and not so resilient. I think he may have heard us talking about permanently removing the security system and trying to send our resident ghosts home for good. Anyway, I think he knows down deep that his friends may be leaving. Nope, I think he is disconnected," James added with an understanding shrug.

There was a click, low and soft, in the strange vibrational hum that seemed to be building. *The house is using the energy, but who or what is benefiting?* James wondered as he surveyed the small radiating cracks in the hallway wall.

He lowered himself onto one knee and ran his hand over one of the larger cracks, which was around six or seven inches high and an eighth of an inch at its widest point. He peered closely, trying to get a sense of the extent of the damage, and stood.

"Well, fuck," he muttered, rubbing his hand on his jeans, as if he could transfer the cause of the damage to himself through touch. Motioning to Jessica to follow, he took large, purposeful steps, stopping at Alena's door. A rush of air moved past him in the hall; there was substance to it as he turned around. Jessica stood; nothing and no one else was there.

Turning back, he refocused, shaking his arms, then he tapped the doorknob with one finger. It was cool to the touch but not freezing. Relieved, he opened the door slowly. Alena was in bed, wearing her yellow chickadee pajamas, Mrs. Kelly held just below her chin.

"Daddy," she said, her small voice mixed with the low symphony of sound that moved through the house.

Jessica pushed past James, taking a seat on her daughter's narrow bed. Alena had thrown back the covers when she'd seen her parents, intending to run to them. "Sweetie, it's OK. You and Mrs. Kelly stay in bed." Jessica met Alena's eyes, feeling guilty that her sensitive daughter would pick up on every nuance in her voice and would know she was lying. Hell, she didn't know if anything would ever be OK again.

Another flash of light lit the hallway, drawing their attention back to the task at hand. "You OK, sweetie?" James stood beside Jessica, placing a hand on her shoulder as he looked down into his daughter's frightened face.

Alena hugged her favorite toy tighter and nodded her head "yes" as Jessica pulled the covers up under her daughter's chin. "We will be right outside the door," Jessica said, trying to be reassuring while keeping the fear out of her voice.

The air was becoming heavy. It was a sign that the world with yellow walls was close. The two dimensions were merging. *The wake will be stronger than ever,* James thought.

Closing their daughter's door, turning toward a glow at the end of the hall, they stood together, gazing at the unearthly spectacle that was filling the small space with a swirling, shifting glow. It started as a rectangle of brilliant, intermittent light that moved up to the ceiling, then out toward the walls, where bright yellow framed the edges. Unidentified voices and sounds ebbed and flowed from the flickering scene, much like watching a movie screen when a reel has broken.

Little Harold appeared from nowhere, moving dreamlike past them without hesitation. As he approached, he lifted his hands, checking for warmth.

Then, as if sensing Little Harold's presence, bright particles of translucent color moved out from the depths of the light and toward him like fingers reaching for a prize, electrifying the carpet and walls.

Little Harold's face filled with excitement, his smile wide as he closed his eyes, his shoulders moving up, taking a deep breath. "Cookies! I can smell them!" His words seemed to float in the vibration.

Transfixed, Jessica, James, and Tracy stood watching as Little Harold approached the ethereal world, the edge of which was moving like a curtain caught in a gentle wind.

"Harold?" A small, barely audible voice came from behind

them. James looked over his shoulder to see Jeffrey standing against the wall.

Jessica looked past her sister to Jeffrey, her motherly instinct taking over as she knelt down next to him. "Don't be afraid," she said, looking into his face, his large eyes reflecting the light in the hallway.

Jack emerged from his bedroom at the end of the hall. "Hey!" He shouted to be heard over the buzzing in the air. He was cradling Jeffrey's catcher's mitt. In the center of the mitt sat Harold's well-worn Rawlings baseball. Even at the tender age of ten, Jack knew that these simple childhood things, items that were once connected to tragedy and sadness, now carried within their etched leather and stitching an offering of forgiveness, healing, and friendship. Moving past Tracy and his parents, he stopped in front of Harold and Jeffrey, who were standing a few feet apart, and placed the mitt and ball on the floor between them. All three boys looked from one to the other, knowing their secret friendship was coming to an end.

As if waking from a dream, Jack backed away slowly and joined his parents, squeezing in to make a place between them.

A small hand touched Tracy, startling her. Looking down, she saw Alena grasping her hand, Mrs. Kelly wedged in the crook of her arm. Alena looked at the spectacle, the beams of light painting her curls with gold, her green eyes looking like jewels. Tracy patted her hand, giving reassurance, then they both turned back to the hallway and the world that was manifesting before them.

Suddenly Alena let go, twisting from her grip, Mrs. Kelly's tail dusting the floor as she disappeared into her brother's room, returning with Racer 8. She looked to her mom and dad, who nodded their approval, her small steps now slow as she placed the car next to the baseball and catcher's mitt.

Jack began to protest, but a glance from his mother stopped him.

Jeffrey stood in place, his shoulders curling forward, attempting to become small. He lifted his head to give his words strength. "What if no one is there for me?"

Little Harold seemed to hear him and whirled on his heel, stepping boldly into the golden rectangle, one shoe still visible at the edge. Fragments of color swirled and bloomed where he entered, then came together, his outline appearing in silhouette on the other side as bright particles twinkled around him. Then he backed out slowly, as if exerting great effort to separate himself from the light, and he joined Jeffrey.

"I asked my mom and dad if you can sleep over, you know, stay with us," Little Harold said, smiling with a wisdom five times his apparent age. He reached down and picked up the catcher's mitt, handing it to his friend. "You'll have a home." He looked for the baseball that had rolled a few feet away, resting next to the wall. He ran to it, scooping it up, then tossed it to Jeffrey, who caught it with his catcher's mitt effortlessly.

Jeffrey looked down, realizing what he had done, and beamed.

The boys stood together, watching as bright colors shifted within the light in flittering movements. Dark silhouettes also stirred, their voices muffled, low, and distant. Fractured words struggled to be heard as snippets of conversations traveled through the air, getting louder, then retreating like waves on a beach.

A tall shadow approached from within the light. "Harold," a male voice called out, deep and familiar. "Jeffrey," the figure spoke again, revealing his features as he moved closer, coming into focus like a photo developing in a darkroom tray.

Harold Sr. stood tall, sparks like small falling stars bouncing off his glasses. He was wearing the same outfit as when he had first materialized to James. His eyes flickered as he surveyed the hallway. There was a stillness about him as he held the moment, then rested his gaze upon Little Harold and Jeffrey. "Time to come home, boys," he called to them, the underwater quality to his voice coming in ripples, the strength of tone rising and falling. There was movement behind him, a shift in the shadows as a small boy stepped out, making himself known.

James stepped closer to get a better view of the boy, who appeared to be no older than five or six. He was wearing jeans rolled up at the ankle; a blue, short-sleeved, button-down shirt; and sneakers. He had delicate features; short brown hair with curls sticking out just above the ears gave him an oddly familiar, elfin appearance. Recognition moved across the boy's young face, hazel eyes twinkling from under thick brown lashes as he gave a nod and smiled.

James had no doubt who was standing before him. He knew the face from old snapshots on the time-travel wall and in picture frames on the bedroom table. Yes, he knew him well; he had his eyes. "Dad?" he whispered, his heart expanding, the world falling away, and, in that moment, it was just the two of them. The soul of the man who taught him, guided him, and molded his life now stood an arm's length away.

James Allen Sr., age six, stood at the edge of his world, smiling up at his forty-nine-year-old son. His eyes shifted to the hallway, looking slowly around, stopping at each face, nodding beatifically as if holding court.

From behind James came a squeal. "Jimmy!" Little Harold was on his toes as he waved to his baby brother, a hand gripping Jeffrey's arm, overcome with excitement.

Harold Sr. looked down at the boy and then to James. "Your father meets his brother at the age he was when he arrived here after the accident," he said. The affection in his grandfather's voice was warm and loving as he placed his hand on his youngest son's head. "You see, we can be whatever age we wish here, and your father enjoys playing with his big brother the way they both remember. Heaven is what you want it to be." His smile widened with a love that reflected the unearthly light surrounding him. He looked again to his son, then back to his grandson.

James locked eyes with his grandfather, then looked down at the small boy. "My God…" His words caught again in his throat, making it hard to swallow, moved by the sheer impossibility of it. He lowered himself down onto both knees, so he was face-to-face with his father, who stepped closer.

"Hello, James." His father smiled, his eyes becoming triangles in the changing light.

"Is it really you?" James asked, his words filled with wonder as he took in his father and the unbelievable smallness of him. *My God, he is so young,* he thought.

James's father cocked his head, then glanced at the floor and the edge of his world, the wavering border looming like a dangerous cliff. Looking up, he took a hesitant step, then another. With his third tentative step, a bright shimmer filled the air, swirling with color. Materializing as if from nothing, he now stood outside the curtain of light.

"My Dad." James held out his open hand as an offering of recognition. They could read each other's thoughts, an invisible bond that neither world could break or bend. In response, James Sr. placed his hand in his son's. James responded with a gentle squeeze, then opened his fingers to inspect the tiny, vibrating hand, which was perfect and unmarked by time. The last time he held his father's hand was on his deathbed, the knuckles large and swollen with arthritis, the skin mottled, scarred, and callused with age spots and a life of hard work.

His father leaned in close. "I'm never far, Jimmy," he whispered, the brilliance of the otherworldly plane suddenly very warm. The magical scene then broke apart into fragments. The weight of his hand disappeared as small particles of color and light filled the air, momentarily suspended, then found each other and reassembled.

James blinked, his hand still open, then saw that his father and grandfather were standing together again, back in their ever-shifting world.

Getting up from his knees, James felt unsteady as he took a deep breath. The air felt cool as it filled his lungs, his face warm, a vibration still running through him. He stood mesmerized at the sight of his father and grandfather side by side, the extraordinary gift of time and communion making it hard to find his bearing. He felt a gentle touch at his shoulder. Jessica was there, taking his hand, entwining and wrapping her fingers in his. She felt good and solid, her presence giving him strength. It was as if the world were revolving in slow motion.

Harold Sr. smiled, answering his grandson's thoughts. "Until forever, Jimmy," he said, meeting his eyes with a nod, then motioning first to Little Harold and then Jeffrey. "It's time to come home."

Little Harold bumped his shoulder against his friend's arm and lifted his chin. "Come on, don't ya smell the cookies?" His elbow nudged Jeffrey, his melodic laughter filling the hallway.

Jeffrey shook his head in eager agreement. "Yes, I smell them." A smile replaced the sadness and fear that had held him for so long. Then they stepped together, the fluid dimension of their world coming to life, sensing their closeness, moving to meet them. A mushroom of small, colorful particles drifted outward, then inward, enveloping their return as they shimmered, broke apart, and came together again on the other side of the glowing curtain.

James and Jessica stood together. Close behind them Tracy and the kids were motionless as they watched the magical reunion. The distraction, however, kept everyone from noticing the black shapeless mass that clung to the ceiling a few feet away.

The darkness that moved within the shadows was making itself known with a guttural, mewing cry, causing James to look up. Jessica turned, letting go of his hand and running toward the kids, needing to get them out of harm's way.

"Run!" James yelled, standing between the undulating mass and his family.

Tracy, in tune with her sister, gathered Alena into her arms just steps away from Jessica, who was pushing her son from behind as they headed to Jack's room, which was the closest to where they stood.

The keening noise grew louder, the black mass moving like a storm cloud, rolling in, then expanding. James was alone, staring up at the darkness that seemed to be defining itself, the anger and hate emanating from it like the heat from a long burning fire. It elongated like the liquid substance in a lava lamp before molding itself into a black humanoid shape. A sharp crack of a sound like distant thunder came from all around, and in those last few seconds James thought he saw the figure dive into the light before the ethereal doorway closed and disappeared.

A blanket of dusky light stippled the hallway. Coming back into himself, he squinted, letting his eyes adjust. Lifting his hands, he inspected them closely, moving his tingling fingers, the memory of his father's hand still warm, the magic of the moment leaving an indelible mark on his heart and soul.

There was movement behind him, a door opening, drawing his attention and causing him to turn. On the floor, where the dimensional doorway had existed just moments before, sat Racer 8.

2023

Chapter 58
Legacy

It was one of the hardest days of Jack's life. The storm released a constant drizzle, running over the boughs of the trees, intent on framing the pain of those who stood around the gravesite. Despite the weather, it was a tranquil spot at the southwest corner of the Mission Hills Cemetery, the names of generations of the Allen family carved deep in granite and marble, the headstones' macabre calling cards of a life lived, an RSVP to a party no longer ignored. A weeping angel, covered with years of dirt and grime, stared at him from above the gravestones. The overall neglect of the property highlighted the pain of the family as they mourned.

On the day of the heart attack, James had been working on replacing part of a broken porch railing. There was always something needing repair, but it was a labor of love, and he enjoyed it. He and Jessica would often talk about the importance of caring for a home where future generations would reside, a legacy of great importance for all who dwelled there, both in this realm and the next.

Before his death, James had contributed greatly to his company over the years, giving the younger tech designers someone to look up to. His innovations earned worldwide respect, expanded his company's product base, and made him a legend to those who came after him. When he retired, he'd reached the position of SVP of Product Development, giving him a healthy bank account, treasured time with family, and endless hours tinkering in his beloved Geek Shed. Jessica, at sixty-five, retired a few years earlier than James, giving up test correcting for tennis lessons.

Alena had wanderlust and followed her dreams to New York, where she pursued a stage career, becoming a big success on Broadway. Her first love was musicals—big, bold musicals. Her strong voice and stage presence made her a hot commodity, and the offers fell at her feet. She embraced the classics, and her latest role was the tragic Éponine in the long-running *Les Misérables*.

Jack took another road, marrying the girl of his dreams right after college, settling down, and planting roots like his parents. A software-design engineer like his father, Jack worked at a data analytics start-up, while his wife, Amy, moved right into an entry-level marketing position at Starbucks, giving them both the security needed to start—and then support—their small but growing family.

Weeks after the funeral, Jessica decided to spend less time at the house, finding the emptiness and loss of James too much. His memory filled every corner and every room, making the mourning of him harder, the small, emotional cuts continuous and draining. So she made a hard decision and moved to a condo on Lake Union to be free from the memories. She split her time between the Pacific Northwest and Arizona, where a few of her friends had found life more tolerable in their golden years with a little sunshine and a daily tennis game.

Almost six months went by, and the Allen home needed a family. Jessica approached both children, but it was Jack and his wife who accepted Jessica's invitation to make the Queen Anne house their home.

Jessica had sold or given away most of the older furniture that wasn't original or built for the house, leaving many things in the attic and Geek Shed to go through and possibly use. Excited to have such an expansive house to live in, with a yard for the children to run and play, Jack and Amy worked to give the home their own special touch, with new paint and a few changes here and there, coupled with her mid-century modern style. There were only a few things Jack insisted on when discussing the house with his mother and wife prior to moving in: the main hallway would continue the time-travel tradition; the playroom must stay untouched; the kitchen's bright, cornflower blue tiles would continue to warm the heart of the house; and the Geek Shed would be Jack's, leaving the rest of the house to Amy to make her own.

When cleaning out his father's things, Jack took great care categorizing and storing each book, journal, and remnant of James's dreams. Over time, upgrading the old, detached garage was a necessary priority, and Jack installed a new door and a functioning heating system so he could be warm while he mourned his father during the colder months. Time went by, and the Geek Shed was always in a state of flux. Jack spent his Sundays trying to wrap his head around his father's obsession with quantum physics, dimensional existence, and parallel universes.

He filled, wrapped, and packed boxes to withstand the years, preserving and organizing the contents methodically and with great care. Jack was working from the farthest end of the shed, moving a section at a time, when he came upon two large black plastic bins with no labels, tucked in the very back corner under an old inflatable wading pool. Opening the first bin, he found two hardcover journals dating back decades sitting on top. The pages were filled with notes, diagrams, and theories, telling the story of a man searching for the truth of what he had created. At first glance, James's story could be misconstrued as the rantings of a man on the edge, gripped by the realization and terror of what he had created and subjected his family to. As he sat, lost in time, Jack heard his father's voice in each word. His recollections, however, did not mirror his father's. His fragmented memories were primarily filled with wonderment and very little apprehension, his imagination filling in the story where the edges blurred.

The rest of both bins held old equipment. He let his hand touch the bundled wires and cables, the motion-tracking IR cameras, speakers, routers, system monitors, and keypads breathing life into his detached memories of childhood. After several hours, he closed the lids, placing the containers back in the corner in a feeble attempt to block the cascade of memories these objects triggered.

As time went by, Jack became obsessed with his father's journals. He spent hours reading them over and over, all while comparing James's work to the current high-tech options available.

There was a real need for a system with such abilities, Jack realized. The world was suffering from a growing paranoia, with bad actors hacking video feeds and computer cameras. Did the system really have the abilities described in his father's journal pages? His father was far from a madman, yet notes about his long-dead grandfather and children caught between worlds haunted Jack.

Surrounded by his treasured possessions, Jack began to dream of his father. He missed him so badly, and the possibility of seeing him again was all-consuming. Was it a dream that he had played with a boy named Harold, his belongings taking up residence in his life? Could he actually spend time with his father again? *There is only one way to find out,* he thought. In the morning, he would pull out the large, black plastic bins, dusting off the contents. Then, with great effort and hard work, he would reconfigure and reinstall his father's system, tweaking, updating, and incorporating available current technology. His father was onto something, and, who knows, maybe the world was now ready.

The End

Within the wake, love floats endless,
Where time untethered
Finds renewal and forgiveness,
Anchored from the shore.

—The Changing Veil

With Gratitude

To those who have supported me along my journey, thank you with all of my heart.

And to Bill Chappell, you are, and will always be, the king of every Geek Shed. Thank you for sharing your amazing knowledge with me.

Printed in the USA
CPSIA information can be obtained
at www.ICGtesting.com
JSHW021318061023
49634JS00003B/8